Delicious Torment

by

Christine Tripp

Delicious Torment

Cover Art by *The Wild Rose Press, Inc.*

The Wild Rose Press, Inc.
PO Box 708
Adams Basin, NY 14410-0708
Visit us at www.thewildrosepress.com

Publishing History
First Tea Rose Edition, 2020
Print ISBN 978-1-5092-3006-8
Digital ISBN 978-1-5092-3007-5

Published in the United States of America

Once they were away from prying eyes, Ralph kissed her. "I am sorry."

Lily giggled. "Never apologize for kissing me."

Ralph sighed. "No, Lily. Vincent's friend has told him some reporters are looking into you. I live in fear that they will reveal your Russian adventure."

"Adventure is an ironic turn of phrase for what happened. You know of it and will still marry me. Bella, Olivia, and Honoria will still be my friends. Threats are only effective if one might lose something of value." Lily struggled to remain calm in her terror. The power of gossip could warp her scarring personal history into a weapon to use against her. A tale where Lily was a child prostitute and was not worth her hard-scrabbled dignity. Blood pounded in her temples, and her stomach churned. Yet Lily smiled. What else could she do when fear was swallowing her whole?

"I wish I could be as strong as you are." He laid delicate kisses on her eyelids. "I hate that there is anything I cannot protect you from. I wish that this were something simple as a dragon, which is to say, easily slain. But this situation is truth mixed with lies and innuendo. I have no idea how to fight this."

She buried her face in his chest hoping he would not see how false her bravery was. "We will fight it together."

Dedication

To my darling husband Nicholas:
You are as loyal as Ralph, as witty as Vincent,
and as diligent as Sebastian. You are my true love.

~

To my beloved daughter Pandora:
You are my dream come true and I adore you.

~

To Mr. Jim Burke: thank you for
everything you have done for me.
The world truly needs more teachers like you.

Chapter One

There has never been anything quite as wonderful as a hot cup of tea, sweetened with heather honey, to greet one upon returning home from a long journey. Tea has a near-magical ability to mend the nerves of travel and ease the wounds of homesickness. The best advice is to wire your servants to have tea at the ready on your arrival.
~Aunt Penny's Advice on Living, May 1885

His heart soared and sank high with the moon and low with the gentle waves. Smooth familiar shores punctuated by dangerous rocks rose into focus across the dissipating sea. Ralph had never thought his homecoming would be lit by moonlight and covered by fog. The details of the English coastline gently crept into view, and distant city lights nagged the corners of his vision. The reason for his singing pulse and plunging doubts was quite plain. After two years with only two quarrelsome brothers as constant companions, how could he not miss London? His eyes glazed over; he could never forget the sights and smells and, most of all, the society. He squinted at the approaching docks for any sign of his old friend, Sir Barton. He was so hungry for the sight of his agreeable, knowledgeable friend. But there was no sign of him. Perhaps his eyes were failing. Hopefully he was wrong. It was hard to breathe without the air bringing a smile to his face as he came closer to his bright city filled with dark secrets.

The last two years had been trying in unanticipated ways. Oh, how he wished the time away from the *ton* had provided a chance for harmony between his brothers. In hindsight, expecting civility had been a fool's errand. Vincent (who was equal parts curmudgeon and charisma) had used every opportunity to make Sebastian look foolish. Sebastian (who was equal parts honorable and humorless) never let it be forgotten that he was Vincent's superior in every aspect. Ralph feared that the tour had enlarged the rift between them. Instead of dulling their rivalry, their insults were sharper and their tempers shorter. They were like boxers who had spent years training to fight only each other.

Their trunks were unloaded, one after the other, onto the docks. The three ruddy porters were shadows, except for their faded crests, sewn proudly onto their livery at chest level. The modest light reflected the blazon of a roaring silver lion supporting a sword, rampant against a field of burgundy. Ralph's mouth turned up in a small smile as he fondly remembered his father's frequent and boastful explanation of the details of the crest and how desperately he loved those tales.

Ralph put on a toothy smile for the servants as if they were old friends. The appearance of these starched men changed the temperament of the night. The salty air of travel disappeared, only to be replaced with the warm butterflies of an eager homecoming. Their confused attempts to return Ralph's pleasantries were unpracticed. They were used to the duke and duchess's air of indifference. Ralph straightened his back for a second, right before his façade melted again into sincerity. Barton's distracted silhouette darted toward him through the fog.

"Ralph!" Apparently, Barton believed that the best way to greet a groggy and sea-worn companion was to shout at him from close range. If only he had brought tea with him.

Ralph's ears throbbed and rang after the too-loud exclamation. In Barton's exuberance, he nearly trampled a young lady. Ralph reflexively bit his lip and half listened to Barton's hurried apologies. Some things never changed.

Barton was a man out of time. His appearance was somehow precisely the same as before Ralph had left for his tour. His brown hair was disheveled by the sea air. His dark-brown eyes sparkled behind his spectacles like a warm cup of coffee. Ink stains streaked his gloves and shirt. His crooked cravat proudly protruded from his coat. Barton had clearly become absorbed in some scientific study and only remembered Ralph at the last moment. Maybe the absent things in the lives of absent-minded geniuses were friends and family. How very lonely.

Ralph grabbed his calloused hand and shared a grin. "Ahoy, Barton!" There was no pretense; he could be as loud as he wanted. This was just like greeting each other back in school. Giddiness leapt up in him, making his lungs fill and burst with happy words.

"Glad to be home?"

"You cannot begin to imagine. Have dinner with us tonight. I need to be caught up on London. Does it smell the same? It's fine if it doesn't."

"Of course! Although, sadly, I must report it is

much as it was before—foggy, soggy, and full of marriage-minded mothers. I do have an invitation to a musicale tonight, but it appears that Lady Serena is not attending. I will also bow out."

Ralph's eyebrows lifted in suspicion. "Lady Serena? Are you courting her?"

Men rarely turned red at the mention of a woman, but there was a first time for everything.

"No. I'm still striving for an introduction. Miss Snowe promised to assist me, but Lady Serena had proven quite elusive."

"Lord Snowe's daughter?" It was surprising that Barton and the young hellion were acquainted. Ralph stilled for moment as he searched for Vincent's nickname for her—"Lily the Lion Tamer." Of course, her notoriety must be great if a recluse like Barton knew her reputation.

"Hm. Oh, yes. Lovely girl," Barton said distractedly. "Oh! Your brothers. I should greet them as well."

As Barton exchanged the smallest of small talk with Vincent and Sebastian, Ralph tapped his fingers to wring out his new anxiety. What was the source of Lily's great fame? The last time they met, she feared being a wallflower. It had been six years since their awkward introduction at her brother's wedding. Awkward was insufficient.

Simple concern and complicated fears filled Ralph until they overflowed. His stomach was a knot of anguish and hope. Hope that Lily's isolation was over. Distress for her independence in the menagerie of London society. She might have recovered from her childhood trials. She had seemed buoyant back then, at the "ripe age" of fourteen. It was too hard not to wince. Barton would be too distracted to read lines of regret or concern on her face. If Ralph wanted to find out if she was still weighed down by her past or had cast it off, he would have to do it himself.

Before he left for his tour, Ralph had asked Christopher about Lily's story. Christopher Snowe was Lord Snowe's son from his first wife and Lily's only sibling. Ralph had desperately hoped that Lily had invented it. He hoped she wanted to impress him with some dramatic and tragic tale.

Such hopes were foolish and convenient. Christopher confirmed Lily was telling the truth. Ralph's face felt numb and prickly, like being touched with ice and rough wind. Even now, just at the memory of it, he went numb. His eyelids were heavy with memories and guilt for things he hadn't done. It was a strange thing to carry such responsibility for someone else's failures.

Despite Sebastian and Vincent's falling out with Christopher (which went unexplained), they both spoke glowingly about Lily. Vincent would often muse that she was the only person worthy of his wit. If she could tame Vincent, then surely she could do so to the multitudes of lesser men in London society. Sebastian hoped she would marry a diplomat. It would do wonders, in his informed opinion, for Queen and Country. That was probably true. Obviously, such a plan was perfect for her as well. Even at fourteen, Miss Snowe had been well travelled and had perfect table manners. Except for her habit of being a bit of a wine thief. But even that was a forgivable sin. Lily only stole the best vintage and year.

He intentionally breathed deep to take in the air and odor of London as his brothers and friend climbed into the carriage. It smelled damp and homey, like the smell of his comfortable drawing room in the early morning before the fires were lit. He was home, and his arms and legs and head felt like they were filled with something lighter than air.

He focused just enough to hear Vincent's droll commentary. "Your grin makes you look like a simpleton. But that's fine, because Sebastian makes everyone look clever by comparison." And just like that, the air was thin and unwelcoming. It was familiar, but just crisp and formal enough to fill him with doubt.

"I am glad to have the Mandevilles home at last," Barton said. Barton's flat, toothy smile was hiding something. This was an attempt at cheerful misdirection.

"Not as glad as we are," Vincent said jovially as he clapped Ralph's shoulder. He was in one of his rare good moods. "Tell me, Barton, is this"—Vincent waved his finger at Barton's ink stains—"the latest fashion for men? Should I fetch an ink pot as soon as we get home?"

Barton smiled at the gentler-than-usual teasing. "No, no. Lord Snowe asked me to review some scientific treatises he acquired before he gives them to a friend. I promised Lily I would give her a review soon and did not wish to disappoint her." Ah, that was the reason for his distracted nature. Hoping for a good scandal was simply too much.

Ralph hoped someone would ask about Lily instead of the treatises. Barton could go on for hours and hours about every experiment if permitted. Clearly, there was not time or patience for a lecture on chemistry or engineering right now.

"How is my little lion tamer?" Vincent asked. His syrupy tone held too much delight in her nickname.

Ralph recoiled in fear that Vincent had read his concerns. The secrets Lily had shared lay coiled in his chest always threatening to spring forth whenever her name was mentioned.

Barton blanched at the question, and Vincent clarified. "Lily. I'm talking about Lily."

"She is well, very well. She is a diamond of the first water."

Ralph's brows draped low over his eyes, and his jaw dropped hard. How could they be talking about that gangly girl? Perhaps thin girls who were all limbs were in fashion this year.

Barton continued, oblivious as always. "Not the great beauty, though. That distinction belongs to Lady Olivia. It's said that Lady Olivia has never attended a ball without having every dance claimed."

"Lucky girl," Vincent said. His smile was too loose and too content. "But if Lily is a diamond, is she at least a sharp one? Can she still cut a man down with a few quick words? If not, I'm going to be distraught."

Ralph snapped his mouth shut, and his brow unfurled. At least her reputation was intact.

Barton flashed big, confused eyes. "I don't believe that I have ever seen Lily be anything but polite. All proper and lovely, all the time."

"It must be just for me then. Thank goodness. I am back to remind her that men adore women with soft looks and sharp words. Plus, wit has a way of inspiring wit. If she has become dull, I will be on my worst behavior until she returns to shape." Vincent smiled widely, and the corners of his mouth turned up just a little. He looked altogether too satisfied. He clearly had a vault of insults reserved just for her. How very unfortunate. She had suffered enough already.

"Vincent, do you have a *tendre* for Miss Snowe?" Sebastian asked his question smoothly, and his voice was lower and more relaxed when he said her name. There was subtle hope in Sebastian's tone. If Vincent had a new sparring partner, he might torment Sebastian less.

"That is vile!"

Ralph stifled his laugh as Vincent turned a shade of green.

"I have always looked at Lily as a sister. I am equally incapable of respecting anyone, male or female. I can enjoy a lady without romanticizing her. Now, if Lily happened to become a fallen woman, I might reconsider. Only a fool would let that opportunity pass. Although I am not villainous enough to make fate turn on her in such a way."

"Jesus, Vincent! She's a child!" Ralph exclaimed. He immediately regretted it. First, he rarely swore. Second, he never raised his voice no matter how provoked he was. And last, Miss Snowe was now twenty and no longer a child. His heart was on his sleeve, and hot, angry blood rushed to his face. How very embarrassing.

Even if she wasn't a child any longer, the idea of her being a fallen woman was repulsive. The imaginary details of such a thing sickened Ralph. Obviously, Vincent's insensitivity, not his hidden knowledge of Ralph's fixations, was the cause of his remarks. The idea of Lily Snowe (whose very name implied purity) being someone's mistress was a vile fiction. His fists clenched, and his jaw set firm at the thought of her being passed from feckless protector to feckless protector. No, it was merely a joke. She was meant for more.

Ralph's eyes were wide, but they saw nothing. His body was still, but his thoughts were galloping horses, threatening to bolt. Why was her fate so troubling? Why fixate on this woman? She was flourishing in the tepid garden of London society. She had been resilient when she recounted her kidnapping and rescue. She remained composed amidst tinkling wine glasses and pleasantries. Although she had been born with title and privilege, she had almost been a child bride.

Her quandary was the sum and summary of contemporary moral failure. Her situation was entirely due to the indifference and polite deference of the people whose role it was to protect her. Her story was a chain of neglectful family, of friends too polite to object, and of crimes unreported to authorities. After all, kidnapping was a crime that only the lower classes performed or suffered. Lily had trusted her secret to him, and he left without helping her. His actions made him part of this chain of neglect. His guilt bound his heart, and his body ached with regret. Regardless of adoration or wit, her name would always carry a measure of remorse with it.

"Ralph...when did you meet Lily?" Sebastian asked cautiously. Even in strife, Sebastian was unfailingly polite.

"Christopher's wedding."

"Ah," Vincent uttered as though he were a wise

man. "That explains everything."

The three men nodded in disparate accord. Ralph couldn't stop his head from shaking. What a farce—this explained nothing. A sigh hissed from him like angry steam.

"Is Christopher still abroad?" Sebastian lacked the audacity to completely change the conversation. But he did try.

"Oh yes, he's doing quite well. He returned home for a fortnight last autumn. However, Lily was at a house party, and the two passed each other. That was quite sad," Barton prattled. For someone oblivious to gossip, he was certainly aware of Lily's exploits.

Sebastian and Vincent exchanged rare looks of trust in the tempered silence. What hidden meaning was behind these events, and why wouldn't they say anything? It was frustrating not knowing more, but to pry into his brothers' affairs would be too rude. Anyway, they were home at last.

****

The Duke of Bridgewater's Mayfair townhouse was the pinnacle of style in London. Ralph's mother labored endlessly on its decor and presentation. It was like a needy fourth child who never quite grew up. The entrance stood imposing and high, and the Carrara marble reflected a tremendous echo. Each of the twelve sitting rooms had a different theme, even if the theme was simply red. Someone had once referred to their home as a warm hug. His father's townhouse was more akin to a stiff handshake, but it was home nonetheless.

After he crossed the threshold, Seraphina Mandeville moved quickly to meet him. Her elegant feet murmured on the floor, and she stayed as silent as an actor waiting on a cue. Ralph loved his mother, but by God, she was intimidating. Her hair was the color of pooled moonlight and rested against alabaster skin. Her eyes were nearly silver. She resembled the terrifying fairies of myth, the sidhe. People said Seraphina Mandeville could cut you from good society with only a flick of her wrist. This was a total falsehood (it took a full wave of her hand), but it was a rumor she actively nurtured.

His father, Grayson Mandeville, Duke of Bridgewater, followed his mother. His Grace was a tall, thin man whose black hair had grown streaks of gray over the years. He was half a legendary man and half the statue of a legendary man. He was made of equal parts history and life. That shone in his larger-than-life walk, his elegant fitted coat, and his voice. It never rose, but it never fell either. His parents were salt and pepper. His mother was essential to everyday life, and his father was very expensive. One of them couldn't sit at a table without the other. Ralph winced at the weight of authority and age on his parents. His father smiled. What relief—a sincere expression of homecoming. That look was usually reserved for a favorite book and a comfortable chair. That look felt like a warm blanket to a cold traveler.

"Sebastian! And Ralph! I'm so glad to see you home! Where's…?" Their mother's voice froze in a tense pause as her eyes passed over them and scanned the room.

"Your Graces. Lovely to see you again," Vincent muttered coolly. He leaned casually against the wall, making himself seem small and as though he were simply observing the family from the wings. Like a gilded fly on an elegant wall.

For the second time that night, Ralph couldn't stop his wince. Their mother's lack of greeting would fuel Vincent's feelings of rejection. Vincent lived in Sebastian's grandiose shadow. It was no wonder he was heavy with hostility.

"Ah, there you are, Vincent. We have missed you boys so much." Seraphina Mandeville smiled past her faux pas. "I have arranged a ball to herald your return."

"Splendid, Mother," Sebastian remarked warmly. "May I see the guest list? Vincent and Ralph can entertain Father and Barton while we are gone."

"Of course, darling. I am thrilled we are all together again," his mother replied. Sebastian whisked her away into the morning room. Ralph hoped he saw Sebastian wink at Vincent, but Vincent made no move to acknowledge it. Any gratitude for this gesture would remain hidden.

"Actually, I'm quite exhausted. I'll go have a lie down before dinner," Vincent stated. He heavily climbed the stairs and disappeared. His hollow stomps echoed with familiarity until he found his room and quietly shut the door.

Ralph's father sighed and sank deep into a burgundy chair that sat in the foyer and was never intended to be used. His hands perched passively on his lap in defeat. Ralph shrugged, but his shoulders were fuller and heavier with stress than before. Barton politely examined his pocket watch during the family spat. His dark eyes focused hard on the time, counting the seconds of awkward silence. Naturally, houses this big had plenty of space for rivalry and jealousy. And for good or for ill, this was home.

Chapter Two

It is incumbent upon every great hostess to recall exactly how every guest takes their tea. For popular hostesses, this can be taxing and overwhelming. I keep a diary of every guest I host and how they take their tea. Before my neighbor comes for tea, I look in my diary and see that she enjoys cream and one sugar. I have several notes about her, including her aversion to citrus treats and preference for chocolate. The expectations of society can seem daunting. However, Aunt Penny is here to guide you.

~Aunt Penny's Guide to Living, May 1885

Lilianna Elsbet Snowe breathed deep and fought hard against the presumptuous ball of white fur. It was truly a battle of wills. For some reason, Lady Olivia had given Lily a white kitten for her birthday. The wretched creature had come with a name: Sugar. Lily understood irony, but associating sweetness with this creature was questionable, even in jest. Today, Sugar had decided she was a mountaineer and Lily's curtains were the best climb in the world. Two maids and a footman were trying to get Sugar down, but Sugar was a formidable opponent. After all, she had nine lives.

Lily grabbed the letter before her with a slight dip of her head to the footman. Her eyes narrowed to examine the silver and red seal, and she hid her annoyance. Why didn't he join forces to thwart the evil cat? It appeared other things needed attending. Clearly, his top priority was looking imposing and daft at the same time. Luckily, it was a task this footman was uniquely capable of performing.

Sugar leapt farther from Lily, springing from the curtains with surprising finesse. She landed on the padding of a soft chair on the far side of the room. From there, she catapulted herself to the long, adorned mantel and ran its length. So cunning, and always just a hair's breadth from being caught. She knocked down a beautiful clock Lily had purchased from a kindly old shopkeeper in Austria. There was a snap of wood splintering and a crash as one piece of glass shattered into thousands. The embellished faces of the angels on the front lay in pieces. Yet, the most troubling detail was the strange look of ambivalence on the kitten's face. Her expression had not changed, despite all the noise. The sort of commitment needed to create such chaos should require emotional investment. How disappointing that this furry anarchist did not have a sadistic grin. But the world didn't always make sense, and this kitten did not either. Taking advantage of the commotion, Sugar darted from the room. The maids removed the shards of glass and broken angelic faces. Their delicate expressions were frozen in positions of serenity. Thomas the footman gave chase to Sugar, and he shouted, "I'll fetch her, miss," as he trailed away.

"Do." Her voice felt firm and cold in her mouth. She sliced through the cool wax seal of Bridgewater on the letter. "I should like to make the beast into a muff."

The maids giggled, and Lily pulled her letter close. *Miss Snowe,*

Upon my arrival in London, I heard you were a "diamond of the first water." I know this can't be true, and it requires a good refutation. Has London inverted its sound judgment entirely? May I come by for tea to see if my lion tamer has tamed London?

Yours,

Lord Vincent Mandeville

Her smile was light and silent in the chaos of the house. Vincent was finally home. At every port of the Mandeville brothers' tour, Vincent had sent her a letter and several gifts. Those letters were stored safely in her nightstand where she kept all her secrets and improprieties. She always laughed after reading them, even though they usually followed the same formula. They contained at least two insults, a half compliment, and a question to keep the conversation going. This was Vincent's way. His jabs were always followed by a compliment to remind her that he never meant any harm. Vincent had proved to be a loyal friend. And his gifts were a welcome respite against the curated life she was expected to lead.

Lily fumbled to grab her pen on the far table and quickly scribbled her reply.

My lord,

You are always welcome, my dear Vincent! I would never forfeit an opportunity to prove you wrong. I expect your attendance for tea at four o'clock. If you are late, I will deny you any cake.

Yours,

Lily

P.S. Please refrain from seducing my chaperone, Olga. I know she will tantalize and tempt you, but I really must insist.

She folded the page and began to seal the letter, then paused and hastily scribbled an extra line.

Also, do you like kittens?

Lily handed the letter to the glossy-eyed footman and gave him further instructions. She bounced up the long stairs for what felt like forever to find out if Olga had woken from her afternoon rest. Olga had not. She was probably tired from all the seduction. At least Sugar was finally behaving herself. She had curled up in a ball near the old woman's chin. Lily cupped her mouth and struggled not to laugh. The pair looked like Father Christmas napping.

She stopped her thoughts just in time—right before melancholy set in. The sight of her chaperone brought up her father's memory like an unwelcome, sad fog. In the years since Christopher left, much had changed. Her father had tried to stay in Britain and succeeded for a pitiful two years. His wanderlust had strained his temperament. So, he began planning trips for himself and Lily. After four months, he became bored with London and ventured off to the countryside. They began in Dover and slowly made their way west and eventually north. Then it was off to Wales, then Scotland, and then Ireland. Papa just couldn't keep still in any one place. Finally, Papa introduced Lily to the queen and court. He was then free to wander, and he promptly set himself off to South America.

She was alone and terrified, but she had survived. And memories like this passed through her like ghosts.

****

Vincent arrived with violets in hand at 3:59. Lily beamed with an authentic smile and floated toward the sitting room. Her hands confidently smoothed her pink tea gown with rosettes embroidered on the lapel. At least it was not the predictable bounty of lilies most men brought her. What a welcome departure. Men never registered the sarcasm of her numerous exclamations of "Lilies? How very original of you." For all the endless hours of preparation she put into her beauty, the creams, salves, cinches, and coats, the least a man could do was be creative. Of course, Vincent would remember that she did not care for violets. This made the flowers exceptionally thoughtful.

"Lion tamer? Not you!" He pointed at her accusingly. "Where is Lily? Where is the mouthy girl I used to know? Have you killed her and taken her place? I do not remember her lady's maids being so alluring." Vincent donned the guise of a lost little boy, but like most youths, his impish grin shone through.

This was a clumsy provocation, so she cleared her throat and glared. He deserved to feel particularly childish. Lily laughed and softened her gaze. "Welcome home, Vincent!" She moved to accept the violets.

He moved them out of her reach and smiled. His brow furrowed in a caricature of sincerity. "For the temptress named Olga. I have also composed several limericks."

Lily giggled silently behind her hand as Vincent leaned close and bowed. His hand extended away as he gave Olga the flowers and kissed her hand. The old woman was clearly charmed, and her eyes shone with a mild happiness masked by the weight of great age.

"*Ich möchte mich recht herzlich bedanken,*" Olga murmured.

Lily poured the tea as Vincent reclined into a pillowy cream William Morris chrysanthemum chair closer to the windows. It was a prized chair, and every man who came into the room made a priority to sit in it. She recalled exactly how Vincent preferred his tea.

She offered him the cup, and he bit into a scone while glaring at her. "Vile creature. Horrid wench. How dare you present me with this enchantress and then ask me not to pursue her? You know as a gentleman I will obey your wishes. Harpy." The last epithet came at a delay. He had manufactured a pronounced glare that would have intimidated a young baron or governess. She could only laugh at such an obvious pretense.

His casual bon mots were obviously intended to show he was well read. Of course, he would tell her as much even if she didn't ask. And she suspected that he harbored a deep feeling no one wanted him. She recognized in his easy criticisms that he was much like her. She was content in heart with him; she had found a true brother. They both felt rejected and coped accordingly. She did so through elaborate dresses and perfect manners. He did so by trying his best to make ladies blush.

"Olga comes from Germany. Do you speak German?" Lily allowed herself a grace and rested her back against the settee. How very naughty—ladies were not supposed to ever allow their backs to touch any furniture.

"No. Greek, Latin, French, Italian, and Spanish. But I have the mouth of a sailor in any tongue."

"Well, then. I will have to teach her Greek, so you may court her. I will find a suitable method of compensation. And no, you may not pay me in insults." She smiled across her teacup at him.

Vincent returned the smile. "You really have

18

become quite beautiful, Lily. Any serious beaux? Is there a matching Franz to Olga?"

Lily shrugged, and a sigh built in her, getting harder to repress. "No. I have had a few proposals, but I always tell them we would have to wait for Papa to come home, and that dulls their ardor."

Vincent frowned like a judging father. "Not even Barton."

She let out a crack of laughter. Laughter was better than a sigh. "Barton. Gracious, no! Whatever gave you that idea?"

"He was the one singing your praises."

It was a strain to read his expression when he averted his eyes. Evidently, he was trying hard to seem disinterested. Lily smiled and batted her large eyes innocently. "No, I am still very much independent. And, between friends, I rather like it that way."

"Hmm." Why would he give such a noncommittal reply? "Are you attending the duchess's ball tomorrow night?"

Vincent was behaving oddly. Compliments and an entire conversation without a single remark about her intelligence or dress? Only one instance of calling her a harpy? He couldn't be planning on courting her. She adored him the way she used to adore Christopher. She truly did not want to lose him, but she would never want to be his wife.

"Oh, yes. It was ever so kind of her to invite me."

Vincent's nod was fast and relieved. "I bought you so many gifts, but my valet hasn't finished unpacking my trunks. I'll send them over later. I'm eager to have a daughter of my own to spoil. It was rather fun picking out gifts for you."

"Are you looking for a wife, Vincent?" Her mild shock trilled through her voice.

"I think I am. Could I count on you to help me? You know everyone and are privy to all the gossip. And you know she must be flawless, delicate, and impervious to insult."

Her heart was light, and her relief spilled over her face like clean water. Vincent wanted a wife but not her. But the dilemma made it hard to suppress a laugh. What woman would want a husband who vowed to love and barb her until death, and possibly further?

"Of course, I would love to help. What do you desire for your life?" Lily asked.

Vincent inhaled. "My God, that is a heavy question. I am not fond of society. It irks me to see the constant fanfare for those born first and little regard for the rest of us. I would like to further explore my house. Ralph and I split the Marquess of Cornwallis's estate in Norfolk, and I agreed to keep the vicarage. It was a refuge during Cromwell's terrors and has secret passages and hidden rooms. The house needs a woman's touch, desperately."

"And in which fashion should the home become? Baroque? Georgian?" Lily pressed. Vincent could easily become distracted by his interests. That would not help in finding the ideal wife.

"I truly do not care. I have collected a great deal of art and literature and simply want to display them. I enjoy a touch of Gothic aesthetic if I must choose but not overtly gaudy. I am more interested in a grand library and art gallery. I want a home *de lettres* as it were." Vincent grinned with pride at his pun.

Lily chuckled. "But what do you want from a

wife?"

Vincent sighed. "I prefer blondes. She must be curious and well-read. An air of mystery is always welcome. I prefer a woman who has very little family or a family I enjoy. Though, as I do not want to marry you, that seems impossible. And, of course, a woman who will not be harmed by refusing invitations. I dislike society, and therefore a popular wife would make us both miserable," Vincent finished.

"I shall begin my search for a mysterious blonde who is well-read and dislikes society. I am eager to find the perfect woman. This way I can ensure your wife and I are friendly! I would hate for us to not be friends." She had twenty prospects in mind, but none of them fit perfectly.

"As would I," Vincent said cryptically. "Now. Tell me all the gossip."

She inhaled sharply. The air filled her lungs with purpose. She would require a lot of breath. This was going to be a long afternoon.

Chapter Three

There are certain aspects to hosting a ball that only the best hostesses pay mind to, but that every hostess should. Always be mindful of the fact that most ladies are sewn into their dresses and the most fashionable dresses are heavy. Therefore, the ballroom should be well ventilated and stocked with ample refreshments. If one is hoping to encourage romance, have boughs of roses to perfume the air.
~Aunt Penny's Advice on Living, May 1885

From his vantage in a small alcove, Ralph could tell his mother's ball was a remarkable success. It was perfectly attended. And more importantly, it was ventilated. There was nothing worse than an overcrowded, overheated ball. Out of reflex, he patted his brow before he withdrew his dry hand to his side. The tendency of the crafted appearances of the aristocracy to wilt under heat was well understood.

The warm candlelight clung jealously to the gilded walls, adorned with mirrors. Debutantes glided about and socialized in an elaborate pantomime. His eyes wandered up and down the bodies of the ladies below him on the dance floor. They flowed amongst the men like water around rocks, and their dresses were too elaborate for anything other than a grand ball. Although the pools of light collected their share of dancers, there were always dark spots in this world. Candles and gaslight were poorly suited to illuminate beauty. Did he prefer the light or the darkness? His elation diminished to a sliver of doubt.

The Duke of Bridgewater's ballroom was famous for its marble floors and the Bridgewater crest inlaid in the middle of the dance floor. Large Ionic columns encircled the room and shouldered the second-story walkway. Twin staircases gripped the sides of the room in a frozen, stony embrace. Ralph and his brothers used to spy from the walkway on the balls held during their childhood and see the couples who had sneaked up there to tryst.

But the final details—those that less-skilled hostesses would have neglected and only the truly elite would notice quickly—engaged the senses of smell and taste. He felt the boughs of ivy hung closely from the columns and smelled the delicate white roses dangled in closely bunched clusters from the chandeliers. He had sipped modestly from the lemonade fountain set to flow over two large blocks of ice to refresh. His eyes drank in the beautiful sprawl below. It was the type of excess that made the justice of his small world so dubious. It was a world where so few held so much. A handful of impractical dresses and waxed moustaches at a party was bad enough. But a waterfall to drink from in an opulent ballroom?

There were sooty hands and empty stomachs just blocks away. Ralph choked back his impolite thoughts and focused on something more palatable. He had previously resolved to develop a skill and work. So many of his peers were men of leisure who would never have these uncomfortable thoughts. The worry that sat on his shoulders, the one that slept with him at night and woke him in the morning, was the tendency for these critical thoughts, when unspoken, to disappear. Observing injustice without critiquing it dulled the senses and made one indifferent to suffering and wrong. There was a hypnotic effect in the daily luxuries of his life. If only he could resist them.

Vincent, who had joined him in his refuge, extended a hand toward him, brandishing a flask. Ralph took a swig and recognized his father's best whisky. The second drink was biting and greedy, and he downed it before handing Vincent back the flask. It was a pity that Sebastian couldn't hide with them, but he was besieged by mamas and debutantes. Soon—too, too soon—Ralph and Vincent would have to join him. Vincent, a man who would never let a single critical thought escape the privilege of being stated out loud, was a welcome presence, and Ralph ignored his own anxiety as Vincent prattled.

Ralph abruptly turned his head as a brilliant gem masquerading as a girl swept onto the ballroom floor. His heart stopped. She was the perfect height, so if she tilted up her face in a moment of passion, their lips would meet. Her hair crowned her perfect face in an elegant arrangement. Her distinctive skin shone out in contrast to the alabaster or cream-colored hues of the women of the ton. It struck him as more dusky, like French or Italian women. Her eyes sparkled and swirled like tiny oceans that shifted from azure to gray to green depending on the light. Even from this far away, the light caught and held their distinct color. And her lips smiled, so plump and full they made every other set of lips pale in comparison. She washed over every sense like a feast of beauty.

She levitated gracefully through the room on a cloud of forced niceties, smiles, and curtsies. Her dress flowed around her long enough to cloud her feet from view, but just barely. Could she float? Upon further inspection, the dress skirted the floor in a most fashionable bustle cut. He drank in the warmth of her shoulders and enticing collarbone. White details and pink rosettes adorned the sky-blue satin dress on the skirt, train, and neckline.

A crack of Vincent's laughter snapped in his ear like a taut whip. "Miss March lost her hairpiece. Look, Ralph! It's caught in her dress! It looks as though an elegant rat is following her. Nonetheless, it is the best suitor she will find."

Even though he tried, Ralph couldn't tear his eyes away from the exotic beauty to gawk at the unfortunate spinster. Of course he would pursue her. She had turned his head without trying. But hopefully she would be an intelligent quarry; appearances could be deceiving, after all. She greeted Sebastian, and Ralph frowned. No matter. He would simply explain to Sebastian that he deeply wanted her, and Sebastian would step aside. Or be shoved. He simmered. How base was his desire?

Sebastian leaned forward to say something close to her. He was too close, really. She smiled broadly. Before, she had a Mona Lisa smile of bemusement and mystery. But now she looked happy and liberated. How enviable. Then she laughed and teasingly tapped Sebastian with her fan. The fire of his jealousy climbed his face until his eyes felt steamy. No matter. He would simply recruit Vincent to help him beat Sebastian about the head until he was ugly and could no longer utter bewitching words. Or he would convince Sebastian to talk about sport or hunting. No woman he had met cared about these subjects, but of course they would nod along politely.

A rose flew and hit her in the face. He whirled around quickly to search its origin. It seemed to come from his direction. Sebastian leaned forward to pick it up, and the beauty looked directly at Ralph with her frozen, perfect smile. Oh no, she was looking at Vincent. Vincent grinned with a deviousness that made Ralph's stomach tighten. Sebastian followed her gaze and raised an eyebrow. The lady whispered something to Sebastian, and they shared a polite and measured laugh. She began to move closer, wielding her seductive smile and slapping her fan against her glove menacingly. Her elegant mouth tightened. Her playful discipline and enticing frame could make men cross their legs.

"I never should have bought her that," Vincent muttered.

Ralph reflexively furrowed his brow. Vincent had bought several ladies' items on their tour, but one only bought things for a lady one wished to court or perhaps a mistress. Did this woman fall into either category? No matter. He would convince Sebastian to avenge himself upon Vincent. Once they were married, then Ralph would have to insist his beauty stop flirting with his brothers. This envy was a dreadful thing, as it was powerful enough to turn him against his closest friends. But that was the exact sort of thing some women might find enticing, so he'd best tuck that idea in his back pocket.

"Vincent! You terrible man!" she sang with a

smile. She closed in and presented her gloved hand. Her accent was pure upper-class English. While not exotic, she was still a beauty.

"A pleasure to see you as always." Vincent leaned forward and kissed the air above her glove.

The lady smiled and feigned slapping the back of his head with her fan.

"Foul play!" Vincent exclaimed while pretending to have an injury. Ralph had never seen his brother as a hand kisser, so this was likely a farce.

"Oh yes, hurling flowers across a ballroom is fair, but smacking a head desperately in need of it is foul play. You are in luck I didn't have anything larger or more embarrassing within reach, or your head would be in quite a bad spot," she joked. Her wide smile revealed perfect teeth.

"No, but I am a scoundrel and you were neglecting me. Besides, what would you advise I throw at you? Sugar is not here. My flask? Ralph?" Vincent asked.

It was nice to be included in their banter.

"Oh, how nice to make your acquaintance again, Lord Ralph." She smiled and presented her hand.

She was poised like marble lit by soft candles before him, unmoving. Oh dreadful, he was supposed to say something. He fumbled for his manners. "I beg your pardon, but I don't believe we have met." He leaned close to the beauty, kissed the air above her glove, and breathed deep. She smelled of jasmine and vanilla.

A pout fluttered across her face. No face could have lips that full—they were the only thing that could steal attention from her eyes.

Vincent interjected quickly, before the silence

turned sour. "Ralph, this is Miss Snowe. Give me your dance card, Lily. I want to twirl you about."

How very, very stupid of him. His memory of a clever street urchin was an illusion cast by time. This woman was different. But people rarely became less interesting between the age of fourteen and twenty. No, she was exotic. Her dress and diction implied exquisite taste. She had been afflicted with a winding, complex life, but there were no wrinkles on her face. Ralph shut his mouth and clung tight to his breath. He could not stop his craving, but he could not act on it either. As a vulnerable child, she had trusted him with her secrets. If only he were an unscrupulous person. The sort who would compromise her and make her his own. But his heart needed to atone for abandoning her in her time of need. His senses were aflame, and he opened his mouth. "Miss Snowe, may I also request a dance?" Why would he, a duke's son, be so nervous?

"Of course, my lord." She purred her words into him, and his legs almost trembled. At least it sounded like a purr.

"Please call me Ralph, as you are such good friends with Vincent. If I don't indulge you, how can I expect you to indulge me?" Ralph leaned forward and emphasized the word "friends." He must move fast to discourage any romance between his brother and his Lily. If he claimed her last waltz, that meant he could escort her to supper. The butterflies in his chest flittered with unease and excitement.

"And you must call me Lily," she answered. She lit up with a seductive smile at Ralph before spreading her fan and peering over it at Vincent. "Thank you for all of the gifts, Vincent. I love everything."

It was a lovely fan of mother of pearl carved to resemble lace. And so, if Lily liked fans, Ralph would buy her every fan in London. He would have hundreds of roses arranged to look like a giant fan. This was a new challenge, but if he pursued her, he had to distinguish himself.

"It is my calling to spoil you and all your progeny. Your children will have to be spoiled by me as well, kind Uncle Vincent. I found a fountain in Greece that revealed one's fate, and mine was to be a Snowe spoiler. When Sebastian looked in it, the fountain showed him a long and boring life. So we know it was right."

Lily sighed in the face of this rivalry and rolled her eyes. "I ought to be mingling about. And you two! Stop playing wallflower and appease your adoring public. You know as well as I do the function of men is to be pretty and charming and laugh politely at my jokes." She spun around so fast that her skirts lifted just barely off the ground. He couldn't stop tapping his foot with eager nervousness as he waited for his waltz. As she moved farther away, his questions grew. Would she return his affections?

If she did, the rules of their class required a complex process of courtship and appeasement directed at the ton, their parents, and any potential critics of their match. If she did not, it would be much the same but with a different result. But the steps and courtesies were the only way to avoid scandal. If he were villainous, he could seduce her. But the knot in his stomach reminded him that he was both a third son and the sort of man who would never sabotage a woman out of desire. Only a detestable man could destroy one who'd had a difficult life. She lit up Vincent's face the way only a best friend might. Compromising her should be avoided. Obviously, his desires couldn't outweigh the risk to her reputation.

Of course, Ralph would regret that decision every lonely minute without her. A bump from a stiff aristocrat adorned in a lush black coat shocked him into consciousness. The aloof rich man glided away from him without apology. Ralph had unwittingly led himself into one of the pockets of shadow between the candles and the lamps. Sometimes the lightest moments were accompanied by the darkest.

Chapter Four

Attending a ball is fraught with difficulties. As ladies, we are sewn into our dresses and squeezed tightly. One must eat a hearty breakfast the morning of a ball, if one does not wish to swoon at the ball. I recommend eating three small meals after breakfast but before the ball. Of course, one should drink the lemonade offered but never the punch.
    ~Aunt Penny's Advice for Living, May 1885

Lily adored balls. Of course, it was a tremendous effort to look this beautiful. She hadn't eaten since teatime, and her tortured stomach ached underneath. But she breathed in deeply and tasted the power she had over the room. She was young and beautiful and desired. She walked amongst the most notable members of Parliament, and they loved her. Balls were like fairy tales come to life. And obviously, the stifled desires of the men around her were like fragrant roses that she never needed to pluck. She danced and talked, awash in feelings of worth and control she never got from romance. The rush of attention and glamour rose in her, like an arc of light joy from her toes to her head, titillating and comforting. Especially after she had been abandoned by parent after parent and friend after friend. The thin heat of desire floated around her like pleasant cloud.

However, it was lovely to see Ralph Mandeville again. He looked less harsh than before. He was too sweet to wear a glare like that. What a paradox. He still resembled a Norse deity, but a nice one, like Baldur. She marveled at his piercing blue eyes and bit her lip a little. Pain brought composure. She had not seen him for what, six years? How were his eyes perfectly frozen in time? Of course, everything else about him had matured in the most delightful way. His hair shone less yellow and now more golden. His face had grown less gaunt and sturdier now. He appeared as an excellent synthesis of Vincent and Sebastian—he lacked the derisive demeanor of the former or the long-windedness of the latter. However, his intentions were not clear. If she asked Vincent about Ralph's infatuations, he would tease her even more.

She gripped another man's hand tightly as Ralph drew farther away. She might have been honored to be the Earl of Coningsby's first dance partner when he returned to London, but he was too intimidating. His title sounded like a hedgehog, but he danced well all the same. His gaze darted away subtly. Lily had caught him stealing glances at Lady Olivia. Oh dear. If those two got married, then half of London would go into fits at the loss. But upon further reflection, the stodgy heir and the beautiful suffragette would be an excellent match. It was, for lack of better term, quite adorable.

She had room on her dance card for only a few new partners, so the Mandevilles took up every spare place. Barton moved reliably but poorly, and he missed several of the steps and trampled her toes. She had ensured a bucket with cool water and ice would be available for her aching feet afterward. She sighed a little. When would he stop interrogating her about Lady Serena? She couldn't help him because Lady Serena was on Lily's list of brides for Vincent. Serena and Barton would not suit. No, Barton needed somebody who would drag him out to events. Lady Serena was far too timid. Although Barton would probably argue Vincent and Serena would be an odd match—a caustic man and a shy, but intelligent woman.

Her next partner, the Marquess of Berkeley, waltzed wonderfully, but she knew enough to keep her distance. He was a renowned rake and was courting her friend Honoria. He smiled to himself, as if removing her petticoats one by one in his mind. But he had the advantages of handsomeness and wealth. Many women found exploring those qualities to be an appropriate use of the brief intimacy.

As she whirled with Vincent, he flouted convention by twirling her about. Her toes never left the floor, and her fine dress flitted about her. Her heart flittered, and she twirled vivaciously and danced a circuit around the drably attired debutantes.

Finally, there was Mr. Adrian Rose, Honoria's brother. He was an exceptional partner and entirely too handsome. During each dance, she could feel her partners' eagerness and it gave an intoxicating power. She smiled before she could stop herself. Judging from the occasional wandering of hands or breathlessness during the movements, her charms were potent. Men seeking wives had cravings, and she had to avoid being too enticing or suggestive. She carried herself flirtatiously but conventionally. She did not crave scandal, but she knew the women of the *ton* lived vicariously through gossip and melodrama. Everyone simply adored watching the calamity, but no one wanted to suffer the consequences.

Before her last waltz, Lily disengaged and sped to the lemonade fountain. Despite her repeated comments about how being parched was afflicting her conversation, no enterprising suitor had fetched her a drink. Apparently, she was too pretty to be listened to attentively. Her feet ached. How long would it take to be free of her dress? She locked eyes with Honoria across the long floor and tapped twice on the fourth prong of her fan. Cards and Scandal were scheduled for two on Thursday. She couldn't wait. Finally, the last waltz began, and she clung tightly to Ralph Mandeville.

"Miss Snowe, may I escort you to supper?" Her ear tickled as he whispered into it.

"Is it already time for dinner?" Her hopes seemed too obvious. Her feet ached, and she trembled with hunger. Her body was a lithe tree thirsting for rain.

"After the song." Had he proposed they flee immediately for a snack, who would have said no?

"Oh, of course! How did you like your tour?" Travel was a subject she could speak about with anyone. Describing a lavish vacation provided a way to talk about wealth without seeming gauche. After all, how many lower-class people could take a grand tour?

"I liked it very much. I thought of you often."

She bent her knees a little to seem dainty and diminutive as he smiled down at her. Men could be so conscious of their height. But that was not important— he had thought of her? How unexpected. Her heart swelled and sang with relief. How very charming, but she couldn't tell exactly why. He thought of her? Most travelers thought of her father and his writings.

"Whyever would you think of me?"

"I thought of your opinions of St. Petersburg, Italy, Paris, and Moscow. You were right. St. Petersburg is far lovelier," he replied. His words were measured and respectful. Too measured.

She swallowed and cleared her throat before croaking out, "Of course." Before she understood what gossip was, and before she truly understood what her mother had intended for her, she had confided in a handsome man at her brother's wedding. That man was Ralph Mandeville. She secretly hoped he had forgotten. But of course, he had not. It was salacious. It was a scandal.

She felt trapped because she was. She couldn't walk away to get her bearings without creating another scandal. She breathed deeply and focused on her feet. She kept her feet moving in perfect time, smooth and practiced. If she could finish this waltz, then she would be decent and safe. There was only one moment at a time, and each moment would pass.

"Miss Snowe, I would never tell anyone else about your…adventure."

This short declaration shattered the tension. Her heart and stomach flooded her with relief.

Lily smiled up at him. Her best defense was overwhelming charm. And just like that, the jeweled mask of her charisma slipped back on. She would command her circumstances. She would dazzle Lord Ralph Mandeville with every sense, and he would forget she had ever been to Russia. If she flirted well enough, he might even forget she was Christopher's sister. But the risk of her "adventure" potentially becoming public cast a constant shadow on her. All her armor, all her reputation, could be rent and thrown away like counterfeit silk if the truth was uncovered.

"Now, now...you are given leave to call me Lily." She focused and traced faint hearts on his shoulder. His suit looked smooth but felt rough.

"Perhaps a nickname?" She tried to follow his eyes, which were staring at some point just beyond her. How very frustrating. Either he remained oblivious or tried consciously to avoid her eyes.

"Hmmm...." She feigned thought while licking her lips. Most men would be trying to caress her or glimpse her breasts. This one could not keep his eyes off the windows. "My father calls me Little Tomato?"

Ralph snickered, and his eyes dropped to hers. "If you are a tomato, then I am a pineapple."

She threw back her head in a laugh. After all, men loved when ladies found them funny. "I am so glad you dislike it. It isn't very elegant, is it?"

"No, but I suppose the name came about when you were young and less refined." She liked this because he was still holding her gaze tight. She couldn't blink.

"Apparently, when I was an infant, I was fond of screaming and turning red. With a tuft of hair to resemble a stem, I reminded my father of a screaming tomato." This flirtation was going poorly, and she needed to right it. "Perhaps we should choose what I remind you of?"

"That would be wholly inappropriate," Ralph breathed. "Would *miliy* be acceptable?"

"Do you mean the Russian word, or do you want to call me 'my lily'?" Either way, this presented a romantic suggestion. *Miliy* was Russian for sweetheart. Maybe her charms had worked. She continued to write tiny hearts onto Ralph with her gloved fingers. Her body bent into his; this would force him to hold her tighter. She gazed into his eyes and realized they were mirrors of her own but in a dazzling blue reserved only for tropical waters.

"While I meant the Russian, most people will assume the latter. I would like to call on you tomorrow. Would that be acceptable?" he asked as the dance came to an end.

"I would adore it," she breathed and paced toward dinner. How astonishing. His interest was an ill match to his actions. Then again, his words were not a good pair for her actions either.

"Tell me, do you like tulips?" His hands slipped into hers and squeezed gently.

If only she could kiss him. Not out of lust, but something kinder. So many men just assumed things, such as all women love roses and value the language of flowers, but he asked. It cost him nothing, but it meant everything. He was exceptionally courteous and kind, but was he courting her or following in his brother's footsteps? His words were flirtatious, but his hands remained properly placed.

"They are, in fact, my favorite. In the language of flowers, tulips mean love, or royalty." At last, in a chair and off her feet. She quietly chastised herself for thinking a man would know or care about the language of flowers.

"And roses mean your suitor lacks creativity," Ralph said. So, he could be funny if he tried.

Her mouth broadened, and her eyes glittered in relief. The tension deflated from her slowly, like water pouring out of a very small hole in a very large bucket.

One could always tell one's host opinion by where one sat for supper. Lily was in the "tolerated but neither liked nor disdained" category. Among her ranks were Honoria and Adrian Rose, the Marquess of Berkeley, Bella, and Lord Amesbury. Olivia was near the Duchess of Bridgewater, to showcase her status as a special favorite of the duchess—lucky girl. But Lily had avoided the dregs at the other end of the table with the Earl of Castleton and Lord Grey. How truly hellish.

"I saw you dancing with all three of Bridgewater's sons. Should I be jealous?" Berkeley asked, his dark blue eyes sparkling. What a terrible flirt.

"Indeed, my lord. You are no longer the only ducal heir at events."

"Pssh. I knew them in school. Sebastian is dull, Vincent is rude, and Ralph is too proper to steal a lady's affections." How sadly correct. Berkeley had every superficial charm, coiffed and unkempt all at once, and was oddly handsome for a ginger. Well, perhaps not a true ginger, but he had a red hue to his brown hair.

"Frederick's biggest advocate is Frederick," Honoria interjected. Of course she called Berkeley by his Christian name. Her voice rang out high and sweet, like a bird chirping at a pretty sunrise.

"Honestly, if you would agree to be my wife, I wouldn't have to be." Berkeley stretched his long arm closer to Lily, nearly clipping her wine, and pointed at Adrian. "Rose, can't you force her?"

"Oh yes, that will convince me. Every girl dreams of the day her brother forces her to marry a good friend." Honoria smirked. This was more levity than Lily would have shown.

Berkeley sighed, and his gaze wandered back to

Lily. "I suppose I shall have to find another bride. Miss Snowe, would you like to be a marchioness?"

Oh no! She forced a giggle. "I don't believe I am properly educated to be a duchess, my lord. I think you may want an earl or marquess's daughter." Berkeley was the grandson and sole heir of the Duke of Wharton. The lady he married would have a castle and more money than the pope.

"Good lord, no." Berkeley leaned close, and his chin almost rested on her shoulder. "I like Honoria because she has a level of contempt for nearly all titled men. I like you because you have seen the world and know more than the average debutante. I'm extremely particular, you see."

"So, it just happens that the women you have the pleasure of seeing have the qualities you are particular about. Perhaps Miss Beauchamp?" Her smile teased just as much as she wanted. He would quit flirting with her if there were another woman to seduce.

"She is beautiful, but I require a wife that will tell me to be quiet. I don't think she will," Berkeley mused.

He was right on both points. "Perhaps Lady Olivia? She is well educated and unafraid to speak her mind."

"At the first disagreement, we would kill each other." Berkeley sighed. "I have contemplated every woman I know, and not one will suit me. But—" He hesitated, leaned close again, and whispered. "Perhaps a few, like a harem."

"Then perhaps you should travel." Lily reached languidly for her drink to insert a space between them. "Many lords find American brides. Visit New York or Boston."

He considered the words. "It will take a few weeks

to plan and to convince Serena…but I think it's a marvelous idea! Thank you, Miss Snowe."

She chastised herself in silence, again. In her head, she heard words she could never say out loud. Lady Serena was Berkeley's sister. After the death of their parents, he was protective and always with her. She had forgotten that they were related despite the two of them being constantly together. Berkeley was so gregarious, and Lady Serena always lurked alongside him like a pretty shadow. This complicated her matchmaking. Or it accelerated it. Who could tell which?

"My father will be returning from South America in a month. You may wish to delay until then. I could host a dinner so you may have an expert advise you."

Berkeley chewed his goose. "Are you certain you will not marry me? You are the epitome of a helpmate. In any case, I will delay until I can speak with Lord Snowe."

She blandly returned to her meal. It was annoying—how many machinations and manipulations did she have to contrive just so everyone could be happy? Her frustration boiled and rose higher. If only everyone would acknowledge her consistent correctness.

As the party began to break, Vincent wound his serpent-like arm under hers. How gauche to touch a woman like that! But since he had twirled her about earlier, this would be an afterthought. She waited pensively for her cloak with Olga. Several gentlemen stole glances at her, their eyes lingering in one direction while their feet (and wives) went in another. Several ladies were stealing glances at her dress.

"Lily, can I call on you this week?" There was an

urgency in Vincent's voice.

"Certainly. Tuesday, I am going to Southampton's fete, and Thursday, I am invited to tea at Miss Rose's home." Home was too far away, and she couldn't focus on her cloak and Vincent at the same time.

"I may come along with you. The Roses are my cousins, you know."

Lily knew something few others knew. Vincent's mother began life as Seraphina Rose. Lily rarely heard anything of them, but it appeared Vincent might view them as poor relations, regardless of their wealth. Seraphina certainly viewed them as lesser.

"Absolutely not. Call on Honoria some other day. Honoria's teas are exclusive and only for the elite few. I will host you any other day, however. Ah, at last." The footmen drew near and brought her cloak. It was silver silk. Her cloak felt like a cold hug made of moonlight. "Goodnight, Vincent. I will see you soon."

"A mysterious tea for glamourous women only? I will have to find a dress in the appropriate size. You know I love nothing more than a mystery."

****

Ralph caught up to Vincent a minute too late to see Lily off. What a bit of relief and a bit of a disappointment! Vincent was saying his goodnights to a few more guests and began to make his way up the stairs. But he took too long. For a churl, he talked too much.

"I'm going to call on Miss Snowe tomorrow. Would you like to accompany me?" Ralph spoke slowly on purpose.

"Always."

Vincent's eyes twinkled with devious spark, but

Ralph had more important things to worry about.

"You are very good friends. That makes me happy. Do you know her favorite flowers?" Ralph asked forcefully. How surprising.

"Hmmm. She hates violets. She finds lilies blasé and roses overrated. I believe she has a fondness for tulips."

"Excellent." He flashed his most disarming grin. He knew precisely how to obtain a most flattering bouquet.

"Would you like to meet just beforehand? I need to look at bachelor's apartments," Vincent asked as they rounded the hall of the family's bedrooms.

Surprise crept into Ralph's face causing the smile to vanish. "May I accompany you? We could get a place together. I am in favor of such a thing. Well, if you don't mind."

The unstated motivation, of course, was to rescue Vincent from the delicate offenses that residing with his mother would bring. He had seen Vincent seethe in her presence. Providing diplomatic distance between the two of them could improve everyone's lives.

"I would be delighted. Is there a reason you wish to live elsewhere?" Vincent sounded curious.

How to disguise his own feelings…maybe a simple shrug would be enough. "Courtship is never facilitated when it is subject to spectators, but on the other hand, I have never lived alone. Eton, Oxford, our tour, here. I should know about managing a house."

"And whom do you plan on courting?"

He stopped sharply at his door. "Since you adore a mystery, we will call this woman Miliy."

Vincent growled. He loved to learn secrets and

hated them being withheld. "Who the hell is Millie?"

Ralph was certain Vincent would follow him, but he did not. Ralph poked his head out the door to see Vincent frowning at a small slip of paper. Whatever this missive was, it saved Ralph from irritating banter. Ralph sighed gratefully for its presence.

Chapter Five

Homes are like shoes. If it doesn't fit, it isn't your shoe. The requirements I have for a home are as different as they can be from my closest friend's. I love light colors and clean lines with lovely open spaces for entertaining. My friend prefers dark rich colors with small tables for card playing. I believe a woman should see a man's home before she becomes attached to him, as these differences can truly break any bonds.

~Aunt Penny's Advice for Living, May 1885

Ralph wished house hunting was more entertaining. Vincent and the leasing agent gushed loudly about the seventh house of the morning. Vincent had very strict ideas about any home he would occupy. He refused a flat outright. And the house could not have many windows, as Vincent's precious art faded in sunlight. Vincent also preferred a house without running water, as the pipes allowed steam and that would also harm Vincent's collection. Why not use a house as a house, as a comfortable place to recline and read?

"I believe you will enjoy this next home." The leasing agent, Addington, shouted from another floor, obviously struggling to maintain his enthusiasm. "It was built during the window tax, so it has very few windows. And sadly, Lord Stallwell has fallen on tough times, so he cannot afford plumbing."

"His misfortune benefits me, and perhaps we could convince him to sell, if I like the house," Vincent sang cheerfully as they entered a gloomy red brick home. How could he sound so cheerful when he had just heard of another's misfortune?

Although Vincent inspected the whole house, Ralph's eyes caught the sight of bookshelves, and he sped toward the library. Why must he wait to see Lily? What could she do with a house such as this? Rumors spoke volumes about her being the most fashionable woman in London, and typically fashionable women lived in fashionable houses. She would be aghast at the dark and dank house he stood in.

The house was sober and tall, contrasting with Vincent's all of a sudden too-sanguine tone. How could he honestly relish less convenience in favor of preserving his musty tapestries? The answer struck Ralph harshly as soon as the thick library door shut behind him and Vincent. It wasn't for Vincent at all; it was for the multitude of coquettes he would parade in front of his collection.

"What do you think of a relief of the sun, perhaps lit with candles for special occasions? I will need some light to read by, and I cannot suffer a boring wall," Vincent whispered, as if he was trying to keep the room's renovation a secret from it.

"I suppose. Since you will, after all, be using it to entertain," Ralph replied and shuffled closer to the blank wall.

"That is quite true. Nothing is more seductive to a woman than a man with an extremely large collection." Vincent smiled at his own joke, which was an almost endearingly confident habit.

"We will have to impose some limits on such acts; we wouldn't want the house to acquire a sordid reputation, brother." Ralph tried unconvincingly to mirror Vincent's smile. When being serious, it was important to appear as though not serious at all. To do elsewise could seem very demanding.

"Pray tell, what sort of limits do you have in mind? One woman? Two women? An entire cast of a musicale? The queen's court?" Vincent could clearly go on like this for hours.

"Consider the remark withdrawn. You may indeed bring the entirety of the queen's aging court here for the purpose of seduction. I am sure of your success." Ralph was actually joking now.

"If you must know—and you are practically begging for me to tell you—there is but one for now. And maybe…for quite some time to come." The words struck Ralph, a quick verbal lightning strike that made this into something far different than mere banter.

"So, Miss Haverford is a serious prospect?" Ralph's mouth was numb as he asked.

"No more serious than yourself and Lily. I am assuming your intentions, but it is unlikely you do not have every step of the wedding planned. You are such a young man, but you have the temperament of a dowager."

Ha! Vincent was seeking to deflect the conversation, so Ralph must have found an area of sensitivity. But giving up on this line of questioning was the only way to avoid being overcome by the intense feelings and dark secrets that Lily and weddings brought to mind.

"I may have the temperament of a dowager, but judging from the house, you clearly have the taste of one. Perhaps we could bring a stuffed chair, and sit it right in that corner." Ralph pointed to the farthest, dustiest corner in the library. "And then you could drink your bitter tea and eat your dry toast in solitude."

"Why, brother...you have wounded me. I am hurt to my core. How could you say these things? How could you...know me so well? A chair with bitter tea and dry toast would be perfection. But you are being evasive; how far off is your proposal?"

Ralph could no longer escape the current of his joy or the undertow of his memories. Lily was perfect for him. He felt deep in the warmest part of his heart that their union would be joy itself. But weddings, much less marriage, had left a mark on his affections, and worries, for Lily.

Lily had changed a great deal since her brother Christopher's wedding six years ago. Ralph had been haggard after a night of too much drinking. She stole his glass of wine and glared at him as she drank. He vividly remembered her steel gray eyes daring him to stop her. Those eyes were too wise and too sophisticated. At the time, she looked and acted at least twenty. But a twenty-year-old should not have been a wine thief.

"How old are you?" Ralph asked. He didn't need to observe etiquette with a wine thief.

"I turned fourteen last month." She sat high, still beaming sophistication as she ate a bite of asparagus. She used the correct fork and somehow managed to speak elegantly through mouthfuls. She was either too lowborn to care about the rules or too highborn to care about the consequences. How wrong those assumptions had been.

"And so, at the tender age of fourteen, you are an expert in fine wines?"

She had raised her head at just the right angle to gaze down her nose at him. Surely this girl was a lost princess of some exalted kingdom. No one would look at a Mandeville that way without the money or the title to back it up. "Of course not. I merely wished to taste the wine to make certain it was perfect. This wedding must be flawless."

This delicate creature made him stifle a hard laugh. She clearly took pains to look thin and dour and judgmental. She had the affect of a dressed-up doll whose years of service to a child had turned it very cynical. "And why, pray tell, must it be perfect?"

She rolled the pretty clouds that were her eyes. He was convinced for a fleeting time that she was touched in the head. Surely a creature so small couldn't contain the temerity to be both dismissive and a wine thief. The tiny, well-dressed contradiction narrowed her gaze before she spoke. "It has to be perfect for Christopher. He deserves it for being the best brother in the world."

She was Christopher's sister. Christopher had a sister? Christopher had practically lived with the Mandevilles for the past six years as Lord Snowe traversed the globe. How peculiar for Christopher not to have mentioned a sister. But Christopher rarely spoke of any of his family. What mischance had made him so silent?

"My apologies, Miss Snowe." This poor pretty thing needed kindness. The youngest siblings needed to care for each other. In a poor family, cruel families called them runts. In a family of means, they were usually creatures of leisure. That description did not fit either of them.

She had smiled magnanimously. "Please call me Lily, my lord."

He couldn't help but smile. The contradiction filled him up with a feeling of light, syrupy absurdity. Lily was a faerie's name, light and charming. Ralph sounded like a heavy brick. It was the sort of name you gave a builder or a grocer. "Thank you, and you must call me Ralph."

"I shall, thank you for the leave." Her elbows touched his as the game course was being placed.

"Tell me, Lily. Is this wedding breakfast perfect?" The duck was savory, and there was a lot of it.

She gazed at the room before she shrugged. "As perfect as English society will allow. They try to strangle the creativity out of things. Have you been to the Continent? I'm terribly fond of Italy."

It had been strange to hear her words come out of such a young mouth. Youth typically meant inexperience. Was this a way of illustrating she was worthy of high regard? An illustration of experience purchased a great amount of credibility in certain circles. She certainly had nothing to prove to Ralph at the time. "I have not. My brothers and I are planning a tour when I finish at Oxford."

"When will that be?" Apparently, she was already trying to assess him. Her interest seemed sincere.

"We will be gone three years. We hope to leave immediately after I have graduated."

"Hmmmm." She had stretched the sound out endlessly. "Italy is phenomenal. I prefer Florence and

Venice. You should also visit St. Petersburg."

"St. Petersburg, as in Russia?"

"Of course, Russia. It is very beautiful but underrated as their…imperialistic actions in Crimea and the Balkans have caused immense destruction. However, much of the Empire is beautiful. Moscow is interesting but not as European as St. Petersburg." Her words were quick, and she did not blink.

"When were you in Russia?" Why the hell Christopher had never mentioned any of this? But asking would have been unfair to the girl.

"I arrived in September of '76, but Papa rescued me in March of '78. I am not fond of Russian winters." She had replied as casually as one might order tea.

"What did you need rescuing from?" There were many meanings to the word rescue, and he had hoped it was a youthful exaggeration.

"Papa felt that I was too young to marry," Lily answered simply.

Her words hit Ralph so hard, his jaw locked up. They filled him up, and air seemed thick as though he were drowning. For the next few seconds, his breath was shallow and his thoughts were hard and heavy as rocks. In 1876, Lily would have been *ten*, but her father didn't rescue her for eighteen months. She used the word rescue, and given her explanation, that meant she had been taken by force. This was why Christopher had been quiet about his sister. What a tragic life for such a whimsical young lady. Why would he keep a personal tragedy secret to them? Their family that had indulged Christopher in their company for years. And why, although he would have been young as well, had her brother not intervened?

"Who...?" Ralph croaked, trapped in the terrifying position of not wanting to know but desperately needing to. He could barely breathe in the heavy water of the situation. Even reflecting on it years after the fact was difficult.

"Who took me? My mother." The word "mother" was spoken with such hatred, not that he blamed her. Even after years of listening to Vincent's invective, nothing could rival that tone. She forced it out of herself like an unwelcome cough. It was not just the intensity, but the disdain and fear. Lily must have thought of her mother like an ugly porcelain thing, worthy of utter contempt, but who would shatter at the slightest indelicacy. Lily's restraint made this anger so sincere. "Or who wanted my hand? Several men. I am considered a great beauty in Russia." She had said this with the same dour and nonchalant tone that had condemned the wine.

It wasn't her beauty that attracted these monsters. She was three or four years older now, but he could imagine how she looked before. She had maintained all her childish features, with her too-large eyes and too-wide mouth. She was quite beautiful, but back then she must have resembled a doll. They had wanted her because she would look childlike for years. His anger had welled up from his feet to his shoulders, like it would explode in flames from every pore. But as always, it had stopped before it reached his head, and he kept his feelings to himself.

"As well as in England," Ralph had reassured her.

Lily had preened with a boastful smile. "However, most men were not able to afford to pay the dowry for me. It is reversed in Russia, and mother set my dowry high so I would live in luxury. I suspect she needed money though, and that was the true reason for the extravagant amount."

Ralph had tried to breathe as the game course was removed and they waited for the first jelly. He recalled hoping she was a liar and falsifying the tale. But later he had confirmed the story with Christopher.

"And so, finally a man offered enough money and I was to be wed. Then Papa came and took me away, and he promised I wouldn't ever have to marry if I didn't want to. We left Russia in quite a hurry."

He appreciated the air that filled him up after the discomfort of the conversation. It had been beautiful to be able to breathe again. He didn't remember holding his breath. What Lily had endured was terrible, but she wasn't ruined. Her past had scratched her, but she still glittered dimly through her opacity and judgments. She might even live unscathed from the affair and become happy ever after.

"We left Russia and crossed the sea to Turkey and spent a while there. I loved the spices they had everywhere. We then went to India and all over Europe, and Papa bought me so many presents. I had to have several footmen accompany me everywhere!" Her excitement had visibly built up, to where she was almost standing. She was less chilly and more comfortable in her speech. Her hands folded in her lap, and she had leaned forward as she spoke.

"Lucky you!" He had to admire Lord Snowe's reaction. Protecting a child by disguising the guards as footmen was clever.

Lily nodded earnestly, her head swaying inches from his face. "I know! Ralph? When I come out, will you help to make sure I'm not a wallflower?"

He had laughed. A hundred rays of light were hitting his face after a long storm, or at least it felt like it. She was still just a girl, despite everything. "I promise, Lily, you will never be a wallflower. If I am able, I will attend your debut only to find every dance claimed. And I will have to fight to fetch your lemonade."

Lily had smirked with a queenly grace. "Marvelous."

They discussed the other wedding attendees and spoke long into the morning. Ralph never forgot her or that conversation. Did knowing her past make his interest in her wrong? She was strong and talented and no longer needed saving. However, he had met her as a child, and he was a full-grown man. She had been hurt, and while she showed no signs of harm, the past must have still haunted her.

Obviously, he needed to treat her gingerly and to show her the utmost respect. To court her as the perfect gentleman. He would follow every rule and never push any boundary. He would give her every opportunity to tell him no and listen to what she said. He promised himself that he would be the most restrained suitor in the history of the kingdom.

Vincent tapped him lightly, shocking Ralph away from his internal world of promises and worries. Ralph grumbled a thoughtful "We have only recently returned. Plus, such a proposal and such a wedding must be perfect."

"Tick tock, brother. You will never have a perfect moment, so you must make do with the least imperfect one you can find."

Chapter Six

When one is planning a garden party, one must arrange for alcoves in which conversation can occur. I prefer small outcroppings of benches amongst one's garden to be the perfect respite during a party. Adorn them with potted herbs of mint or eucalyptus, as they will not attract bees.

~Aunt Penny's Advice for Living, May 1885

Ralph's thoughts swirled so fast, he stumbled dizzily as he entered his mother's garden party. There were three dozen guests within arm's reach, but he couldn't spy Lily. His back stiffened as his gaze flitted back and forth like a pendulum. He had not missed the constant garden parties and balls during his tour. They served a function, but it felt a bit like playing the violin while Rome burned. And what might women achieve if they were not segregated to the domestic realm? If his mother's intelligence and energy could be put to anything else, she could revolutionize the world. However, a duchess must entertain. And her son must attend her events.

There was no Lily to be found, but her friend Lady Olivia and Olivia's mother, Lady Banbury, glittered brightly at the far end of the party. The two stood together, arms linked, whispering and smiling. They looked like the goddesses Frigga and Freya, both golden blonde with brilliant blue eyes. Lady Banbury only looked old in comparison to her daughter, who had delicate ears and whose coy half smile was impish and joyous. Lord Banbury had his hands full with the two gorgeous and devious creatures.

"Lady Banbury, Lady Olivia. It is lovely to meet you both again." He bent at the waist, rigid and formal.

"As it is for us, my lord." Lady Banbury smiled as she and Olivia dropped into a less formal curtsey.

"Is Miss Snowe in attendance?" That was a miscalculation. Never reveal your intentions too quickly. He should have made conversation about the weather or the sandwiches before inquiring after Lily.

"Sadly, no. Her chaperone has a cold, and Lily could not attend." Lady Olivia pouted before donning a fox's grin. "My, my. Have you taken an interest in Lily?"

His jaw dropped, and his mouth filled with cold air as he pondered his mistake. How could Lady Olivia be so blunt? Did all suffragettes have such boldness? But she might be a useful ally in the campaign for Lily's heart. "I believe so, but of course we must be further acquainted."

"Come sit with us." Olivia smiled and extended a gloved hand to lead Ralph and Lady Banbury to a set of benches near a water fountain. "Do you have a cigar or a pen?"

"Olivia, what are you playing at?" Lady Banbury asked. Her voice was thick with warning. The two women were perfect mirrors of each other, separated only by time and temperament.

"Poor Lily has no one to interrogate prospective suitors, with Lord Snowe always roaming the earth. I shall be Lord Snowe." Olivia grabbed his pen and chewed on the end like a cigar. Her brow furrowed. She moved closer and feigned a gruff expression. "And you should be her mother."

Given what he knew of Lily's mother, he would much rather speak to Lady Banbury. "Very well, but you must tell me about Lily."

Olivia nodded and gave a grunt. "Ay, you have a deal. Now…how do you intend to provide for my little tomato? She has expensive tastes, you know."

He caught his laugh before it gave him away but just barely. This beautiful girl was trying to intimidate him. "Well, I have an estate in Norfolk, and I studied economics at Oxford. I am skilled at investments. Lily will want for nothing."

"You are planning on having a career? How very progressive of you." Lady Banbury's words made him nervous about the idea. It was better to change the subject.

"How does Miss Snowe have expensive tastes?"

Olivia cocked her head up at him in confusion. "Surely you have seen her gowns. Lily does not have her dresses made from a fashion plate, but rather, Lily is a fashion plate. She dreams of her new patterns and has the lace or fabric crafted for her. Far too many of the frocks here are copies of Lily's ideas."

"Is that not as expensive as a gown for a ball or a trousseau?" Were women not meant to come to the marriage with a year's worth of clothing?

"I have no idea. She secrets herself to Ireland to have her designs made. I know she has the minute details of her garments crafted for specific events. For the duchess's ball, I noticed the rosettes on her gown had tiny ships sailing into London. There is absolutely no one in London, perhaps the world, who puts as much effort into her ensemble as Lily Snowe." Her explanation was satisfying and revealed just enough to be useful.

"Fascinating," Ralph muttered.

"Ay!" Lady Olivia returned to her overblown impersonation of Lord Snowe. "Now, my Lily has been abandoned by nearly everyone. Can you promise me that you will remain close to her?"

"Lily has not been abandoned." It was worse. She had been exploited by her mother but rescued by her father.

"I beg to differ, my lord," Lady Banbury interjected. "Most people do not recall Lily's introduction, but I do. Lord Snowe introduced her to the queen and then simply felt the need to flee to South America. I understand he is an explorer, but he is a father first. The rigors of our society require an introduction before anyone can pay a call, and no one knew Lily. She would go to the parks and try to make friends, but no one could speak to her until they had been introduced. It was heartbreaking, as a mother, to bear witness."

Poor Lily. "How did she come out of this quagmire?"

"Your brother." Lady Banbury smiled. "Lord Vincent Mandeville, through a campaign of insults, arranged for Lily to be invited to one of your mother's balls. He then introduced her to every person at the ball, and made it seem as though Lily was a special favorite of your mother's. From then on, the poor lamb was drowning in invitations. Lady Belasyse and myself decided to take her on. Olivia was away at Cambridge, and I had very little to do with my days, so I decided to adopt Lily."

"Lily once spoke to me of that time. She said she was confused as to which was lonelier; no one speaking to you at all or only being spoken to in hopes of a better connection. I did not have the heart to tell her, but that is the nature of society." Olivia straightened and returned his pen. "I am afraid your brother has caught my act and now believes I have a parrot growing out of my head."

Sebastian's confused face was right behind him, watching closer than he had a right to. When had his brother become so sneaky? "I promise to explain that you were simply being an excellent friend. And I do promise to keep Lily very happy. I am delighted she designs her own patterns. I vow to encourage her to do it further," Ralph murmured to the small circle.

Lady Olivia smiled brilliantly. "And I shall to encourage your suit to Lily. I'm sure you will suit very well. You may even grow to love each other."

"I believe that is the aspiration of all brides and grooms." He stood up and brushed his lap off. "If you will excuse me, ladies, I should greet my brother."

"Good afternoon," mother and daughter sang.

This conversation, though useful, did nothing for the nerves. After all, even if he declared his intentions, it would not erase the hardships in her past. Lily had been treated poorly by both of her parents.

People thought of Lord Snowe as a hero, but Lady Banbury had a point that no man should just abandon his daughter. Lily's world was far more complicated than Ralph had understood.

However, with the support of her friends, he could begin pursuing her openly.

Chapter Seven

Conversations during courtship should attempt to reveal the soul of a man. One can usually find this by watching his interactions with his mother, servants, and friends. He should be kind but distant from all three. One does not want a meddling mother-in-law, servants that take liberties, or friends that don't respect a wife. Alternatively, a man who is disrespectful of any of these is not worth one's time.

~Aunt Penny's Advice on Living, May 1885

After waiting for what had felt like forever, Ralph followed Lily into the Duke of Southampton's Piccadilly townhouse. Long waits were a toll paid on any elite invitation. Lily's chaperone and Vincent followed behind Ralph and Lily, but far enough behind to make mischief possible for everyone. Vincent's friendship with Lily was useful, but their closeness made him roll his eyes on occasion. While calling on Lily had been easier, how would she behave when not being teased and tormented by his brother? How much of her measured smile came from formality, and how much from sincerity? How much was for him, and how much was a product of Vincent's humor? Twin waves of joy and anger welled up in him. The joy came when he thought he was in her favor, and the anger when he thought he was not. How very powerful this woman was, even if she didn't know it. Then again, she probably felt like a prisoner, with her every move inviting misinterpretation.

Southampton's title was ancient. As the fourteenth Duke of Southampton, Alastair Belmont had acquired a great deal of art and artifacts when he inherited the title. Everything Southampton possessed was of some historical importance. Even his townhouse, which sat quietly in Piccadilly when most fashionable people had moved to Mayfair fifty years ago. The ostentatious home was built just after the Great Fire, and it sat comfortably in its neoclassical style. Its opulence stood out in gilded ego amongst the false humility and discretion of the other homes. The friends' footsteps echoed in the domed hall. Ralph caught Lily gazing at the cherubs painted over the ceiling, who were in turn watching over guests. They peered down with a little curiosity and a bit of indifference. The rigid suits of armor and weapons reminded every guest that a Belmont had fought in nearly every war since the battle of Hastings. The whole house reeked of status and noblesse oblige. Clearly, the Dukes of Southampton kept trophies for centuries.

Southampton lounged with a younger girl in a room with vaulted ceilings. They sat too comfortably for aristocrats. Southampton looked much the same as before. He was stately, just over six feet tall with mahogany brown hair and dark blue eyes. When he wasn't smiling, he had the gift of appearing commanding. Ralph smiled in secret confidence. Southampton was actually shy and nervous in crowds.

The lady at his side reclined like an alluring cat. Her appeal almost boiled over. She wore her auburn hair down in curls, as a child would. But she was no child. Her figure was hourglass-shaped with an ample bosom and tiny waist. Her smile began at her plump mouth and travelled up to her jade green eyes. His arousal by this woman stung the back of his head with guilt. Better to consciously stare at Lily. Hopefully, she had not read his mind. This irrational fear was rooted in something. Was his depth of affection for Lily so great he needed to feel guilt for such a light thing?

"Lily, who is the little goddess?" Vincent asked, trying his best to seem casual.

"The true reason for Southampton to host a garden party. I believe that is Lady Aurelia, as she is due to come out next year. Southampton cheats. Well done to him," Lily explained without a hint of judgment.

"Southampton is clearly a good brother. I could not imagine Sebastian hosting a garden party for Ralph and me." Vincent groaned. He leaned too quick and too close into Lily.

"No, your mother merely hosted a ball. Don't be maudlin." Obviously, her chastising was good-natured. She reclined into Vincent and breathed with a false sense of seduction, "Olga will be sad at your infidelity, Vincent."

"She bears such a burden well," Vincent stiffly replied.

As they approached the duke to be received, the weight of the rules of courtship were crushing. Ralph could be near Lily but never alone. Decorum allowed him to buy her small gifts but never touch her unless dancing. They could converse but not about anything "impure," a term which no one could define. It only appeared capable of definition after one had transgressed. Although admittedly, Vincent could have come up with an alphabetical list of debaucheries if asked. Ralph's frustration was a throbbing vein in his head, and he had only been courting her for four days. Given the mental and physical stress, he may not survive an entire month. If the goal of courtship was marriage, a union of two persons, then why did every step need to be measured and judged by others?

How could intense passion provoke love and hate at the same time? He wanted her more and more. The desires of his body and mind were visceral aches. They were constant, uninvited companions. It was too confusing. He had a responsibility to her, of course. He needed to be more than just another feckless man promising protection but never delivering. But her beauty was so great that even his tightly gripped mind could not come up with pure motives. He wanted to crush her body under his, taste her mouth, and…It was entirely inappropriate to remain silent and think of tupping in polite company.

The invitations and garden parties were just vehicles through which society could observe and intervene in the marriage market. The banality and uncritical acceptance of this system by his peers was loathsome. But he couldn't become a libertine and ask her to be a wanton. After all, he was bound by more than just his base needs. He was a good man, in spite of his lusts. However, just thinking of Lily as a wanton was too distracting. As he regained his composure, he stopped just short of walking into a tree. How could he be so preoccupied?

After being received by Southampton, they walked the gardens. Vincent preened and spoke too loudly to

Lily's chaperone in bad German and Greek. Was it possible to get away with a seduction if that seduction was in a foreign language? That would be a useful loophole. Lily walked with grace. She was a painting of a lady in a garden come to life. How did she fit perfectly in every situation? Even her dress seemed from a dream—a lovely lilac day dress with enamel pansy buttons. And upon further inspection, the embellished lace cuffs had decorative teacup designs on them.

"How lovely!" Lily sighed and touched his arm. The light touch made warmth arc through it in a way that made him forget what they had been discussing. "Southampton has bluebells! Some people won't plant them because they flower early in the season and don't bloom for a July garden party."

"Are you fond of gardening?" Opinions were the gateway to her mind, so he needed to know her opinion on everything. Her thoughts on politics and how she preferred her eggs were of equal importance. Oddly enough, he didn't know either.

"Not inordinately. I enjoy gardens, but my thumb is not particularly green. I assume I will marry a man with an estate where I can plan a garden." She wandered farther into the garden and away from the other guests with a knowing half smile.

He wasn't a literary man, but the pointed imagery laid before him was obvious—an invitation to journey farther into an unchaperoned garden, dark and enticing. So pungent a metaphor for what he was undertaking, it almost hit him in the face not to have seen it before. But like everything that tempts, this seductive opportunity was a knot in the stomach instead of a gasp of pleasure.

Confusion was brewing; yearning, curiosity, and guilt stirred in his mind like a harsh tea.

"Vincent, Sebastian, and I have estates in Norfolk. Mine is neighbor to Vincent's. In the middle, truly," Ralph babbled. He caught himself in half step—frozen like a rabbit that just found out it was in a hunter's sights.

"Where will you live during the season?" Lily asked over her shoulder. Her words always melted him.

It was all he could do not to kiss her. They were far enough from the other partygoers, and Vincent was distracting Olga. It seemed almost engineered to tempt him. It would be so easy to simply pull her body into his and press his lips to hers. And yet, how could he treat her that way and be any different from the other men who had promised her friendship and protection, then failed? Why couldn't either half of him, the one that wanted her body coiled around him tightly or the one that wanted to be her shield, just agree with the other and let his struggle be over? Wishes would not relieve the tension in him, the unique ache of desire that swelled when the prospect of transgression came up.

"I haven't considered. I suppose I shall have to find a house. I would only be in town for socializing. I have no seat." She had never discussed politics, so did she care? Most people assumed all lords sat in the House of Lords. All dukes' sons were lords, but only the heir would hold a seat.

"You could build a new house! I hope to design one; I have so many ideas."

Her eyes were alight, and his smile beamed in happiness and envy. How could he not—he had found her passion.

"Are you interested in architecture?" Hopefully this was where her heart lay. He could study architecture for years if that would win her hand.

"I am better at the home arts than the architecture. I have brilliant ideas, but the mathematical components intimidate me. If I were wrong, the house might collapse. It is the way of my dresses. I may have the ideas, but I need a seamstress to sew them. I tried and accidentally sewed my left arm closed." Her blush was arousing, even though it was platonic.

"What do you have in mind for a townhouse?" And before he could stop himself, he pulled her close, so he could inspect her arm. "Lily, I apologize for this, but your arm looks fine. Are you quite sure of your injury?" They were still far from any other person, and he would have discussed anything to keep from behaving inappropriately with her. Even an ill-toned joke. The subject of architecture, as dry as it was, was a welcome distraction. Maybe his mixed feelings were deeper than he thought. But she was soft and lacy, and her eyes were locked on his in a way that threatened to make his hidden thoughts very public.

Her smile was polite, though—no teeth showing and big dimples. "Well, I'm fond of the Queen Anne style. I have a vision of the vestibule being a dodecagon shape. I want the ceiling to be a *trompe l'oeil* of a Japanese parasol with cherry blossoms. I think a teak column with a table built around it would resemble an umbrella handle. Oh my, I am rambling. I do apologize." She pressed her back against a tree. The bend of the tree caused her back to arch.

How many layers of torture could he endure? There was the enticing posture Lily had chosen. The slope of her backside pushed firm against the tree. The branches of the trees ensured that her face and breasts pushed up toward Ralph, highlighting the narcotic allure of her swelling femininity. She could twist away if he tried to ravish her like the beast he felt like. His heart leapt into his throat, and her body drew closer and closer. His pulse surged, and the world swirled in front of him like the whole forest shared in his excitement. But before his heart hammered his will into submission, he would claw his way back to polite subjects. Ones that were not soft and lacy. Ones that did not smell like perfume. He would regret doing this at some point.

"Miss Snowe? Ah, and Mandeville." Lord Amesbury appeared down the path with Adrian Rose. Amesbury seemed indifferent to the scene before him. Adrian Rose, who was hardly a rake, but was an observant man, arched his mouth in the manner of a disapproving fish. He righted it as soon as Lily spoke.

"Pleasure to see you again, my lord and Mr. Rose," Lily answered. She disentangled herself from the tree, and Ralph, and gave a polite dip.

He bit his lip and must have nodded politely. If they saw this for what it was, they overlooked it for now. How irritating. Just another reminder that the rules could be bent or broken without punishment, but that such indulgences were arbitrary.

"I say, you have wandered far from the others," Amesbury noted in his least judgmental tone. Or perhaps he was chastising and just bad at it.

"We were walking with Vincent and my chaperone. They are over by the willow tree," Lily said as she pointed to Vincent and Olga, not half a minute away. "Is Miss Rose in attendance as well, Mr. Rose?"

"She is, and she is besieged by Berkeley at the moment," Rose answered. He clearly knew what happened based on his practiced response, answering only what was asked.

"I believe I should rescue her. Excuse me, gentlemen." Lily gave another curtsy before collecting Olga and walking out of view toward the party.

"I thought you liked Berkeley, Rose," Amesbury asked lazily.

Ralph remembered Amesbury from Oxford, when he was only the second son of the Marquess of Hastings. After his brother passed, Harrison Staverton became Lord Amesbury. He had matured into the title. While he was well kempt, lines were beginning to form under his hazel eyes. His sandy hair was shorter than he kept it in school, and he had gained weight.

"I do, but I like my sister more," Rose replied with a smile. Ralph's cousin closely resembled Vincent. They shared the deep brown hair and pale blue eyes, but it was more than that. They both looked disdainful regardless of their mood. However, Adrian was one of the best solicitors in London and had a very promising career ahead of him.

"Ah, hello, Rose, Amesbury. Lily stole my dear Olga from me. I'm so happy to see you, Rose. I have been planning on visiting you," Vincent blathered and drew into the group.

Rose looked surprised but wary. Of course a man practiced in the courthouse had an excellent poker face. "Really, whatever would you need of me?"

"Friendship, of course," Vincent said jovially. "I am famously sociable and renowned for my good wit." Vincent said this without a hint of irony. But no one would be gauche enough to correct him.

Ralph's eyes couldn't help but follow Lily as he tensed. He might have missed his chance.

Chapter Eight

One of the greatest luxuries afforded the modern lady is a small tea with good friends. Faithful friends will allow you a freedom found almost nowhere in the world. I have a friend who adores dressing as though she were a duchess and insists on only feminine topics of conversation, as she is the only daughter with six brothers. Therefore, it is my pleasure to indulge her. A good friend should accept you as you wish to be, even if you desire to wear a ball gown for an intimate tea.
~Aunt Penny's Guide to Living, May 1885

Lily was doing her best to sit in Honoria's drawing room, but her hands kneaded her cards in frustration. Her worries sucked the air out of the room; she felt like she couldn't breathe when she thought of the embarrassment. How could she escape her shame? Southampton's party was a humiliating debacle. She had practically begged Ralph to kiss her. Amesbury and Adrian, two eligible men, saw her presenting her breasts and attempting to seduce Ralph. And it had not worked! For a moment, he seemed like he would lose control. She knew a man's subtle lurches before they caved in. His mouth was dry, and his hands fidgeted. And from their breathless conversation and his precarious fixation on her body, maybe it was working. But his resolve held too long. Maybe she should travel with her father, protected from her private shames. But Ralph was comfort and the physical love she craved. Her heart swelled and hammered when she thought of him. No, he was assuredly not interested.

The worst aspect of her behavior was her failure. He didn't kiss her; he didn't touch her. He just asked her about decorating. She had enticed him away, flashed her delicious naked skin, and twisted her backside in a pose that would make a nymph blush. But there was no evidence of her success. Maybe if she acted more like one of the columns they'd discussed, he would give in. Perhaps the Mandeville brothers, including Ralph, would only ever view her as a sister. She had always thought that, as soon as she wanted a husband, she would simply have to choose one. But if Ralph was her choice, and he denied her, was she was wrong about everything?

"Lily, are you in? It's two secrets to call," Honoria chirped in Lily's ear.

She held a pair of jacks and sevens tightly, a decent hand. She tossed a red chip into the center of the table. "Raise to five."

Cards and Scandal was Honoria's idea. It would foment a tremendous uproar if the *ton* knew that four of the most eligible debutantes met to gamble. Playing for money came off very gauche, not to mention the potential illegality of it, so they bartered secrets.

Olivia Pembroke was the Earl of Banbury's only child and the most beautiful woman in decades. This was both common wisdom and accurate. Olivia radiated beauty with her buttercream hair and sapphire eyes. She lit up every room as if she had swallowed a star and the stardust seeped from her. Olivia was also an outspoken suffragette and feminist. She attended society parties and lectures at Cambridge with equal zeal, but she considered her studies her highest priority. Olivia's biggest flaw was how annoyingly accomplished she was.

Lily's other close friend, the Honorable Miss Bellatrix Beauchamp, sat across from Lily. From the moment they met, Lily's whole body felt like a warm smile every time she saw Bella. Bella possessed a more muted beauty than Olivia, but her elegance made her very pretty nonetheless. Sadly, her painful shyness disguised that she could sing better than a nightingale. She also had a special trick in that she could remember every word she heard and could detail nearly everything she had seen. The granddaughter and ward of Lady Belasyse, the unofficial matriarch of London society, Bella had a profile that rivaled Lily's own. Although Bella and Lady Belasyse contrasted in meekness and boldness, their bond ensured they prevailed in any contest of wits or wisdom.

Miss Honoria Rose was the eldest of the Rose daughters and Adrian Rose's younger sister. Honoria delighted in flaunting her commoner's style of beauty. She took pride in her brilliant red hair and charming freckles. Her green eyes sparkled with an impish gleam every time an old biddy gave her beauty advice to rid herself of her freckles. She absolutely refused to allow society to shape her, and in that way, she was like Vincent.

"Does anyone know anything about Miss Marlene Haverford? She appears to have just materialized from the ether," Honoria asked as she checked the pot.

The mention of Miss Haverford was like hearing

the brakes on a steam engine, and Lily failed to stop her eyes from rolling. Midroll she took note of the crème-colored ceiling. "I cannot bear to be near her. I wish I knew why, but something about her sets my teeth on edge."

"She lies. It's very odd, but she is quite a chameleon," Bella whispered.

"You can't fault her for that. Damn, I fold." Olivia lay her cards down. "I heard Mrs. Jennings is her sponsor. She's a dear but not very...cunning."

"A polite manner of declaring her a dunce. But, pray tell, why can I not fault Miss Haverford for her mercurial personality?" Honoria asked. She displayed her hand, a full house.

"We are twenty years. She is older and in her first season. She has perhaps three seasons before she is on the shelf. She must cater to every man she meets if she hopes to be married, especially if he likes a long engagement," Olivia answered. The implication, of course, was that her verbal jousts and public criticisms would be sufficient to condemn her to spinsterhood.

Miss Haverford was quite tiresome. She was the only consistent topic Vincent ever talked about. Lily tried hard to suppress a smile when he gabbed about her butter-colored hair. It lay in perfect complement to her cow-brown eyes. Of course Vincent would never describe her as a cow. Why did she care that Marlene had captured Vincent's wicked heart? It couldn't be jealousy of Vincent's affections. Something about Miss Haverford manifested as untrustworthiness. On the other hand, it could just be that Miss Haverford was new and not a friend.

"How goes the suffrage? When will I be able to

vote?" Lily asked Olivia, hoping to change the subject.

"It goes miserably. Unless and until every woman agrees we need the vote, no woman will have it. It is a power that only men can bestow, even with a queen for nearly fifty years," Olivia lamented. "It is ridiculous to base women's rights on men's whims."

"Don't be dejected, Olivia. Progress is long and arduous, but each generation contributes more and makes the world a better place." Honoria's smile was honest, and she winked a little for extra persuasion. "In addition, if it is a mere whim, then we are merely one elegant dress from Lily away from suffrage. After all, men cannot be led by logic alone."

There was one man Lily wished was less led by logic.

"I did see Berkeley at a debate. He was cheering for the communists. Is the future Duke of Wharton going to give away all his money?" Olivia asked slyly, changing the subject to fluster her companions.

"Frederick is not a communist. He merely believes that everyone should have a base standard of living: a roof over their heads, hygiene, and food in their stomachs. He's rather fond of the investment economy and enterprise because it encourages progress. Before it, people could not leave bad jobs and remained trapped by the village of their birth. But it would be silly for him to give all his things away. It wouldn't make any difference. Frederick says we must change the system in which we live," Honoria answered. She shuffled the cards with a flair only scoundrels should exhibit.

"Isn't it hypocritical of him to advocate for the poor while being so wealthy?" Olivia countered.

Lily envied Olivia's elegance as she sipped her sherry. How could her tone sound so warm yet so studied?

"Of course not. It would make Frederick less powerful, and his fortune could not provide for all the poor in London. No, he'll continue to be a thorn in the side of the powerful for many years to come." Honoria's voice trilled with vigor.

Honoria's unusual defensiveness stirred in the air. Maybe there was more below the surface.

"That seems logical; a powerful man in Parliament is worth millions," Bella mumbled.

"Honoria, did you really reject his marriage proposal?" Lily felt the words leave her mouth, and her stomach tumbled in instant regret. Olivia gasped, and Bella nodded as they threw their chips into the pot.

"I have rejected nine of his proposals. And that only includes the marriage proposals. There may have been other proposals as well." Honoria smiled as she raised to ten secrets.

"But he will be a duke!" Olivia cried. "And he's ever so wealthy. And he's kind and generous. And I don't have to say it, but he is incredibly handsome."

Olivia was right on every account. It wasn't uncommon to reject a proposal, to make a man work for it, but to reject nine was just foolish. And according to rumor, Berkeley was a good and attentive lover. It was unheard of for anyone to reject a ducal heir, but especially a mere miss. Honoria must have lost her mind.

"I have heard every woman he beds is happy for the pleasure," Bella added.

Lily needed answers. She raised her eyebrows

intently at Honoria. "Do tell, Honoria. Why will you not marry Berkeley?"

"No one has won that high a pot," Honoria teased.

"Pssh! We are friends, you can trust us," Olivia pushed.

"How much would you trade it for?" Bella asked.

Honoria bit her lip and tapped her fingers pensively. "Perhaps five hundred pounds?"

Lily resigned herself to never knowing this secret with a sigh. Some things she was better for not knowing. Life was immensely simpler when one knew which keyholes one should not peep through. Sadly, Lily had learned this lesson in an embarrassing fashion when she found one of Christopher's gentleman's magazines.

After the game had ended, Olivia turned and whispered, "How many of Honoria's chips do you have?"

Lily counted the red chips. "Twenty-two."

"If we three combine our chips, we will have seventy-eight. Surely that's enough for part of the secret," Olivia said.

This wasn't a bad idea. "Very well."

Honoria's pout and blushing cheeks teased a big secret indeed. This had to be a true scandal. "This is all very underhanded. However, I admire cleverness. I cannot marry Berkeley because my heart belongs to another."

Such a revelation crackled like thunder and stunned the room. Lily's mouth became dry and her mind raced, grasping at the disparate threads of their memories to solve this mystery. A pity that it was Honoria's secret, Lily mused. Her mind coiled and got into position to strike—she would figure it out.

Oh, the possibilities were endless. Honoria wouldn't fall in love without some hint of affection. That meant it had to be a former suitor or possibly a servant. Surely there hadn't been any other suitor than Berkeley? Honoria nearly always accompanied him and Lady Serena. Of course, Lily had heard of women who only enjoy other women's company, but Honoria didn't strike her as the type. Maybe Lily should just avoid intrusion—maybe it was none of her business. Of course, that had not deterred her before.

Apparently, while Lily thought, Honoria had been scheming. "Lily, I own all of your debts now. I want to trade them for you helping my sister with her coming-out wardrobe. A debutante wearing your dresses might land the son of a duke."

Miss Aurora Rose was far too pretty for Lily's comfort. She looked half doll and half duchess, and that could be a very dangerous thing for such a young woman. Aurora had a slender frame and a perfect face with large round jade eyes and hair the color of deep chocolate. And Lily envied her nose. It was adorably upturned and tiny. Aurora's mouth even rivaled Lily's. Lily needed to get married before Aurora's debut or else the comparisons would begin. With Lily being the older and less exciting of the two, she had more to worry about. Assisting Aurora in poaching Lily's marriage prospects would be dreadful.

"That would be delightful. Perhaps you should invite Lady Serena, as I have not yet met her." Lily tried hard to lie without a hint of her turmoil. And in the way that only two women can, Honoria and Lily decided to investigate each other.

Chapter Nine

I find Wales to be an underrated jewel in Britain's crown. Of course, most English find very little charming north of Bristol, but I find it to be some of the most beautiful land in the Empire.
~Aunt Penny's Guide to Living, May 1885

"I don't understand why we are going to Wales. I thought you went to Ireland for your fabrics," Honoria whined excessively as she, Lily, and Olga bumped together and arranged themselves tightly in the train car.

"I tell people that I go to Ireland, but actually, it is Wales." Lily could not stop fidgeting, and her fingers tapped nervously against her dress. It was hard to be still and calm.

"Ah. Much like how you seem to be infatuated with Vincent but secretly prefer Ralph," Honoria teased.

It was too much to suppress her groan. "Is there any person with such low intelligence as to actually believe that I would prefer Vincent to Ralph?"

"Yes. Most people prefer Vincent," Honoria answered tartly.

"I do not, at least not as a husband. Vincent is a friend—the best friend anyone could ever have," she argued, eager to beat back this point. "But I would murder him if he were my husband."

Honoria chuckled like an imp. "I have never asked, but how did Vincent earn such loyalty from you?"

She froze. No one had ever asked before. "If I tell you, I must insist that you cannot repeat it to anyone. Not even Bella or Olivia."

"Of course I will not. I shall shave my head before I break a confidence," Honoria vowed.

Lily breathed in, terribly unsteady. She despised reliving that day. Her eyes glazed in hazy recollection. "Sebastian and Vincent were friends of my brother Christopher. Sebastian more than Vincent, as Sebastian and Christopher had been friends since their first year at Eton. When I was fourteen years old, Christopher married Clara Richmond. Three years later, Clara tragically died in the birth of their child, who also died."

"My condolences. You never speak of your brother," Honoria murmured and patted her hand. The warm touch was reassuring.

"No, I do not. After burying his wife and child, Christopher turned maudlin and mean. He took to drinking gin, every day from morning till night. I despise the smell of gin. To me it smells like death." Lily grimaced. She crinkled her nose—even mentioning the dry juniper scent of gin was disgusting.

"Fortunately, it has fallen out of fashion," Honoria asserted.

"Yes, it is fortunate." Lily's mouth was dry. Recalling this was like being in a trance, like it happened to another person. "I recall clearly that the house began to fill with tension. It was as though a mysterious gas had filled the rooms, and I was terrified that if I did one wrong thing a match would ignite to explode all around me. I, in my wisdom, decided to let some air inside the house in the form of an informal dinner with Sebastian and Vincent."

Honoria gave a nervous laugh. "I would be hard-pressed to think of any event with Sebastian as informal."

"Sebastian can be quite informal. As a child, I thought the Earl of Coningsby sounded like a title for a stately hedgehog. Sebastian still makes hedgehog noises at me. And Vincent still calls me his little lion tamer, as he believes I had tamed lions in my time in Russia." Lily focused to continue, lest Honoria ask about Russia. Please let her avoid the subject. "The dinner went smoothly. Afterward, Sebastian suggested foregoing cigars so I could join them. I made conversation with Vincent, but I must have said something wrong that made Christopher tell me to go to bed."

"Do you remember what you said?" Honoria sipped something and set it down, leaning closer to Lily. Being so close felt more intimate, and that warmth did not sit will with Lily. Not while discussing this dark tale.

"No, but I tend to verbally spar with Vincent. I rose from the table, and as I walked down the hallway to the stairs, I could hear footsteps behind me. I was so afraid that, whatever those footsteps were, whoever they belonged to, I was in trouble. Before I could turn, a hand gripped my shoulder to turn me, and Christopher slapped me. He was so angry. He told me I had embarrassed him in front of his friends. His eyes filled with rage, and I was too afraid to move." Lily felt the hot and searing tears streaking her face, and she could barely contain her shock. Those tears had appeared from nowhere. She could not blink them away easily.

Honoria moved to sit next her and wrapped her arms tightly around her, crushing her in soft traveling clothes. "I am so sorry. I had no idea that happened to you. You don't have to say any more."

"It is fine. Before I knew it, Christopher had his hand around my throat. I had never thought of myself as small or frail, but my brother's hand around my throat suddenly made me feel as though I were a rag doll in a dog's mouth." Lily's moved her hand defensively to her throat without thinking. Try as she might, she could never forget that night. "I remember darkness enclosing me and faint purple dots began to appear. Then suddenly, right as I thought I might die, I dropped to the ground and begin to rasp for breath. Sebastian had punched Christopher and knocked him to the ground. It was such a haze, but I could hear Sebastian shouting, 'Never hurt a girl. Never hurt your *sister.*' Vincent lifted me, and once again I felt as though I were a doll, but this time I was a cherished doll. He ordered tea with honey and took me to my room."

"Thank goodness! What happened next?" Honoria asked, still embracing Lily.

"Vincent helped me out of my dress. I was honestly more mortified about my state of undress before a gentleman than I was about my brother. However, Vincent reassured me that he would never feel lust for a girl who is injured. He read *Alice's Adventures in Wonderland* to me until Sebastian joined us. They both vowed to be my new brothers until death.

Christopher and my father had a tremendous row, and Christopher left to never return." She shut her mouth tight. It would be a misstep to mention how glad she was to be free of her brother.

"I certainly understand why you would never marry Vincent now. I imagine, in a world where people hurt and betray you, having one person to simply be your friend is immeasurably comforting. I am very sorry you had to go through that, Lily," Honoria whispered with wide sympathetic eyes.

Lily nodded. Vincent and Sebastian were perfect as they were. She never wanted to change their relationship. "Thank you. Vincent took to the role of big brother more than I could ever have wished. During his tour, he wrote from every port and sent endless gifts. He makes me feel as though I am worthy of being adored by a brother."

Honoria chuckled. Anything to cut the tension. "I could never see Adrian as being anything other than an adoring brother, especially toward Aurora."

Could Adrian Rose be enraged? No, he was too evenhanded and calculating to ever allow himself to be controlled by his feelings. "No, neither could I."

"I will keep your secret. It frightens me to know how many closed doors have such violent secrets beyond them. It is no comfort, but you are not alone," Honoria assured. Honoria hinted at a secret, and she knew one of her own.

"Bella?" Lily asked. No one should have to endure her miseries.

Honoria nodded. "Her father is a monster."

Honoria's face was stone. Beyond the balls and gilded chandeliers, London had endless horrors. It was frightening that such things occurred just beyond the beautiful gas-lit streets. However, society never treated the victims as innocent. Rather, if anyone knew what Lily and Bella had endured, the blame would rest with the ladies. It was an injustice, but it was one society comfortably perpetuated year after year.

Chapter Ten

When preparing for a dinner party, pay close attention to the seating arrangements. If the hostess cannot find any reason for two people to converse, then they should not be seated next to one another. The conversation could spawn from something as simple as he has investments and her favorite cousin hails from York.

~Aunt Penny's Advice on Living, May 1885

Ralph couldn't hide his foul mood as he stomped up the too-short stairs to his parents' home. He only had a few seconds to grimace in private before entering the audience of family and servants. So those few seconds had to matter. Of course, the expectations of his family demanded the serene expression of indifference and piety all people of station had to exhibit. He had been wrestling with his courtship of Lily for three weeks and making the sort of attempts that previously had been unavailable to him. It had been progressing well. His heart swelled with more certainty with every encounter, but he owed her more than a mere suitor. His mind raced with warm vigor and hot ambition when he thought of her. His fantasies leaked into every encounter they had, and he replayed them over and over, finding reasons for hope and drifting to troubled, exciting sleep. But the memory of her hardship was a heavy anchor. His secret guilt for failing her in her youth had affixed itself sternly to his passions. Her father was due in town next week, providing Ralph with a chance to finally ask for her hand. But what he'd seen yesterday still filled him with bile. He had spied her at the International Inventions exposition with Lord Fane. Detestable Lord Fane.

Fane had escorted her around the fair. Watching them walk about the exhibits, even knowing they were there together, broke his heart and filled him up with steamy anger. He raged as Fane tried to touch her while "showing" her this or that. The lack of subtlety meant Fane felt comfortable with Lily, which was loathsome if true and worse if wrong. Vincent had to drag Ralph's angry visage away when Fane cornered Lily and tried to kiss her. Ralph didn't recognize himself yesterday.

But before the world of London society placed its eyes back on him, when he was in the limbo-like antechamber of his parents' home, all by himself, he couldn't repress his grimace. Vincent called men like Fane "moths." According to Vincent, moths circle flames listlessly until they get too close and are burned. Fane circled around the earthbound sun of Lily's grace, until he got too close and came away scorched.

In fairness, Lily had rebuffed all of Fane's attempts. She was polite but not encouraging and held herself well. But Ralph couldn't stop this anger. It flowed through him in the reddest shade of blood. It wasn't fair, but he was angry. His anger captured him. Disgust filled him like brackish water at the thought of remaining an unwitting prisoner of this powerful and unexpected jealousy. How could he both lust for and want to protect her at the same time? He was courting her; it couldn't overcome his other sensibilities. Her lips and eyes were powerful liquor, but he did not enjoy feeling intoxicated. He was a lone sapling, battered by opposing winds until he lost his roots. And Lily was the storm. He'd have time for this poetry later.

He and Vincent entered the burgundy sitting room shoulder to shoulder, where the other guests for his mother's dinner party waited. Although the house was equipped for gas heating, a footman would casually intrude to add wood to the fire. A well-stocked marble fireplace in a heated room subtly reminded Ralph of the wealth that the duchess showcased when company called. Lady Belasyse and her son Lord Belasyse were in attendance with Miss Beauchamp. Unfortunately, Miss Haverford was present, but so were Barton and Sebastian. Lord and Lady Banbury were there with Lady Olivia, though Olivia was speaking to Lily in the distance.

Lily was radiant again. She wore a peacock-blue dress with gold peacock feathers embroidered on the skirt and royal purple embellishments. The dress gave her eyes an emerald hue, and her hair glistened in the light. She had a healthy glow and blush as she leaned forward to conspire with her friend. If only she could wash over Ralph and cure his insecurity about Fane. Ralph pleasantly and somewhat indulgently remembered the way she had rested against the tree at the garden party, where he had wanted her so bad it pained him. He was picturing that again when he heard a decidedly too cheerful voice.

"Ah, there's Lily," Vincent said a toothy exuberance as he dragged Ralph over to her. "Good evening, Lily. And Lady Olivia."

Both women dipped at them in light curtsy. "Good evening. I am so pleased to see you both. Everything is better in your presence," Lily greeted.

"I am delightful company, but Ralph has been in a mood since we attended the fair," Vincent announced. Maybe Ralph could smother his brother in his sleep.

"Oh dear! Did you not enjoy the fair, my lord? I thought the folding table was ever so cunning," Lily inquired. She was eager and appeared earnest in a way Ralph rarely saw.

"It was very crowded, too much so for my comfort," he answered.

"Yes, it was. Although I wish there had been one more in attendance." Lily gave a pointed look at Lady Olivia.

"I apologize, again," Lady Olivia whined.

"Oooh, discord. Do tell," Vincent pried. Attempting to dig would be perceived as interest, so hopefully the women would enjoy retelling the tale in greater detail.

"Olivia was supposed to be escorted to the fair by Lord Fane and begged me to accompany them as an additional chaperone," Lily began. She tucked her chin in a little when talked, hiding her embarrassment as if it was a second chin.

"Lord Fane is an absolute lecher, and it is rumored he is forceful with women," Olivia said quietly.

"Three minutes into the fair, Olivia had to leave because she had a headache. Although I never doubt the sincerity of a friend, those headaches also plague me when in the presence of insufferable men. So, I was given the unhappy task of rebuffing his advances." Lily glared at Olivia.

Relief and anger wash over Ralph, like being half inside and half outside in a powerful snow. "My lady, how could you leave her with him?" He growled, his jealousy turning to protection. Wrinkles of concern crept on Lily's face. Apparently, his normal veil of niceties had slipped. Caution be damned; he was too furious to hide it. How could Olivia have done this to Lily?

"Fane is a…Oh, what do you call the people who believe that one must breed well to have better offspring?" Lady Olivia asked.

"A Darwinist?" Lily offered.

"An aristocrat?" Vincent suggested.

Lady Olivia chuckled. "Yes, a Darwinist. He wouldn't harm Lily as she is too dark for him. Fane wants a beautiful blonde. Although if you ask me, why intelligence and good breeding is tucked in the hair rather than somewhere else seems like a bit of a flaw in his theory. He didn't hurt you, did he, Lily?"

Lily shook her head. "No more than the average suitor. A grope here, a pinch there, and of course he tried to kiss me."

"Which is even stranger considering that many Darwinists are bald and have no hair at all." Vincent beamed proudly. His contribution landed flatly and did not divert the conversation.

"No man should behave in that fashion with a woman he is not engaged to." He barely had time to register Lily's confusion before his mother interrupted to call for dinner. Ralph usually avoided puffery, but something about this situation was vexing. If a man could change his affections so fluidly, then he deserved some punishment for his insincerity. The dark fugue of his private irritation from a few moments ago was returning, but if he focused on Lily's face, it disappeared. She was pure magic bound in a pillowy cloud of satin and musk perfume.

He was seated between Lady Olivia and Lady Belasyse. Lady Belasyse was very likeable. She was ancient and had married into one of the oldest titles in Britain. Her French accent and avant-garde wardrobe stood out in any crowd. She knew everything about everyone. Yet she spoke so bluntly and forthrightly. She said whatever she thought, for good or for ill. It was rather like playing roulette. One never knew where the ball might land. She was only allowed such indulgences through her title and by her association. But she had earned enough fame through her flamboyance to make most people a rapt audience when she spoke in violation of social taboos.

"Tell me, young man, would you like to marry my granddaughter?" Lady Belasyse asked with her thick, determined French accent, despite forty years of living in London.

Miss Beauchamp was beautiful, although she was nearly uniform in color. Her light brown hair perfectly matched her eyes. She seemed to have been painted without cleaning the brush and was all over taupe. Her graceful coil of hair framed a face that seemed far too young to fit her body. She was a true casualty of Victorian fashion, as she was quite beautiful, but she was tied up in a bodice and dress. If she wore something in a Swiss waist, she could turn any man's head.

"Thank you for the kind offer, my lady, but I must refuse," he replied.

Lady Belasyse's practiced sigh told its own story. "Yes, Lily speaks so highly of you. I had hoped you might take a liking to my Bella. I fear she will be overlooked by the little men of England."

"I could be of assistance. My brothers and I know most of the men in London. Let the three of us think on Miss Beauchamp and find her a suitable suitor." When one's good neighbors are in need, it is necessary to help them. After all, Miss Beauchamp was Lily's friend. If he got on well with her friends and their husbands, then they would have a happier marriage.

"Thank you. You will make a fine husband. It is unfortunate that the fashions of today seem to be preventing a great deal of marriages, but one keeps hoping for the future," Lady Belasyse said as the soup arrived, tinting the nearby glasses with steam.

"I beg your pardon, my lady? How do the fashions prevent marriages?" The soup was carrot with a hint of ginger, but still too hot to eat.

"The bustle dress with the tight skirts and high necklines. In my day, we had hoop skirts and low necklines. One could easily catch a husband with that," she opined. "Imagine what it is like to court a woman in a tucker, no corsets, and abundant modesty pieces adorning them. It is rather like this." She placed the puffed sleeve of her dress in front of a candle, far too close to the flame. "Now, tell me how you will go about getting to the fire?"

"Perhaps I am oblivious, but how would that help marriages, my lady?" Hopefully this old sage would stop speaking about dresses and explain her theory.

"I understand that you are courting Miss Snowe? Surely you have tried to…storm her citadel? A hoop skirt and low necklines make that easier." Lady Belasyse tilted her head up in confidence.

His cheeks were warming up from embarrassment and too hot soup. "Of course I haven't. Lily deserves to be respected." But unlike others, his respect was sincere. And she deserved better than another man who claimed to adore her only to leave her.

"Oh my. You believe that, don't you? My dear, men have been pushing past the rules of courtship since the rules were written. Women fend off the advances of men they don't want and fall prey to ones they do. That is the true courtship ritual," Lady Belasyse explained without blinking or nodding. She was a queen in her element.

"But surely the rules mean something. Surely they are there for a reason."

"If there is a reason, it is the same reason that people dance. They like the motions. But no one would ever confuse the steps of a waltz with the passions of the dancer."

The pieces began to fall into place. Vincent's constant pursuit of the old woman. Lily always inviting Ralph to sit near her. She was teasing him with the ghosts of future touching. He should have known. How many couples had he seen kissing and more in his parent's ballroom? He had assumed they were all married, which in hindsight showed incredibly naiveté. He was truly an idiot. Ralph felt as though his intellect was a meringue, apparently dense but just puffy on the inside. His credulity—most of all his belief in the decency of people and a rigid adherence of social order—bothered him. It is painful to be the final person to understand a thing.

"My lady, do you know what happens when a man doesn't try to cross those boundaries?" he asked. He hoped the answer was that everything was fine.

"The ladies tend to assume the man is not interested. However, as the hostess of a small house party this weekend, I could speak to Lily on your behalf." Lady Belasyse batted her lashes, showing a glimpse of the girl she once was. She probably lived off mischief alone in her advanced age.

Naturally, her remarks were worrisome. Even though he'd courted Lily properly, his anxiety welled up and threaten to spill out of his mouth. Was he any better than the lechers who pursued her, if they were all doing it for the same reason? Or did something more sincere lurk behind these stirrings he could barely restrain—something more than lust or worry for the welfare of a woman who had been so often cast aside? Losing her would be tragic regardless of his intentions. But his heart stirred like a tempest in a teapot when he thought too hard about it. Better to choke down the insecurity and be thankful for any help.

"Thank you, my lady. My heart thanks you. I had not heard of the house party. Any exciting guests?" He fumbled for an invitation. How smooth and not at all obvious.

"No, it is the ladies' retreat. Bella and her friends flee town at least once a season to refresh. I do adore it; they make me feel young again." Lady Belasyse sighed, her eyes welling up with liquid ennui. "Prior to you thinking anything sordid, I assure you they will only be reposing and walking in their basquines and shawls." Trying not to imagine Lily in that state was a foolish thing, but this daydream would arouse him. Perhaps that was her motive; she was a tease, after all.

"A retreat sounds splendid. Perhaps I should implore some friends to have a weekend at Brighton." The soup had finally cooled enough to eat, but he didn't touch it.

"We went to Brighton last August," Lady Olivia offered. "This year, Lord Belasyse offered his house in Devon. However, those of us who are not engaged will be having a weekend in the south of France in August."

"Why not an engaged woman?" Would courting Lily separate her from her friends?

"Once a woman is engaged, she usually wants her fiancé with her. These weekends are to be free of the expectations of men." Lady Olivia pushed her course aside without touching it.

"I have never expected anything from a woman." Apparently, such interludes were important to women.

Lady Olivia laughed in light-hearted dismissal. "Of course you do. You expect us to wear pounds and pounds of clothing, and to be proper and speak with smiles. And to be informed, but not have opinions. When we are all together and it is simply friends, then we can let our hair down and frown."

It didn't sound altogether difficult to smile, but he considered being forced to smile when one was in a poor state. Wearing a social mask could be painful; the past few moments had been a decent education in that. The "pounds and pounds of clothing" didn't sound pleasant either. Honestly, what did women go through? Perhaps it was time to learn. Although the unjust dance of courtship had worn on him like water on rock for a while, who knew about the stifling effects on Lily?

"Lady Olivia, I would like to be educated on the

trials of being a woman in the world. Would you be willing to help me?" He got closer to whisper it, hoping for sincerity. She would like that.

Lady Olivia smiled a genuine smile. It was different from the practiced smiles where she didn't show her teeth and had a come-close gaze. No, Lady Olivia had a silly smile with too many teeth, and it made her eyes squint. This was more beautiful than the skilled debutante visage she usually wore. "I would be all too happy to lecture you on the rigors of womanhood."

Chapter Eleven

It would appear in the Modern Age that going to the beach has become our new pilgrimage. Two hundred years ago, people traveled miles to see a relic from a long-dead saint, whereas now we all must see Brighton. I confess, I prefer a picnic by a lake when compared to the overcrowded shore, but I have made the visit nonetheless. It is one of the few occasions where dukes and paupers meet.
~Aunt Penny's Advice on Living, June 1885

The Devon sand stretched and yawned its lazy warmth all around Lily's body. The unruly tassels on her large umbrella waved yellow and shiny in the wind. The sounds of the waves and a water bird's call soothed her, and the sun warmed and beamed like unrequited adoration. This place was free of coal dust and the unwashed smell of the city. It smelled like rain and sand. Lily wished her entire life was this relaxed and beautiful, and if she could always wear her bathing suit, that would be lovely as well.

Lily closed her eyes from the brightness, and the smell of water was everywhere. She loved the sea. It changed without direction or intention and tossed and rose forever. The sea in Devon was calm and merely lapped at the shore. The same sea behaved completely differently in Cornwall. It could have a temper that raged and stormed, as it had during her voyages with father. Then again, sometimes it was pensive and mournful with barely a movement to be found. To her father, the sea was a mistress who would support and encourage his wanderlust. Today the sea was acting like an old friend, eager to catch up and babbling. Almost as if it wondered why Lily did not visit anymore.

Bella hummed nearby as she sat up. Olivia and Honoria's sister, Aurora, were chatting on a blanket a few feet away. Honoria and Lady Serena were farther away on a blanket reading. Last summer, there were four of them, and now there were six. If this persisted, next summer ten ladies would line the shores.

"Hmmm. I wish we could always be far from London." Bella sighed.

"I am rather fond of London; I wish we could live as we are here." Lily bloated her stomach, free from the corset that typically gave her pains.

Honoria and Lady Serena both read *Bleak House* and mumbled to one another too quietly for Lily to hear anything good. Lady Serena was far less shy than Lily had ever witnessed. She allowed her golden hair down, and her dark blue eyes focused on the book in front of her. It wasn't that Serena was talkative, as she had barely uttered a word. But her whole body relaxed at the party. When she sat in London, she was a tense spring wound tight with worries. Here, it was like seeing the afterhours of a modiste, when the shop girls or mannequins who were forced into ungentle stillness to exhibit their wares were freed of the imprisoning gaze of shoppers. How refreshing to see all the ladies gathered without the acrimony of competition for gentlemen or heavy bustle of social expectations.

This was one of only a handful of times she had seen Lady Serena. Of course, after a day of observation, Serena bore a strong resemblance to Berkeley. It was easy to miss at first blush. Serena's round face was entirely contrary to Berkeley's chiseled and bearded face. Her complexion was peaches and cream with golden hair, and his was rosier with auburn hair. But if one stared into their eyes, the siblings looked identical. Both had deep, dark blue eyes which brought to Lily's mind a sapphire brooch she had admired once. The rest of their family had dark, nearly black eyes, but Lady Serena and Berkeley had their mother's eyes.

"Bella, would you be willing to try this beauty advice we found?" Olivia asked, interrupting Lily's important thoughts.

"Perhaps, but please tell me what it is," Bella answered.

"We pour lemon juice over your hair and let the sun lighten it," Olivia explained. This sounded utterly stupid. Bees might attack poor Bella.

"How long must I let the sun lighten my hair? Would my face become sunburned?" Bella asked. Her smile was forced, with no dimples or sincerity.

"I will fetch a blanket to put over you and read to you. I promise no harm will come to you," Aurora pled.

"Very well." Bella relented and sank again. "But someone must read my book aloud."

"I will," Honoria volunteered. She was right behind the group, apparently creeping quietly to surprise everyone. Aurora ran off to retrieve the blanket and lemon juice. "*Jane Eyre*? Oh, Lord, I detest this book. What kind of society applauds a novel where a woman is locked in an attic?"

"It isn't far from the manner society treats all women," Olivia began.

"Please read the book first, and we can discuss the implications later," Bella pled.

Honoria began to read while Olivia, Aurora, and Bella set upon their beauty experiment. Hands whirled, and voices floated through the air. Serena joined Lily to stare at the ocean. Honoria's sweet voice wandered through the tale of Jane Eyre. In all honesty, who liked that book? Lily harbored no fondness for it. Books with women who were bold and fought the afflictions of fate were far better. Jane Eyre seemed to simply let life happen to her and mourned the consequences.

"Perhaps tonight we should host a séance! And Serena can read our fortunes. Serena knows everything about mysticism," Honoria offered with gleaming eyes.

"Could you tell our fortunes?" Aurora asked.

"As well as any other fortune teller I have seen," Lady Serena muttered quietly.

"Wonderful! Let's do a midnight excursion with the occult!" Olivia cried, apparently assuming no one of ill intent could hear her.

****

At midnight, the ladies gathered in Lord Belasyse's library. A few simple props transformed the library from parochial to exotic and mysterious. A large round table was brought in and covered with a black velvet cloth which looked as if it had moonlight poured on it. Lady Serena had lit several candles scattered around the room, casting competing shadows. Atop the table rested an immense crystal ball, gold coins, a jeweled cup, and a double-edged blade, in perfect ceremonial order. Each item gleamed in the candlelight.

"Lady Serena has visited nearly every mystic in Britain and has learned their secrets. Tonight, the future will be unveiled!" Honoria announced with the same theatrics as at the pleasure garden. "Who shall be the first to have their destiny revealed?"

"Lily!" Olivia volunteered. Lily fought the urge to throttle her and simply nodded.

Lady Serena took Lily's hands into hers and gazed deeply into the orb. Lily watched as the woman's face distorted in the flickers of the lights. Smoke swirled in the orb, and Lily's mouth opened to alert Serena, but Serena began to speak.

"I see a fair man," Lady Serena began.

"Lord Ralph Mandeville, no doubt," Olivia observed from one of the cushions near the windows.

"Indeed. He will propose soon, but only if your father gives permission. He is not the sort of man who will run off with you," Serena foretold ominously. Her face was transformed by the mystic authority she wielded. She became prettier and less kind; her face was luminous and harsh.

Lily's head bobbed. Just one day before anyone knew Papa would be home. She planned for the two of them to spend the day together. She could use that day to promote Ralph. If Ralph offered a proposal, then her father would avoid strangling him. "What else?"

Lady Serena focused again. Her face leaned forward, and her fingers knitted in neat arches near the ball. Her cornflower-blue eyes sparkled in the light. "I see you and he are very happy and prosperous. Two children, both sons."

Lily's body relaxed, but then tensed up again. It was good news of course, but good delivered with a hint of the ominous was harder to take than good given with a smile. She wanted marriage and had affection for Ralph. Secretly, who wouldn't be afraid of motherhood with a mother like Katerina Snowe? Especially being a mother to a daughter. It was terrifying to think of becoming such a monster—someone who would have sold her. Sons were easy. They went off to school and barely needed their mothers.

"Amazing!" Aurora gasped. "Would you be willing to teach me how to future gaze?"

"I will reveal my secrets after. Who is next?" Lady Serena asked, unblinking and imperious, her pretty blonde hair shocking in the blackness of the room.

"I am," Olivia offered.

Lily stood, and her legs wobbled a bit. The air pooled thickly and smelled of sandalwood. Lady Serena truly possessed gifts and predicted that she would marry Ralph. Again, this news made her happy but uncertain. Lily returned his affections, but given his hesitation, she could never be completely certain about them. The rituals of courtship that he strongly held to constrained his sincerity. Which was, unfortunately, his most endearing trait.

She hummed, but she didn't care enough to listen as Serena gazed for Olivia. She foresaw suffrage would occur in the next century and not this one. That news did not sit as well with Olivia as Serena's prediction for Lily. Olivia started arguing until she decided that biting her lip and appearing entertained was more appropriate. Bella was next. Hopefully she would not eternally be overlooked.

"I see your future husband. I cannot see his face but rather his character. He is what one might call 'a diamond in the rough,' as it were. You will see what no one else can and will fall deeply in love," Serena predicted, almost in a chant.

"Will I ever have to see my father again?" Bella whispered, obviously terrified. Very few people knew what Bella's father had done to her. The horrible beatings she took simply because she was female. How in the hell could a man could profess to believe that women were the more physically fragile of the sexes and then force them to endure physical violence because of their gender? She had squeezed the pillow in her hands so tightly it was nearly a ball. It was hard to not be angry on behalf of such a sweet girl.

"Once more, but not for a while. And you will finally be done with him forever, and he will not haunt you," Serena promised.

The pillow fell to the floor, and relief soothed into her like the soft candlelight. Grappling with her own neglect and abandonment was emotionally impossible. Understanding her own suffering through Bella's was much easier. The news that Bella would no longer live in fear shot through Lily like heady joyful champagne.

Bella seemed taller as she stood. She looked stronger. Aurora was next and eagerly took her seat before Serena. It was a strange thing that people who suffered must seem strong, but that the people who saw suffering must seem sad. It was altogether inappropriate that one must learn the potency of one's own tragedies by seeing others experience them vicariously.

"What of my future, my lady? Will I marry a wealthy and handsome man? Before Honoria?" Aurora asked excitedly while Honoria stuck out her tongue.

"I see you adorned in jewels. I cannot see if he is

incredibly handsome or wealthy, but you will be adored. And as Honoria refuses Frederick, I see you marrying before her."

Aurora clapped and laughed. "It has been foretold, Honoria! I'm telling Mother!" Aurora was apparently pleased in the manner that only a teasing younger sibling can be pleased.

"I'm certain it won't be news to her," Honoria said with a roll of her wrist. "And now Lady Serena will reveal her secrets for those interested."

"No, thank you, your ladyship. It was most enjoyable, but I don't need the stigma of being both a suffragette and a witch," Olivia announced as she stood.

"I shall join you, Olivia," Bella called as she hurried to catch up to Olivia.

Lady Serena waited a few minutes until after they left. "It is all false. I have been to countless mediums and mystics, and not one has been real. We burn incense to perfume the air while giving an illusion of spirits. The crystal ball has a hose to pump smoke into it and everything else was just guessing,"

Lily gasped. What a deception! "But you saw Ralph and me marrying!"

"No, I began with a fair man. Lady Olivia spoke of Lord Ralph Mandeville in an intimate tone, and so I knew he was courting you. I know you love your father and would not tolerate a man who did not respect him."

"Ralph won't propose then?" Her heart suddenly felt heavy, sinking to her feet. She hadn't realized her desire to keep him close until Serena made him seem distant. If necessary, she could cause a scandal. In that case, Ralph would most assuredly marry her. But the costs of such a thing, the doubts they would both have about the truth of their love, could be too much. The pain of losing a thing she did not yet have stabbed her heart like a dagger, pointed and deep. She grabbed the soft purple pillow from the ground, calming and focusing on this strange emptiness. Did she love Ralph?

"I have no idea, but if the rumors are correct, he is going to. The future is mercurial, but some things are easy to see." Serena granted a smile.

"But what of my husband?" Aurora asked.

"You are so charming and beautiful. Men will form a queue for the privilege of giving you gifts. You are not even out yet, so be patient. I think you will love being in the marriage market." Serena comforted the girl.

"What of Bella? You spoke of her father." Lily's tone hardened, and Serena blanched. Bella's abuse was a secret. She needed to know how Serena ferreted it out.

Serena nodded, and her brow crinkled in sympathy. "I could hear the fear in her voice. I didn't want to give her false hope that she would never see him again. Instead I hoped that if she knew the next time she saw him would be the last that it may help her overcome her fears."

Bella was not shy by her nature. She had submission beaten into her. If Serena's fortune-telling had any effect on Bella, it could make her braver. There didn't seem to be much harm in allowing Bella the idea that she might be free of her father once and for all.

"We must swear to never tell Bella the truth; she must believe Lady Serena's future will come to pass."

"I swear." The three women swore in unison. There was power in this secret because it was kept out of love.

As they began to leave the library, Honoria stretched out her tiny sun-kissed hand and pulled Lily back a step. "What I am about to say may have dozens of explanations, but I must ask for your help," she began.

"My dear Honoria, what pains you?" Honoria was normally a light thing, but her tone was dark.

"I am afraid I am growing overly suspicious. I have seen the same maid at both my home during Cards and Scandal as well as here. It is possible that my mother sacked a maid, and she was lucky to get employment with Lord Belasyse. Or perhaps his lordship is wooing my mother. Or—"

"Honoria!" Lily snapped in the loudest possible whisper. She could be here for hours listening to the possibilities Honoria's overactive imagination had dreamt up.

"Yes, of course. Would you be willing to host the next Cards and Scandal?"

"Certainly. Do tell, what does this maid look like?" Most maids looked alike, as their uniforms tended to obfuscate their particulars.

"She is about Aurora's age with blonde hair. Every time I see her I think of a cat. Deceptively lazy and ready to pounce." Honoria frowned at her description.

"Ah, I see you remember Sugar," Lily teased.

Lily climbed the stairs to her rooms and dreamt of the vision Lady Serena had given her. Ralph was exactly what she wanted in a husband. He was attractive and sweet. Their conversations were lovely, and the rumor had it he was also skilled with finances. Most importantly, his loyalty inspired her. He would never leave her for foreign soil or the next mountain to climb. No, in her heart Lily knew Ralph would put down roots and she could grow well nestled with him. Her heart's faith could convince her head's doubts with sweet, poetic whispers of a better future. How tantalizing and comfortable.

The sea moderated the night's chill and the day's heat. In the stillness of the night, Lily's cravings were sharp and her heart needy. Knowing with confidence that they might be together soon made her body heave and race with apprehension and excitement. Only if there was a word for what she felt. She pulled the covers into the shape of a body and held them close. She needed the weight of something near her. Her mind ambled through lusty fictions about the frolics they would have. She fell asleep to whispering dreams that were both seductive and normal.

Chapter Twelve

A difficulty with living in a great house or simply an old house is how very outdated they are. Take heart, dear readers; Aunt Penny knows a few tricks to update your home on the cheap. If you are in possession of a sewing machine, replace your curtains and upholster sofa and chairs to harmonize. Take care to make the curtains heavy to keep the room warm in winter.
~Aunt Penny's Advice on Living, June 1885

Ralph strolled down the street from his house and headed to Lily's. If not for Lily, this would have been the most difficult fortnight of Ralph's life. Thankfully, Lord Snowe would return to London in just three days, and Ralph's efforts would pay off. Obviously, the best path to resolving both his immeasurable physical craving for her and his guilt would be asking for her hand. Or at least it would reconcile both his physical hunger and his mental anguish. He simply needed to secure Lily's agreement and eventually her father's. This compact, rather than a sweaty *tendre* in a dark garden, was definitely the appropriate way forward. Although the latter sounded better than the former. He could taste his freedom, like a prisoner nearing his release. Hopefully, he would appear contrite enough.

Like everything Ralph did, this careful seduction was planned well in advance. It began with Lily's dream home. This would be the perfect way to convince her that he was the best husband for her. It took a few days to find the right house and the right location. He wanted a lot, not a house. Unfortunately, Mr. Julian Archer also wanted the house and proceeded to raise the price. Ralph won the house, but lost an additional ten thousand pounds for the victory. That stung, but it was worth it.

Once he had acquired the house, he needed to tear the horrible building down. The police arrested the laborers he hired under fear of a political protest. Although labor organization was contentious, this made very little sense to Ralph or Adrian. Then, someone else hired away the next batch. Then, once Ralph had found some men recommended by his father's vicar, bloody Lord Castleton decided the building was too precious be destroyed. How vexing.

It seemed that Castleton, whose earldom was in Essex, had enough influence to halt the destruction of what Castleton felt was a historically important house. Who could have anticipated such a stupid possibility? What was so uniquely valuable about the dilapidated house? How would renovations be a black mark on London's history?

Adrian promised to handle the Castleton situation while Ralph moved on to finding an architect. Vincent was incredibly helpful in this point, as he knew many talented but penniless people. Vincent also insisted Ralph hire a tapestry weaver and a muralist. Since learning that Ralph was designing a home, Vincent's natural eagerness to impress people with his knowledge and style had become hard to contain. Luckily, a firm word from Ralph stopped Vincent before he hired a stained-glass artist. After all, Lily should be the one to make decisions about their home.

Lily's butler was taking too long to answer the door, so Ralph tried as he might to ease his stomach with a few calming memories and deep breaths. All his happiness—hell, his entire future—lay in the spun lace of one woman's hands. It was agony. How much drier could his palms feel or his mouth become? Nothing compared to this anxiety. The walk from Lily's door to the sitting room was like walking the plank.

"Good afternoon, Ralph. Where is Vincent?" Lily asked, while looking over his shoulder. She was as fresh as the sun after a tormenting night. He needed her in the way sunflowers bent toward the sun, and only she would suffice.

"He is meeting with Mr. Enright." Where were the right words to propose? Sadly, Ralph knew his faults; he was more planner than poet.

"I am unfamiliar with the Enrights. Did you make their acquaintance during your tour?" Lily asked while gesturing for Ralph to sit close to her.

"Hmmm? No, Mr. Enright is an architect," Ralph answered. Perhaps he could recite poetry. Lily brought to mind "She Walks in Beauty." He simply needed to recall it.

"Oh, how wonderful! Is Vincent updating his estate? Or has he purchased the townhouse? I hope he can negotiate a house with both running water and great art. Elsewise he will never find a wife," Lily lectured as she poured tea for him. Her body moved like a swan's, both poised and relaxed. In his mind's eye, he moved like a naked child in a snowstorm, battered by snow and harsh winds.

"Mr. Enright is hired to help me build a house. He loved the foyer you designed." He had to stop speaking about Mr. Enright long enough to concentrate. How did the turn of phrase go again? Was it "what's best of dark and bright met in her effort or her aspect"? He should have studied the damn poem before he came here.

"I beg your pardon. Why would your architect know of my entry hall?" Lily asked abruptly. Her eyes were blue anger, and her teeth flashed. Ralph stopped trying to remember the poem. She sounded the way his mother did before she punished him. What had he done wrong?

"I rather loved the idea and…" Why was she was turning red?

Lily's color deepened, and she did resemble a tomato. Which would have been adorable if he were not so confused as to why.

"You are going to put *my* entryway into *your* home? Are there any other beloved ideas of mine you desire to steal? I dreamt of a turret in the master bedroom, with a glass roof for stargazing. Would you like that in your home as well? What of the drawing rooms and their integrated bookcases?"

"Well, yes, if you would like to…" His tongue felt swollen, like it tripped over words and couldn't find them. This was going terribly. She was shrieking, which rarely led to a marriage. Except the worst kinds of marriage.

"They say Vincent is the cruel Mandeville. But no, it is you, Ralph Mandeville! I have humiliated myself for you, and yet you continue this campaign. I need so few kindnesses, and yet you try to ignore me. I will not allow it!" Her tears had started their journey from her eyes, and her feet paced away in whispering fury. Her hands flew to her forehead, as if the anger in her brow would explode and ruin the teacups.

Only a drastic gamble could change the situation. "Did Lady Belasyse speak to you last weekend?"

Lily stopped her pacing. Her eyes were filled with venom, and her lips were pursed in rage. "I beg your pardon?"

"You attended Lady Belasyse's house party last weekend?" Ralph held still for her to nod. "Did her ladyship speak with you about me?"

"No, Lady Belasyse had a summer cold and spent much of the weekend recovering. She is quite old and needed to sea air to help her," Lily babbled. Her red face and dark eyes were clearly confused as to why they were speaking of Lady Belasyse.

Well, if he was going to marry her, he needed to calm her down enough to ask. People described Ralph like they would a train: reliable, dependable, and decent. He needed to correct her perception of him and how he felt about her. He crossed the room and pulled her to him. And finally, after a lifetime of longing, he kissed her.

His arms moved of their own accord, grasping her limbs until they felt like folded silk against him. Her fingers kneaded deep into his back. The lusty beacons of their bodies met together and melted and separated again and again.

He had kissed several women. They were mostly barmaids and women on his tour. No woman tasted as sweet as his *miliy*. His hands desperately hungered to explore the terrain he had been dreaming of. He stroked the hair just above the nape of her neck. Finally, Lily was in his arms and he never wanted to let her go. She had a tension that ran from her head to small of her luxurious back that intensified and diminished. Like one sort of passion was mingling too much with another.

"Lady Belasyse—"

"Why would you speak of a septuagenarian woman after kissing me?" Lily breathed.

Ralph hadn't noticed, but he was happy to see he took her breath from her. "Lady Belasyse was meant to explain that I had been laboring under the notion that one does not kiss a woman one admires." Ralph stroked her cheek, the too-soft, too-warm face of his woman. Now that he had touched her skin, he didn't want to stop.

"You only kissed women you did not admire? That seems foolish." Lily smiled up at him. Her smile was holding back something. Perhaps she wanted more too?

He exhaled and chuckled, but it was too quick, and the laugh sounded like a whip cracking. "No, but I thought if I hoped to marry you, then I ought to respect you as my grandfather would have done."

Lily rolled her eyes. "I am fairly certain your grandmother was kissed often. I have read some libertine novels. They were indecent. And although your grandfather may have been quite decent, if he kissed me the way you did, I think your grandmother would be quite jealous."

He needed to regain control of the conversation. "Lily, I came to ask you to marry me. Will you?"

Lily reached up and pulled him into her. When Lily kissed him, she slid her tongue into his mouth. Her hands roamed his chest and crawled to his back. Her bold hands pulled his body into her. It was so hard not to carry this too far. Warmth pooled in the center of her body, in a place hidden and locked away. He almost exploded with a desire to be in that secret, balmy place, and a flood of images of her unclothed silhouette mounted on him pulled him away from the immediacy of this important moment. It pained him to, but he eventually pulled away from her.

"Yes," she whispered.

"Wonderful. Would you like to meet Mr. Enright so we can build your dream home now?" It sounded more hesitant than it should have. He gasped these words out. They were little lies. Lies, like he was interested in anything but the curve of her mouth and way she grabbed eagerly when touched. He instantly regretted rekindling the argument, but if that was the only way to preserve this moment, then all he could do was try.

"Oh, I am so embarrassed! I thought you were going to build a house for another woman and only saw me as Vincent and Sebastian do. I truly apologize," she moaned. She was very forgiving of his restraint.

But his excitement still swelled, and the firm arch of his longing was still reaching for her. "No, I should have been clearer in my intentions. You see, from the moment I saw you, I have been conniving to make you my wife." Ralph smiled at her.

"Truly? Oh, that eases my mind. I thought you were resistant to my charms, and I kept trying to persuade you." Lily laughed. Her large eyes held more relief than any words could express.

He didn't want to laugh. He had nearly lost the woman he loved because he believed the common wisdom. How could he not know the unspoken rules of courtship as well as he knew the unspoken rules of the rest of society?

What was the point in spoken rules if there were hidden codes in the world? What purpose did the pretense of purity further? If the only hopes of success were to rebel and disobey, then a world premised on piety and obedience would be torture. If containing the passions was critical to order and morals, then why did an act of rebellion feel so truly meaningful? Why did the world of faceless, knowing antagonists simultaneously chastise people for such misbehavior, and then do it themselves? It was maddening. But the feeling of his guilt fleeing and the empty places filling with passion turned him away from such bleak questions. And his guilt was largely forgotten. How quickly worries fade when passions were roused.

"Shall we be off then?"

"I must change my dress. I couldn't possibly walk in my tea gown. I won't be long. Wake Olga, will you?" Lily's voice trailed far away into the deep house.

Ralph sat on the settee and began to eat a fairy cake while staring at the old woman. She was quite possibly the worst chaperone ever to watch over a young lady. It was harder liking Lord Snowe the more Ralph thought about him. What kind of father left his only daughter with an old sickly woman who did not speak English? And from what rumors he had heard, this Olga woman had attempted to cause a scandal with Vincent. Ralph's beloved Lily was left with no one to care for her or protect her, which was Snowe's duty. Happily, Ralph would not have to endure Snowe's presence that often, and thus he may not hate him as much.

A half hour later, Ralph shook Olga midsnore. "*Spaziergang*," he said. That was one of the handful of German words he knew. Piercing her slumber proved harder than he thought.

"*Wo ist mein Lily liebling*?" the suddenly protective woman demanded.

The only word Ralph understood was Lily.

Lily glided down the stairs in a lilac walking dress of satin woven with silver pinstripes. "Shall we, fiancé?"

He couldn't stop smiling, and he let the word echo inside of him. "Of course. We should probably not touch in public until after the engagement dinner. I should hate for your father to refuse my offer and it damage your reputation."

"Yes, that is the sensible path. Besides, I can sneak a kiss or two. It will be fun. I forgot about the dinner that is held by the bride's mother and my mother..." Lily frowned at the mention of her mother.

"Plenty of ladies are motherless. I am certain that we will find the right person to act as hostess." He tried his best to assure her, holding her hand as he stroked her palm.

"I'm sure Lady Belasyse and Lady Banbury will fight over which one will step in." Lily laughed. "Tell me, where is our home to be?"

"I bought Lord Gunn's house in Hanover Square. It is still there, but I am hoping to destroy it." Ralph smirked; just saying he hoped to destroy something was a bit anarchist. Or maybe he was just happy to maneuver away from the uncomfortable subject of Lily's mother.

"We may not have to. We could maintain the

facade and simply remake the interior," Lily mused.

Lily's idea might save them from the endless hurdles imposed by Lord Castleton. "We will speak to Mr. Enright. I want you to have the home you've always dreamed of. Lily, I wanted to speak with you about an idea that has been bandied about. How would you feel if I took on a career?"

Lily went pale. "It depends. What sort of career?"

"I am rather talented at investing. I have a system I designed that yields very well."

"Would you have to leave to research these investments? I know most money is made in foreign countries."

"No. I thought I would lease the third floor of Adrian Rose's office building. The law and investments are so closely tethered. We may end up sharing a great many clients." But why would he travel for research? The idea was pleasurable but silly.

"If you are home every night to warm my bed, then what should I care about how you spend your days?" Lily rolled her wrist dismissively.

"Some ladies may have an issue with a gentleman who earns a living." His fingers tapped his side, steeling his nerves. This wasn't worth worrying about.

"Some ladies think corsets belong on women who are with child. There was once a gentleman who demanded a divorce because his wife was not smooth as the nude statues he had seen. If one asks enough people, one will find a plethora of stupid ideas. Our marriage and household will be made of what we like, and everyone else can go to hell for all I care."

This was so illustrative of why he was desperate to marry her. Somehow, she connected his career to corsets, then to sexual mores, and finished by telling society to go to hell. He was never anything but himself in her presence, and he would never have to pretend. She deserved the same sense of security.

"Are you trying to tell me that you are not as smooth as the statues I have seen?" he teased.

Lily batted her lashes at him. "I'm afraid not, but I am much softer."

Chapter Thirteen

When greeting a loved one from a journey, it is important to be consistent. No matter the length of time of their journey, we must all behave as though we have missed them for years. My father often goes to town, and even if it is for a day, I behave as though I have missed him forever. It warms his heart to be missed, and it is so little effort upon me to express how much I love him.

~Aunt Penny's Advice for Living, June 1885

Lily smoothed her hair for the fifth time in ten minutes. She had always preferred Liverpool as a port, and her father acknowledged that by arriving there. Her breath caught sharp in her throat. She had not seen her father in over two years, and well, Lord Snowe could make anyone nervous. But that was normal anxiety, and this was overwhelming. She had invited Olivia along to calm her; sadly, she was having no effect.

This might be the last time she fetched her father. Without her to return home to, the fear that he may never return haunted Lily. Of course, she would have to convince her father to agree to her marrying Ralph. It was hard to tell whether her father wanted her to wed or not. She hoped her father would be happy with her choice, but she needed to present the idea carefully.

"This is riveting!" Olivia exclaimed. "I have never

met a ship at the docks, but it is overwhelming. I had no idea they were so large. We truly are living in an age of wonder. It's amazing."

Lily smiled. This was quite the familiar scene. She had been to ports all over the world, and after a while they all looked the same. There were always faces so happy to see their home. There were the faces of people who had never been here before and were curious about the locals. There were the tired captains and the beleaguered shipmates. The only difference was the weather.

Lily looked to the dock meant to harbor her father's ship, empty. "His ship is late. Would you like to see what is for sale?"

"Certainly, back to the shops then?" Olivia asked as she began to stroll away.

"No, we merely need to look monied as we walk toward the train. I am hoping to find some silks or other such fabrics." The silks would fit just right in an Indian sitting room off the master bedroom she and Ralph would share.

"How will we shop by walking around?" Olivia dodged a heavy man as he lumbered to his ship and passed by.

"Sailors are occasionally given a bit of their cargo as a reward. If they have no use for the item, they try to sell it. Pretty ladies can get decent items for little." It was better to omit that the sailors often wanted sex instead of money. But there were one, two, three, four policemen within sight, so they were safe.

Two hours later, they were clearly overburdened with crudely wrapped packages. Her arms were shaking, but there was nowhere to put them down.

Olivia had purchased jewelry, hairpins, and fabrics that were probably stolen. But again, it was better to remain silent on these things. Lily found rich Chinese-red silk, fit for a brothel. But it would be perfect for a dressing gown and chemise made for her trousseau. She had also found some saffron and lace from a Spanish sailor and curry powder from an Englishman. But nothing could rival her joy as the American ship crept slowly into view. America was a great unknown, outside of the bottles of syrup for soda and medicines purchased from American sailors earlier.

"What do you plan on doing with the syrup?" Olivia asked as they watched Lily's father's ship get tethered to the dock.

"Sir Barton has a carbonation machine. I thought he might make us some sodas." Her nerves rattled up from her anxious, tapping feet all the way to her skirts no matter how much she resisted.

Olivia clapped, calling even more attention to her than the usual gawking. "You should have a soda fountain at the wedding! Oh, how fashionable you would be."

Now this was a clever idea. The best path to fashionability was to be daring while not offending the older generation. But no time to think—her father's head bobbed closer, only to be blotted out by the shoulders of a giant man who was presumedly looking for his beanstalk to get home. "I shall see if I can and if Ralph likes the notion. There is Papa."

Papa, or as the world knew him, Lord Aidan Snowe, was unmistakable and impressive. He stood at just over six feet and had jet black hair, even in his sixties. He was chiseled out of rock and earth, with shark-like black eyes. He wore a beard streaked with gray. This was an ironic contrast to the impervious youth of his hair. His intimidating mask was formidable, right up until he saw Lily. His face broke into a wide smile and revealed him. Here was the silly Papa she knew and loved!

"Little Tomato!" Papa bellowed. His arms strongly hugged her, lifting her. The air swished coolly under her feet and dress. The faces of the crowd raced by as she flew in his arms like a happy ballerina. It was a struggle not to kick Olivia or any other passersby. "I have missed you so much I thought my heart might give up!"

He set her down. She was three years old again. "Welcome home, Papa. This is my friend, Lady Olivia, the Earl of Banbury's daughter."

Papa inspected Olivia *thoroughly*. It was good that he remained married to her mother. This was the only time in history someone thought that. "A pleasure. You are nearly identical to your mother. I imagine that you cause as many scandals as she does."

Olivia looked as though someone had just told her the queen was a tortoise in disguise. Lady Banbury was the soul of motherly grace. "I am plagued with a progressive reputation, but my mother steers far from any hint of debauchery. Unless she is more secretive than I imagined."

"Pssh! Tosh!" Papa motioned to some men to assist with his trunks and the ladies' packages. "Emilia Forrester, yes? I remember it well. She was promised to a laird in Scotland, McDonnell or McDougal…no, MacDonald. In any case, he returned home from the war and hosted a ball to meet your mother. The Scot decided to invite several fashionable and influential lords, including the Earl of Banbury. By morning, your father and mother eloped, and the laird tried to sue your grandparents. I don't recall how the affair was settled, but apparently the *ton* no longer cares. The only part of the story they care about is the ending. Which was a marriage, of course."

But everyone adored Lady Banbury. "Gracious, Olivia, you were born under a cloud."

"That feels natural to my character," Olivia answered. They entered the hot railway station into a thick crowd.

"Ah, have duels been fought for your favor? Lifelong friends turned to enemies over you? If not, surely the fog has gotten into men's eyes, as they are blind." Papa navigated to the platform and met the train, barely on time.

"No!" Olivia laughed. "I am graduated from Cambridge University and am a suffragette."

"I fail to see the conflict," Papa said. According to the timetables, there was a slight delay in the connecting train to Paddington.

The snicker crept out too eagerly to contain it. Papa had spent far too much time away from the *ton*. Lily cleared her throat; it was time to steer this conversation away from Papa's practiced flirtations. "She is the great beauty. They tend to marry quickly and not have any thoughts to distract their husbands."

"Barbaric. I taught my girl to always think. Besides, a woman voting is logical. Why should half the population not be allowed to have any say in their lives? And by the way, there are many simpletons among my sex. I know we hide it well." Papa gave the sort of half smile he used when negotiating.

"We could use more men such as you in Parliament. I suppose you will be in London for Lily's wedding?" Olivia blathered.

Papa raised his eyebrows and surveyed Lily. "You cannot marry. You are a child."

The train screamed onto the platform, and it was easy to find a first-class car. Once seated, it was appropriate to confront this...misconception. "I am indeed old enough; I am twenty. And Lord Ralph Mandeville has expressed a desire for wedded bliss."

"Pffff. Who is this man? Mandeville... Christopher's friends? The boring one or the ratbag?"

Her laugh was uncomfortable, but it was necessary to flatter a man who resisted you. "Neither. Ralph is their younger brother. I care deeply for him, Papa. Please don't interfere."

Papa chewed his lip, probably fighting his urge to bully her into forgetting this idea of marriage and growing up. "Lady Olivia, surely you think this is a terrible idea?"

"No, my lord." Olivia was suddenly bereft of language. Pity she had not been so afflicted before she mentioned marriage.

Lily offered her father his favorite meal to enjoy on the train to London. Hot coffee, a lamb pie, a pork pie, and lemon biscuits. "He is a wonderful man, Papa. I know you will like him."

Papa drank his coffee and smiled briefly before his face returned to the interrogating glare. "Tell me, Lady Olivia, how does an educated suffragette support this marriage?"

"Marriage to a man like Ralph Mandeville would

be wonderful for Lily. He utterly adores her, and he is very handsome. More importantly, he is rumored to be a financial genius, and he is renowned for his loyalty. He will always protect and help Lily in whatever she wants to do. I heard that he is actually considering buying a factory to weave her designs," Olivia answered.

Lily couldn't help her bad form and stared at her slack-jawed, but what on earth was Olivia talking about? Ralph was a "financial genius" who was rumored to have plans for a factory? But Olivia sounded convinced. Ralph would be the first man to love her and not leave her. Ralph fit perfectly with her, and Olivia was selling him well to her father. She needed to finish the job.

"And we know his family well. Vincent and Sebastian were always about. He was so respectful during our courtship, I thought he did not like me. I believe he will allow me to have as much freedom as I desire. This is an excellent match for *me*, Papa."

Papa chewed his pork pie in thought. Thankfully, Olivia remained silent as well. He broke the quiet as soon as he was done. "If you think this is the best path for you, then I trust your judgment. I simply ask that our relationship not change. I demand to see you at the docks when I arrive, and I want you to keep illustrating my adventures." Papa negotiated softly with her. That was good.

"Of course, Papa." Her smile was as large as she could make it. The countryside sped by just outside the window. Everything was lining up for her, and finally her future was bright.

Chapter Fourteen

In this modern age of travel and information, I have been considering the best manner to announce large events such as an engagement or birth of a child. One once wrote letters to one's entire family and acquaintanceship, but with the speed and ease of a telegram, I no longer believe it is necessary. I believe one may send telegrams to one's immediate circle and publish the event in the newspaper. After the engagement dinner or baptism, of course.

~Aunt Penny's Advice on Living, June 1885

Ralph slouched in his mother's rose sitting room for tea. Slouching was altogether appropriate for a day like today. Every waking moment had been spent negotiating with Lord Snowe. Snowe was obsessed with ensuring Lily would have independence and insisted on protecting her as much as he could in the marriage settlements. Snowe never pretended to withhold permission for their marriage. He was merely a ferocious advocate. He respected Lily and wanted her to be her own champion. That was respectable enough, especially the low opinion Snowe had earned during Ralph and Lily's courtship. Perhaps Snowe had decided his daughter could be left alone and flourish, but that wasn't the world they lived in. The shadow of a man's absence could be as potent as his presence. But it was warm and soothing to know Lily would never be alone.

Of course, the day was not over yet. There was announcing the engagement to his parents and brothers. In truth, Vincent's potential reaction set him on edge. He had been closest to Lily. Vincent might take umbrage to her choice of Ralph instead of nursing a platonic love for him. Although, the rest of the family would be thrilled; Lily was intelligent, beautiful, charming, talented, and popular. She was the perfect wife for him.

"I have heard your point, but I disagree and will not alter my behavior." Vincent snapped him from his thoughts. How very selfish of him.

"It is foolish to continue. I refuse to allow this," mother announced firmly. Her hands were shaking, so this was clearly false bravado.

"I apologize. I was woolgathering. What is the matter?" Ralph asked.

"Mother is unhappy with the current living situation. She would prefer we all live under the same roof. Vincent disagrees, as do I," Sebastian explained with a shrug. "Are you feeling well? You appear beleaguered."

Where was the duke when you needed him? "Is Father not joining us?"

"He is at Avebury Park. Apparently, there is poaching, and he needed to investigate." Mother sank deep into her chair, digging her heels in.

Although announcing without his father was not ideal, delaying longer was simply impossible. "I will send a telegram to him later. I have wonderful news. Lord Snowe and I signed the settlements today, and Lily and I will marry in August."

"Huzzah!" Vincent shot up like a cannon blast. His hand firmly clapped Ralph's back, and he dashed out of the room shouting. "I'll fetch the cigars! And start planning the best bachelor's send-off in history!"

"Felicitations, Ralph. I couldn't be happier for you," Sebastian said with a hug. He was proper and measured but not surprised. If boring, patrician Sebastian agreed to the match, he should feel more confident. Apparently, Sebastian thought Ralph could earn the hand of a beautiful woman. How flattering!

"Ralph, darling, are you certain you wish to wed so quickly? You are only twenty-five years old, and neither of your brothers has married. Don't you think you should wait until Sebastian has married?" Mother asked. Ralph felt the tension grasping his shoulders, as Seraphina never voiced an objection without a reason.

"No," Sebastian answered, plainly and seamlessly. The single word hung in the air and seemed heavy with potential argument.

"Mother, I love Lily and cannot wait. Sebastian does not want me to wait," Ralph answered through his confusion. He had been courting Lily every day for nearly a month, so marriage wasn't a surprise. His mother should be overjoyed, but instead she was being absurd. His mind again raced to fathom what on earth she might have against marriage to Miss Snowe. This let him ignore his statement that he loved her.

"I don't doubt that you love Miss Snowe. I am simply trying to understand the urgency," mother said calmly but forcefully.

"I fail to see why Ralph and Lily should delay. I am thrilled we will have an August wedding. Do you plan on marrying in London or her father's estate?"

Sebastian asked, trying to move on from their mother's odd behavior. This was a risky tactic, as refusing to answer Seraphina's objections might mean they would be aired later with greater force.

He hesitated in answering, mostly because he had no idea what Lily would choose. Was this how Vincent had become bitter toward his family? Ralph and Sebastian had never been in competition before, but even the hint of it caused their mother to advocate for Sebastian. Vincent and Sebastian had spent their lives in competition. Did their mother always behave this way? He did not like this aspect of his mother's character and was beginning to doubt her reasoning.

"Father locked the Cubans away, but I found these cigars from India. I also found some Scottish whisky," Vincent said jovially as he returned. "What has happened?"

"Mother is unhappy with my upcoming nuptials," Ralph said between gritted teeth.

"I am not, but it is traditional for the eldest to wed first," Seraphina explained. She stared at Vincent the whole time, curiously.

"If Sebastian were courting anyone, then that would be a discussion worth having. Sebastian is not and therefore is not going to wed any time soon. It would be farcical to expect Ralph to wait until Sebastian weds for the sake of tradition," Vincent explained as he clipped the cigars and handed them out. "It is unhelpful to cause a scene over an idea that cannot pass. You can be excited for the marriage or not, but it has my support."

"Here, here," Sebastian remarked warmly.

Ralph smoked and drank with his brothers in

silence for a few moments. Eventually Mr. Rodgers, their father's butler, entered and broke the tension. "Lord Ralph Mandeville, there is a Lady Olivia in the drawing room for you."

"Lady Olivia? Send her in here," Mother said.

"Why is Lady Olivia here?" Vincent asked.

"I have no idea. She and Lily are close friends. Perhaps something has occurred," Ralph explained, hoping she was merely here to offer congratulations and that Lily was safe and comfortable.

Lady Olivia entered and dipped a curtsy. She was clearly surprised to see Ralph's family. Her fetching brown tweed dress perfectly matched her jacket. It was the first time Ralph had seen her outside of a dinner or ball. She resembled a suffragette perfectly. This was a revelation—Olivia was not just a beautiful debutante but also an educated and passionate woman. Ralph's head swam with pleasant surprise to see her this way.

"Good afternoon, Your Grace and my lords. I have unfortunate news, so perhaps we should find a private room?" she asked Ralph.

"Olivia, enough with the cloak and dagger nonsense. Say what you came to say," Mother said firmly. Firmer than she would have been with anyone else. But Olivia was her special favorite, and Mother hated secrets.

Olivia sighed. "If it were not for your upcoming wedding…Congratulations on that by the way…"

"Olivia," Mother warned.

"Yes, I digress. I would try to verify this, but your wedding is soon, and I wanted to warn you. So, you may wish to investigate rather than react—"

"Olivia!" Mother snapped.

"Right. I attended a suffrage meeting where I met a woman named Susan Petty. She is engaged to a man named Edward Sedgwick. He is a young barrister. In any case, Miss Petty bragged about how Mr. Sedgwick would soon be the most successful barrister in London once he won the case he was working on. According to Miss Petty, in this case he would unseat the Duke of Bridgewater because he is not the rightful heir to his title." Olivia finished and swallowed.

The whole room felt a peal of silent thunder. Ralph's mouth itched and felt impossibly dry, and he immediately regretted not insisting on a private discussion.

"Preposterous!" Sebastian dismissed.

"Who could be the heir?" Vincent asked.

"Thank you, Olivia. Would you like to stay for dinner?" Mother asked.

"Thank you, but I cannot, Your Grace. My mother and I are invited to Lily's house for a sampling of the wedding—err…There will be so many surprises. It will be spoken of for years to come," Olivia said as she dipped again and began to take her leave.

"My lady, what kind of surprises?" Vincent asked, walking toward her. "There will still be a wedding. You will allow us the opportunity to tell Lily ourselves of this development, won't you?"

"Oh, of course! Sir Barton is teaching Lily's footmen to work his carbonation machine, so there will be a soda fountain. And Lord Snowe bought an ice cream machine in Kentucky. This will be a perfect wedding to close the inventor's exposition," Olivia blathered at Vincent. His intensity clearly unnerved her.

"I see. Well, do have a lovely evening. Do you

require an escort?" Vincent asked.

"Thank you, my lord, but my maid is outside, and our home is just four doors down. Good evening." And with that, Lady Olivia was finally able to take her leave.

The room was tense, Ralph was tense, and his adoration of Lily seemed far away.

"Mother, this accusation is impossible. We will not have to worry." Sebastian tried to reassure not just Mother but everyone.

"It could be. Father was a second son. Perhaps Uncle Anson was thought to have died in Crimea but was merely injured. After years of striving to regain his memory and his legs, he is coming home. With the aid of a one-armed prostitute by the name of Brunhilda, of course." Vincent snickered, clearly enjoying his tale.

"Vincent, do stop. We do not need to weave fanciful tales," Ralph pleaded. Although, had this been a less-dire situation, Ralph would have enjoyed hearing more.

Mr. Rodgers entered the room once more. He was carrying a silver tray with a missive. While they waited for his mother to read the telegram, Ralph thought about what Olivia had said. This accusation would devastate his parents and Sebastian. Vincent and Ralph were secure without touching the Bridgewater estate or monies. He supposed that the entire family might be able to weather the storm. They would be poorer and without title, but they could survive this.

Mother sighed. "There was a constable waiting for your father at Avebury Park. He attempted to serve your father with a summons for this matter, but your father claimed the privilege of his peerage. The constable departed and informed the judge involved that the privilege was claimed, and the judge did not dare to go further than that. Grayson will be on the next train. I am retiring to think until he returns. Take heart, my boys. There are two arenas in which the Mandevilles are peerless. We can fight in ballrooms and backrooms, in rumors and reputations. Our family has never feared what happens when words fail us, and we must make war. Whoever is waging this suit has no idea what will be unleashed." The dramatic snowfall of his mother's fair skin and platinum hair twirled stylishly as she left the room.

After Mother had left the room, Sebastian turned to his brothers. "I shall fetch Father and hire Adrian Rose to defend us from this ridiculous endeavor. All I ask of you is not to upset this situation any further."

"Huzzah," Vincent muttered. "On the sunny side, Lily won't mind this scandal at all. She is like you—both loyal and stalwart. She is much better looking, however."

Ralph emptied his glass and refilled it. He hadn't thought about Lily or the wedding. He should have though. She should not marry him, and if her father loved her, then he would forbid it. Ralph would let the settlements go and not sue Lord Snowe. If he broke the engagement, it would be a clear signal of guilt. No, Lily would have to be the one to end it, and it would kill him. But if his feelings for Lily were love, then true love meant giving her the best outcome he could. His world was crumbling and showing the cracks of too much wear. Lily was the only one that could save him, but he had to release her. How cruel and wicked this prospect was. Could he ever survive?

Chapter Fifteen

To undergo a trial is a dreadful thing. To witness someone you love enduring a trial can be twice as painful.

~Aunt Penny's Guide to Living, June 1885

Papa had only been home for a week, and Lily was already exhausted. Every night was attended by a cavalcade of admirers and hangers-on. Because of Papa's relaxed and modern demeanor, people believed they could come to his home unannounced and at all hours. She was barely sleeping. Who knew at what hours they would leave? She longed for the nights when she had wept out of loneliness.

Last night, she had hosted a dinner party for the Marquess of Berkeley, Lady Serena, and Viscount Melgum, and instructed the butler to send away anyone who called. It was the first night she was able to relax and have a pleasant evening. Papa convinced Berkeley to visit Paris, Florence, and Barcelona before departing for Canada. From there, Berkeley's itinerary was filled with cities to keep him in America until November or perhaps even December. It sounded thrilling, but Lily's travels wore hard on her, and she simply wanted a home of her own.

In truth, Lily had always hated her father's home and being forced to live in it alone. It stood as a silent witness to the litany of troubles that she had endured. She was daily forced to pass the spot where Christopher had strangled her. The morning room had not changed since her mother decorated it nearly twenty years ago, and her father refused to allow Lily to change it. The lush pillows drank her tears of loneliness and seemed to mock her. Every inch of the house was a painful reminder of her past, but her new home would be made of memories of Ralph.

Tonight, Lady Belasyse was hosting Lily's engagement dinner. Lily had decided to allow Lady Banbury to act as her mother for the wedding and Lady Belasyse for the engagement. Lady Belasyse had two daughters and was skilled at hosting dinners. Lady Banbury had not been able to have her own wedding, and Lily thought she might enjoy the process.

Lily finally spotted Ralph; relief washed over every inch of her body. Lily smiled and crossed the room to greet him. "Good evening, my lord."

"Lily. May I speak with you, privately?" he asked as he guided her by her elbow to the hall.

"Ralph, is something bothering you?" Lily asked.

Ralph was behaving oddly for the first time. He didn't seem happy to see her. His formality was harsh, and his eyes were stony. "Why have you not called off the engagement?" he hissed.

Lily cocked her head. Perhaps he had suffered a head injury. Vincent aside, mental illness did not appear to afflict the Mandevilles. "I beg your pardon. Why would I do such a thing?"

Ralph sighed. "Lily, my family is under attack. Father may have to go to defend his title. And if we lose, your reputation will be injured. I was certain that your father must have told you…"

"Papa has been occupied. Ralph, we have settlements signed, and it's too late. I would never abandon you in your hour of need," Lily explained, although this discussion was idiotic. She did not leave people. They abandoned her. She was not about to permit Ralph to escape her and their affections.

"I will not fight you if you end the engagement. I give you my word," Ralph said. His eyes sank, and his mouth hung in a perfect reflection of his downtrodden and miserable mood. How could she comfort him? She was a close companion of her own fears but had until this moment not visited with Ralph's or those of anyone else. This was not due to a lack of understanding, but until now no one had been close enough to let her see their fears. She had heard the cries of Bella and Olivia, but their fear was a distant thing compared to whatever caused this present hardship.

"But I will fight you. You promised me, Ralph. You promised we would be married and that I would be protected and safe. I never cared about the Duke of Bridgewater's social ties or estates. I care about you. I need you. I need a home. You are the closest thing to family I have ever known, and I will chase you for eternity. Know this, Ralph Mandeville. I will fight you every step of the way if you try to end our engagement, and I will win."

With that, Lily marched back into the lounge while holding her head high and blinking back her hot tears. She had behaved terribly, and she sounded shrill and like a hag. Why did she persist in such behavior with the one person she needed to charm? Ralph was likely filled with regrets. He never should have courted her.

But Lily was like a starving dog that had finally stolen its favorite morsels. She would bark and bite anyone who tried to take away what she had needed for so long.

She had begun to realize that she had never had the home she needed. Lily wanted a home that was stable. A home where voyages to far-off lands were rare and included the entire family. Lily couldn't blame her father or Christopher. They simply did not have it in them to foster a young girl to make her feel safe and secure. Ralph could provide a safe and stable home and always be her warm place. She simply needed to drag him to the altar.

At dinner, Lily was seated between Vincent and Sebastian and across from Ralph. She chose Vincent to converse with. "Tell me, Vincent, have you had an opportunity to meet Lady Serena?"

Vincent stared at the ceiling and tried to recall. "No. I have met her brother on several occasions, but I have not met the lady herself."

"That is a pity. She is fond of you," Lily teased. Nothing provoked Vincent such as the idea that anyone held him in high regard. He had a desperate need to prove them wrong.

"Why on earth would she be fond of me? I know I am the prettiest Mandeville, but she cannot form an attachment on that. Unless she is incredibly superficial." Vincent preened as he stole Lily's wine before sipping it and making a face. Vincent had clearly forgotten that ladies' wine was always watered down.

"She enjoys your critiques. Even the one of *Pamela*, which most women of means find to be quite a delightful book. She quoted it at dinner last night," Lily answered.

"I see. Why were you having dinner with Lady Serena?" Vincent asked absentmindedly. His head swayed deliberately while looking for someone to bring him more wine, but the footmen were clearing the first course and were preoccupied.

"Papa was helping Lord Berkeley plan his tour of North America," she explained.

"That is unfortunate. I rather like Berkeley. When is he leaving?" Vincent asked.

"I believe not for at least a fortnight. Berkeley, Lady Serena, and Lord Melgum are visiting a few European cities first. I think they will not arrive in Canada until August. Lord Melgum is planning on moving to America permanently, if you can imagine," Lily answered and cringed as a maid dropped a serving spoon.

"Berkeley said Melgum had planned to move. I cannot imagine what he could be thinking. Melgum is the heir apparent to an earldom in Scotland. He is essentially abdicating his title. I wonder who will inherit it now?" Vincent mused.

"I am uncertain. I enjoyed my time in Scotland. From which part does Lord Melgum hail?" Her eyes danced and delighted in the roasted quail with mushroom stuffing. Quail was her absolute favorite dish, and it was terribly sweet of Lady Belasyse to recall this fact. She smoothly tasted the dense and gamey meat.

"I believe he said Aberdeenshire. I have been to Edinburgh and Glasgow, but I have not explored the countryside of Scotland. Is it scenic?" Vincent asked. Obviously he was on his best behavior.

"Oh yes. It's beautiful. Lovely hills of heather and

sunsets made of violet and orange. You should plan a visit. Perhaps purchase a kilt for the wedding," Lily baited.

"Perhaps for the winter sports," Vincent mused, and Lily could finally see how low the Mandevilles were laid. For Vincent to let opportunity go by to mock kilts, the Scots, or Lily meant something dire had roosted in his mind.

"Tell me about this trouble, Vincent. Ralph has not yet informed me. At least not at length," Lily whispered.

"Rose claims they will not be able to prosecute in a criminal court because the House of Lords will not hear the case. However, if we lose in the civil court, then the House of Lords may take it up. He is taking a chance at getting this matter resolved outside of both the courts and the Parliament," Vincent explained. However, it was useless. Lily had no idea what the case was or who was pursuing it.

"Vincent, I don't understand. What is it that they are alleging?" Lily asked, still whispering.

Vincent frowned at her. "There is a man who accuses father of usurping the title of Duke of Bridgewater. Father was a second son, and his older brother died during the Crimean war. Both Father and Uncle Anson served in the Light Brigade under the Earl of Cardigan. This man alleges that upon his return to London, Father bullied the dowager duchess into hiding. That he knew that she was with child. Nine months later, she birthed a boy who would have been the rightful heir, but Father abducted the wee babe. The dowager allowed it because she was terrified of Father," Vincent whispered conspiratorially.

She was silent as the footmen took away the delicious quail. This ordeal would be horrendous for the Mandevilles and by extension for Lily. Lily knew (but suspected the Mandevilles did not) that the *ton* disliked Seraphina Mandeville immensely. Her snobbishness and need to exclude "undeserving" people left many resentful of her. Seraphina made it perfectly clear that she had never liked Lily or her father. But they were going to be family, and Lily would have to help. As much as Lily wanted to see Seraphina hoist on her own petard, she couldn't allow the rest of the family to be injured.

After supper, when the men and women separated, she had to find Ralph. He leaned pensively against the wall outside the dining room. He was clearly exhausted from this lawsuit and fear of the consequences of it. Understanding dawned on Lily. She may have been a child at the time, but she remembered the feeling of impending doom and the paralyzing terror that was its constant companion well. It was a heavy rock that weighed you down and blocked out the light.

"The English legal system is one of the best in the world, although there is much need for improvement. I, for one, think there are far too many hanging offenses. But it is much better than it once was. In the middle ages, justice was a trial by ordeal. One would undergo a massive amount of pain to prove one's innocence, and if the accused could not endure it, then he was guilty. While our legal system may have improved, as a civilization we still test others in this fashion. It is tempting to push away your allies during this time, as shame desires isolation. But it is the wrong move. This is the time to forge new bonds and solidify old ones."

Lily moved toward Ralph while making her speech.

"Lily, I'm sorry—" Ralph began. She could see by his softened face and bow of his head that her words meant something to him.

She pressed her white-satin-gloved finger against his lips. She didn't want to hear his words. Be it a sincere apology or a further excuse to end their engagement, those distinctions were not meaningful to her. "However, once you win, you are rewarded immensely. You will always know how to fight, and you will learn who is worth fighting for. Personally, I think I was bestowed the magic ability to see which people are truly evil beyond those that are merely irritating. I also believe that I am rewarded with you, the person I dreamed of."

Ralph crushed her into him and kissed her. The warmth of his body and the pressure of his embrace brought to mind being bundled in blankets during a winter storm. She felt snug, invulnerable, and warm. In a world that was never truly safe, she had found her refuge and needed to return the favor. Ralph may not have been a wild romantic such as Heathcliff. Although he was not Heathcliff, he was her Mr. Darcy…if Mr. Darcy had fancied Lydia instead of Elizabeth.

"I don't deserve you," Ralph murmured as he released her and allowed air between them.

"No, you don't. But luckily, I deserve you," she said with another kiss that silenced him for a full minute. Real love, true love, was not the absence of strife or happiness forever more. No, love was knowing that you would never fight alone and there would always be one person by your side.

Chapter Sixteen

I am fond of gardening, and I have come to understand it as a metaphor for life. One must handle manure for truly beautiful flowers, and if you allow weeds in your garden, they will choke the life out of your growth. For every problem one will face, I have found a garden-inspired solution. Of course, common wisdom will tell you that one must have a garden for anything to grow. I have been experimenting with window boxes to grow tomatoes, carrots, celery, and peas with wonderful success.

~Aunt Penny's Advice on Living, June 1885

Ralph was in hell. He was certain of it. He had the world in his grasp but could not take hold of it. He silently contemplated the universe that should have been, as the foul scents of carefully prepared coffee and toast wafted past him. If this lawsuit had not occurred, he would be rushing to the altar with his perfect bride by his side. He would not be tormented by her kisses. He would ravish her every moment he could. Everything would be right in the world, and he would be a settled, happy man. Lily had told him, in no uncertain terms, he was her home. He would never be like the men who had abandoned her. If he could persevere through this lawsuit, then he could find love and validate the toil and hardship that he had endured throughout his courtship. And it would diminish the perils Lily had suffered throughout her life.

He walked down the street after leaving Barton's home. The papers were lampooning his entire family. Mother was deemed to be a calculating shrew. Father was a dithering moron. Sebastian was a dull snob. Ralph was so boring, he had to resort to marrying a foreigner. Vincent was ridiculed for every cutting remark he had ever made and called "The Malicious Mandeville." Vincent's only response was that "The Mandevillain" would have been better and that perhaps he should join the clergy as everyone loved a handsome man in black.

As he approached the house, there was a dim light in the library. Vincent must have come home from Miss Haverford's early. Ralph was in no mood to hear about the obnoxious woman and sneaked around to the kitchen. However, as he entered Ralph heard Vincent humming "Three Little Maids." Vincent was frying a sandwich and smiled when he saw Ralph.

"Good evening. I was at *The Mikado*. Lovely show." Vincent slid the sandwich onto a plate and handed it to Ralph.

"I thought you were paying Miss Haverford a call," Ralph stated as he bit into the sandwich. It was truly odd, brie and strawberry jam, but it tasted magnificent.

"I saw her earlier. Sutherland and Osborne hoped to cheer me and accompanied me to the theatre. It was wonderful to simply experience something beautiful with my fellow Londoners." Vincent grinned as he toasted his own sandwich.

Neither brother spoke for the moments while Vincent cooked. Ralph knew that Vincent must be exhausted. No one could prepare for this onslaught. It was draining to face the news every day and have it be only upsetting. They should have avoided the papers for their own good, but neither of them could. It was there, and they had to read it, even if it hurt. Especially if it hurt.

Ralph followed Vincent to the library, only to have his brother reach back and gently push Ralph against the wall. Vincent was not facing him but spoke. "I believe you have the wrong house. Or depending on your temperament, the right one."

There was someone in the library. He could not see around Vincent and had no idea who or what the visitor wanted.

"No, Vincent. I am here for you." A woman spoke. Slow and lazy with confidence and deliberation.

"Oh, are you a gift? Very well. I shall put on the saucy chambermaid uniform, and you go fetch a spoon. I will refer to you hence as Mummy," Vincent chirped. It was hard to suppress a chuckle.

"I am familiar with what you think is wit. I am not your mother, so you cannot shock me. And I am not your friend, so you will not charm me. You will listen. I am here to aid you in this crisis. Are you interested in help, or would you like to continue referencing *The Pearl*?" she asked. She sounded well educated and definitively upper class, but not familiar.

"By all means. I am desperate to know what a plucky girl with a high-priced companion's wardrobe can do to help. How long have you been out of the nursery, by the by?" Vincent moved into the room.

This was the best moment to take advantage of the moment to steal a glance, and so he did. The woman was dressed as a pirate. She was beautifully proportioned, and the ambient light highlighted tiny gold strands that escaped the flamboyant plumed musketeer hat. She reclined on Vincent's favorite red velvet armchair and stretched her legs on one arm. She seemed to be seducing Vincent, but at the tender age of perhaps seventeen or eighteen, she didn't know the fire she was playing with.

"My age has nothing to do with the Shadow Society. They sent the warning to you, did they not? They said you were chosen?"

What the hell was she speaking of?

"You have my attention," Vincent answered as he rested against his desk.

"That implies they view you as the threat to them. Yours is not the first family they have targeted, but they have changed immensely. And it appears they were sound in their judgment that they could warn you, and you still would be vulnerable. They are smart enough to play with you. Think of how smart you think you are, Vincent. Then think of how confident they must be to treat your family and fortune as a game."

"Who are they? What do they want from us? Who is this other family?" Vincent asked. Coming from anyone else, those words would seem panicked.

Ralph struggled not to barge in and demand to know what was happening. Vincent was forewarned? This is a coordinated effort? He breathed slowly to trust his brother and would mandate answers later.

"The Shadow Society, from what I have learned, is a secret society bent on revenge. Someone in your family has wronged one of the members, and this is their vengeance. I will not reveal the other family, as they have gone through great pains to hide their injury. I will, however, tell you what the Shadow Society did to them." She stretched out her hand, and Vincent gave her a fourth of his sandwich.

"Well?" Vincent prodded as she chewed.

"This family, who we shall refer to as the First, had a tremendous fortune built up after centuries. The Shadow Society stole all of it, except for twenty thousand pounds intended for the daughter's dowry. The lady has yet to come out, though she was meant to this season. Instead, the family has been trying to rebuild their wealth. Although it is difficult to go from Croesus to a pauper overnight." The pirate swung her legs down and waltzed to his brandy. She poured herself a glass before offering Vincent one.

It would be easy to argue that he could do a great deal with twenty thousand pounds if the first family would trust him. It was unlikely that the family had a man such as Ralph within their ranks. It was harder and harder to bite his tongue, remain in the shadows, and eavesdrop. But it was the wiser position.

"And how does a child learn all of this?" Vincent asked.

The pirate laughed a child's laugh, full of amusement. "I am but a part of a much larger organization. We call ourselves the Black Swan."

"Another secret society? Though I rather like the idea of a black swan. So different from a black sheep," Vincent mocked.

"A reactionary club. We formed to stop the Shadow Society and help the victims of their treachery."

"And you? Who are you?" Vincent sounded angry

for the first time.

"I am but a quiet girl of no consequence." Her answer was full of confidence that proved her words were lies.

"Why would you care? You do not resemble a crusader, and we are far from innocent of a crime. Vengeance rarely is unasked for," Vincent challenged.

"Do you know why power fails, Vincent? Because every power is a great tree. Deep in its roots, there is always a tremendous jealousy, and so it thirsts angrily to grow and grow, until only it survives. And the only powers that survive are the ones that convince us that they are beautiful to behold. Wealth. Religion. Justice. Every one of them is full of jealousy because they know that the others have something they cannot. And so, they make war just as the Shadow Society makes war. The things we hate most are the ones we aspire toward. I will not see lives wrecked for the sake of power."

"How does one obtain membership to the Black Swan?"

She grinned. "I will have to discuss the notion with the other members. We will be in contact with more information about this lawsuit. It may not be I. It might be another member."

Ralph managed to duck into the shadows just as she walked out the room. Her curves swayed as she left by the front door. He had to wait a moment before he entered the room. Vincent was staring at a painting of a silver star. Ralph cleared his throat far too loudly to break the silence up into little pieces.

"You were warned?" Ralph demanded.

"In a fashion. Do you recall Mother's ball?" Vincent asked.

"Very well." How could he not? It was the night he met Lily.

"I found a missive in my pocket—a warning from a group that calls itself the Shadow Society." Vincent dug in his desk to produce the slip of paper.

Ralph looked over the note.

THE MANDEVILLES HAVE BEEN CHOSEN

"Why didn't you mention this?" Ralph demanded.

Vincent shrugged. "I could not know if it was a jest or if it was serious."

Ralph nodded. "I'm going to sleep. Hopefully, this group will help us."

The next morning, Ralph left his townhouse shortly after his breakfast and walked to Rose's office. But he veered off to find Lily. Of course his duties and responsibilities lay in working with Adrian, but a siren's call was overwhelming him. Lily had a fantastic ability to focus Ralph after he saw her. Before he had even thought of it, he was at her door. As the butler guided him into the morning room, he realized it may have been too early.

Lily entered wearing a cheerful white morning dress but appearing fatigued. "Ralph, it is early. Is anything amiss?"

"No. Well, nothing new. Is your father about?" Ralph asked. Where was the frightful brute?

"Papa was reveling late last night, so he will not wake until noon at least. Do you need to speak with him?" Lily asked.

He wrapped his arm around her waist and pulled her close to him. He began to kiss her neck eliciting a soft moan. "I missed you terribly, *miliy*." He groaned before capturing her mouth with his.

"Oh, my darling. I wish we were to wed tomorrow," she whispered into his ear.

"I must resolve this suit before we wed. I will not jeopardize your name and future," Ralph said sternly. Perhaps if she accepted this, then he could as well.

Lily leaned her head on his shoulder. She was small to him, and he wanted to protect her. "Then we must work together to correct this fiasco. I cannot tolerate being apart from you much longer. Every night I lie in bed without you is a crime."

Ralph tilted her chin to meet her eyes. "Once we are united, we will never be parted again. Lily, I promise I will never leave you," Ralph vowed and was rewarded with a deep kiss.

"I need you," Lily whispered as she pulled him into her. "I need you now."

He groaned in agony. "We cannot. If I were to get you with child, the world would know."

Lily nodded. "There are...other intimacies we could do."

His eyebrows jumped at such an idea, and his heart hammered. "How do you know of such things?"

Lily giggled coyly. "I have been to Khajurado and Pompeii. Although I cannot speak to how pleasurable it will be. They carved the oddest expressions. The ancient people were much more libertine, with their bawdy notions unbounded by disapproving mamas."

Ralph's head swam with the possibilities of what Lily saw. He had been privy to a copy of the *Kama Sutra* with one of his friends at Oxford. The Indians were a dexterous lot. As for Pompeii, half the exhibits had to be hidden for fear the indecency would cause ladies to faint.

Ralph kissed her once more. He should be canonized for his strength in the face of overwhelming temptation. "I will savor the idea of…other intimacies."

"And what should I savor?" Lily asked before nibbling his earlobe.

Ralph struggled with his hands, choosing to rub her arms instead of the places he longed to touch. "Much the same, I suppose. I hate this as much as you do, *miliy*. As soon as the trial is over, we will wed. I promise."

"Or the first week of August. Whichever comes first," Lily said as she straightened his necktie.

The first week of August was still nearly five weeks away. He was in torment, but he wouldn't alter his life. He had Lily, and his worst day near her was better than his best day without her.

"I must be going to Rose's office. I will find a way for us to be together, Lily." Ralph rubbed his thumb against her plump lower lip.

"I know. If you don't, well, I have already threatened to follow you to the ends of the earth," Lily teased. She kissed him once more as though it could mend his broken world. And in truth, her lips seemed to erase most of his worries.

Ralph smiled as he left Lily's townhouse. He hadn't relaxed. In fact, he was much tenser than before-but in a better way. He had simply needed to be reminded of who he endured this debacle for. He loved his family, but he fought so that Lily could be his wife. Everything in his life was a calculation of risk and reward, but Lily was all rewards. She asked for so little, but he wanted to give her everything. She was the only person whose presence had never been an encumbrance or cost. She was always sweet and free, and for that gift he would never stop trying to please her.

Chapter Seventeen

A garden party is best held when one's flowers are full bloom. A lawn without blooms feels as though it were a ship wrecked upon the shore. When hosting a garden party, I like to use elements that I have grown. I enjoy putting mint in my lemonade and serving fresh strawberries picked only that morning. Anyone can purchase such items, but if you can grow them, it makes the party so much more intimate.

~Aunt Penny's Advice for Living, June 1885

Lily uncoiled with relief to attend Lady Belasyse's garden party. The event was meant to display support for the Mandevilles by all, but it was not as well attended as Lady Belasyse had planned. It was remarkable how naïve they were about the *ton*'s true nature. The *ton* behaved like fair-weather friends. Adversity had a way of shaking the fickle people from one's life. Those who stood by you while your life was in tumult were the only people worth knowing. Everyone else was merely extra.

It was a spectacular afternoon, and Lady Belasyse clearly had a passion for roses. She studied them and bred them in ways that Lily did not truly understand. Apparently, it was an honor to have a rose named for you, and Lady Belasyse coveted that honor to an extreme. Lily mused as to what name Lady Belasyse would choose. Perhaps it could be the Hélène rose or the Belasyse rose. Lady Banks had the Lady Banks rose, so the Lady Belasyse rose was not out of the realm of possibility.

Lady Olivia stood next to Lily. "I am keeping note as to which of my suitors is in attendance. I may have to cull my list of admirers to this lot. Ralph excepted, of course."

Lily smiled at Olivia. How annoying that someone so beautiful should also be clever and kind. If there was justice in the world, Olivia would be the callous factory owner's dim wife. In truth, Lily was eternally grateful for Olivia and for all of her friends' loyalty. These past months would have been unbearable without their support.

"A lady should be happy with these men. You could marry the Duke of Southampton or his younger brother, Lord Drake Belmont, or the Earl of Coningsby. Mr. Rose is in attendance, and he was on my list of men to pursue myself, before I met Ralph. And I believe I saw Lord Amesbury wandering about earlier," Lily explained.

Olivia nodded. "It's a lovely day. Your dress is stunning."

Lily preened with busy hands because she had to be perfect in this dress. She was especially proud of it. It was a cream bustle dress, but the bunting was fabric cut to resemble ivy leaves with pink satin rosettes dotting the gown and dragonfly buttons on her chest. The hope was to elicit the idea that the garden itself was trying to shelter her. Lily was inspired after a picnic at a fairy mound, and she liked it best when her dresses told a story.

"Thank you!" Lily said.

"How are you faring with Miss Aurora Rose's new dresses?" Olivia inquired.

"Quite well. Aurora is the Roman goddess of the dawn. I am working with dawn colors since Miss Aurora Rose is impish and playful," Lily explained.

Olivia looked thoughtful. "I rarely see dawn, with the exception of winters. What would you consider dawn colors?"

"Lavender, peach, sunny yellows, robin's egg blue, and pinks. As a child, I would confuse Aurora with Iris, so I may be creating a pastel rainbow. Regardless, I am most excited about her dress for her coming-out ball."

"I cannot keep my tongue sheathed any further. You should be creating dresses for everyone, Lily. You have far too much talent to keep it hidden. Do not hide your light," Olivia burst out.

"Olivia, I am not a modiste. I have no skill with needle and thread. Merely skilled with sketching," Lily explained, trying hard to justify her mixture of fear and pride.

"You can hire seamstresses. I implore you to think on this," Olivia pled.

"The House of Snowe," she mused out loud before dismissing the idea. It was absurd, if for no other reason than the Duchess of Bridgewater would never allow it. The indulgence of styling oneself was already a potent token of independence, and Lily moving beyond it might invite serious rebuke.

"The House of Mandeville. You are so lucky, Lily. All the ambitious ladies will be desperate to befriend you once this scandal is over. They will attend every party and dinner you hold just for the hope Coningsby will see them. You will be akin to Saint Peter," Olivia meandered, though in her babble she compared Sebastian to heaven.

"I adore Sebastian, but he is far too interested in politics to maintain proper conversation," Lily answered.

"Is he?" Olivia muttered. She began to look lost in her own mind before snapping back to Earth. "Here comes Miss Haverford. We have not yet been introduced. Please do the honors."

Lily wanted to spare Olivia and simply refuse to make introductions. Lily desperately desired to tell *someone* what an obnoxious twit Marlene Haverford was. If Lily ruled the world she would send Marlene to Australia, or at least push her in horse dung. Obviously, the only reason she tolerated Marlene's presence was because Vincent was smitten with her. However, decorum mandated she just smile.

"Good afternoon, Miss Haverford. Lady Olivia, I present Miss Haverford." Lily tried to not sound as annoyed as she felt.

"How do you do, Miss Haverford?" Olivia asked, now donning the mantle of a queen.

"I am well, my lady. And how does this afternoon find you?" Miss Haverford asked. She exhaled the phrase in a low purring voice. She was not elocuting like a proper lady.

"Quite well. I am always best in the company of my friends." Olivia grinned and looped her arm with Lily's.

Miss Haverford raised a false smile. "I fear I am ignorant of our host. Is there anything I should know about Lady Belasyse?"

"We are close friends with her granddaughter, the Honorable Miss Bellatrix Beauchamp," Olivia began.

"Bellatrix? What an odd name," Miss Haverford mused, and Lily resisted the urge to yank the curls at her hairline.

"Bella, her mother, and her grandmother were all born in France. Albeit with English lord fathers, Miss Haverford," Lily answered.

"Ah, it seems half the *ton* has foreign-born mothers," Miss Haverford said giving a pointed look at Lily.

"Of course it does. After all, most noble families trace their lines to the conqueror. And where does your family hail from, Miss Haverford?" Olivia asked.

"Northumberland," Miss Haverford answered. Of course, as Northumberland was where cows generally came from.

"Lily, here comes your fiancé," Olivia said, then whispered to Lily, "He looks like he is going to ravish you."

Ralph, Vincent, and Sebastian walked to the ladies with somber footfalls and pensive shoulders. To Lily's gaze, Ralph was on the edge of his careful control. Sadly, Lily knew it was a lack of sleep and overwork that gave him that air. Even in the throes of lust, Ralph was capable of buttoning his coat. But today he had missed a button. Ralph and Vincent shared a valet right now. This was mainly because they were squabbling over which one kept Barrowman and which one had to find and train a new valet. Ralph argued that he was to be married soon and should have the more experienced valet. Vincent argued that Barrowman had been with Vincent longer and knew Vincent better. Lily felt such pain for him, and for all the Mandevilles. They were struggling to stay afloat.

"Good afternoon, Ralph and Vincent. Lady Olivia, Miss Haverford, may I have the honor of presenting Sebastian Mandeville, the Earl of Coningsby." Lily performed in a rehearsed pleasant tone.

"Miss Haverford. Lady Olivia, it is lovely to make your acquaintance, as both my mother and Miss Snowe hold you in such high regard," Sebastian said stiffly.

"Why, my lord, I was about to say the exact words. You stole them from me." Olivia flirted.

"You were going to call Sebastian 'Lady Olivia'?" Vincent smirked.

Olivia didn't bat an eye. "Oh, I call everyone Lady Olivia. It saves me from having to recall names and titles of everyone I meet, which can be quite tedious. It runs in the family, you see. My great-aunt Matilda calls everyone Barty."

"Touché, my lady," Vincent said.

"Would you care to take a turn about the garden, Lily?" Ralph asked, in a gesture completely out of character for him.

"Of course, dearest." Lily dipped to the remaining group before joining him.

Once they were away from prying eyes, Ralph kissed her. "I am sorry."

Lily giggled. "Never apologize for kissing me."

Ralph sighed. "No, Lily. Vincent's friend has told him some reporters are looking into you. I live in fear that they will reveal your Russian adventure."

"Adventure is an ironic turn of phrase for what happened. You know of it and will still marry me. Bella, Olivia, and Honoria will still be my friends.

Threats are only effective if one might lose something of value." Lily struggled to remain calm in her terror. The power of gossip could warp her scarring personal history into a weapon to use against her. A tale where Lily was a child prostitute and was not worth her hard-scrabbled dignity. Blood pounded in her temples, and her stomach churned. Yet Lily smiled. What else could she do when fear was swallowing her whole?

"I wish I could be as strong as you are." He laid delicate kisses on her eyelids. "I hate that there is anything I cannot protect you from. I wish that this were something simple as a dragon, which is to say, easily slain. But this situation is truth mixed with lies and innuendo. I have no idea how to fight this."

She buried her face in his chest hoping he would not see how false her bravery was. "We will fight it together."

Chapter Eighteen

The Good Book tells us to do unto others as we would have done unto ourselves. It is for this reason that whenever I know someone is undergoing strife, I imagine myself in their situation. I create a care package of tea, heather honey, and scones. Scones are but a culinary canvas for one to paint upon and are perfect for whatever is in your kitchen. I have had great luck with bright lemon, rich pumpkin, and tart cranberry. I promise if you bring your neighbors some scones, you will brighten their day.

~Aunt Penny's Advice on Living, June 1885

Ralph sat in the Roses' library with his brothers and Adrian. In the past few days, Ralph had alternated between struggling to get out of his bed in the mornings to wanting to murder far too many people for his busy mind to bother counting. Vincent kept barging into his bedchamber every morning and forcing him to participate in life. It was not altogether unpleasant, but the physical exhaustion of his mental state was devastating.

The exhaustion began after the papers began running stories on Lily. On the first day, they merely questioned her fashionability and referred to her as "The Gilded Lily." Then the press discovered that her mother was pregnant with Lily when her parents married. They questioned her legitimacy. And finally, the revelation came out that she was the artist in all of Lord Snowe's books. There were bare breasts in some of those renditions. Knowing that the hand of a sixteen-year-old girl drew them made the whole matter indecent. It was foolish, and it didn't make any logical sense, but they were ravaging her. Without any care for the destruction or power they had over innocent life, they printed the darkest moments of her life. They made her an unwilling actress in a play she never auditioned for. A production that was performed in front of a hateful audience for someone else's salaciousness and profit. It would make any sane person rage.

Today they were in Adrian's library, as his law office was surrounded by reporters. Ralph liked the Roses' home. It was closer to Soho than his parents' home and built in the Georgian style. If Ralph were pressed to describe the Roses' townhouse in one word, it would be clean. The white house had a black door and black iron gate with bright green topiaries. The entry had a black and white checkerboard floor with a simple black table and mirror. The library was entirely blue with two leather chairs near the fireplace. He could tell the two cream chairs that seemed out of place had been brought in for his brothers (from perhaps the drawing room). Everything was in straight lines and organized. In the midst of Ralph's chaotic life, this was paradise. Someday he would seek to explore the entire home.

"Well, gentlemen, I finally have some news," Adrian announced.

"I'm sick of news. Unless it is good, we should discuss the weather." Vincent brooded.

"It isn't good or bad but simply is. We finally have a date in court, July 27. Or a date for a preliminary hearing before a steward. It is different from a civil court for reasons of jurisdiction." Adrian was clearly losing his audience, so he calmed himself and moved on to something much more easily explained. "We also have the accuser's name, Mr. Bartholomew Edwards. He is recent from the Yorkshire Asylum. We have not heard from the dowager duchess," Adrian explained.

"Why hasn't she responded? She could make this entire situation moot!" Sebastian exclaimed. This ordeal had stretched Sebastian's ability to be stalwart in every situation. The man was close to snapping his tether.

Adrian shrugged. "I am as confused as you are, I assure you. I have sent over a hundred missives, be they telegrams or letters, and not one has been answered. On the other hand, we are assuming her ignorance rather than her malfeasance. The simple motive in this case is that her negligence enriches her while her assistance keeps her in what she might think is an unjust condition. I suppose we could force her hand if she were compelled to appear."

"I will go to her." The offer escaped Ralph's mouth before he had even thought of it.

"And to the asylum. We will investigate further and be back before the trial begins," Vincent added.

"If you wish. We have hired investigators. But lords tend to open doors others are locked out of," Adrian said.

"It's settled then," Ralph said. He hoped Sebastian wouldn't want to come with them. Sebastian had been threatened and harassed the worst of the three brothers.

"What are we settling?" Miss Honoria Rose asked as she entered the library with Lily behind her.

"We are going to investigate the dowager duchess and the man accusing our family of wrongdoing," Vincent answered.

Miss Rose handed Adrian a missive and said, "Marvelous."

Adrian cleared his throat. "The long and the short of this case is that it confounds our system of justice. A judge will not have adequate jurisdiction to decide this sort of matter; the duke can claim the privilege of his peer status. That would make this a matter for Parliament to decide. However, that assumes he is a duke. If you assume the correctness of the assertions—"

"They are patently false, and entertaining them—" Sebastian glowered with a disciplined tone that could set a Prime Minister on edge.

"—is part of the nature of our defense. You see, the jurisdictional issue must be decided prior to adjudication of the legal question. Claiming the peerage and its privileges is a way of placing the question in front of the judge prior to his reaching the claims themselves. Only then, by claiming the privilege—" Adrian interposed, only to be interrupted by Vincent.

"—we place what is a Parliamentary determination before a legal one, and judges fear to tread a path reserved for lords. So, we turn a legal question into a political question. That is risky but brilliant, Adrian."

"It has the effect of stalling things a bit, but also gives the appearance that the duke is not afraid of this question. A client that appears scared appears guilty. It is an unfortunate turn of the human mind that people who are innocent and afraid to lose appear guiltier than confident people who are of bad character." Adrian had experienced the loud, angry tears of many people who were innocent but very nervous. Obviously, his gambit was for the duke to maintain composure.

"You know, that is so strange. It is claimed that the meek shall inherit the earth. But everywhere I go, it is the bullies and the extortionists who seem to seek the most and sometimes win. Why is that?" Lily turned the dryness and heat of the conversation into a bright glow rather than leave it a crackling mass of words.

It was hard to admit, but he enjoyed the direction of her rhetoric. "The Marquess of Berkeley," he said, glancing toward Miss Rose, "would say it is because the rules are unjust and produce an unjust outcome because the people who set them are an unjust people."

"That can't be true. There are surely enough good people to prevent such difficult things. Or surely in our nation, that cannot be true." From her tone, Lily half agreed with such sentiments, but even a contentious debate was preferable to Sebastian and Vincent fighting with Adrian and each other.

Ralph replied, "We shall try to be the good people, then."

"On the subject of Berkeley, he sends his regards and apologies for not being in town to assist the Mandevilles." Miss Rose deftly changed the subject.

"Has he arrived in America then?" Vincent inquired.

"No, they are in Dublin. Frederick has finally been granted access to the Royal Irish Academy, and I am positively green with envy," Miss Rose lamented. Though if she were green, it would look becoming against her ginger hair.

"Honoria, we could go to Dublin right now if it piques your interest," Lily said with a confused expression.

"No, Serena and I have an interest in the Tuatha de Danann. The Royal Irish Academy was gifted the Books of Lecan and Ballymote. Both are pivotal manuscripts," Miss Rose explained.

"The Tuatha de Danann? Invaders from another world of unspeakable beauty and power? If I recall correctly, are they not all trapped in fairy mounds?" Vincent asked.

"Indeed, that is the legend. They are in the underworld with the sidhe," Miss Rose answered.

"Have you written to Uncle Evert?" Adrian asked with a wink.

Miss Rose's mouth formed an O, and she smacked her palm against her forehead. "It has never occurred to me. Oh, how could I have been so foolish?"

Adrian chuckled, and Ralph sensed an opening. "Would your uncle have helped you see the manuscripts?"

"No," Adrian answered. "Uncle Evert is the Earl of Strange, and he lives in Hopes End. It once was a castle and scriptorium until a fire ravaged the castle in 1398."

"I beg your pardon, but what is a scriptorium?" Lily asked, and Ralph was grateful as he did not know either.

"A scriptorium is where they would, before the printing press, create manuscripts. Imagine the hours that went into these works, and a fire breaks out. The legend tells that the authors secreted away a treasure trove of manuscripts and hid them in the dungeon. The dungeon remains as part of the rebuilt house but is largely used for storage," Miss Rose explained with a dramatic flourish of her opening palm.

"Honoria and I spent much of a summer searching for the books. You ought to write Uncle to seek an invitation to stay in his home this winter," Adrian advised.

"I shall. Cousin Sabrina is Aurora's age. I'm surprised he hasn't asked Mother to sponsor Sabrina," Honoria said with a confused expression. Honoria's eyes cast to the telegram in Adrian's hand. "Well, get on with it. What did Frederick say to you, Adrian?"

"He and I are developing a scheme, and he had an idea. It was nothing terribly important," Adrian said as he swept the missive into a pile of correspondences upon his desk.

"Oh, yes, nothing provocative in that pile. Everyone look this way. Adrian has nothing interesting over here," Vincent mimicked sarcastically. "Adrian, we are family. We will understand if you tell us it's none of our business."

Adrian sighed. "In all honesty, I wanted to invite Ralph into the scheme, but I was going to wait until the suit was settled."

How intriguing. Ralph was pleased that Adrian thought so highly of him. "I would enjoy a distraction from the suit. What kind of scheme is it?"

"We plan to purchase estates from indebted gentlemen and…revitalize them," Adrian offered.

"How do you intend to do so?" Sebastian asked.

"In all honesty, that is the reason we hope Ralph will join us. If the estate is profitable, we will leave it alone and create a resort out of the house if it could become one. If the estate is not profitable and within a reasonable train ride to London, we wish to build houses for the middle class and create a village with a department store there," Adrian explained.

There were so many questions about this scheme. "I am eager to discuss this more. Perhaps when I return from Lancaster."

"May I ask that we wait until Friday to leave? I am hosting a tea," Lily asked, sensing that the room's temperature had changed.

"Oh, Lion Tamer, we intend to visit an insane asylum. That is no place for a lady. They are hellish." Vincent tried to dissuade her.

"I have experienced a Russian winter. Hell would be pleasant in comparison," Lily retorted.

Chapter Nineteen

It is peculiar how much the past haunts us. Yesterday, I discovered a trunk of my great-grandmother's clothes. Inside I found clues to the woman she once was. I had never met her. However, I instantly missed her. I wanted to know the girl who wore such charming jewelry.
~Aunt Penny's Advice for Living, June 1885

Lily never missed Katerina Snowe. Katerina was a selfish miserable creature who had felt the need to constantly remind Lily how much prettier Katerina was than her daughter. Katerina had done a world of damage to Lily and never thought twice about it. Even if Katerina were to return and profoundly apologize for every act of cruelty she'd committed against her only daughter, how could she ever be forgiven? Not that Katerina could ever admit she was wrong.

Still, it was easy to miss the idea of a mother terribly. Or to envy her friends who could enjoy their mothers and be comforted by them. The traditional engagement rituals represented painful rites of passage without a mother to smooth them out. Lily's face flushed with embarrassment and she excused herself so often so the others would not see her tears. She was alone, and there was no one who could possibly understand.

It would be less painful if her mother were dead instead of simply gone. A dead mother could never hint it was Lily's fault that her mother was absent. In the stillness between her sobs, she blamed herself for her mother's callousness. If she was worthy of love, then her mother would have loved her. This emptiness felt so unfair; murderers' mothers wept for their hanged sons, but Katerina couldn't bear to do anything for her. But thankfully soon, the wedding would be over, and Lily could continue pretending she was whole once more.

Pulling herself out of the maelstrom of misery that was Katerina Snowe was hard, and Lily failed more often than she succeeded. The best way was to remind herself that, were her mother present, she would be forced to submit to her every whim. Her wedding would have transformed into whatever Katerina wanted and would have centered on Katerina. And even worse, Katerina had seemed to enjoy making Lily feel small and worthless. The reminders helped, but the empty space where her mother should have been haunted her heart.

This mountain of latent bleakness may have been unearthed by the wedding—or perhaps it was the presence of the reporters in Russia. What if they unearthed the abuse she endured? The scalding worry rose up in her throat, and she couldn't shake it. How was it so simple to be ashamed of actions beyond your own control? She should just tell her friends and let the *ton* go to hell. And her sorrow grew deeper by fathoms when it brushed up against the uncomfortable truth that none of this scandal was her fault at all.

Olivia, Honoria, and Bella had gathered for Cards and Scandal, but no one was gossiping much. They were oddly quiet as they gambled and ate tea sandwiches. Not one lady had requested a sherry or anything stronger than tea. The specter of the papers catching them was omnipresent. How depressingly boring. Even Lily's dress, a mere gray silk with a white overlay, hung limply. It was like wearing a fog.

"Ladies, I have a confession to make." Her words shook free and stretched into room. "There is an event in my past that may cause you to regret our friendship, and I need to tell you now."

Olivia cocked her head. "I am certain that nothing you could say would cause me to regret our friendship."

"I hate to test your sentiment, as I value your friendships above all." It was hard not to fidget and preen out of nervousness, and she caught herself staring at her gloves. If only she could propel herself into the future. If only it was done, and she could lie light as a feather in bed for the night. "When I was a child, my mother decided to return to Russia and took me with her. Of course, you already know that. Whilst there she tried to...well, there isn't a polite or delicate way to frame it. My mother hoped to sell me to a man who would take me as a bride."

Olivia gasped, but Honoria cleared her throat and looked daggers at her. "That is dreadful. Obviously, you did not wed, and therefore something must have intervened."

"My father found me..." She was trying so hard to talk, but there was something in her throat that would not let the words out. Better to push past it while she was still brave. Maybe if she told the story, she could be unaffected by it. Her mouth moved in gushing pantomime, but no words came, only sobs. She burst like a broken bottle of wine. Once broken, nothing could stay inside. She hated the fat, too-hot tears on the sides of her face, but they had a life of their own and were determined to escape.

Bella wrapped her arms around Lily and began to rock. "There, there. It's over now and far away. You're safe now. It's not happening now."

"Reporters...going to come out!" Not even she could understand herself. She had never cried over the years. She was too strong to cry. But she was so very wrong.

"They wouldn't write about this, Lily. They are the fourth estate. They have ethics." Olivia's thin, cold arms hugged tight as she tried to calm her. But nothing could work.

"Have you been avoiding the papers, or have you simply gone mad, Olivia?" Honoria asked confidently and leaned into her words. "They no longer have ethics. They only care about selling papers. If they find out about this, it will be printed."

One would have thought Honoria's words would have hurt, but her honesty was a relief. She was so exhausted from the constant bravado and stoic demeanor she had to wear. Bella was comforting, and Olivia was trying to ease Lily's heart, but Honoria was forthright. Being naive about the future didn't change its potential darkness.

"Even if it does come out, no one will fault Lily! I refuse to think so poorly of the world," Olivia bit off.

"They always blame the woman. There is an expression in French—'cherchez la femme,' or look to the woman. In other words, how can we best fault the woman?" Bella lamented. She hadn't blinked, but her eyes narrowed in expressive worry.

"Bella is correct. We need to lie," Honoria said. "This is not an environment suited to cultivating sympathy, and after the way they have ravaged Seraphina, the press is apparently targeting high-born ladies. We simply lie."

"Should I have kept it a secret?" Was it wrong to inflict her secret upon them?

"No, of course not!" Honoria came to Lily's side, but Bella rocked her firmly, almost maternally. "This must have weighed on you and colored your world. That is the nature of secrets. They are invisible hands around your neck, and you are simply waiting for them to squeeze."

Under her tears, her face shook. It was such a relief for her friends to know her secret, but Honoria's metaphor reminded Lily of the incident with Christopher. On the other hand, people rarely cared that a man hit a girl. Honoria grabbed Lily's right hand and squeezed it tightly while Bella stroked her hair. Lily appreciated Bella's close embrace, as she knew Honoria had provoked her with the reference of hands on a woman's neck. Olivia, most likely feeling left out, cuddled into her left side. She was being entombed by well-dressed ladies. It didn't feel unpleasant. Their perfumes even harmonized with her jasmine— Honoria's lilac, Bella's orange blossoms, and Olivia's orange-scented soap. They mingled together like a sweet summer day in the garden.

"We will lie and cheat and reveal the secrets of others to protect you, Lily. I refuse to allow this to hurt you," Honoria vowed.

"Honoria is correct," Bella said. She stopped

hugging and rang for a servant. "We must rehearse what we'll say. Lies are found in the inconsistencies of a story."

If any reporters had been present at Lord Snowe's townhouse, the true scandal would have been how much four small ladies ate. They discussed the details of Lily's youth and agreed that simply saying Lily had lived with her maternal grandmother could sufficiently misdirect the press. She calmly recalled some details about her grandmother (whom Lily was named to honor). After an hour, they were laughing at Honoria's impression of Lady Grandview. After two hours, her mind felt a thousand miles from her troubles even though she was sitting in the same room.

After Bella and Honoria left Lily's townhouse, Olivia remained and hooked her arm into Lily's and pulled her backward. "I will be voyaging to Lancaster with you."

Lily cocked her head. This was unexpected. "Olivia, it isn't going to be a pleasure junket. I am marrying into the Mandevilles. You don't need to endure the hardships that will occur."

"Lily, you are my closest friend, and quite frankly the reason I have not gone mad. I need to be with you. I will be there making certain you will never cry again." Olivia's words were practiced and even. She drank more tea, a common tactic to cut off any further discussion. This tiny woman poured and drank her tenth cup of the afternoon.

"Oh, dearest. You are not going to go mad. You will be quite all right in society with me wed." This was her best attempt at reassurance, so hopefully it would work.

"No, Lily. You have no understanding of what I must be subject to. For the crime of wanting a voice in my own government, I am insulted daily. I have been told I am too stupid to see what will occur if women vote. Men frequently believe that I am a suffragette because I am a virgin and seek to correct this." Olivia hung her head and sighed.

"Oh, Olivia!" Lily cried, not realizing until afterward how loud she sounded. Why had Olivia kept this burden to herself? Not that Lily was any better.

"My father has hired men to protect me. They can stop most attacks, but I have been pelted with rotten food and screamed at. I truly don't understand. If you are a Darwinist or faithful soul, why would we have a world where half the population is useless and created to be enslaved? In the animal kingdom, the female fulfills a more useful role nearly every time. Why would humans be the exception?"

It was easier to shrug than to grapple with the question. "I never knew people acted so cruelly. After the wedding, I will join you at the marches. I may not be able to be as involved as you are, but I will stand with you."

Olivia smiled. "I would love another voice, but shouldn't you ask Lord Ralph Mandeville before you commit?"

Lily laughed. "I will let you persuade him on the train to Lancaster. One voice can change a mind, so you simply need more voices, my dear."

Her heart stirred in harsh conflict. The dark storm of fear that had blown in with the scandal had subsided to a dull rain. Had the worst had come and gone, or she was in the eye of the storm? That was the nature of her secrets. Even once known, they could lie in wait until convenient and then rise to sabotage her. But in the face of such hardships, the only thing that mattered was the potent bond between her and the people who would stand with her, no matter how dark the storm raged.

Chapter Twenty

I firmly believe that when one travels by rail, one should carry a satchel of the following: a book, an orange, paper and envelopes for writing, a pen, five shillings, and an umbrella. One cannot be assured of good company or refreshment, hence the book and orange. However, if one should happen to make a friend on the train, then one must exchange envelopes to maintain the friendship. Finally, I believe one should always have a few shillings and an umbrella due to the unpredictability of the world.
~Aunt Penny's Advice on Living, June 1885

Ralph had been waiting forever in the London Euston Railway Station for Lily to arrive. Long enough for his legs to ache, his shoulders to feel heavy, and for light fatigue to settle on his mind exactly when he needed it to go. The balmy beginnings of a London summer rolled over the station with waves of eager heat and hesitant sunshine. Everyone—Sebastian, Miss Haverford, and others—was seeing Ralph and Vincent off to Lancaster. How very awkward. He stared at his feet and winced, trying to ignore Vincent's whispering crude innuendo into Miss Haverford's ear. His patience was nearly gone, but thank God, here was Lily! But who was that accompanying her?

Lily walked with Lady Olivia, which was quite a

surprise. Behind the pair were their lady's maids and Olga, and behind those three were two footmen rolling trunks. This trip had gone from him and Vincent to eight people. Ralph's cheeks flushed, and he wanted to beat his hat mercilessly.

"*Miliy*. Is there no way to have…less company?" Ralph spoke evenly, sincerely trying for the least irritated he could sound.

"I am afraid much of this is my fault, my lord. I insisted Lily not leave my side during this period of the press attacking her. My father insists that I am well protected, and I am not allowed to travel without two footmen…ever." Lady Olivia stared deep into him with a sympathetic smile.

But why would Lady Olivia need to journey with them? There was very little patience or time left to argue. "Very well, we should be getting on the train. Goodbye, Sebastian."

Sebastian extended his arm in his dark jacket and shook Ralph's hand. "Best of luck to you. Lily, please take care of them. Lady Olivia."

"Lady Olivia," Lady Olivia said with a nod and wink, gaining a genuine smile from Sebastian.

"Ah, is Olivia joining us? Wonderful, now I will have someone to talk to," Vincent joked. He approached the group with Miss Haverford still married to his arm. "Sebastian, would you be willing to escort Miss Haverford to Mrs. Jennings's home?"

"I would be delighted," Sebastian replied warmly before pivoting away like a guard in a beefeater's uniform.

The "merry" band of travelers boarded the train to Lancaster and waved goodbye to Sebastian and Miss

Haverford as they got smaller and smaller and finally vanished from view. Ralph was next to Lily, while Vincent sat too comfortably between Lady Olivia and Olga. Within seven minutes of the train leaving, Olga slumped over into sleep and began to snore. Lily cuddled into Ralph, and her hair tickled his neck enough to make him laugh.

"Are you planning on taking a honeymoon, Lily?" Lady Olivia asked.

"No, I want to spend some time at Ralph's estate," Lily answered and turned up to face him. "Do tell us about it, Ralph."

"It is in Norfolk. I bought it a few years ago, and the house was in desperate need of repairs. Vincent will be our neighbor."

"What good fortune! How did you manage to have your estates so close?" Lady Olivia leaned in to bypass the snoring chaperone.

"Are either of you ladies familiar with the Marquess of Cornwallis?" Ralph asked.

"I am. He is over sixty but tried to court me. Why do men keep insisting they age like wine? Don't they understand wine turns to vinegar?" Lily asked eagerly, and Vincent and Lady Olivia shook with silent chuckling.

"He had four estates; two were entailed. I purchased the Norfolk estate, over three thousand acres, and divided it with Vincent. We are twenty miles from Sebastian's estate." His explanation was too long, but it felt good to show off a little for Lily.

"I got the vicarage, which I named Nightingale Lodge. Marlene is not fond of the name. That is a disappointment," Vincent said.

"And I named my estate Water's Edge. I hope you like it," Ralph said to Lily as she delicately traced hearts on his thigh.

"And what does one grow in Norfolk? My father's estate is in Surrey," Lily asked.

"The usual things. Wheat, lavender, and sugar beets do very well. I am experimenting with growing saffron. Did you know the spice comes from the stigma of very pretty purple flowers?" Ralph babbled. It was hard not to react to Lily's teasing. She seemed to delight in tormenting him, but of course he loved every second.

Lily giggled. "Your estate grows sugar and spice and everything nice?"

He couldn't suppress a laugh. She could never truly know how she unmade him. "I had never realized it. But yes, I suppose it does."

"Ugh. You both are boring. Shouldn't you be trysting or reciting poetry to one another?" Vincent asked.

"Oh, my darling Vincent. Estate growth and development is poetry to Ralph. If you cannot understand his language, then I see why you are bored," Lily drawled.

"Oh? Enlighten me as to the subtext of Ralph's poetry," Vincent teased. It was irritating to be the subject of conversation but not included in it.

She rolled her eyes far away and focused on Vincent. She sat up, and Ralph felt the acute, cold vacancy where her body had just lain. "Ralph's estate is where we will live as man and wife and where we will be fully united. The lavender will perfume the air and our baths. The sugar beets will sweeten our cakes and pancakes. The saffron will spice our food, giving it an earthy flavor and golden hue. This will be our life together, and it sounds heavenly."

Lady Olivia sighed. "I'm terribly jealous, Lily."

He wrapped his arm around Lily's shoulder and kissed her temple in pure love. She was well travelled and exotic but craved the mundane. Of course, perhaps in some parts of the world, there were places that believed an estate in Norfolk was exotic. It would be adorable to watch her walking in the spice bazaars of India or dreaming of a field of wheat in Surrey.

Once they arrived in Lancaster, Vincent and the servants went to the hotel and arranged rooms for the night. Ralph had the pleasure of escorting Lily and Lady Olivia to a restaurant for lunch. This was a necessary rest, and he could sit drowsily while the ladies discussed the upcoming wedding. Apparently, Miss Honoria Rose had decided to craft swans made of white roses for the wedding. Perhaps she was a member of the secret society known as the black swan. She was so close to everything and rather clever.

After lunch, Vincent escorted the ladies shopping. That would give Ralph just enough time to arrange a carriage to visit the dowager duchess. To the best of his very studied recollection, his father had never owned an estate in Lancashire. His curiosity was high, so he moved fast. Being fluent in bureaucracy, Ralph had visited a few clerks and accountants to uncover more than any man should about this place. The most boring men held the most important and interesting information.

Ralph finally caught up with Vincent at the hotel. His breath came in thick rasps, and his sweat was cooling him off. "Where are Lily and Lady Olivia?"

"Lily found a weaver who would weave tapestries of Lily's design. She and Olivia are scheming about what to commission."

He smiled. Most tapestries were depictions of coats of arms or symbolic emblems. Lily had it in her to design something fantastic, such as a unicorn hunt or a dragon slaying. Their home would be interesting to say the least. Who wouldn't trust Lily's eye for fashion? However, sometimes fashion was not long lasting.

"Ah. I have been researching the dowager duchess's holdings." His voice was even for being so out of breath.

"Lady Jocelyn. She was only a duchess for two years," Vincent interjected with pointed eyes. Obviously, this was a sore matter for him.

"Longer than either of us will be a duchess," Ralph countered. It wasn't worth arguing about though. "Her title is not what interests me, but her estate. Did you know our family has never owned land in Lancashire?"

"I hadn't really thought about it. Avebury Park is in Hertfordshire, and Sebastian's Marble Hall is in Norfolk," Vincent said.

"There is also a small estate in Hertfordshire for Sebastian's son should he come of age while Father is alive and duke. There lies the question. How does the dowager duchess have a house in Lancaster?"

Vincent considered this. "I have no idea. I honestly don't care enough to be curious."

"Father bought it for her. According to gossip—"

"Which is always reliable," Vincent interrupted.

"Nevertheless. The dowager duchess wanted to return home and refused to accept the customary house that the dowager duchess of Bridgewater would receive." Maybe the usefulness of the information would quell Vincent's snark.

"I have seen the house. It is where Mother will live. It's very generously situated," Vincent said, finally interested.

"Indeed, but Father simply purchased a house here and settled monies upon her to last her life. I feel that is appropriate, but the dowager duchess felt differently. Apparently, she felt she should be kept in the lifestyle of a duchess and be given twenty thousand pounds per year."

Vincent groaned and threw his paper far away. "This is all very frustrating. One could argue Lady Jocelyn pressed for more because she was with child. Or one could argue this is evidence that she would have fought for her son to have everything."

Ralph nodded; it was nice when Vincent agreed with him. "Indeed, but now we understand why she is slow to help. She doesn't like us. At least we know she will be hostile."

Vincent shrugged and leaned back into a chair. "I suppose it is better to know who one's enemies are. I have your room key. I must be off to Liverpool on an errand Sebastian dreamt up. I shall see you in the morning, much as we used to in our travels. Oh, I do have a hint of good fortune to come. My friend Osbourne—you know the fellow that runs the magazine my critiques are published in? He has informed me that the *Pall Mall Gazette* will have an exposé that will end the papers writing of us. I have no idea what it is, but I imagine we will be all the happier for a reprieve. After reading the vicious lies about Lily, I am ready to burn every paper in England."

Ralph gazed at the paper in Vincent's hand. "Gilded Lily Strangled by Brother!" was the headline. What utter nonsense. As if Christopher would ever lay a hand on Lily. Although, that would explain the distance between Lily and her brother. However, Lily had never mentioned such a thing, and Ralph already knew her darkest secret.

Ralph nodded and accepted the cool metal key. It would be nice to know what Vincent was up to, but of course Vincent had said exactly as much as he wanted Ralph to know. Seeing Lily would be a tempting way to end the night, but it was after dark and that was forbidden. A warm bath and his hand tonight were the best he could hope for—just like every other isolated, unhappy night. When would everything be done with? Then he could spend a month with Lily in his bed and not have to leave from inside her.

Chapter Twenty-One

There are a few things in the life of a woman that men will never understand. To me, the most important one is the little ritual just before bed. Personally, I like a hot bath and a good book to send me off to Dreamland. Although sometimes that is not sufficient...
~Aunt Penny's Guide to Living, June 1885

Lily was carefully sketching in her room. She had ideas for tapestries, and if she paid enough, she could have them made. She would of course have the banal tapestries of Water's Edge and Ralph's coat of arms, but she truly loved the idea of tapestries that would make a whore blush. Perhaps Ralph, shirtless, riding a horse. Or Lily reclining in her undergarments. These ideas amused her like welcome fantasies, but instead she must focus on scenes from their courtship and show how much she adored her husband. She would, of course, be an ideal wife. Ralph deserved nothing less.

She sighed happily in the foreign space. She loved hotels. Just as much comfort as home but with more privacy. Servants were always simply around, but they were not for conversation. How could she help but feel even lonelier? At hotels, servants had to knock, and she was free to lounge in her dressing gown and belch if she needed to. It was liberating, especially since Olga had been poached by Olivia for the night.

There was a key in the door, and it twisted. She gulped in fear and terror shot through her for the first time in a very long time. The Chinese screen was the only thing big enough to hide her, so she tumbled behind it and peered out. The door creaked closer, and the shaft of outside light blazed in for a few seconds. Fortunately, Ralph entered and removed his coat and hat. He was so nonchalant—perhaps he had no idea he was in her room? Vincent must have had arranged this. He had, after all, made Olivia paranoid and needing Olga to stay with her. Well, Lily was never one to look a gift horse in the mouth.

Lily unfastened her dressing gown to reveal the soft cotton nightgown underneath. Damn, why had she not brought the sheer nightgowns she had made for their wedded life? She walked as silently as she could, only the pads of her toes touching the hard floor. The silk slippers did not help.

"Darling, you are in my room," Lily purred. Hopefully that sounded as seductive as it felt to say.

Ralph jumped in an adorable sense of misplaced fear. "My God. Lily." He blushed too much.

Lily poured him a cup of tea and tried not to giggle. Best not to try his nerves. "I apologize for frightening you, but you frightened me."

"Vincent said this was my room; he must have gotten confused. This is a disaster," Ralph murmured more to himself than to Lily. There was nothing disastrous about this.

"I don't think it was an accident, Ralph. I think Vincent assumed we would want to share a room," Lily explained slowly. She nodded as she spoke, and hopefully Ralph would catch on.

"But we are only engaged! We are not meant to be alone after dark and never in a bedroom!" Ralph exclaimed.

It was hard not to roll her eyes. "I am going to be rude and blunt now. I hope you will forgive me. Do you honestly think people only stuff it up at night? Do you believe my gulf of Venus refuses to open during sunlight hours? Will your torch not light in daytime?"

"Jesus, Lily!" Ralph cried. She touched a nerve, even though she wanted desperately to touch something else. "Where on Earth did you learn those terms?"

Lily shrugged. "Sailors talk loudly. The language is not important so long as we are to be married next month. Our lives are tethered and bound together. Stop letting trivial details, such as the law and God, come between us."

A nervous laugh escaped him. "Those are very important things, *miliy*."

Even as he said these words, the wanting poured out of his eyes, fixed on her body. They traveled along her neck to her breasts with hunger. She needed to be bold, and waiting for Ralph would mean waiting until everyone agreed he could have her. It was a simple thing to let her dressing gown fall and pull her nightgown over her head. She stood fully naked before him, the shivering breeze in the room making her tense. She felt free and cold. This was the ultimate risk. If she faced rejection, she would forever be a fool. But the second this doubt started to enter her, Ralph finally moved. At last.

He kissed her and crushed her into him, allowing her to feel warmth again. His hands roamed down her back to her curved and magnetic bottom, where he lifted her into him. Her skin felt malleable and everything turned hot instead of cold. She coiled around him like a snake; her legs bound tighter and tighter around his hips. It was such a pleasure to have finally seduced him. They fell on the bed. The softness behind her felt amazing. Ralph's weight was on top of her, and she pulled him into her even closer. She longed for them to always be tangled in one another. To be crushed into something so soft, pinned under the weight of passion and delicate warmth, was surely half heavenly. And half something much more indulgent.

Ralph parted from her and began to disrobe. Lily smiled and ran her foot up his trousers, which forced him to chuckle. "Let me undress, *miliy.*"

Lily pulled his waistcoat off and tugged at his suspenders. "I can help."

Ralph winked at her. "I can undress, little vixen."

"It is unfair. I never realized how much less clothing men wear until now," Lily whined while Ralph unbuttoned his shirt. For such a worldly man, he took a terribly long time to undress. "Although once I ruin you, Ralph, you will be lucky if I let you wear anything at all."

"I apologize for my gender being less…poufy. And I promise to ruin every part of you before you ruin me." Ralph grinned at her, while his gaze and exposed flesh set her skin aflame. His rising member came closer than ever to her face and breasts. It was too big and inflamed to be extinguished anywhere but deep inside of her. She was in complete control of him as long as he was contained. How glorious it was. Why not tease a little more?

"Hmmmm. I would prefer it if you simply never

wore a shirt at all. Regardless of how ruined you might be after this." His midsection was delightful, and more colorful than she thought it would be. Her soft tongue licked his stomach, tasting the salt of him, and his muscles tightened. Men quivered too, apparently. "How do you get these ridges?" Her eyes were on his chest, but they couldn't help but flick downward. She hesitated, not wanting to make Ralph conscious of his build and his endowment.

"Sebastian and I box, and I enjoy riding," Ralph answered as he removed his trousers. How curt. Once he was set on this path, he became quite focused.

"Do all men look like you?" He had similar tone and definition of Michelangelo's *David* but with a light lining of golden hair. Lily was eager to see his member in the flesh—was it the Renaissance interpretation or the Roman? Oh, it was quite exciting to see the devilish thing. It was somewhere in between, although she didn't have a lot to compare it to. It was a hard and lusty thing, desperately responding to every coo or wink she made. And when her face or hands touched him, it would rise farther, almost like it wanted her too much to let Ralph make choices. She had found a part of him that could never resist her. She ruled it, and in this hot and singular moment, it ruled him.

"No. I am young and fit. Most men of our class are older and…doughy," Ralph answered and lay down next to her on the bed.

His lips were on hers once more, and her body was alert and alive in his hands. Her hidden parts were melting from the inside and seeping out of her body. Ralph seemed to want to touch every part of her, and his hands were frenzied. He pulled her on top of him and began to stroke her spine.

"I have plans and ambitions concerning the things I will do to you. But tonight, *miliy*, I give you the control. Whatever you desire, I will give you," Ralph rasped.

"I have no experience!" Lily whined. "I don't know what I want."

Ralph kissed her fingertips. How sweet and reserved. "Let's begin with kisses. Do you like kisses on your lips?"

"Yes," Lily murmured and felt another deep kiss. She was faint with wanting, but now she felt frenzied and needed so much more.

Ralph moved to kiss just above her collarbone. "And your neck?"

"Yes," Lily moaned as his soft lips pressed into her pulse. His hot breath teasing her.

Ralph moved to her breasts and began to kiss them. He suckled her nipples, his tongue tracing circles. How could she not cry out in her pleasure? Ralph smirked and continued his journey of kisses. His lips were tracing down her stomach, and he rolled her so she could recline. She felt a tremor of anxiety. He was headed to her prannie, and she was nervous. She felt so nervous about down there. He seemed to be looking for something, and Lily was about to ask him to stop, when he found it. How strange that she had not.

Lily had been in possession of her body for twenty years, and yet Ralph found a hidden spot. He discovered a small island of pure sensitivity. Ralph nibbled it, pulled it into his mouth, and ran his tongue around and across it. Each movement conjured a moan from her, although she tried so very hard to remain quiet. Lily was on a cliff, and she was going to fly.

Suddenly, an unfamiliar sensation overcame her. She was going to die and began to cry for God. As her spirit exploded out of her body, she was quite shocked to find herself still alive and in Lancaster. Her unbound body breathed deep, warm and wobbly. After a moment, she sighed and rolled over. She wanted a warm body to curl into, but Ralph was past her reach, fetching a towel to clean his face.

"What was that?" Lily asked lazily. Was it appropriate to ask for more, or to take a cat nap?

"Which aspect? What I did or what you did?" Ralph asked her as he washed his face and threw the towel on the wooden floor.

"Either. Both," Lily answered. She was so very naked right now, so she sat up and hugged her knees to her chest.

"I had a lark, and you found your pleasure. Did you enjoy yourself?" Ralph walked back to the bed and kissed her shoulder. That kindled the flames in her once more.

"I thought I was dying," Lily said. How embarrassing to not know what had just happened inside her.

"No. Would you like to stop now?" he asked.

"No. I thought we were going to…I have heard it is painful." She sounded awkward and ached with a little vulnerability.

Ralph pulled her on top of him, once more. "Whenever you are ready, lower yourself. I won't be able to last long. I promise next time I will. But I have been craving you. Longing for you."

He was kissing her neck again, and her lower portion was impaled on him. It hurt, but the fear was worse than the pain. Ralph moaned and began to thrust into her. The pain subsided so she could move in rhythm with him. So much separated people from one another. Clothing, society, and the silly rules laid down by others. Yet, in this moment, he was as close as possible. Suddenly, his face contorted, and he groaned. Did her face also look so ridiculous when she found her bliss? Then she felt his cock move from her, and it felt as though something was missing again.

Ralph panted, lifted her off his lap, and laid her on to the bed. He bundled her up with the protection of the blankets and lay close to her. Lily lifted her head to he could slide his arm around her shoulders. Lily had never been so warm or wanted in her life.

"Is this how it will be when we are wed? Sleeping together after making love?" Was this unwarranted sleepiness a punishment for finally enjoying herself?

"You will be lucky if I let you sleep, *miliy*," Ralph answered. However, he was a sweet liar; his eyes were closed, and he was close to sleep.

As Ralph began to breathe heavily, not quite snoring, Lily snuggled into his chest. She had found her home. This warm naked place, all alone with each other, was just theirs. As heavy sleep began to overtake her, she tried to stifle her laughs. Who could have predicted all the world's best things were in Lancaster?

Chapter Twenty-Two

The truly upsetting times in one's life are never polite enough to wire ahead or even send a note. Rather, I find when life is about to shatter all about you, it is when you are most assured of your place within the world. The solution is to prepare for what may come and to remain calm. Troubles are advantages in masquerade dress. We must be diligent to find solutions. Trust me, dear reader, I know Trouble well...

~Aunt Penny's Advice for Living, July 1885

Ralph hovered in the delicate and bizarre space between sleep and wakefulness. He had never contemplated the amount of acrimony and ritual that built in men who eschew the company of women. The philosophers of old with their theories of the humors understood that lust spoiled men like time can turn wine. So many hardships were forgotten when such ubiquitous cravings were satisfied. In the most generous interpretation, society sensibly tried to restrain men's craven impulses and to weave layers of hardship and ritual to stop passions from bleeding into action. Because once those impulses seeped past the bounds of the acceptable, then none of the ritual or pomp mattered much. The power of social contrivance and guilt was waning and temporal, and the keepers of tradition knew it.

But he ought to scurry whilst her lady's maid assisted Lily with whatever it was ladies did in the morning. He had never seen his mother before ten and had never been privy to what women did in the morning. He moved as a quickly as he could, dressed silently, and slipped from the room. When they were married, he would watch Lily wake every morning. She slept beautifully, and he wanted to kiss her awake.

He ventured to Vincent's room and rapped at the door. How could he not? After a great deal of noise, Vincent opened the door. Of course, Vincent would look dreadful at this hour. His eyes were red with the heavy liquor of sleep, causing the gray of his pupils to look shockingly teal. He smelled of whiskey and was still in last night's shirt.

"Good morning. I need to shave and wash my face in your room," Ralph said. He pushed past Vincent.

"Right, because women do...magic in the mornings. How did you enjoy your room?" Vincent asked as he collapsed on to his bed. He tried to hide his face from the sun, but it was not working.

Ralph sighed. "Very different."

Vincent cocked his head. "Oh dear. That is not what Lily would want to hear."

Ralph began to wash his face. The water was too warm. "No. With most women, swiving is pleasurable, but when you are in love with a woman...you are born again in a world with no words and only sunlight. All you are able to do is feel the fleeting warmth and fight the insecurity that someday you must return to the sullenness from which you emerged."

"Ugh. I want to fall in love and babble poetry in

the morning," Vincent lamented from under the covers. His voice was lower and smaller than usual.

"You are not in love with Miss Haverford?" If only he could rid Vincent (and by extension, himself) of Miss Haverford.

"Marlene is beautiful, and we have a great deal of common interests, but…no. Of course, most marriages are not based on love, but companionship is wonderful for a long happy life." Vincent was digging through his coat and pulled out a lemon. He began to peel it. "My mouth tastes of death. I drank far too much last night. You'll have to go see Jocelyn without me."

Ralph frowned at the meager excuse. Vincent never drank to excess or alone. "Who were you with?"

"I went to see Christopher, in Liverpool. I find conversations that involve unearthed secrets and whatnot require whiskey. This was a two-bottle conversation." Vincent began to eat the lemon noisily. The bright citrus perfumed the air lightly, humming along amidst the background of poor hygiene.

"What did you discuss?" Perhaps Vincent would finally tell him why Christopher had fallen out of favor with nearly everyone.

"Sebastian and I swore we would never speak of it, but it was in the newspaper and few seemed to care. Shortly after Clara's death, Christopher got drunk and tried to strangle Lily. It was a long time ago, and she is completely recovered. But the press found out. Sebastian and I want to know how they heard the story. Christopher had told Viscount Lake after a rowdy night with Lake and Julian Archer in Amsterdam."

It was hard not to punch the mirror. "I vow, once we are married we will have the most serene and dull life imaginable. Days and days of placidity and watching the wind sway the grass."

Vincent laughed. "Have you decided not to marry Lily? To marry someone entirely different? Lily is far too sociable for country life, and it would be a travesty to hide her. This is life. Well, it is the life of a lord. We must attend balls and garden parties while participating in the pageant of idealism that has taken hold of the world. Or"—Vincent grinned for this part—"the illusion we have forced on it. Lily will masquerade as a humdrum wife while designing rooms and ball gowns. You will manage your life, but any expectation of control is a fool's errand."

"I just want to be happy and for Lily to be happy," Ralph said. This statement should have been uncontroversial.

"It is interesting. We have so much that others crave, such as abundant meals and great houses, and yet mankind constantly finds a path for unhappiness. I imagine the middle and lower classes romanticize the balls and boughs of roses. They see the gilt but not the constant backstabbing and acrimony," Vincent said as he finished his lemon.

"The gilt but not the guilt?" Ralph asked.

"Very good turn of phrase. My point is that no matter where you lie on the social scale, you will find strife. It is as natural as breathing. Stop telling yourself that once the suit is settled or once you are married, you will find peace. You will never find peace. After you are wed, you will have children and the roof will leak. Today, you are off to have breakfast with two beautiful women, and you will be well fed. That is most men's dream. Enjoy the life you have," Vincent lectured.

"I shall, but the irony of those words coming out of your mouth is overwhelming. Sebastian has his own problems. Stop being angry over something that you cannot change." Wait, did he just say that to a hungover Vincent?

"I find you impossibly annoying when you are correct. I promise to spend the day in quiet contemplation. I shall try to unwind the decades of dislike. Or I will sleep and ignore this conversation. Either is equally likely. Go to your lovely fiancée," Vincent said as he threw a pillow. It missed Ralph, but not by much.

He traversed the lobby of the hotel. It was hard to stay patient. There were little pockets of people huddled around newspapers. Please let it be anything other than yet another tale of the Mandevilles and their treachery. When a maid faints to the floor, it must be something worse than mere treachery.

Ralph rounded the corner, to the restaurant. Lily and Lady Olivia sat huddled too close. There was trouble. Lady Olivia was reading to Lily, and Lily was completely still. Lily stared ahead and wore a mask of stoicism. Of course, Lily was only still when she was trying to hold herself together and not react. Whatever Lady Olivia was reading was unmaking his Lily. He needed to stop it.

" 'But,' I continued, 'are these maids willing or unwilling parties to the transaction—that is, are they really maiden, not merely in being each a virgo intacta in the physical sense, but as being chaste girls who are not consenting parties to their seduction?' He looked surprised at my question, and then replied emphatically: 'Of course they are rarely willing, and as a rule, they do not know what they are coming for,' " Lady Olivia read aloud. "My God, this is outrageous!"

Ralph snatched the paper from Lady Olivia. It was the *Pall Mall Gazette*.

" 'The Maiden Tribute in Modern Babylon.' " Inside was a well-written and detailed story of the ease with which a man could purchase a child for coitus in London. Ralph's mind resisted the details of the story; reading tales of children brutalized and used until death near his home broke his heart. This sort of barbarism scalded his blood. How could this happen in the heart of the Kingdom, the seat of English manners?

"Something must be done. This is a national travesty," Olivia cried. She was so sincere, and her voice felt like rallying cry.

"Olivia, look around," Lily said calmly. Much too calmly. "There will be a moral panic. We must be calm, or people will riot."

"We should go to see the dowager duchess and avoid any panic," Ralph urged.

"Oh, yes. I must fetch my shawl. It is cooler here than in town," Lady Olivia said as she stood. "I shall be back soon."

Ralph nodded as she wandered out of sight, then grabbed Lily's hands. "Are you feeling well enough to pay a call, *miliy*?"

Lily smiled. He hated this smile as he knew it was false. "Yes, I could use a distraction."

"If you need anything, then I am very happy to oblige," Ralph offered.

"I know. I am happy this story has been told, and it will hopefully help many children. I realize how lucky I am. The house was ablaze, but I am not burned," Lily answered.

"But you felt the heat. I find the best path to feeling strength is to do something about a problem. Parliament will handle the laws. Perhaps we should make donations to the homes for children?" Hopefully suggesting things within their power would comfort her.

"I am less concerned for orphans. You read the exposé; it is mothers selling their children. I have no idea how to stop greedy women from handing their children over to a brothel. Some are prostitutes themselves and don't know how else to live. I want…I want to give these children hope," Lily opined.

He tried hard to smile. "Think on it for a while. Hope does spring eternal. We simply must plant some seeds for those children."

Chapter Twenty-Three

To pay a call without proper notification is the greatest gamble a young lady can make. It is entirely possible your hostess will be not at home. It's equally possible she does not want to see you. And there is of course the third option that she is ill. The rules of etiquette are not in place without reason. Though I hear most young people claiming so.

~Aunt Penny's Guide to Living, July 1885

Lily was surely a terrible person. Or at least she wore the mantle of a terrible person when she thought too hard about her feeling of relief. When she thought about the last few days, her body ached as if her bones were hollow with guilt. It was fortunate that the article, "The Maiden Tribute in Modern Babylon," had brought to light the horrifying possibilities for young girls in London. But shamefully, she felt ecstatic that her story would never be told. Her mind soared with selfish relief that, even if some resourceful reporter found her mother, the story would be a drop in the bucket. Lily felt like a villain as she delighted in the suffering of others. Not their suffering, which hurt her immensely, but the subordination of her shame by their pain. Fear could make a villain out of the best people.

It was uncomfortable being a villain. It was better to try and move her mind away from it. She gazed out the window of the carriage as they traveled to Grandview Manor, the dowager duchess's estate. How could people name estates with absolutely no regard to location or truth? Was there a registry of great house names so no two lords had the same names for estates? After all, armorials had to be registered. Adrian Rose would most likely know, especially since he had a scheme to purchase many estates.

"Adrian!" Lily cried out. Clearly, that was a mistake.

"I beg your pardon, *miliy*?" Ralph asked.

Grand ideas tend to snowball and take form before one's mouth can properly enunciate the word. This happens whether they are genius or terrible. The larger an idea, the more difficult it is to explain. She needed to calm herself. "Mr. Rose spoke of an investment scheme he was forming with Lord Berkeley. Do you recall that?"

"I do," Ralph answered.

"No," Olivia answered.

"They were buying large estates from poor lords and had ideas to transform them, and they hoped Ralph might join them," Lily explained to Olivia. "What if we took one house and made it into a school for service? The young girls in brothels could learn to work in service, and we could buy the children as well."

Ralph was quiet; this meant he was considering the idea. "I am not comfortable buying children, but perhaps scholarships would be better. Opening a school would be a great deal of work, but I believe Rose and Berkeley would be intrigued by the notion."

"A few of the ladies in the suffrage movement are teachers. Perhaps I could inquire with them about proper school management. We would not want to have a whisper of impropriety at our school," Olivia rattled. At Lily's raised eyebrows, she continued. "Oh, my darling. You did not think I would sit in the garden whilst you helped the helpless, did you? This is my reason for living. I suspect Honoria and Bella will wish to help as well."

"We must wait to discuss this with Rose and Berkeley before we speak to others. But I generally agree with you, my lady," Ralph said. His tone was even and firm. "Perhaps we can get others involved. And it would be a marvelous way to retire older servants who still have much to offer."

Lily followed Ralph's eyes to Olga, who was sleeping soundly. Lily wanted to persist in the discussion; she should. However, they had arrived at Grandview Manor. The view was decent. It had endless pastures with few trees and even fewer hills. She had to admit she liked the house and its flowers and trees. The foliage splayed out, verdant and lush, and colored the yard before the house came to view. It was a Tudor-style timber-planked house (which Lily found hilarious considering they were in Lancashire and heading to York), although the Tudor reputation for excessive gardening was not applicable. Perhaps the dowager duchess could be a lovely woman after all?

As they entered the hall, the Tudor splendor continued to overwhelm. Ralph stole away from the group to give the butler his calling card and asked for the dowager duchess.

"I am afraid Her Grace has vacated to France for the season," the butler informed them, mired in confusion.

Lily sighed. How terribly coincidental. "Oh, how dreadful! We have written to her in the hopes she would host us on our journey to Glasgow. I understand now that she cannot, but might we trouble you for a luncheon?"

The butler was obviously at a crossroads with himself. Lily knew servants, particularly ones that had worked their way to being butlers and housekeepers, took immense pride in providing exquisite service. "Of course, miss."

"We shan't be a bother. Allow us to walk the grounds while we wait. I know servants are given little time off, and I feel terrible trespassing upon you," Lily pressed on.

"Oh, no, miss. I insist you rest in the drawing room," the butler said as he began to lead them into the house.

The interior was darker than expected. The vaulted ceilings conspired with small and elegant friezes to make it seem like there was a silent gallery watching their every move.

"You are ever so kind. What shall I call you when I tell of your hospitality?" Lily asked.

The butler beamed. "I am honored. Please call me Mr. Cartwright. The housekeeper is Mrs. Bertrand, and the maids are Mary, Lucy, and Sarah."

Something struck Lily as wrong. This was a large house, and with only five servants, the work would tax them immensely. "Does the dowager duchess have any children?"

"No, miss. She had a niece that lived with her after Her Grace's sister passed," Mr. Cartwright answered as they entered the drawing room.

Lily stared in contemplation as he opened the curtains. It was time to invoke Vincent. Vincent had taught Lily the best lie was the truth. "Mr. Cartwright, I have deceived you. We seek the dowager duchess because a man has come forth to claim he is her son. Of course, if you speak the truth, then he has no claim on her estate."

Mr. Cartwright reddened. "I have been with Her Grace for thirty-three years. Her husband himself hired me, as a footman! She has never been with child. Who spread these lies?"

Well, that worked splendidly. "I do apologize for burdening you with this. The Duke of Bridgewater has hired a lawyer to fight this slander. But…perhaps you would be willing to swear Her Grace has never birthed a child?"

"I certainly would, miss. Mrs. Bertrand will join me, and she has been with Her Grace for thirty years. I shall get cook to prepare the luncheon."

After Mr. Cartwright left the room, Ralph pulled her close on the settee. "That was a gamble. What if the servants are complicit with the lawsuit?"

"That requires the duchess to be complicit, and we do not yet know if she is. Regardless, she has not been to this house in at least six months," Lily answered. She gave a sly smile and cocked her head. Hopefully she could charm him.

"I noticed that as well," Olivia added, cutting the flirtation back.

"I am oblivious. How did you know the duchess hadn't been here?" Ralph asked.

"There are not enough servants," Olivia answered. "When one is managing a house, one needs more servants even if it is one person. The dowager duchess is not here to give her blessing to replace servants that have been relieved and accepted better offers."

"Precisely. If Jocelyn were here frequently, then the number of servants would indicate that she is financially in need. She may not be a willing participant in the lawsuit. She still may be involved, but her servants are not." Lily spoke and continued to smile, feeling warm and proud of her deduction even in the cold room.

"Well, thank you for being so bold." Ralph leaned in close to whisper, "I love you when you are bold."

Her skin flushed. How could she feel like she was sweating and freezing at the same time? And why couldn't they just return to their room, so she could fall asleep in his arms once more? She had never slept so well in her life. She had awoken to golden sunshine, and a million worries had been cut free from her. And after reading "The Maiden Tribute in Modern Babylon," it was important to feel protected once more.

The lunch was mediocre. Of course, it was the sort of fare that is celebrated by an uneducated palate. But she intentionally raved to Mrs. Bertrand and Mr. Cartwright as though it were the most lavish meal she had ever dined on. After a tedious exercise in writing Mr. Rose's office and home addresses along with the trial date, she and her friends ventured back to the hotel. It was quite fortunate that Vincent had stayed behind, as he rarely knew when to butter up. In truth, her heart filled with syrupy joy to have helped save the Mandevilles. They would be her new family.

****

After lunch, Lily, Ralph, and Olivia returned to the

hotel. Vincent was tucked into the corner of the lobby sending a telegram. His natural glee at creating a secret shone in his focused eyes.

Evidently, they were easy to spot, so he closed the distance and greeted them. "Good afternoon. How was your visit?"

Ralph couldn't contain his pride. Bragging about Lily came naturally to him, or at least it appeared so. "Lily convinced the butler and the housekeeper to testify that the duchess has never been with child nor given birth to a child."

"I am impressed. Ralph, perhaps you could make arrangements for us to go to York?" Vincent suggested. He patted the pockets of his coat as though looking for something.

"If you will excuse me, I am going to have a lie down," Olivia said as she pulled Olga by the elbow. Her eyes glimmered, like she knew a secret—and maybe she did.

After Ralph kissed Lily on the cheek and left, Vincent leaned in to whisper in Lily's ear. "Come to my room. I have a surprise for you."

"What is it?" She despised surprises. She couldn't stand waiting to know what they held.

"Be patient! Why must you always seek to spoil the surprise?" Vincent asked.

"Because you insist on teasing me! At least a hint?" Lily begged as they climbed the stairs.

"I ordered a massive tea service. That is all the hint you shall receive," Vincent answered as he plucked her elbow sharply and led her down the brown hall.

"I am peckish. The dowager duchess's cook did not prepare for guests." The lunch had been truly insipid.

Vincent opened the door to his room and revealed right inside an elaborate tea service, with a dozen puddings, fairy cakes, jellies, and blancmanges. He crawled under his bed to find the real surprise—a box of foreign fruits. "Chinese gooseberries."

A gasp shook through her before she could catch it. "My favorite! Thank you, Vincent!"

Vincent tried to give Lily the box but was met with a forceful hug and a kiss on his cheek. She couldn't believe he had found them. "Stop it."

"Pish. I am going to be your sister. Do you have a knife?" She smelled the egg-shaped fruit. It was a treasured delicacy.

Vincent handed her a knife and sat next to her. "I want to have a wedding photograph taken of you and Ralph. Would you like that?"

"Absolutely! I believe Honoria will be using her camera at the wedding breakfast. She loves photographs without posing." She used a spoon to dig out the moss green fruit as though it were a soft-boiled egg. Nothing tasted quite like Chinese gooseberries.

Vincent's demeanor changed; he sat up and moved half a step away. "I know what happened, Lily."

She stilled and starred at the tiny black seeds of the gooseberry. "Please don't think less of me or Ralph."

Vincent groaned. That was the groan of a man who didn't want to explain himself. "I don't care about your virginity, Lily! I know about Russia."

"I see." She remained unmoved. Hopefully if she didn't move, then he would just move on and insult the latest play he had seen. Honestly, she would prefer he judge her for seducing Ralph.

"Why did you never tell me?" There was a

desperation in his voice that was strange for him.

"Nothing actually happened. It was all just a possibility, but it never came to fruition. I don't tell you every time a gentleman has cornered me at a ball and I fear he may rape me. Why should I tell you about events that were years ago and thousands of miles away?"

Vincent paused, his face leaning closer and his mouth forming words that refused to come out. Obviously, he was struggling not to follow the path Lily have laid out for him. "Lily, I am trying to protect you. You can tell me every instance of fear you feel, and I will defend you."

"You and Ralph are so alike." She gave a small smile, but she still stared at her fruit.

"Does Ralph know? I thought it was 'years ago'?" Vincent sneered. He was getting angry. But Vincent had never once been angry with her.

"Well, I told him years ago when it was relevant!" Lily snapped. Apparently, she needed to argue about this. It was ever so much easier to be angry then to accept the selfishness of the people that had harmed her. And how dared Vincent? How dared he be angry at her for keeping but one secret when he kept too many to count?

"When did you tell him?" Vincent exploded.

"I was fourteen and unbelievably naive and stupid. I sat next to the most beautiful man I had ever seen and was dreaming of marrying him. So, being a vazey girl, I tried to impress him. I thought I was worldly and sophisticated at the time. I even begged him to dance with me at my coming-out ball. I was a bungling idiot," Lily barked. She was talking so fast it was easy to trip over her own words. If she had to recall this, she would only do so once.

"Did you think child selling was sophisticated? It is the worst aspect of our primal selves, Lily," Vincent lectured. How dare he moralize, given his language, behavior, and teasing!

"I know that now, you prat! Again, I was fourteen years old. I have regretted my words for five bloody years. When Ralph did not attend any of the balls or dinners, I assumed he saw me as you and Sebastian did, as a sister. I hoped he forgot my tale and forgot me. But he didn't, and I struggle with him knowing that part of me." She wailed. Why couldn't men understand when they had gone too far?

"Lily, do you blame yourself for what happened?" Vincent asked. How could it be that even Vincent, who had always been her comrade at arms, didn't understand? Yet, he was softening toward her. Maybe he had forgiven her silence.

"Of course it was my fault! Every bit of it was my fault. If I had been a good girl or prettier, then my mother would have loved me. There is something evil and broken in me. My own brother became violent with me. I am so wrong and horrible, I can't bear to be near myself." Hot tears streamed down her cheeks. It was one thing to tell her ladies, with whom she shared secrets and the private burdens of their gender, this terrible secret. But confessing to a man she cared for, and who was known for his malice and wit, was a bit of nightmare.

Vincent grabbed her and pulled her into him. "I love you, Lily. There is nothing wrong or broken with you. Sometimes bad people have children. It is not the child's fault, and the fact that you feel responsible only proves that you are not evil. Truly bad people cannot apologize or take responsibility for their actions. People, including nearly everyone who has ever met you, love you."

Lily continued to sob into his chest for what felt like an eternity. Finally, she stole his handkerchief to blow her nose and dry her eyes. "Thank you, Vincent."

"I will only say this once, and if you repeat it, I will deny until my death. You redeem me. I am a vile man, and petty, and rude, but I helped you. And so, in my eyes I cannot be the worst person on earth," Vincent said with a smile that attempted to be comforting and a bit scandalous.

"Why must you speak of yourself in such a fashion? You saved my life and helped me again and again. You are every bit as virtuous as Ralph and worth the admiration you consistently diminish." Her anger was seeping out. It was a nuisance to have to comfort the person she was exasperated with, but he was a good friend.

Vincent had never explained to Lily why he felt the need to vilify himself—she definitely would have remembered that conversation. Rather than doing so on this occasion, he picked up a jelly and smeared it across her face too fast for her to leap out of his clutches. "You looked hungry."

"Did I? Have I ever asked you to feed me?" She grabbed a particularly delicious-looking strawberry cream cake by the serving plate. She was seething with rage. Her hair was ruined as was her dress. The fopdoodle. Her dress was stained, and she was going to destroy his fine suit. Vincent was, after all, notoriously fastidious in regard to his clothing.

"No, nor have I ever wanted you to feed me," Vincent answered.

Vincent tried to back away from her. Her long legs flew farther than he had ran, and she tripped him. He fell backward, and she, the wild beastie that she was, sat upon his chest. She took handfuls of the soft, sweetened cake and smeared them on Vincent's face and hair. "Darling Vincent, so hungry."

Vincent licked the cream off his lips like the sarcastic jackass that he was. "Thank you. I was quite in need of a sweet."

"And now, you must be thirsty," Lily sang as she poured the cream on his head. She paid extra care to ensure his necktie was soaked.

"Please stop now," Vincent pleaded. But that was not good enough, obviously.

She stood up in the primmest manner she could, only to sit next to him and hand him his handkerchief. She began to eat a piece of delicious shortbread. "I am very happy that I am marrying Ralph. I truly never imagined I would marry for love, but I love him so much, I can barely see anything but him. Additionally, I am so pleased you will finally be my brother. I don't know how we could have remained friends without alienating my husband."

"You would never have married a man who would have not allowed you to be friendly with me. I am glad you are marrying Ralph as well. You both deserve the greatest marriage in history, and I believe you shall have it with one another," Vincent agreed.

Lily smelled the sweet air as light sugar and cream dripped onto the polished floor.

Chapter Twenty-Four

There is a bit of romance to the rituals of yesteryear when we were forced to take carriages and wait for weeks for a letter. It seemed as though the world had more time to think about their lives and create philosophies and great novels. Then again, I hate to wait, and taking the train ensures I can do my shopping and come home the same day.

~Aunt Penny's Advice for Living, July 1885

Ralph regretted taking the train in lieu of a carriage to York. The journey would have taken longer, by days, but a picnic with Lily would be heavenly. Being in the countryside only to have the landscape speed by was an inferior experience, and he wanted to walk in nature. Did he feel this way because he was away from the city or because he and Lily were spending their nights together? The air smelled sweeter, and food tasted better. While he would grow accustomed to this new reality, his life was just a splendid bit of perfection at this moment. Of course, it had to get worse by definition.

He held, but was not really reading, a report containing information and speculation concerning potential investments. Lily sketched with great intensity, close enough to see but not touch. The worst sort of distance. From his few disguised glances, it appeared to be a morning room with stained-glass windows of morning glories. Vincent read in uncharacteristic and patient quiet. Vincent was better behaved with Lily and Lady Olivia than he ever was with their parents or Sebastian. Lady Olivia was reading three different magazines and switching between political news, ladies fashion, and a suffragette magazine. The only sounds were the rushing machinery of their transport, uneventful without being uncomfortably so. The hum in the background was surprisingly peaceful and serene.

"Good morning, Lady Olivia, Miss Snowe, Lord Ralph Mandeville, and Lord Vincent Mandeville," Lord Amesbury said as he entered the car.

"Amesbury, what are you doing here?" Vincent asked.

"You wanted membership to the Black Swan, and I am here to give it to you," Amesbury said as he sat next to Lady Olivia. To invite oneself into a car and then solicit a conspiracy required confidence.

"I beg your pardon, Lord Amesbury, but what is the Black Swan?" Lily asked. Ralph barely knew himself, but guilt stirred and stabbed him at him for not telling her.

Amesbury raised his eyebrows and removed his hat, revealing his sandy hair. "Oh. I thought you would have told Miss Snowe and Lady Olivia. Apparently, your notoriously large mouth did not disclose our secrets. I'm impressed, my lord." His head turned toward the resolute women while ignoring Vincent. "I have been trying to find a reason to recruit the Cards and Scandal group for a while, and you were keeping them out of the game."

Lily and Lady Olivia exchanged a panicked glance. How very curious. Vincent shifted in his seat. "What is Cards and Scandal?"

Amesbury sighed. This was clearly a distraction for him, so he made himself comfortable. "The peacock struggles less if you pluck the feathers quickly. I am going to quickly reveal secrets and give instructions. I ask that you save any questions for when I have finished. Cards and Scandal is when the four biggest gossips exchange their knowledge in a game of poker. They drink, smoke, and gamble. We have tried to spy and infiltrate, but it's impossible to find a route in."

"That is by design," Lily explained.

"I hope you will recruit the other ladies." Amesbury dropped a wink. It was hard not to throw the charming, flirtatious man off the train. Sadly, the windows were fastened shut.

"We might if you tell us what the Black Swan is," Lady Olivia said.

"Of course. The Black Swan is a defense against the Shadow Society. The Shadow Society is a virtually unknown group that wreaks havoc on upper-class families. They are the worst sort of villains, the kind you know by deeds and not words. We know almost nothing of their membership or motives. We do know they have attacked before and will most likely move on to another family. That is, if yours should survive. The Black Swan is small, but you will help us grow."

"Yes!" Lady Olivia cried. She had sat up a little before she caught herself and tempered her enthusiasm. "I have been disheartened by the lack of victories for women. Give me a dragon to slay, and I will follow you." Her exuberance was a gust of wind that stirred the room.

Lily nodded. "Indeed. I am so exhausted by feeling as though my fate is forever in other's hands. I will gladly assist you. Especially if they seek to destroy what I have with Ralph. I want to be more in the world than just pretty or a frame for nice dresses."

Amesbury smiled and began to dig through his coat. "Bertie thought you might be eager to help. So here you are, ladies. Welcome to the Black Swan."

Amesbury handed Lily and Lady Olivia small black boxes, the sort designed for practicality and not fashion. Each box contained an onyx swan brooch and a silver star hairpin.

"Gorgeous," Lady Olivia breathed.

"When you need assistance, we ask that you wear the brooch. If you have useful information, then please wear the hairpin," Amesbury instructed.

"Where is my hairpin?" Vincent whined. Admittedly, he had gotten through half a conversation before needing more attention.

Amesbury rolled his eyes and offered another box. "For the gentlemen. We thought Coningsby would accompany you, but alas, he remains in London."

Vincent's box opened easily and contained two silver stick pins. One was a silver star with a diamond in the center of the star. The second was an onyx swan with a diamond for the eye. Despite Ralph's discomfort with Amesbury flirting with Lily, Amesbury had exquisite taste. Perhaps Amesbury did not choose these. There was a feminine quality about them. And Vincent was initially approached by a woman.

"I assume the same code follows for men as women," Ralph asked. His fingers drummed on the seat as he waited for Amesbury to nod. "What of the woman?"

"Oh yes! I love a voluptuous blonde. Where is the saucy pirate?" Vincent asked.

Obviously, Amesbury was distressed at Vincent's rhetoric. He had the look of a man whose host had asked his opinion on a particularly bad glass of wine. Clearly, he was trying to contain his displeasure and remain somewhat truthful. "She is my sister. She is only sixteen. Please do not speak of her as though she is an actress. And she is returning to London with the evidence of Her Grace the Dowager Duchess of Bridgewater's lack of children. You were very clever to get the servants' testimony. We stole pictures of the Dowager Duchess of Bridgewater during the years of her marriage showing she was never with child."

"Ah, we did not think of theft," Lily said.

"Why perform illegal activities when one can be sweet as sugar and get what one wants?" Lady Olivia asked.

"I suppose were I as pretty as you, my lady, I would be able to receive whatever I asked for," Amesbury bantered.

"And what does membership entail? Will we be required to break laws? I'm not fond of seeing my bride hanged for a minor offense." Ralph's ire was raised. Lily could not be placed back into danger.

"No court would hang a lord's wife, but I take your point. We need to discover the members of the Shadow Society. Who would have reason to harm your family? Once we learn who the members are, it is likely we will discover more," Amesbury replied.

"Are we to know the other members of the Black

Swan?" Vincent asked.

"At this time, it is the people in this railcar and my sister. The leader is Bertie, and I take instructions from him." Amesbury plucked a spot of lint from his trousers.

"When will we meet Bertie?" Vincent asked.

"It is unlikely that you will ever meet Bertie, but once the Shadow Society is no more, I believe he might consider it." Amesbury's lack of flirting seemed evasive.

"We could use the investment group as cover," Lily said. It was important that *someone* was planning whilst the men were discussing Bertie, the putative leader.

"Brilliant! And the school, the one for former child prostitutes, will allow us to speak to former servants without rousing suspicion," Olivia agreed.

"I'm afraid I am lost in the conversation," Amesbury noted.

"Mr. Rose and Lord Berkeley are designing an investment scheme. Naturally, they desire Ralph's talents. Vincent and Sebastian will follow. The scheme is to purchase estates. Due to the economy being so volatile as of late, many lords are long on creditors. Rose and Berkeley wish to make the estates into resorts or little villages with department stores and a middle-class life," Lily explained in a near whisper. Her voice was quiet enough to draw everyone in.

"But we want to have one estate as a school for service. Imagine a place where the children from 'The Maiden Tribute in Modern Babylon' could learn to work in service," Lady Olivia added.

"Yes. The scheme will allow members of the Black

Swan to visit estates and review finances without raising alarms other than that of an investment group. Besides, I think having a man who understands the law is important to any group such as the Black Swan," Lily concluded.

Quelle surprise! Lily was much better at espionage than he was comfortable with. The investment group would hide a great deal of investigation. "We will have to invite Mr. Rose as well as Miss Rose into the Black Swan. Are you interested in having two more members?"

"Certainly, as well as Miss Beauchamp and Coningsby. I don't believe that Berkeley needs to be involved, and I'm not sure he would agree with a secret club," Amesbury babbled.

"Will you be joining us to York?" Lily asked.

"Yes. There is a lady I am considering recruiting. She is the daughter of Lord Hume," Amesbury began.

"Hume? Doesn't he have a position with the Home Secretary?" Vincent asked.

"Yes. Lord Hume oversees the insane asylums in Her Majesty's kingdom," Amesbury said with a wolfish smile.

Chapter Twenty-Five

There's nothing quite a soothing as walking in nature, and parks are mankind's path to nature in an urban setting. It is heartening to see many lords donating land so that all citizens can partake in the beauty of the empire. I am in the firm belief that there is no country more beautiful than Britain, and it is enlightening for all citizens to witness its splendor.
~Aunt Penny's Advice for Living, July 1885

Lily and Olivia walked arm and arm with Olga and their lady's maids trailing uncomfortably close to them. Her ease was hard to project. She was furious as she passed the stone buildings on the streets on York. How dared Vincent interrogate her and yet withhold this Shadow Society? How could Ralph keep secrets from her? She would not trade abandonment from one set of family for deception by another. Being betrayed by the two people who swore they would protect her? That was intolerable. It felt like steam exploded from her elegant bun.

Of course, they thought they were protecting her in the way men protect women. Men felt women were fragile and easily wounded, and so thrilled as they kept them in the dark. Lily was not made of glass and could handle the situation. The disappointment with Ralph was overwhelming, whereas Vincent merely stung. She was strong, and she had proved herself again and again. But it appeared she still needed to prove it more.

"Do tell. What is it like?" Olivia asked. This temporarily snapped Lily from her fury.

"I beg your pardon?"

"Lovemaking," Olivia whispered close enough to make Lily blush. "What does it feel like?"

"Oh, we should not discuss such things on the streets." She stumbled painfully, half from the ground and half from the question.

"I don't see why not. Many men take whores in the alleys. But let's go to the park," Olivia said. Olivia pulled hard on Lily's arm to cross Clifton Street and sit on a bench. The perfect place to discuss the finer points of intercourse.

"I believe the Earl of Harcourt owns this land. The city hopes to have a park, but Harcourt is resistant to donating it," Lily babbled. How did one avoid such a direct question?

Olivia snorted. "If you ever wish to see Honoria spit venom, mention Lord Harcourt. I have never seen her so vexed, and she refused to elaborate as to why he angers her so. Never mind. Tell me all of the details."

Lily sighed. Why did she have such curious friends? The true aspects of Ralph that she liked best could never be understood by another. She adored the quiet moments when they could simply be. Those lovely and simple minutes as he read his investment reports and she reclined with a magazine. The subtle haze of comfort that hung in the air. Her much-longed-for safe place manifested in the cozy interludes of absolute peace—a serenity she had dreamt of and thought she would find only in Heaven. Lily had never been consumed by thoughts of divinity or destiny, but it was impossible to not see how perfectly they complemented one another and how sublimely they came together.

"It is not unpleasant, but when he is inside of me, I feel protected in a cocoon made just for us. The world melts away, and it's just Ralph and I. Sailors speak of hidden lands such as Atlantis or Shangri-La, but paradise exists on earth when you are as close as possible with someone you love. But he does something beforehand, and that is my favorite aspect of it."

"It sounds heavenly. What does he do?" Olivia asked. She smiled the same way Vincent smiled when he was very bad.

"There is a small…I truly don't know what to refer to it as—a berry-like part of my naughty bits. When he touches it, I feel a flush of warmth engulf my body, and when he kisses it, I feel the most pleasure I have ever felt. The first time I thought I was dying and my soul was escaping my body." A deep blush overtook her face, and she wished she could make her body smaller.

"You know, we are all so jealous of you. Bella especially. She was half in love with Ralph before she saw the way he looked at you," Olivia said as she stood and dusted off her dress.

"But she never mentioned!" she cried. She couldn't hide her guilt. She adored Bella and hated hurting her best friend.

"Bella wouldn't, and she never will. I only know because we were standing next to one another when you two were dancing. Don't think on it. Bella will find a man as honorable as Ralph. Or she can join Honoria and me in spinsterhood," Olivia said as she began to walk toward York Castle.

Lily rolled her eyes. Such histrionics. "You won't be a spinster, Olivia."

Olivia grimaced. "I might. The queen has decided to make an example of me."

"I don't follow." She was utterly lost as to Olivia's meaning.

"Her Majesty despises feminists, especially suffragettes. She refuses to attend any event in which I am also in attendance. I will no longer receive invitations to the bigger events, and no man with political ambitions will marry me. I have become a pariah," Olivia lamented. She couldn't even look at Lily as she said it. She knew how much it hurt to hide one's fears and pains.

Lily felt the air leave her body. It was utterly unfair to attack a woman for wanting to have a little control of her life. "But she's the queen! How can she hate a woman for wanting power? Her husband was made to be a consort rather than her equal."

Olivia shrugged. "It is strange, but women who are anti-feminist are more extreme than men. They seem to think that I personally want their husbands to fail, and that I hope for every wife to be forced to work. I do not, but they will not listen."

Lily put her arm around Olivia's shoulder and pulled her close like a righteous mother. "To hell with Her Majesty. If she will not attend events to which you are invited, I will never have her at my parties and neither will anyone who wishes me to attend. She is an old woman with a horrible son. She can bugger off for all I care. Her influence is waning, and history is long. Progress will not be held back forever."

"I am fortunate to have a friend such as yourself. I will always be in your debt, but I will be happy just for your friendship," Olivia sighed.

They spent much of the afternoon trying and mostly failing to cheer Olivia from her doldrums. The world was attacking Olivia and expected her to be docile. Lily wouldn't let her. In fact, she had to start campaigning to make feminism fashionable. She was so furious—not angry, but hot with a fury that would melt steel. She forgot for a moment who she was. The notion that a queen would seek to use her soft power, the power of exclusion and whispers, to pluck the emerging rights of women from them (and in doing so, use her voice to silence others like her) made her heart burn and freeze. This was the sort of anger that kept you in a cage. The type of rage you were always thinking about and confronting. It was impossible to avoid because it struck at her core. The hypocrisy and false benevolence of moralizing oppression could tie a reasonable woman's head in knots. If only she had something to shout at; the lack of such a thing made her madder because she didn't know who would listen. After all, she was a woman. And if "woman" was a slur, her anger would remain sincere, but it would be unheard by those in power.

She flew upstairs, took a bath, and ordered dinner to her room. She was a tempest in a teapot and might explode at the wrong person. Baths always soothed her. She loved to scrub herself soft. If Lily were to touch her cheek and feel anything but smooth skin, she felt wrong. It would be wonderful if she could rinse free the past day's strife and wash it down the drain. Once cleaned, she rubbed in lotion to soften her skin and donned her nightgown. She began to feel like herself again and hunted for something to read.

Newspapers were not an option, as the news depressed her. She had no desire to read about anyone worse off than she that she could not help. And of course, no desire to read about anyone better off than she either, and so novels were out. She was limited to what was available at hand, which meant settling for Ralph's report on investing in the textile industry. It was dull, but at least it did not upset her any further. It was easy to understand why the workers in such factories were unsettled. She would hate to work in the factories given the conditions factory masters bragged about. Let alone what they hid from the reports.

"You were missed at dinner. Are you reading my reports?" Ralph asked as he entered their room and removed his hat. He tried to come close, but her eyes raged at him.

"Yes, and I was too angry with you to dine together in any polite manner this evening," she answered while staring at the papers. Her tone was drawn, and she intentionally closed her mouth after she stopped speaking.

"Would you please enlighten me as to why you are angry? I believe I know, but I would like to hear exactly what I have done," Ralph asked evenly while he removed two bottles from his satchel and rolled them toward her.

"You knew for weeks that it was not just one man attacking our family, but an organization. I deserve better than to be treated as a child. Is that how you see me? As merely a large child, to be coddled?" she asked heatedly. He needed to answer.

"No, I don't, and I'm sorry. You deserved better, and I will make a point to be more forthright with you in the future," Ralph vowed. His eyes were sheepish and apologetic. This was the right response, but very deflating.

"Yes...well, now I have all of this anger and no direction. That is vexing," Lily stammered while biting her lip. It was frustrating. She had prepared for a long drawn-out argument, but he was being so irritatingly reasonable. "I had really clever arguments at the ready, and now, well, to use them would be cruel."

"I would love to hear them. Perhaps you could tell me while I make amends?" Ralph suggested. There was clearly a plan of some sort.

"How do you intend to do so?" Lily asked. Her cheeks flushed red with memories of their nightly dancing.

Ralph smiled and took her by the hand. He led her to the bed and removed her nightgown faster than she had ever done herself. Her body tingled; she was nude and excited. He gently laid her on the bed, but to her surprise he had her lie on her stomach. This was new. The weight of his body loomed over her, then finally rested at her buttocks. She was nervous and fixed her eyes firmly on the beige wall. But soon, she felt a liquid on her back, and Ralph's hands began to massage it in. The splendor of his wide hands finding parts of her back she never knew needed kneading was intense.

"Do let me know if I am too harsh with your delicate skin," Ralph said as he focused on Lily's shoulders. Was this part of the "dance" she had missed before?

"Mmmm. No, this feels remarkable. Where did you

learn to do this?" Lily asked after he finished with her shoulders and moved to the center of her back.

"While we were in France, I fell off my horse whilst hunting. The doctor swore by Swedish massage, and I admit that it relaxed me utterly. I have been craving a massage myself, but I needed to apologize to you. And I don't believe that you know how to massage," Ralph explained.

"I could learn. Perhaps we could alternate nights." She moaned. It felt so good.

Ralph kneaded into her lower back, and Lily heard herself purr. She could feel the pressure and movement in her fanny and grew excited. Ralph leaned against her and breathed lightly in her ear. "Do you feel better?"

"Yes." Lily smiled.

He rolled her over and kissed her deeply. He tasted of madeira and cherries. "Do you want me?"

"Yes," Lily gasped.

Ralph kissed her neck and slid his fingers in to find her center. His fingers swirled around her while teasing and exciting her. He moved his lips to taste her nipples. In turn they stood at attention. "I love your breasts. Do you like it when I lick them?"

"Yes," Lily rasped.

She was eager for him, and he slid inside her easily. As he began to pump, he pulled her legs to his chest. "God, I love you. Do you love me, Lily?"

"Yes!" Lily roared.

Ralph sped his movements and his stroking of her bud to match them, overwhelming her. "Are you mine? Are you mine, Lily?"

Her release was close, and she felt the dizzying nearness of it. "Yes, oh God, yes!" Lily screamed while the flood of pleasure washed over her. She and Ralph found their release together, and in that moment, they were truly one.

Chapter Twenty-Six

There are three daily newspapers and nearly thirty weekly newspapers and magazines. The post may come up to twelve times a day. We are overwhelmed with information and very little of it is uplifting. It can be frustrating to choose between being well informed and maintaining an optimistic outlook. I choose to read the news two hours before tea time and then put it out of my mind. I enjoy knowing the news, but for my peace of mind, I cannot dwell upon it for too long.
~Aunt Penny's Advice for Living, July 1885

Light and wakefulness exploded around Ralph again. He must have been tired, because the world had changed around him while he slept. Lily quietly read a magazine next to him. She lay on her stomach, indifferent to his opening eyes. She was still nude, with her chestnut hair coiled around her body. Seeing her without clothing was quite a revolution. One would have never guessed she had peach-colored nipples against her honey skin. Today the arc of her thighs and the way they led to her round backside proved irresistible. He admired her, and all of a sudden, Lily pushed her rump into the air and wiggled it with a coy giggle.

He couldn't help it; he had to smack the wriggling thing. "What are you reading?"

"Aunt Penny. I have never missed one yet," Lily said. She batted him with the magazine. Clearly, she was going to be quite a tease.

"Who is Aunt Penny?" Ralph asked as he kissed her shoulder.

"She writes an advice column for poor upper-class and middle-class ladies about how to live as though they were wealthy," Lily answered as she turned over.

"You are neither impoverished nor middle class." Although talking with her was quite satisfying, it was much better to touch her. He delicately kissed her breasts.

"No, but she has endless wisdom. Aunt Penny thinks every woman should know how to cook a meal, start a fire, and tend to a wound. I had to learn, but should we ever need to, I can make a delicious soup and sew a cut after cleaning it. I appreciate my cook far more now," Lily explained.

This slightly disheartened Ralph, as he was still kissing her breasts. "What sort of soup could you make?" This was surprising.

"Curried carrot soup. If I am to cook it, must be flavorful." Lily giggled as he kissed her stomach.

"I once made a decent Welsh rarebit." That was the best bragging he could do.

"Isn't Welsh rarebit simply cheese on toast?" Lily asked while propping herself up on her elbows.

"No. It is a cheese sauce, but you add ale and mustard to it for flavor." It was morning, so anything sounded good, even a Welsh rarebit. But why were two members of the gentry exchanging cooking tips?

There was a knock at the door, loud and urgent. "That will be Marlow. Send her in, will you?" Lily

asked.

He let Lily's maid in and began to dress hastily. Watching Marlow transform Lily's wild mane into a neat bun was surprisingly arousing. Ralph sat, intrigued, and observed. The morning rituals of women fascinated him. First Lily washed herself, starting with cleansing her face with a mixture of soap and sodium bicarbonate. Then her hair was tamed, and her eyebrows manicured. Then Marlow carefully dressed Lily. First were her stockings, then her all-in-one, followed by her corset. Then Lily held fast to the door frame while Marlow attached her bustle (this was fascinating to Ralph as it resembled a lobster trap he had once seen). Finally, they draped and fastened her dress. It was near impossible to restrain himself, but he had to wait patiently as Marlow literally gilded the Lily. The little incidentals such as gloves, hat, and jewelry were like garnish to an extensive meal.

Another knock sounded, this one less ominous. Ralph opened the door to see Vincent, not the breakfast he hoped would be there. "Good morning."

"I have just suffered through the most annoying breakfast in the history of breakfasts," Vincent announced as he entered the room.

"Please come in. What was so annoying about your breakfast? Did they burn your kippers? Or perhaps your toast?" He truly did not care why Vincent was upset with his breakfast, but it was important to be kind.

"This little brown creature, Miss Hume, would not cease in asking me questions. She is studying the mind, which I suppose makes sense, and she is dogged in her pursuit to 'fix' me. I may not survive," Vincent complained.

"Then you will have to seek to avoid her," Ralph suggested.

"I cannot. Nor will you be able to. Amesbury agreed to let her study us in exchange for assistance with entry to the insane asylum and a viewing of their private records. Also, she is the newest recruit to the Black Swan. How very vexing. She wants to know about my feelings toward our family," Vincent groused.

Ralph blanched. Letting someone discuss such things with Vincent would unearth all sorts of unpopular opinions. "That sort of thing is best kept private, is it not?"

"I agree, but we need her help. This is my conundrum. I need this loquacious church bell to keep ringing, but I have no interest in reciting Mother's ill deeds." Vincent jumped at a knock at the door and moved aside for the breakfast trolley. Thank goodness.

Once the porter had finished and left the room, Ralph resumed his conversation with Vincent. "Well, perhaps you could retell her what is already in the papers."

"Fortunately, the papers did not print the worst memories of Seraphina." Vincent sighed.

Oh, no. This was a relief but also a reminder of Vincent's pain. "What were the worst memories of Mother?"

"She and I have the same weapon, death by a thousand insults. It is almost impossible to find one time that she was horrible, but there are a million half-horrible memories. I was the invisible man far too often. Mother only loved and cared for Sebastian," Vincent reminisced. He refused to look anyone in the eye when he complained about Mother, probably because it would reveal some hidden pain.

He considered Vincent's words while he buttered his toast. Mother did advocate for Sebastian with a vigor that had only insulted Ralph once. He couldn't imagine suffering from it for his entire life. Yet he loved his mother, and Vincent did as well. It was confusing to hold two such diverging concepts in one's mind at the same time. How do you love the person who makes you feel small? Of course, Vincent insulted everyone and people liked him well enough, but Ralph was certain Vincent would not insult his own child.

"Perhaps…you could negotiate an agreement for Miss Hume's silence. If not, I still think speaking about Mother would help you. I have only been in competition with Sebastian once, but you were so clever, you were always in competition with him in school, despite his being two years older. If Miss Hume could help you have as good a relationship with Sebastian as you have with me, then I support this idea absolutely." Maybe Vincent needed a new friend.

"What of Mother? Won't she be angry at me for telling tales?" Vincent asked.

Ralph shrugged. "I was given to understand that you love vexing Mother. You might as well benefit from it."

****

Lily, Olivia, Miss Hume, and Olga walked the grounds of the York Insane Asylum like silent ballerinas tiptoeing to their marks. The men were resolute that the ladies not enter the asylum, as there was cause to believe that it may contain tuberculosis. Lily could accept this idea, for how could she be comfortable seeing in reality the "treatments" she had read about? Reading about the shackled mad and neglected feeble-minded shattered the mind and hollowed out the heart. Lily was unsure she could be strong and resolute when she saw it. Not that walking the grounds proved much better.

The asylum building was red brick with white quoins and lintel heads. The large clock tower in the center of the roof was higher than it had any practical need to be; and why would she want to know the time in a place such as this? There were plenty of windows. They rose high with rusty bars that allowed the patients to view the expansive gardens. Faces of unkempt misery in the windows peered out at the flowers. It was peculiar to force beauty to exist alongside despair, but Lily might want beauty if she were in such a hopeless place.

"This is the stuff of nightmares," she lamented. She tried to talk in just one breath, to avoid inhaling more of the dewy air. "I hope never to have to live in a place such as this."

Miss Hume snorted. "Unfortunately, especially if one is female, one can be put in a place such as this for nearly anything."

"Oh, my. Have I already committed acts to have me committed?" Olivia asked cheerily.

"Yes, being a woman is often sufficient reason to lock one up. Were you aware that hysteria comes from the Greek word for uterus?" Miss Hume asked.

Both Lily and Olivia were aghast at Miss Hume's language. Finally, Lily cleared her throat. "Yes, I speak Greek quite well."

"Hysteria or calling someone hysterical is essentially saying they are behaving like a woman.

Therefore, the beginning position of a woman is madness. Only by behaving as society demands may they be sane. God forbid a woman does anything beyond the pale and strives to be more than the diminutive hausfrau." They had clearly upset Miss Hume.

"Please do not mistaken my curiosity for objection, but isn't hysteria a medical condition? Is there not a treatment?" Olivia asked.

"Are either of you ladies familiar with the treatment for hysteria?" Miss Hume asked.

"No," Lily and Olivia answered in unison.

Miss Hume raised her eyebrows like she had a salacious secret. "You are stripped down to your chemise and laid down on a bed. It is usually a bed, but sometimes it is a table or sofa. Your doctor applies a vibration device to your clitoris until you…give up the ghost as it were."

Her cheeks were hot and blushed. A stranger being witness to such an intimate moment? Lily wondered how one could reconcile the rush of love after release with a cold and distant doctor. If she were forced to divorce the aspect of lovemaking from her husband, she would grow cold to him. She might even be able to forgive him having a mistress. How very fortunate not to have to live in such an arrangement.

"Yet another reason for women to have the vote," Olivia said with less enthusiasm than usual.

"Ah, that brings me to the questions I had for you. Why, when you are an earl's daughter and renowned for your beauty would you choose to be a suffragette?" Miss Hume asked.

"Olivia is brilliant as well as beautiful," Lily

answered. "When we, as a society, restrict the truly brilliant minds, we are only harming ourselves. Imagine an inverse world in which women are the dominant gender. DaVinci and Descartes are forced to be cooks and maids whilst great women rule the world. It is a crime for the world to tell half the population to simply mind the children. We are only harming ourselves and our potential by subjugating half the world."

"Here, here!" Olivia cheered.

"I absolutely agree with the sentiment, but I truly wish to know why Olivia chose this path," Miss Hume said amicably.

"My mother lost four children after my birth and could not have another," Olivia explained. "My father was disheartened but focused solely on me. He never questioned the notion that I would attend Cambridge University or that I would graduate. I am a bit like Mary Shelley. My parents simply supported me. I believe if he could, my father would happily make me the next Earl of Banbury. But alas, he cannot."

Lily envied her so much it hurt her sides. It was unfair for Olivia to have two wonderful parents when Lily only had one, or at least the ghost of one.

"I see. Well, that is less interesting and unlikely to yield any assistance." Miss Hume sighed.

Lily laughed. "Oh, my dear Miss Hume! A human being just unveiled her soul to you! There will never be another like Olivia, and she gave you a glimpse into the deepest parts of her. Appreciate that for the gift it is and be grateful."

Miss Hume blushed. "I do apologize. I did not mean to offend."

"It is of no consequence, Miss Hume. I understand.

The study of the mind is unfamiliar territory. You wish to map a piece for yourself. Perhaps one aspect you may wish to explore is the treatment of the treatment. That is to say, when one is exposing oneself to you, be as gentle as you would if they were naked and wounded," Olivia suggested.

"That is a promising idea. How very brilliant," Miss Hume said jovially, her voice getting deeper. Or at least it could pass as jovial for her. "Miss Snowe, may I ask you a few questions?"

"Certainly, Miss Hume." Lily braced herself for whatever Miss Hume was seeking.

"Why did you choose Lord Ralph Mandeville and not Lord Vincent Mandeville?" Miss Hume inquired.

Lily laughed. "I could never view Vincent as a husband. He is much more of a brother to me than my own brother. I believe we met when I was four and he chose me to be his sister. Sebastian feels like a brother to me. They even swore an oath to make me their sister. I am pleased Ralph was not a part of the compact, or else I would be conflicted."

"But Lord Vincent Mandeville is handsome, and you are beautiful," Miss Hume argued.

Lily giggled. "There are many handsome men, but I see Vincent as a brother. And I am happy to have him as a brother. I could not tease or pour cream on his head were he a man. Trust me, this is the best for all parties. Sebastian and Vincent wanted a sister, and I wanted a family to fill the roles they have chosen. Sebastian, though less warm, has protected me and aided me time and again. Yet no one asks why I have not chosen to marry him."

"Why did you not look toward Coningsby?" Olivia

asked.

Lily sighed and wondered if orphans and wards had to endure this scrutiny. "Sebastian is a brother to me. Even if not, I do not believe I would be the ideal wife for Seraphina's golden child."

Olivia and Miss Hume chuckled. Olga managed to inject a "Sit now?" She was the best sort of chaperone—always tired, never a terrible scold.

How bizarre that the gardens of a madhouse should be so peaceful and pristine. With Miss Hume's revelation that anyone could be interred for any number of mundane reasons, what should be done for the twisted faces in the windows? Lily's heart raced as she imagined those poor faces of the people she loved in those smudged windows. How easy it was to be imprisoned because of a cruel twist of fate. How would she feel if she were imprisoned for drawing her father's adventures or having lust for Ralph? She would just be another angry face screaming at the injustice of it all, pressed up against a window while time passed and nothing changed. It hurt her heart to see Lord Berkeley's words proven correct. No single man could solve Britain's problems, and only systematic change could make a better world.

Chapter Twenty-Seven

One can never discern the true goings-on of a house by simply looking at it. Inside there may be monsters or angels, but the lovely brick will deceive you and the beautiful gardens will invite you. Be wary of judging the exterior.

~Aunt Penny's Advice on Living, July 1885

Ralph counted his steps quietly to keep focused in the rancid halls of the asylum. The entire building felt musty and damp and smelled of a wet dog. The corners lurked in macabre darkness, and the hallways were sinister roads. Mad howls echoed throughout the air as an omnipresent reminder of where they were. The walls were white tile, as if to relay that this was a place of health when this was a place of madness. It was good that the ladies had agreed to walk the gardens, as he doubted the putrid air would suit creatures that perfumed their hair.

Just when he could not take any more (he had counted to about four hundred), Ralph and his friends arrived at the office of Doctor Dolan. The office was orderly to a fault, with everything in perfect straight lines. The corpulent man inside had a constant rose bloom on his cheeks. Doctor Dolan's cough echoed as he stood, and he covered his mouth with a handkerchief to wipe it before he spoke. "I am Doctor Dolan, and I am given to understand you are Lord Amesbury, Lord Ralph Mandeville, and Lord Vincent Mandeville. Lord Hume asked me to review a former patient's records with you."

"Yes, Doctor, a Mr. Bartholomew Edwards," Ralph supplied. This was going to be a simple conversation.

Doctor Dolan wiped his brow. Even his sweat smelled off. "Ah, yes. Has Mr. Edwards caused trouble?"

"He is claiming to be the heir to the Duke of Bridgewater. What do you know of him?" Vincent asked.

"Bridgewater? That is odd, he used to claim to be one of Victoria's children. Bit of a letdown to choose a duke after believing the queen birthed you," Doctor Dolan began.

"Indeed." Vincent smiled.

Ralph resisted the urge to tell him to stuff it.

"Mr. Edwards came to us when he was fifteen and was attempting to enter Balmoral Castle. He was certain the queen had abandoned him and claimed to need to make her see him. Of course, lunatic asylums are filled with people that claim a connection to the queen. One man tried to assassinate Her Majesty because she did not like his poetry quite enough." Doctor Dolan babbled. This man was lonely for educated company.

"That is very interesting, but why did Mr. Edwards leave the hospital?" Ralph knew enough to remain diplomatic.

"Well, his sister collected him. Said she found a hospital that specializes in providing care for one with delusions such as his." Doctor Dolan's face screwed up, as though he wanted to ask why anyone might inquire.

"When did she collect him?" Ralph asked quickly. Better to seize the moment before he asked problematic questions.

"Late May," Doctor Dolan answered as he looked for his ledger.

"And what did Miss Edwards look like?" Amesbury asked. The office was tidy, unlike Adrian's. It was sterile and unwelcoming, like the inside of a dysfunctional clock.

"She was tall for a woman with brown eyes and brown hair. But her hair struck me as peculiar," Doctor Dolan said.

"Peculiar how?" Ralph asked.

"It was odd. Even tucked into her hat, it looked as though she had a false color. Almost as though she had smeared shoe polish into her hair," Doctor Dolan answered.

Vincent exchanged a quiet glance with Amesbury. "Did Mr. Edwards appear happy to see his sister?"

"No. He swore he did not have a sister, but he had been here for so many years, she would not resemble the little girl she once was." Doctor Dolan moved away and bent down, searching his ledger. He must have found what he was searching for. "Ah. Here it is. Bartholomew Edwards, admitted March 4, 1870. Diagnosed with grandiose delusions and mania. Discharged May 27, 1885, to his sister, Miss Dorothy Edwards."

"Would you be willing to testify at the trial, Doctor Dolan?" This would make everything easier.

"I beg your pardon? To which trial do you refer?"

Doctor Dolan asked.

"Doctor Dolan, we are the Duke of Bridgewater's sons, and Mr. Edwards is suing our family. He believes we stole his title and land," Ralph explained.

Doctor Dolan turned a brighter red and sputtered. "That can't be! What kind of a fool would represent him? This is an outrage!"

"Yes, Doctor Dolan, we quite agree. That is why we are attempting to prove that Mr. Edwards is not of sound mind," Vincent explained and stood a little taller.

"I see. Well, yes, I will testify. I must return Mrs. Edwards' payments in any case." Doctor Dolan was rummaging in his desk drawer.

"Mrs. Edwards?" Vincent asked.

"Yes, his mother. She has paid for Mr. Edwards' treatment dutifully for fifteen years. After Mr. Edwards left, the payments persisted. I must return it to her," Doctor Dolan explained. "Moreover, the guest register will reflect any visitors he has seen recently."

"Yes, of course. Doctor Dolan, perhaps you could give us the payment as well as Mrs. Edwards' address. I don't believe she knows of her son's actions," Vincent pointed out.

Doctor Dolan's face uncoiled into a look of surprise. "I suppose she wouldn't know what Mr. Edwards is doing. I must admit it would shock the world for three lords to be acting as errand boys, but I don't see any harm."

"You would be surprised by what we get up to," Amesbury said. It was taking too long for Doctor Dolan to fetch the address and pound notes.

"I imagine I would be shocked," Doctor Dolan agreed as he handed over the envelope intended for

Mrs. Edwards.

They stepped into the damp yet sterile hallway. The moans were a sharp reminder of where they were. Doctor Dolan's office was truly a port of hygiene in the storm of the asylum. The doctors and staff must have needed some sort of control to keep sane in this madness. He had honestly never much thought of the people who worked in lunatic asylums and wondered if they suffered madness as well. Certainly, lunacy was not contagious, but it must wear on a man's soul to endure this place day after day.

"We are making excellent progress in your father's case but also with the Shadow Society. We now know they have at least one female member," Amesbury noted.

"Indeed, tall for a woman with brown eyes and hair that is not brown. Amazing progress," Vincent said sarcastically. Everyone's patience was running thin.

Ralph shrugged. "It is progress, and I hope once we prevail in court they will show their hand. I had not anticipated this level of sophistication. They prepared for us to investigate and disguised the woman. Every step will tell us more about them. Cheer up, Vincent." He gazed at the address he held in his hand. "Mrs. Edwards resides in Wooler." This would be a far-flung trip.

"Where in the bloody hell is Wooler?" Amesbury asked.

"Northumberland," Vincent answered.

"How did you know that?" Ralph asked.

"There is a family of artists from Wooler, and we have a wood carving by them in our home," Vincent answered. It was clear that this ought to be common knowledge.

"Well, off to Northumberland we go, I suppose," Ralph said, not at all excited about the prospect.

Chapter Twenty-Eight

Nobility is more than birth or wealth. There is a quality of nobility that is only found in the truly great leaders: kindness. It is but a small effort to be kind to those who are lower than yourself, but it is a profound gesture to those who receive it. A man is not worth his salt if he enjoys insulting any person who he views as his lesser.

~Aunt Penny's Advice for Living, July 1885

This trip was like a story told by a drunk. Just when Ralph thought they were close to arriving, the journey persisted. How trying this countryside could be. There was no train to Wooler. They had to take a train to Alnwick and hire a carriage. His only familiarity with Northumberland came from the possible investments research. Northumberland was rich in coal and granite, but the population was sparse, and so Ralph passed on investing. If a coal mine collapsed, would there be sufficient infrastructure to ensure the safety of the workers? Perhaps in a few years when roads and railway stations were built, he would reconsider, but for now it was just rolling green hills.

Selfishly, he was a little sad that the trial would soon start. This little excursion with Lily had been supremely enjoyable—especially the nights. Returning to a cold empty bed and mornings free of her figure as his first sight sounded just awful. He had abstained from her because he knew the moment he had her, he would hate a moment without her. In the country, they had freedom, but once they returned to London, they would be watched carefully and would have to wait until their marriage. If Lily had not orchestrated such an elaborate wedding breakfast, he would have procured a special license and married her tonight. He should have done so anyway.

Lily and Lady Olivia were riding in a separate carriage with Miss Hume, Olga, and the lady's maids. Ralph, Vincent, and Amesbury shared another carriage. The carriage smelled entirely too earthy. It was impossible to not miss the superior, light fragrances of the ladies with Lily's jasmine and Lady Olivia's citrus scents in the air. Or the near endless conversation. Even if it was just Lily and Olivia discussing fashion, they were constantly entertaining. The temptation was strong to sabotage the carriages and find a cottage to live on Lily's soup and his Welsh rarebit until they grew very old.

"Have either of you gentlemen read Aunt Penny?" Ralph asked. This would surely provoke a conversation.

"My sister never misses Aunt Penny. She clips the columns and glues them into a book." Amesbury smiled.

"I have never heard of her. Who is she?" Vincent asked.

"Aunt Penny is an advice column in *Ladies Today Magazine*. She advises middle-class and poor ladies of tricks to live a more upper-class life. It educates you about the thousands of trivial things that only the crème de la crème notice and use to cast out impostors. Her identity is a great mystery. Is she an upper-class lady who broke ranks to help others? If so, many would consider her a class traitor. Is she a middle-class lady who aspires for more? If so, she is an upstart. She could be a governess or housekeeper. Some even suspect she is Berkeley," Amesbury explained.

Vincent snorted. "Berkeley writing as a woman would be hilarious. Is Aunt Penny married to Uncle George Sand?"

"Of course, with Berkeley in America, that theory will die out. We need to discuss what will happen after the trial. I am comfortable with a small holiday from investigating, but we must find the Shadow Society members." Amesbury changed the subject.

"Do we know anything about them? How were we chosen?" Ralph asked.

Amesbury shrugged. "We know they exist and that you are the second family chosen. I believe they choose one family per year, with 1885 being the Mandevilles."

"Hooray," Vincent muttered.

"The 1884 family has put forth an incredible effort to not reveal their misfortune, so Bertie has decided to respect their privacy. There will be an 1886 family unless we stop them. Without knowing the members of the Shadow Society, we cannot predict the next family. Thus far we know there is a woman, but we don't believe she is the head of the Society," Amesbury explained.

"Perhaps we need to try to figure out who would hate us enough to cause all…this." Ralph waved his hands about. It was a struggle to plan for a fight he could not see.

"The dowager duchess hates us," Vincent supplied.

"She has been in France since March, so she could not have been the woman at the asylum. But she could be a member," Amesbury agreed.

"Sebastian and I have been trying to find who has been feeding the papers information about our family. Viscount Lake and one of the Archers were on my suspect list," Vincent suggested.

"Lake might be a suspect. Castleton is an unpleasant jackass," Amesbury began.

"Castleton has been a thorn in my side. He tried to stop me from building my house. Although, Archer also tried to buy it," Ralph said, more confused than ever.

"There are four Archer brothers. The eldest, Tristan Archer, is the Viscount Primrose. Julian Archer is the second son, William Archer is the third, and Baxter Archer is the fourth. Baxter Archer has just left for America last week. I believe he is settling in a place called Oregon," Amesbury explained.

"Baxter Archer was a few years behind me in school. He was…" Ralph struggled to find the words. "Well, to call him an idiot might be extreme."

Vincent laughed loudly and interrupted Ralph. "Oh my, when you have something unpleasant to say about a man it speaks volumes. Poor Ralph, are you having a grim time trying to be polite while calling him stupid? Baxter is an anomaly. Usually droll people can be well informed, ugly people can be kind, and the bad and good are in balance. Baxter is the sort of idiot that would make Aristotle throw up his hands and follow Socrates."

"Baxter Archer is very stupid. Unfortunately stupid. It would be less offensive if he were pleasant, but he is rather of the opinion that might makes right."

His laugh caught in his throat. Baxter was indeed quite an idiot.

Amesbury frowned. "His lack of intelligence does not rule him out, but his moving to America might. William Archer ventured to India and has begun investing in mines with enormous success. The man seems to be able to smell rare minerals and gems. Does anyone have any reason to think he may hold a grudge?"

"No," Vincent and Ralph said together.

"Primrose and Julian Archer are the two best suspects of the Archer family. But Lake is also a likely member of the Shadow Society, as well as his father, Castleton," Amesbury noted.

Ralph had nothing to say, and so he stared out the window. They were making progress. But Vincent was right; they knew nothing. The Mandeville brothers had been gone for two years and had returned to a society that was constantly shifting based on the tiny slights of others, a rocky land, filled with tremors over the smallest of things. His mother could have snubbed the wrong man and brought this upon them. Far too many people were pleased to see the Mandevilles in trouble, and he wondered what they had done to merit such treatment. Of course, the easy reason would be Vincent's insults, but many people enjoyed his wit and criticism.

Perhaps it was time for the Mandevilles to reevaluate their lives and ask why the number of people who would be loyal to them would be so small. All social loyalty was conditioned on the same arbitrary rules that had separated him from Lily, estranged Vincent from Sebastian, and chained others to a dreary, anonymous life in the shadow of families like the Mandevilles.

****

Wooler was a sleepy village of browns and reds in a sea of green hills. Its lush clouds of earth and sky were the exact inverse of the controlled estates on which members of Lily's class vacationed. Quite frankly, she preferred Alnwick, but she had to admit she was not familiar with Northumberland in general. In her travels around the British countryside, Lily hadn't spent much time in Northumberland. For the first time in a very long time, she was out of her element. But from this perch, Northumberland was more nature than people. It had tiny villages along the way, but it was largely verdant and untamed. However, she had found something special about every place she had been, even if it was simply that the pharmacist had an adorable dog.

Mrs. Edwards was the butcher's wife, and so they first ventured to the butcher shop. Lily's gloved hand firmly pushed the creaky door open. Behind the counter, Mrs. Edwards was an elderly woman with white hair and a plump bespectacled face. Her countenance was painted with the sort of rural kindness earned through decades of toil alongside family and neighbors. Behind her, three men worked at butchering. One was clearly her husband, and Lily guessed the other two were her sons.

Mrs. Edwards smiled at Lily. "Good afternoon. How can I help you strangers?"

Lily returned the smile. "Good afternoon. I am the Honorable Miss Lily Snowe, and this is my friend Lady Olivia Pembroke. I am pleased to introduce my fiancé,

Lord Ralph Mandeville, and his brother Lord Vincent Mandeville. And finally, I present Lord Amesbury and my chaperone, Mrs. Olga Schimmelpfennig. Though I simply call her Olga."

"I can see why," Mrs. Edwards said. Of course, the rest of the room agreed with her. "How can they be brothers and both be lords?"

"Ah, when a duke has multiple sons, each one is granted the title of lord. However, people regard this as merely a courtesy, and so our children will not have any title," Lily explained. Commoners loved hearing details of the gentry. Mrs. Edwards would dine on this tidbit for years. Everyone in the village would be bombarded with the retelling of this interaction. "We are here regarding your son, Mr. Bartholomew Edwards."

Mrs. Edwards's demeanor immediately changed from honored shopkeeper to suspicious mother. Her gentle leaning into the conversation was replaced with the retreat of a woman with something to lose. Her hands folded across her waist, and her elbows thrust out from her sides. "What do you want with him?"

Now, this would require a bit of charm. How very lucky they were that Lily was here! She broadened her mouth and batted her eyes just enough to make them flash a little bit—that should do the trick. "As I mentioned, Ralph and Vincent are a duke's sons, the Duke of Bridgewater, to be precise. Mr. Bartholomew Edwards is suing the Duke of Bridgewater. He claims to be the rightful duke and that he was sired by the duke's long-dead brother. As part of this case, he says the dowager duchess is his mother. Since you are his true mother, we were hoping you would be willing to travel to London and testify to his birth and collect him."

Mrs. Edwards looked near tears. "I'm so sorry. I'm so ashamed."

This was terrible. Lily flew fast around the counter to put her arm around Mrs. Edwards, soiling her dress by dragging the skirts through blood. "There, there. We do not blame you for this matter. Someone clearly took advantage of a confused young man and manipulated him. You did not know he was suing the duke, did you? No, I imagine you have never thought of the Duke of Bridgewater."

"Thank you so much for your kindness, my lady." Mrs. Edwards began to cry, and the three men began to walk toward them. It was better not to correct Mrs. Edwards and for Lily to simply scamper back to her party. The three provoked butchers frightened Lily.

"What'd you do to Mum?" One of the younger men glared at Lily.

"Now wait just one moment—" Ralph began.

"No, no, Billy. This nice lady has been kind to me," Mrs. Edwards objected. "Batty has been making trouble in London, and they've come to ask for 'elp."

Lily had never heard of Batty being a nickname for Bartholomew, but maybe the family referred to their insane family member as Batty in a tongue-in-cheek fashion. Hopefully, it was a term of endearment and not an insult.

"Batty ain't been in London. He's been in York," the older man said gruffly.

"I beg your pardon, sir, but Doctor Dolan will be at the trial to testify that he was discharged to his sister in May. We have a letter from him, along with the return of your payments to the hospital," Ralph explained as he handed Mrs. Edwards an envelope.

Mrs. Edwards sighed powerfully, her whole body deflating in a potent shrug. "When must we be in London?"

"The trial is July 27. It should not run more than a week. Please allow me to give you my card." Lily fished a calling card from its bejeweled case. "If you should require anything, please do not hesitate to call upon me."

"Thank you. The Honorable Miss Liliana Snowe," Mrs. Edwards read aloud.

Lily wasn't sure if Mrs. Edwards could read, but the flick of her eyes across the card was reassuring. "My father is a renowned explorer, and I have tasted a fair amount of sausages. If you would like, I could bring a list of some of the sausages that are popular in other countries. Perhaps I could bring one before we depart?"

The Edwardses nodded their agreement. Obviously, in a village without a railway stop, German or Polish sausages would be considered exotic. The fact that a lord's daughter gave them the recipes would add to that excitement. While the rest of their party went to the pub, Lily and Olga went to the dry-goods store so she could write down the sausage ideas. The dry-goods store was owned by the Haverford family. Wait— wasn't Marlene Haverford from Northumberland? How very curious.

"Lily, what will become of me once you are wed?" Olga asked in German.

Lily frowned. She truly had not thought of Olga's fate. "Well, Papa will always have a room for you. Or if you would like, I would love to have your company as a companion. There is also your son. You could always return to Germany."

Olga shook her head. "My son is a grandfather himself now. He has no need for me. I would like to care for someone. I should like to keep caring for my little Lily *liebling*."

Lily giggled and tried not to show how touched she truly was. Lily may not have a mother, but a little old German woman had adopted her as a granddaughter. "Oh, thank goodness. I was so concerned that I may never find the correct way to make *schweinshaxe*."

"Only upon my death bed, little one. Now, you wish to trade Olga's sausage secrets. Let me begin with my mother's sausage." Olga tugged at her cap to recall.

As Lily and Olga discussed sausages (one never argued with a German grandmother about sausages, even when they were simply pork, salt, ginger, and cardamom in various degrees), the shopkeeper muddled through what was no doubt his daily business. Preparing, storing, testing, and grinding. He had the bearing of a middle-aged man, perhaps in his forties, with graying hair and deep brown eyes. Mr. Haverford had very little patience for his young shop assistant. However, he was a man with an attention to detail, and most of his frustration stemmed from a need to provide exemplary service.

Lily had to speak to the man to know if he was related to Marlene Haverford. After all, Haverford might be a common name in Northumberland.

"Good afternoon," Lily greeted as she approached the polished counter. "I was wondering if you have any spices?"

"Of course, miss. Allow me to show you," Mr.

Haverford said.

Lily was disappointed with the selection of spices, but she bought a healthy amount for her sausages. As Mr. Haverford packaged them, Lily tried to make conversation—or gather information. "It is nice of you to hire your son-in-law."

"Oh, Sam isn't my son-in-law," he answered without moving his eyes from his wares.

Lily resolved to try again with less subtlety. "Oh, I was given to understand these stores were family businesses."

"Usually they are, but my daughter went to live with my sister-in-law in London for the season. My Marlene is pretty and might fetch a lord. Perhaps a gentleman. But it will still be better than this village," Mr. Haverford said. Speaking with such sincerity may be a bit guileless, but he clearly wanted the best for her.

Lily passed a handful of coins from her hand to the man. How very dreadful. Miss Haverford felt false because she was false. She was a poor relation. Bella had called her a chameleon, but maybe Miss Haverford behaved like a chameleon by necessity. Poor Miss Haverford was most likely petrified someone would discover her roots and she would be a pariah. Should she treat Miss Haverford differently? After all, Vincent loved Miss Haverford and Lily adored Vincent.

Chapter Twenty-Nine

One of the most important aspects of a dinner party is the conversation. We are told to avoid discussions of the religious, politics, and gossip. Unfortunately, these three subjects often cross over into every other conversation. Because of this, I keep a list of polite subjects to discuss. The rotation of crops has settled many arguments that threatened to be political. Whilst at a dinner of a Catholic and a Protestant, I settled a brewing argument by inquiring about sheep's wool. I will admit it was a dull dinner party. However, my guests left liking each other.

~Aunt Penny's Advice on Living, July 1885

A week after they returned from Wooler, Vincent and Ralph hosted a dinner party at their townhouse. Lily acted as hostess, arranging the seating and designing the menu. The servants were all nerves, as it was known she would soon be the lady of the house. They were right to be afraid. Her menu made a showing of great ambition, and she demanded excellence. Lily had an attention to detail that Ralph had only seen in his mother. Despite the dinner being a mere pretense to recruit new members to the Black Swan, his great love had orchestrated a six-course menu with elaborate centerpieces. How very like her to excel at everything.

Sebastian was, naturally, the first to arrive. His

stateliness was followed by Adrian Rose and Honoria Rose. Then Amesbury and his sister, Lady Stella, crossed the threshold. Lady Olivia and Miss Beauchamp were the last to arrive. Once they were seated and the first course was served, Lily nodded forcefully. Every servant left the room, closing the door quietly behind them. How very theatrical—and intimidating. All eyes were on Lily, and she stared down the table at Ralph.

He cleared his throat and stood. "Mr. Rose, Miss Rose, Miss Beauchamp, and Sebastian, you are invited to join the Black Swan. I turn you over to Amesbury. To my knowledge, he is the leader of our club." Ralph nervously returned to his seat. He was a competent speaker, but rhetorical flourishes were not in his repertoire. Good thing no poetry was involved.

Amesbury stood and deliberately withdrew the letter Vincent had given him from his jacket pocket. " 'ENJOY SOCIETY WHILE YOU CAN. THE MANDEVILLES HAVE BEEN CHOSEN.' Signed by the Shadow Society." Amesbury walked the circumference of the table while the secret lingered in the air. "When one thinks of the unbelievable events of the past two months, they seem unfathomable and chaotic. If we understand that there is a conspiracy behind this, then the events seem less unbelievable. They fall like pieces in a terrible puzzle. The Shadow Society is a club bent on revenge and destruction of whichever family they have chosen during that year. The Black Swan seeks to stop the Shadow Society. By becoming a member of the Swan, you agree to assist with destroying the Shadow Society. The Shadow Society will move on next year, and the next family will need our assistance in surviving the onslaught."

"I wish to join. How does one become a member?" Sebastian asked as he leaned forward.

"Amesbury refuses to let us have a secret handshake. I tried, Sebastian. Truly I did. For now, you just declare that you are a member. For now." Vincent smiled and had clearly amused himself.

"Rose? Miss Rose? How do you feel about uniting to defeat true foes?" Amesbury asked.

"I am more than happy to, though I am unsure how much I will contribute," Miss Rose whispered.

"Rose?" Amesbury asked.

Rose stared out the window pensively. "I suppose I am useful to you, or I would not be invited to belong to such a club."

Vincent snorted. "I would much rather be chosen for usefulness than for simply being one of the chosen family. We have had to walk through hellfire and have a personal reason to hate the Shadow Society. Amesbury, who is here because they are useful?"

Amesbury furrowed his brow. "All of you. I don't see the Duke and Duchess of Bridgewater as particularly useful, and hence they are not here. Every single person present is of use and value. Miss Snowe, for example, speaks, reads, and writes in twelve languages. Lord Ralph Mandeville, were I to wish to purchase an estate in Shrewsbury, how might I be able to make a profit?"

"Wool. Shropshire has excellent textiles," Ralph answered easily. Wool was his favorite investment.

"Ralph studies investment reports constantly, and they have useful information that no one else gleans because it is boring. Miss Rose can pick any lock and solve nearly every puzzle put before her. Miss Beauchamp, what was the first thing Vincent uttered at the table?"

" 'Amesbury refuses to let us have a secret handshake. I tried, Sebastian. Truly I did. For now, you just declare that you are a member. For now,' " Miss Beauchamp recited. Ralph wasn't sure if those were Vincent's exact words, but they sounded close.

"And in May at the Mandevilles' ball, what were the first words you heard him utter?" Amesbury pressed.

Miss Beauchamp sighed. " 'Miss March lost her hair piece. Look, Ralph! It's caught in her dress! It looks as though an elegant rat is following her.' I was surprised to find the brothers hiding and retreated from the ball."

"Miss Beauchamp can never forget any words spoken to her. It is useful, but imagine never being able to forget the tiny insults slung your way," Amesbury explained.

"Fear not, my lord. I have been beneath your notice," Miss Beauchamp said as if she was reading Vincent's mind.

"Your kindness exceeds your memory. Although, to be honest, now you have my attention. And since you are both pretty and modest, you can expect me to harbor a special affection for insulting you." Vincent flattered the demure lady.

"Yes, yes. My point being that every person present is useful," Amesbury said with a pointed look toward Rose.

"Very well, I belong here. Though I second the handshake motion," Rose responded.

"Huzzah! Now you get jewelry. I think the jewelry makes us a rarefied club," Lily announced with a wink to Ralph. Oh, if only he could climb the table to her. Such an elegant and teasing hostess deserved a kiss.

Amesbury sighed and exchanged a look with his sister, Lady Stella. "Do you see?"

"The jewelry was my idea. And if you keep making a fuss, Harrison will devise a new system to signal one another," Lady Stella sang.

"Oh no! I wasn't…I didn't…" Lily stammered.

"It was not you I complained about, Miss Snowe." Amesbury glared toward Vincent as he fetched the boxes of jewelry on the far end table. "Wear the swan if you need assistance and the star if you have pertinent information."

"Is this why you were a maid at both my home as well as Lord Belasyse's house in Devon?" Miss Rose asked Lady Stella.

"I do apologize, but I was dying of curiosity about what occurred during your teas and house parties," Lady Stella explained.

Ralph sipped his wine as quietly as he could. How many homes Lady Stella had entered in the guise of a maid? The servants were furniture, and she had made effective use of that attitude. But Ralph's optimism bubbled deep inside of him. After all, his family was united, his bride-to-be was by his side, and he had a room full of allies to combat the Shadows. Perhaps his darkest hour was finally over. Although sometimes it was darkest before it is pitch black.

Chapter Thirty

A fortnight ago, I was enjoying a cup of coffee in Edinburgh when I overheard two servants discussing their mistresses. Ladies, be respectful of your servants. They know all your secrets.
~Aunt Penny's Advice for Living, July 1885

The chamber chosen by the Lord High Steward for the hearing of preliminary arguments concerning the title of the Duke of Bridgewater was too large for such a small cluster of litigants. The Mandevilles and Mr. Rose, the Lord High Steward and his assistants, and Mr. Sedgwick and his assistant were all dwarfed by this chamber. Its soaring ceilings and large windows amplified every whisper with a cavernous effect. The echo of any word would clang and shudder against the walls with a false importance, as if the room itself wanted to etch the events it saw into its wooden memories. Was Ralph just a character in an opera someone else had written? But the steward's words were both too dreary to listen to fully and too piercing to ignore.

The Lord High Steward selected for this matter was the Earl of Cornwall. The old bird of a man oversaw the hearing from a slightly elevated perch. He was removed from the barristers, behind a desk with elegant timepieces and copious amounts of ink and expensive paper. His assistants were two clerks selected from a prestigious family, albeit a minor one. They were attired in red, like a youthful gilding designed to lighten the appearance of the old, curmudgeonly man. His brown eyes were a little watery and gray at the edges. The wrinkles pooling around them communicated his advanced age. He drawled when he spoke, like a butler who had been forced to carry a particularly heavy tray to an ungrateful family.

"It is curious to me," he began after leaning slightly to take measure of the room. "The parties petition for the appointment of a Lord High Steward prior to the House of Commons bringing forth such an impeachment. Since Parliament is in session, there is not truly a need for such a thing. The normal order of justice might dictate that this formality is unnecessary. And yet, here we are. Gentlemen, explain to me why this is necessary and why I am being taken from my duties."

Adrian's strategy might not be working. The risky bet of making this a political rather than a legal question had complicated things. This strategy made the result much foggier to predict. Ralph leaned into Lily in the next seat over. She had a stern but not unsympathetic face and was dressed in the most conservative fashion she could. He'd had to fight with Adrian over her attendance. Mr. Rose had stated that because of the recent scandal with Lily's past and the hesitation of more backward men to include women in hard matters of state, Lily would be a distraction at the precise time when one was not desirable. But she had been instrumental to the defense of the family, and her reputation had been sullied by the same villains who had targeted the Mandevilles. She had earned her right. And thus, Ralph won the pleasure of her company here.

"Lord Cornwall, if I may. As you know, I am Adrian Rose, and I represent the interest of the Duke of Bridgewater in these proceedings—" said Adrian.

He was promptly cut off by the steward. "I know the identities of the parties and the barristers, Mr. Rose. I know why you are here. What I do not know is why I am here. Please explain to me how I am to be of service to the Crown and to justice in this matter. And be specific."

"Lord Cornwall, although impeachment does originate in the House of Commons, the acts which His Grace the Duke of Bridgewater is accused of contain criminal implications and components. The trying of peers in the House of Lords with the appointment of a Lord High Steward if they are charged with treason or felonies is an established but infrequent feature of our government. Rather than separate the two and wait years while an impeachment and criminal case languish, we asked for your appointment to secure a consolidation of such events. We hope to dispose of these claims expeditiously."

"Lord Cornwall, if I may," said Edward Sedgwick, who was the barrister representing the dowager's supposed son. He was immaculately groomed and attired in a black suit that contrasted with his mop of hair the color of fallen leaves. His brand of slick London English was decidedly middle-class, although it was very highly polished. "The dowager duchess and her son only wish the truth to be heard. The procedure for doing so has been convoluted by Mr. Mandeville and forced through this most unusual channel because of the nature of the claim. We are perfectly happy to air our case here. Our only objection is that without the House of Commons hearing the matter, there can be no accounting to the public on this matter. After all, we must preserve the public's right to know."

Lord Cornwall's face was sour grapes and lethargy. He raised an eyebrow and wore an angry grimace that portrayed that he did not believe or care for these small men. What a bitter old goblin. "I believe that if His Grace desires quickness, then that can be achieved. And if, for lack of better term, His potential Grace seeks a record of the proceedings, we can conduct them with the presence of some of the press. Provided they are not disruptive, and the parties can agree."

Adrian stood up at his table. "This is an austere body, and the presence of the press would disturb the proceedings. To do so would potentially facilitate slander."

"So, I am in the difficult position where one asks for an indulgence and the other objects. We will compromise on the matter. I anticipate this matter only taking two days for resolution. Today, we will take testimony. It is important that no press is here so the testimony will remain untainted. However, tomorrow we can allow a limited number of the press to appear to hear your arguments and my decision."

Anxiety began to boil in Ralph's stomach. A single day to put all the witnesses in order would strain Adrian immensely. And it invited greater uncertainty. But the presence of the press, the same press who had savaged his *miliy* without regard for her well-being, turned this rancor even more poisonous and vile. His face twitched, apparently quite severely, as Lily started to caress his hands.

"This is pure bollocks. I cannot understand why they need be here to embarrass us. I have never been so furious," Ralph whispered. Hopefully, it was a whisper. It was the angriest whisper he had ever made.

"Darling, don't be afraid. They cannot hurt us if they are bound by truth," she whispered back.

"That is my precise concern."

"Well, this is a great crucible. If we come out of this, we will be tempered and hard against their assaults."

"That is true. You are too beautiful to be so wise."

"Why would you ever say that, Ralph?" Lily smiled coyly, and with that she had won his attention back from the trial.

"Because, *miliy*, God does not give with both hands." He understood the subtle language of her hand in his and the unspoken promises it held.

She drew closer and breathed into his ear as her hand squeezed his and she caressed the back of his hand with her other. "Oh Ralph, how many hands do you think it takes to satisfy your *miliy*?" She was far too enticing in the completely wrong place and wrong time. He spiraled into lusty thoughts that he knew were dangerous in such a place. And yet, he was lost in them for a few moments. He only snapped out of this arousal with a name he loathed.

"Mr. Bartholomew Edwards," Lord Cornwall intoned dryly. "Are you of sound mind and character, and do you promise to conduct yourself truthfully?"

"Of course. Yes." Mr. Edwards was an unhealthy, glowing thing, with piercing eyes and a posture that was as straight as a tower yet still seemed crooked. He was dressed in a brown coat and a plain clean shirt. He was so simple and pious looking, it appeared his advocate was trying to drape honesty over him.

"Then please approach me. I will have questions, and then your advocate and Mr. Rose will have questions. You are to answer what is asked but are not required to provide more than what is asked."

"Thank you, High Lord Steward. May I also make a statement?"

"Mr. Edwards, if there is time, I will entertain such a statement."

Edwards continued to sit straight up through the steward's questions. He explored when he had found his identity, how long he had known his lineage, and why these claims had lain dormant for so long. It was all false. What was so repugnant about Mr. Edwards, aside from presenting a threat to his family and world, was that he was an actor so convinced of his own performance, he had begun to think it was real. His delusions had so much fury behind them, he could not help but state them with a conviction that indicated truth. But it wasn't truth. It was pandering sincerity. What a disgusting man.

"I was, in truth, a disguised man for long because of the powerful jealousies this family harbors." Mr. Edwards pointed a finger at the Mandevilles in a bold gesture that appeared intended to shock them. "My mother, while believing that my father's death would place me in physical jeopardy, chose to go along with the Mandeville plot to hide me. She concealed me even from her closest servants and confidants. She knew that my inheritance would place me at odds with Mr. Mandeville and his family. And that they could insult my paternity, imprison me, have me declared mad, or…" He held his breath in a long repose, as if to draw in the ambient attention. "Worse."

"So, you mean to say the dowager duchess hid a pregnancy out of fear? And that the duke, Grayson Mandeville, hid you to protect his false claims? Why then would you wait so long? You are older, and your claim would have matured." Lord Cornwall smiled a little. Maybe the old imp enjoyed this theater?

"In the course of my education, the title was mistakenly claimed by another. That family…" He again paused to stare at Ralph, Vincent, and Sebastian. "They watched the duchess under the pretense of making provision for her and monitoring her. That family has availed itself of our rightfully bestowed titles and lands. They have aggrandized themselves in society, which is perhaps out of a sense of guilt for their knowing transgression."

Lord Cornwall arched the twin rodents he called eyebrows in interest. "So, you do not recall your path away from your mother, as you say you were too young to recall her? Why then do you possess the certainty that she is who you claim? And this detail is critical. If you cannot persuade me, I will stop this as a farce."

"Of course. After the facts concerning my heritage were discovered, they tried to discredit me through incarceration in the York asylum. It is a peculiar facet of our times that when someone contradicts power, they are labeled mad and banished. Surely, we are stronger as a people for such dissent. As Mill has written, in the marketplace of ideas, the truth shall emerge after a collision with falsehood, and truth will be stronger for the collision."

"Quoting Mill is an interesting tack, Mr. Edwards. Were you educated in such philosophy during your maturity?"

"Yes. I had the good fortune of growing up near shopkeepers and merchants who treasure such thinking. It's important to understand such things, even though I am more of a Platonist myself."

Ralph's jaw was slack and then clenched. This threatening imposter was smart enough to cite philosophers on demand. Hopefully, Adrian was wilier and more impressive than this man. Or more ruthless.

"Philosophers will not prove your case, Mr. Edwards. How did you come to know that your father was the duke and your mother the dowager?"

"A woman who was my governess and a close family friend visited me in York. She brought letters she had discovered from the dowager to the family I had been reared by. Those letters revealed the truth of my lineage. I was dubious about the matter, but after reading the letters, I started to remember details about our house in Lancashire. I remember it being remote and the journey being long. I also remembered Mrs. B. She was a housekeeper for my mother and visited me in my mother's absence. She also had a role in secreting me away after my birth."

"Mr. Edwards, you again offer me mere conjecture. Without any of those people present, there is no basis for any credibility other than your word." Lord Cornwall's impatience was a red mask that began at his neck and had begun creeping up his face.

"I thought that might be the case. And so, I brought these." Mr. Edwards rummaged through a satchel strategically hidden under the table. He produced a stack of papers bundled together with twine. "These are records from York. As you will see, I did have a visitor during that time—my family friend and governess. She came on a consistent basis. But she always insisted that she keep secret the evidence of the correspondences with me. However…" Again he paused while staring at Ralph. "I managed to steal one of them." Mr. Edwards grabbed his papers and shuffled to the Lord High Steward. An unsolicited approach of a judicial figure could be a grave slight. The expected provocation was mild but present.

"Mr. Edwards, if I have a need for anything in your possession, I will ask for it. Until then, you will remain seated. Mr. Elrich, please assist Mr. Edwards in selecting the most relevant correspondence and papers and bring only those to me for review."

Adrian interjected. "My Lord, I would ask for an opportunity to inspect those papers as well."

"In due time, Mr. Rose."

The clerk frantically tried to catch the papers cascading to the floor as Mr. Edwards burrowed through the pile. Edwards ferociously looked for the choicest morsels of detail to support his claim. When he found one, he would stick it in a pile and glower at it. After a few moments, a considerably smaller pile sat in front of the Lord High Steward. He began to review it. His sullen face stood in silent rebuke to the boisterous Mr. Edwards.

"Do you have any other facts for me, Mr. Edwards?"

"Only these—according to the genealogy of my father's line, there is a set of distinctive features possessed by the male children. We all have dark hair, are tall men, and the lobes of our ears are attached. You will see from the etching I attached the resemblance between my father and me. So, in summary, I have the trusted history of a family friend, correspondence from the house of the dowager concerning my well-being, a memory of escaping from Grandview with the help of Mrs. B, whom I had no reason to know of, and my strong resemblance to the duke. The fact that other witnesses were intimidated from attending should not discount the legitimacy of my claims."

"I will add the charges of conspiracy to the pile of accusations, Mr. Edwards. Mr. Rose and Mr. Sedgwick, it is nearly tea time, and so I ask that you keep your questions brief. I believe I have covered much of what you would in your examination."

His stomach turned and sweat poured from him at the idea of this sociopath getting more time in front of the Lord High Steward. People thought in stories. Give an idle mind enough cloth and it eventually will make a strange quilt of assumptions that seem reasonable when stitched tightly together. Even if independently the assumptions are quite unbelievable.

He was deep in thought and ignored most of Adrian's questioning, slumping into the chair and leaning into Lily. But Adrian asked a strange enough question to wake him up.

"Mr. Edwards, even if everything you say is true, is there anything criminal about ignorance of the facts? And can you prove that anyone in the duke's household had any knowledge at all of your existence?"

"The crime," Mr. Edwards began with a growl, "is that knowingly or not, I was deceived out of something that should have been mine. And in addition, I have heard from Lady Seraphina's servants that she would take any measures necessary to ensure that Grayson was seated. She desires that the peerage pass to her oldest. I think I see some of her servants seated in the gallery, and so I believe you might hear them soon enough."

"But, for purposes of clarity, you mean to say that even in ignorance, there is a crime. And you demand that, in the name of justice, a peer be punished."

"Yes," Edwards snapped, his chin tucking down and his eyes building in color and redness as if he were about to weep with rage. "It is a crime, and I am here to seek justice."

"And one more question, sir. The attestation of the records comes from Dr. Dolan's facility and is backed by his word. If we are to authenticate this document, we must believe he is credible. Is he therefore credible?"

"Your words are prose, Mr. Rose. I am educated, but you twist words like peasants wrest wine from grapes. What are you saying?"

"That if we are to believe in your records of the visitor, then we must rely on the man who runs the facility at York. If he is credible and the records are credible, you did have a visitor after all. If not, we would have no reason to believe the evidence of the visits or the letters. All we are left with is your word. So, you must choose. Is Dr. Dolan a reliable witness, or not?"

Mr. Sedgwick leapt up while appearing to sense the gambit. Ralph had not seen him so animated since the trial started. "Mr. Edwards claims no special knowledge of Dr. Dolan's character. I will also note that, like all men, the good doctor may be credible in some fashions and not others."

"Yes. But as a witness to the events, Dr. Dolan is or is not credible. Your client is permitted his opinion. In my opinion, the documents showing the visits lack credibility in their entirety. I would not be surprised that a madman would be a capable forger. After all, he has forged a fantasy potent enough—"

"Mr. Rose, you will stop—" Lord Cornwall's voice cracked, and he sat up.

"Shut it, you filthy imposter. You wouldn't know the first thing of me, you lowborn…" Mr. Edwards' snarls revealed his vulnerability to these allegations. Nothing was more dangerous than a cornered animal.

"—to bring a case before Parliament. Tell me how you did it, you common criminal. Did you make them in your putrid cell out of the—" Adrian also sat up, and his professional veneer became beastly.

Lord Cornwall was hoarse and lifted both hands as if he were a conductor. "Mr. Rose, you will stop, or I will eject you!"

"—scraps of paper the doctors would scribe of your many derangements. I'm sure they had a lot to record. Or did the doctor and his staff write them after all?" Adrian paused and stayed still. Tension lanced through Ralph's body, and to his right Vincent had gone pale.

"No! I did not make them! The doctor and his staff made them."

"And we should believe them?"

"Yes, you idiot. We should believe them."

"Mr. Rose, your outburst has disrupted my court and the decorum of the House of Lords. I will therefore allow Mr. Sedgwick to bring forth his witnesses after lunch, and you will receive only limited time for examination. And if you do this again, you will be ejected." Lord Cornwall rose, his clerks following suit and hastily adjourning. Adrian remained seated. When Ralph rose to leave, Adrian grabbed his leg and glared. Ralph observed Sedgwick and Edwards starting to exit through the door they came in.

Lord Cornwall turned and looked back at the bright room. "We stand adjourned until after one o'clock. You are dismissed." Evidently, Lord Cornwall had forgotten to adjourn his court. Although Adrian had just prevented Ralph and his family from making an unnecessary faux pas, Sedgwick had not done so for his client.

Small victories.

Chapter Thirty-One

Public restaurants or houses are interesting. They are a natural meeting place, but one should never discuss private matters within them. Even the most innocuous topics are overheard by strangers. I once noticed a woman listening in rapt fascination as I discussed the renovation of our orangery, which was, I thought, a dull conversation to eavesdrop upon.
~Aunt Penny's Advice on Living, July 1885

Lily crooked her arm through Ralph's, and they trailed after Sebastian, Vincent, and Adrian to a high-brow restaurant that only allowed them in once Vincent had dropped enough names of his Arts Club cronies to sink a small ship. Ralph held her hand tightly in an inappropriate display of affection. His resolute face was a little too rigid; it almost seemed desperate. If only she could comfort him here and now, but the words might seem forced if she said them too soon. Her chair was uncomfortable but fashionable, but she had to take the one next to Ralph. Of course Sebastian had darted ahead to sit at the head of the table. Vincent and Adrian reposed sulkily across from Lily. Adrian had made pains to not sit next to Sebastian, which had resulted in a scramble between Vincent and Adrian for the seat farthest toward the end of the table. Every part of this procedure was pedantic and fraught with barely contained tension.

"That seemed fantastic to me. Did it seem that way to you all? I always wondered why barristers were paid more than barmaids. Now I know. One drives you to drinking, the other merely supplies the gin," Vincent intoned. His nervous tone wavered as if he'd had too much wine. Apparently, he was secretly more concerned than he let on.

Sebastian winced visibly, and then replied in his most overbearing, patrician tone, "If the trial goes poorly, it is a result of a charismatic madman and not the facts themselves. I am sure our cousin has laid a trap for them. Adrian, what is your opinion?"

Adrian was visibly stunned. He had wide eyes, and his chin rested on his hand. "Mr. Edwards is wily and speaks too much. He tells so many lies or half-truths, addressing them all becomes impossible. I am glad our examination of him is over. The other witnesses should be more reliable."

Lily's hand remained nestled in Ralph's. She stroked it affectionately and cooed deliberately into his left ear. "I think that the Lord Cornwall looks like a ferret and has the temperament of a cat woken up in the middle of a good dream."

This worked. Ralph smiled and nuzzled into her a bit farther than acceptable. It was a relief, but they were in public. She glared at the rest of the table. They were shocked at the sight of the betrothed sharing even minor affections in public. She crinkled her lip and glared more, trying to stare a hole straight through them. Luckily, their averted eyes told her what she needed to know. They understood it was not the time test her. Even Vincent, who looked up after burying his nose in a small book he had been hiding, had started to see the tenderness and opened his sarcastic mouth only to be hushed.

Ralph looked at her and whispered, "Did we make a scene? I'm sorry."

She burst with a smile, and she tried to resist laughing and reassure him. "The only people who saw are not the sort to comment. They are surely too polite to do so."

The lunch dragged on, and it was harder and harder to go through the motions of a pensive lunch bereft of any female companionship. Vincent and Ralph bantered about the new house and the design, and they made an especial effort to praise Lily for her expert design. How very considerate. Vincent and Adrian discussed the fine butchery of Mr. Edwards citing John Stuart Mill, and how Mill would undoubtedly revile the idea of slander. How very boring. Albeit, it was comforting to be in the midst of something so impossibly normal. It fit her mood like an oversized glove over a sore hand. It became easy and warm. But it hurt. It still reminded her of the precariousness of her situation and her new family's vulnerability. By the time they began their journey back to the Parliament buildings, her eyes were heavy. She was ready to be done with it.

The room had been heated in their absence. A procession of women, young and old, with fresh faces touched by morning dew and old brows crinkled and cracked from furrowing, had filled in the empty spaces. They were dressed in honest garb made for durability and coarsely cleaned. Who were they? She did not recognize them, but the number of them and their presence was extremely alarming. As she turned to ask who they were, she saw the brothers grab Adrian by his shoulder and march him back to the hallway. How uncomfortable to be abandoned in the midst of a trial. She scurried back to the hall and closer to the conversation to eavesdrop. They had no right to keep these kinds of secrets.

"How did he find so many? And what on earth is their relevance to the case?" Sebastian asked as he froze. He silently waited for Adrian to speak.

"I can see no direct relevance to the facts that need be proven. Certainly, the matter of your paternity is not in question, so their opinion is probably relevant to the question of your family's motives."

She dropped to a knee and hid her face; Ralph was looking around for eavesdroppers. He scanned for a few seconds. But if they were hiding something, she could too. But this dress was large and heavy. She sighed and motioned to him with an inward wave. "Ralph, who are they?"

He strode toward her as quietly as possible, pressed a finger to his lips, and then clearly thought better of it. "There is no use in keeping it a secret much longer. My darling, those are former maids of my family. They have observed us for years in moods both decent and indecent."

Lily understood the great confidence that their family placed on servants. She also knew there were some elements of the family which could be sordid, indeed.

"Do you believe they will defame Vincent? Admittedly, the idea that he has not harassed most them like he does to dearest Olga seems unlikely."

"No. I think they are here to defame all of us, but

especially Sebastian and Mother."

Lily led Ralph back into the courtroom. The remaining maids were seated uncomfortably, and Edwards and Sedgwick were hunched over and waiting. The clerks stood next to the large desk reserved for the steward. The room grew quiet enough for light chimes from outside to fill the air.

Lord Cornwall stepped into the room without ceremony and sat in precisely the same unflattering pose he had prior to leaving. Painters must adore him, as he almost never moved and only had two facial expressions.

"Mr. Sedgwick, as we discussed, you will bring the witnesses. But the examination of these women must proceed quickly and not face the same outbursts as before. I trust you and Mr. Rose understand?"

Both barristers rose, acknowledged him, and then quickly sat. Lily relaxed and expected to disengage and focus exclusively on Ralph. This would be boring, after all.

Within moments, it was evident how critically incorrect her thoughts had been. She sat on the edge of her seat, so engrossed by the servants' recollections, she narrowly caught a few sighs from escaping her. The gossip surged through the room like verbal electricity. Ralph sat back and stifled his anger, and Vincent's eyes were wide and distraught. A few choice moments rang in her memory.

One maid, plain and young, said that "Lord Vincent prattles on about murdering a man he calls Sugar. He does this in great detail, and in the presence of ladies. He doesn't care who hears him." She said this in a seamless recitation, completely free of guile.

Another maid, older and with a broad face and hostile brown eyes, accused Sebastian of "being an immense schemer who was constantly looking in on both of his brothers. Even at an early age, I caught him practicing his speeches to Parliament. And his mother did nothing to humble him. As a matter of fact, the only time a playmate of his stood up to him, the duchess expelled him and his family. She spread falsehoods about the wife's fidelity and their title."

Lily had seen the Duchess of Bridgewater in action. Her ambition seemed redeemable only because she allied herself with the man Lily adored. She had made her share of cutting remarks and veiled threats. If the charge was that her instinct to defend and promote her family overcame proper morality, then such an accusation would be hard to disprove.

"The duchess once threatened to sabotage a rival's entrance into Eton. The young Earl of Coningsby required a specific tutor who had been hired by another household. Rather than negotiate an arrangement to share this tutor, she threatened the other family. If they would not fire the tutor, then she would personally intervene to stop their child from attending Eton."

The room grew chill again. The cold seeped through her collar and spread like an unwelcome whisper. The problem, as she saw it, was the accusations had a slight bit of truth to them to make the gratuitous ones seem plausible. But as she steeled herself for another witness, a slight, thin woman with a small face and too long a nose rose.

"Miss Quick, do you promise to tell me nothing but the truth and to conduct yourself properly in this matter?" Lord Cornwall seemed to have become quicker at this process, and he was starting to sit up.

"Of course, Your Grace."

She listened hard to the details this woman was parroting. She was forty-four and had entered service as a fourteen-year-old. Her words stung with empathy. The poor girl had spent two-thirds of her life in service and had no golden years to reflect on. But her revelation was shocking.

"What exactly did you hear thirty years ago?" Sedgwick asked, winding up like a hungry snake.

"The incident happened after Her Grace received a letter from the dowager. I know it was from her because it had the duke's seal and I could see it marked as arriving from Lancashire."

"What did Her Grace say after she read it?"

"She said that if the duchess was right and the duke was dead, that the title rightly was Lord Grayson's. She said that the duchess was alluding to other circumstances that might force Lord Grayson to show her generosity. Her Grace said she would do whatever it took to make sure Lord Grayson, as he was known before he was the Duke of Bridgewater, would get the title and that they would be protected."

"Why do you remember this so well?"

"Because I remember her saying that the duchess should be tested to see if she was with child. If there were a child, that might change things quite a bit. She seemed upset at that idea. His Grace and Her Grace caught me listening to them. I was asked to resign and provided a reference."

"Your employment was cut short because you overheard this conversation?"

"That is what makes sense to me."

"Do you think the Duchess of Bridgewater would have done anything to protect the lord's new title?"

Adrian jumped up. It was hard not be startled after his barrister leapt out of his chair. "My Lord, this is entirely speculative. This woman is providing stale evidence of an event that no other can validate or disprove."

"I will disregard her opinion on whether or not the Duchess of Bridgewater could or would do anything to protect her husband. Since it is dark and therefore inappropriate to continue to detain these women, we will adjourn until tomorrow. And to remind you, tomorrow I expect to be done with this matter. Your very limited request that the public be allowed to view these proceedings, in lieu of the House of Commons formally filing for impeachment, has been approved. However, their presence must be limited and not disruptive, even in the slightest. We will adjourn until ten o'clock tomorrow."

Thank God. Lily evanesced out of her seat, squeezed Ralph's shoulder, and began to leave as quick as her biting shoes would allow. The lights shone bright and futile against the clattering darkness. Over her shoulder, Sebastian suggested they share a coach and stop to discuss the case. Vincent insisted they go to his and Ralph's house because any other location would be a minor inconvenience. The coach ride was quiet. It was as if the trial had used up all the words in the world and people were done with talking forever.

As soon as they arrived, Vincent insisted on changing into something more leisurely. He left Adrian and Sebastian alone in the parlor. Ralph also left to change.

This was a moment for deviousness. It had become too easy for her now that she had violated many taboos. She might want to do so again with the man she loved. She crept after Ralph and gracefully lifted her dress from the floor. Thank God they had no pets to disrupt her ruse.

Ralph had discarded his jacket and shirt on to his bed and was staring at this closet when she wrapped her gloved hands around his stomach. He started like a spooked animal. She whispered, "Never turn your back on a lady," and then lightly bit his earlobe. He was warm and stood too still. When he finally turned to face her, she did not waste time. Her hands touched the trail leading from his muscled chest, to his chiseled stomach, to his belt, and his pants, and other places where only she was allowed. Her eyes were not on his face. Her gloves were pretty but difficult to remove. She finally looked up once she had visible proof that her efforts were working.

"Ralph, do you suppose your mother is a bad woman?" Lily asked honestly. She was reasonably puzzled.

Ralph's face screwed up in complete confusion. Thinking about his mother during such an intimate moment would be unfathomably difficult to do. "I do not think so. I know she is often overbearing and seems to favor Sebastian, but I am not sure she is bad. I do not believe she would hurt a child or threaten to hurt a child to help her family."

She stroked Ralph again. This time her gloves were finally off. "She appears to have threatened a family over stealing a tutor. She also appears to have spread falsehoods about other families. Is it a stretch to say she might threaten someone else?" And just like that she was staring him right in the eyes. He was aching in an uncomfortable way, and her breath was sweet and hot. And her hands were teasing.

"But that seems to equate all bad things. There is a difference between stealing a loaf of bread from a baker, stealing a loaf from an orphan, and stealing a cart full of it bound for the army. Seraphina has the sort of badness born of harshness. Like the world expected her to sit down and be quiet. To be the sort of wife who holds parties and never potency. But that is not a good reason to do a bad thing."

Lily stood up and kissed Ralph on the neck while keeping her hands in place. His breathing was deep, and she could feel him engorged through his clothes. Her hand reached farther and barely touched its intended target. Her touch made Ralph step back for a second. "I cannot imagine ever not fighting for my family." She stopped and kissed Ralph's neck again. "I would not wish to do something bad though." She reclined on the soft bed and half pulled him on top of her. But unlike his usual practice, he was far too excited to subdue his lust. "Although I want to do something very naughty right now."

His mouth was all over her dress, his hands were under it, and his member so tense and rough that it brushed against her. "I promise I would stop anything bad from happening." Her breasts were bursting out. His hands eagerly groped her. His mouth fought layers of petticoat and cloth to caress her excited wetness. She was more eager for this than she should be, almost enough to let guilt spoil this perfection. That he was so overwhelmed by her, and that someone could find them in this state drove her insane. There was something about the way a mouth fit on her aching parts that made her terribly lusty. She pushed him off and began to unfasten her adornments while smiling. Her breasts were exposed, so of course he could not stand to be away from them. "Ralph, don't worry."

Her remaining clothing fell off, and she was cold for just a few seconds. But that faded; he was quickly kissing her neck and grabbing her while positioning his molten rod to enter her aching body. "I am really nothing like your mother." She laughed at the remark and was overjoyed that her humor had not quelled his passions. And then, precisely before she would have felt him deep inside of her, she heard a crash and yelps of distress from the other room. Ralph immediately started to pull on enough garments to preserve his masculine modesty and rushed out of the room. She could do nothing but repose in the bed for a minute. She was annoyed and aroused, but eventually her intrigue exceeded her modesty. She collected herself and crept through the darkness to the other room to ascertain the source of the commotion.

Chapter Thirty-Two

There is a great power in silence. The discomfort and latent judgment of a silence can be more potent in a situation than a thousand words of condemnation. A good woman knows when to use silence to her advantage.
~Aunt Penny's Guide to Living, July 1885

After he rushed to the parlor, each breath filling him up with fear for his family's safety, Ralph dug his heels in to stop short. Any other day, this scene would make him laugh.

Sebastian had grabbed Adrian by his shirt and thrust the poised barrister against a windowless wall. In the process, he had apparently knocked loose a tray. Several items necessary for the preparation of tea were strewn across the floor like the toys of an invisible but very angry child. Adrian looked both scared and practiced. His eyes were open wide, and his hands were on Sebastian's wrist.

"And you just sat there! You just let them defame us! Those maids were not there for the trial. They were here for show! What sort of a lawyer are you? One that is not entitled to his name!" Sebastian growled.

"You mean a bunch of maids got to complain to a high lord in an empty room. And this happened right after I got Edwards to say that the doctor who will affirm that Edwards is mad is a credible witness." Adrian was angry but also prudent enough to change the subject a little.

"But what will they say in the tabloids? Those maids will have a story to tell, and they will not be bought off!" Sebastian was an angry tide. He was full of unanswered questions and irritation, and his irritation had clearly boiled over. "And you sit idly with photographic evidence that the dowager duchess was never pregnant! It is clearly an error to hire family!" Sebastian lowered Adrian as Ralph touched his arm.

"You can question my tactics only once. I tricked our opponent into agreeing that he is a madman. Since he is the primary source of these allegations, this case will be dismissed before it starts. The Lord High Steward will report to the House of Commons that there is no basis for impeachment. With no further allegations for the House of Lords, my strategy will resolve this whole thing before either house votes or hears anything." Adrian struck a confident tone despite the violence. His focused brow wrinkled in annoyance at the questioning. Of course he was—Adrian was never wrong.

"And what of the photographs, then? Explain yourself!" Sebastian's temper was still rising and ebbing.

"You mean the photographs which were illegally obtained? If used, they would invite scrutiny of ourselves and the allies who supplied them. I was hired to prove the credibility of the duke's title, not to send his heirs to prison." Adrian was a thin, unflappable flower in a torrent of anger.

Vincent wandered into the room—seemingly

agnostic about the breakage of his belongings—and made a show of sitting down with a loud and feminine sigh. He looked like one of Lily's fashionable friends after being snubbed by the most eligible bachelor at a ball.

The other men stopped and stared at the absurdity of his indifference. "Sebastian, Adrian has guided us this far, and he has found a way for our family to sacrifice little to protect ourselves. Thus far our reputation is largely intact, and our estates and titles are still fine. We can expect little more. Let us be thankful for those things." Modesty was never Vincent's strong suit. Neither was seriousness.

Sebastian withdrew into himself like a caged lion. "But you cannot think that we are escaping unscathed? After all, these accusations will be public. Those details will be public."

Ralph was the mediator, so of course he had to chime in. "All families, like all loves, face hardships. And their strength is only that of the smallest, weakest parts of them. There is nothing small or weak in our family. We will endure because we are each other's strengths, and the heavy burden of each other's welfare will make us unbreakable, not broken."

Sebastian stood agape with his hands curled in and his eyes turned dark and introspective. Despite Ralph usually being the stoic, his brothers had exercised utter restraint in the face of his outburst. "I understand. I apologize. I have never said it, but there is much pressure in being the heir. Much is expected of me. There is every chance that I will fail in what I do. I would never say it aloud, but I have always feared failure. If I fall, if I fail, then this burden will pass to you both. So I do everything I can to make sure that you will both enjoy freedoms I do not have." Sebastian paused, and his face was heavier than it ever was. He could pass the words out of his mouth only after letting them marinate in his thoughts for a few seconds. "But, and I mean no offense to you all, I had never thought that you both would be suited to the same task as me. I see now that I was wrong. You are both worthy of my burdens."

"Sebastian, we are all under pressures. Adrian is more strategic and less tactical, and as such he is probably planning to win, as opposed to worrying about minute details or egos. And you are hardly the only man to put his hands on his barrister, I am sure."

"I will brief you more if I can. This is a tricky situation to anticipate, so I have had to think more on my feet than I prefer. And now I must defeat the claims of Edwards and the intrusions of Lord Cornwall." Adrian focused on the chipped cup he was drinking from. He was avoiding any one person's gaze.

Lily had snuck into the room behind Ralph, and her feminine voice was welcome difference. "And the press, Vincent. Adrian must also defeat the reporters who will make stories out of this event." Her face was bright and angry. It was clear her recent experience as a victim of the "Gilded Lily" story was ready to bubble out of her.

"So, he must defeat a madman, a lord, and a pool of hungry sharks that smell blood in the water." Apparently, Vincent found the situation hard to make sense of, even with all the assembled intellects.

"I am a lawyer, not a magician. The madman has largely defeated himself. The lord is disinterested, and I believe he has somewhat made up his mind. There is too high a cost to imposing impeachment. He would risk that the asylums would open and a battery of new 'lords' would emerge."

Sebastian paced a little. He looked firmly at Adrian and asked, "How can you defeat a group of men who have every financial interest in the publicity of our family's dark secrets? If that is the full cost of this debacle, how can you stop it?"

Adrian finished his drink, and then got another. "In days of yore..."

Vincent groaned. He was correct to groan; oration was most unwelcome.

"In days before, there were men who claimed, as con men do, to turn lead into gold. They were called alchemists. The press takes rumors and misery and turns that dark stuff into a profit. They try to make our lead into their gold. I must figure out how to turn gold back into lead."

"I don't understand," said Sebastian.

"I think you have had too much to drink." Ralph tried to keep his voice low and concerned, but he was impatient, and it was late.

"I understand. Please go on," replied Vincent, with a smile. "How can you do that, turning gold back into lead?"

"It is easier than I thought. You must know the secret that they do not. The gold was really lead all along." Adrian then paused and cryptically withdrew to the porch with Vincent.

Chapter Thirty-Three

*There are certain things that we all agree must
exist. We all tell children of fairy tales and Father
Christmas. Justice is a fairy tale. It only exists because
we, as humanity, demand it. But we must continue to
demand justice whenever there is an injustice, and we
cannot allow it to be diminished.*
~Aunt Penny's Advice for Living, July 1885

The gallery of the hearing chamber looked like a
stained-glass painting, with row after row of faces
aligned at every angle. Pens and ink whispering on
paper were deafening as the press wrote their
impressions of the event. The sound distracted Ralph
from his important duty to his family. Lily again sat at
his right, which was a welcome comfort. The Lord
High Steward looked more nervous than Adrian.
Although his ruling had been to allow only limited
members of the public to access the proceedings, Mr.
Sedgwick had leaked word of this as far as possible.
Now most of the London press was in attendance.

"We will come to order. Regarding the claims of
Mr. Edwards against the title of the Duke of
Bridgewater, we will hear testimony from only four
witnesses today. Mr. Rose, you have brought a Mrs.
Bertram from Lancashire."

Mrs. Bertram was ruddy and sweated in the hot

room. She took a seat far away in front of Lord Cornwall and wore a practiced, patient expression. Mothers all had that patient expression in their repertoire.

Adrian began. "Mrs. Bertram, could you please describe your position and knowledge of Grandview Manor?"

"I have been housekeeper for Her Grace the Dowager Duchess of Bridgewater at Grandview Manor. I have been employed there for most of my years and have been a loyal servant." She did not stutter; she had clearly rehearsed this speech.

"Can you provide more detail of the duration of your service and the duties of the position?" Adrian continued. Ralph was more than happy to believe this would be done soon and took a moment to scan his family's behavior. Sebastian appeared entirely focused on Lord Cornwall. Vincent antagonistically looked at the crowd of onlookers. That would never do. Ralph reached out and tapped him to ward off his angry expression, and Vincent started to glare at Lily. He smiled in an attempt at silliness and levity.

"My duties," Mrs. Bertram said after clearing her throat and fanning herself, "when I was a maid included the washing of linens, assisting cook in the preparation of dinner, and running errands and fetching goods in town. I have served there around thirty-six years and served the prior duke before his untimely death."

"So, it is fair to say you have personal knowledge of the habits of Her Grace? Things like her diet, linens, size, and temperament?" Apparently, Adrian knew this path and would not delay getting there.

"Yes. I changed her linens and did her laundry. I

also brought her meals and ran her errands."

"I will be as plain as possible. Was Her Grace ever pregnant?"

"Not to my knowledge."

"It is possible it is hard to remember. Thirty years ago, before the duke died, was she pregnant?"

"No, she was not."

"And have you observed any signs of her increasing? Any change in her diet or morning sickness?"

"No."

"Any evidence in her laundry of symptoms of pregnancy?"

"I feel strange commenting on it here—"

"Please, Mrs. Bertram, so much is at stake. I apologize for your discomfort. Any signs of her pregnancy?"

"Not that I recall."

"Any changes in activity, bed rest, or doctors coming to the house to assist in delivery?"

Mrs. Bertram's face was scarlet, and her embarrassment and fatigue were palpable. "No doctors, no delivery. I have never seen her pregnant."

"And did you ever write letters on her behalf or your own to an asylum?" Adrian asked and glanced away from Ms. Bertram.

"No, I have no business doing that, and I can read, but my writing is shaky."

"Thank you, Mrs. Bertram."

Mrs. Bertram, who apparently thought she was finished, rose a little. She hesitated, looked at Lord Cornwall, and half smiling asked, "Do I have your leave, my lord?"

"I am afraid that Mr. Sedgwick may have questions as well."

She slumped back into the chair, her eyes darting to the ceiling. Obviously, the old woman was apprehensive. No servant would ever wish to endure such questions.

"Mrs. Bertram, or may I call you Mrs. B? I promise to be short and to the point. Did you know the precise date of Her Grace's wedding?"

"No, sir, I did not."

"Do you know her favorite cousin?"

"No sir, I do not."

"Can you recite her measurements?"

"Not absent a reminder, sir."

"And her favorite books and poems? Do you know any?"

"She favored *The Marble Faun*. I do not know much about poems."

"So, Mrs. Bertram, she does not share every hardship and confidence with you? She still has some secrets?" Mr. Sedgwick was insufferably smug, like a too-proud child.

"I suppose she did not tell me everything."

"And she had a private doctor and other maids as well, right?"

"But something like a child, which—" she stammered.

"Please answer only the question posed, Mrs. Bertram." He had been around condescending men before, but never a man so pretentious he laughed at his own condescension and jabs.

"Then restate the question, or move on," Lord Cornwall eagerly uttered. Perhaps he also wanted her testimony and nastiness to stop.

"Did Her Grace have a private doctor and other maids she could have entrusted with the secret of a child?" the grotesque man asked.

"She had maids and a doctor."

"And she may have said something to them?"

Adrian stood up straight. "My Lord, I am of course interested in your hearing the full facts of the case, but such a statement either way would be immensely speculative."

Lord Cornwall concurred. "I will disregard the question and any answer."

And Cornwall tilted his head after his words hung in the air for a few minutes. "Any other questions for Mrs. Bertram?"

"Only this question," said Mr. Sedgwick, with a false air of humbleness. "You said you were better at reading than writing, correct?"

"Oh yes. I write the grocery list every day I go to the market, so I get practice. But I am not a person with many correspondences, because of my family living close to me."

"I appreciate that detail." Ralph recognized the sarcastic tone and reflexively looked toward Vincent. The rake was trying to whisper something to Lily in a futile effort to inspire her to smile or laugh.

"If you do not have correspondences, have you practiced your signature much?" Sedgwick asked again. He feigned contrition.

"Not much. Writing the names of things is more important than a stylish signature in my profession."

"How do you sign your name? If you were to write a letter, for example?" The crowd seemed to tense a little. That made four questions, not one. But Sedgwick was a barrister, not an accountant.

"If it is in a document for Her Grace, a full name, printed. If it is something else, usually I sign it Mrs. B."

Vincent's eyes rolled back in his head. His eyes and tightly bunched face appeared equal parts amused and angry. He was clutching the back of the seat in front of him and smiling.

"That cannot be the best card they have? That the letters to Mr. Edwards were signed Mrs. B? Surely that is a single letter, and the mere presence of such a thing is pure coincidence?" Ralph asked Adrian.

"It is a coincidence. Or not one at all. If we believe there is a force working to frame the family, then they would know enough to sign the incriminating documents with the appropriate initial. I doubt that is a tricky thing to discern, given that Mrs. Bertram has worked at the same house for upward of thirty years." Adrian seemed confident. But then again, he seemed confident when Sebastian had punched him and thrown him against the wall last night.

"Mrs. B. So, tell me, if you had written to a person who had been confined, would you have signed the letters that way?" Sedgwick was beaming. His pleasure coalesced in his overly full grin, like a cat that had unexpectedly caught something. Kind of the way Sugar did when she caught a stuffed mouse. The look was entirely unearned.

"I did not." Mrs. Bertram was cutting her sentences shorter. Perhaps she wanted this line of questioning over.

"However, if you had, would it have been signed Mrs. B?"

"I suppose."

"I am done with the witness."

Lord Cornwall imperiously rose. "You may be dismissed, Mrs. Bertram."

Mrs. Bertram, skirt in sweaty hand, collected herself and hurried straight out of the room. Adrian put his hand out to comfort her, but she resisted and instead walked past and left. Ralph felt a bit of guilt that this trial had both forced her to travel and to potentially contradict her employer. This could jeopardize her future. What about the dowager would inspire such loyalty? But upon reflection, he understood. Mrs. Bertram did not have many options. Past a certain age, women such as her were not seen as assets to the wealthy.

"I have three more witnesses, Mr. Cartwright, Dr. Dolan, and Mrs. Edwards. Please instruct them to be ready, as I will require time to deliberate after their testimony." Lord Cornwall was even in tone and projected a sense of certainty that this could be done today. There was a hum of busy pens and the occasional whispered question in the gallery above. Mr. Cartwright approached the witness box. He had a dignity about him as crisp as a starched collar, and his wreath of aging hair was wispy fog trying hard to grow long enough to obscure his eyes.

"Mr. Cartwright," Lord Cornwall began. "In the interest of expediency, I will ask you to confirm what Mrs. Bertram said. Did you ever observe any indication of pregnancy from Her Grace during your tenure?"

"I did not." Mr. Cartwright was not quiet, but he was far from loud. His accent was hard to place. "And what's more, Mrs. Bertram knows everything about that house. The missu—er, Her Grace, would not hide her pregnancy from her, much less from me and her physicians."

"So, it is your contention that the allegations are false then?" Lord Cornwall asked, leaning his face against his fingers.

"It's no contention because it's the case. Her Grace and the duke discussed the matter of a child but believed that such would be easier after the war. So, you see, it's not possible that this fellow could be her son."

Lord Cornwall snapped to attention, and Sedgwick sat up, wide-eyed and defensive. "You mean to tell me that Her Grace acknowledged she was not pregnant?"

Mr. Cartwright nodded, crooking his eyes a little. "Before he left, the duke asked about that. He wanted an heir, and she informed him that they had not conceived. So like Mrs. Bertram said, it is not possible, unless she was wrong."

"Do either of you have questions? I imagine Mr. Sedgewick will." Lord Cornwall cleared his throat.

"I do. Mr. Cartwright, the dowager duchess is not here, correct?" Sedgwick started without asking permission.

"I do not see her." Obviously, Mr. Cartwright disapproved of Mr. Sedgwick.

"So, she cannot say what she said and did not say? But we are just supposed to believe you."

"I don't care if you believe me. It's true. And this is all a farce."

Lord Cornwall intervened, which was unfortunate because it was quite entertaining to see the patrician grumpiness of Cartwright facing down the arrogant Mr.

Sedgwick. "This is a proceeding of Parliament inquiring about the necessity of an impeachment. It is not a farce. I command decorum be observed."

"My pardon, Lord Cornwall," Mr. Cartwright said, never changing the direction of his angry gaze.

"Thank you, Lord High Steward. So, she cannot speak for herself, and you have taken it upon yourself to speak for her? As a servant?" Sedgwick trailed off disdainfully.

Although the trial was interesting, it was important to focus on the gallery. The hungry blank faces watched with glee. This was all a show. Ralph had once watched a man dip a cow's head into a piranha tank and had seen the fish devour the gross thing until only bone remained. That image plagued him today. It was just entertainment to them. Their rise and fall was just a device to get money. Maybe Cartwright was right. Maybe it was a farce. Sebastian and Vincent were fixed and staring at the witness and Adrian, respectively.

By the time Ralph returned his gaze to the witness box, a stocky man with a ginger beard and glasses with reinforced frames sat there. His coat was expensive but practical and had a fresh set of dew on it, as if he had come urgently.

"Dr. Dolan." Adrian addressed him before he asked, "Was Mr. Edwards a patient under your care in the York Insane Asylum?"

He leaned toward the Lord High Steward. "Yes, he was and is a patient under my care. I must state that I strongly believe he is not what he alleges. I believe he is a vulnerable man who is being manipulated."

"What is the basis of this belief, Dr. Dolan?" Adrian asked, appearing to mirror the doctor's placid demeanor.

"Many personal meetings and a diagnosis based on empirical observations. He has previously believed himself to be related to the former king. His mind is sharp. As he acquires additional information, that information becomes part of his delusion."

"How did you diagnose Mr. Edwards as insane?"

The whole room held its breath. The silence made the billowing wind outside seem terribly ominous.

"Mrs. Edwards, his mother, brought him to the insane asylum in a teary mess. She said he had rejected his father and mother and claimed he was the rightful heir to the throne. He also claimed that someone had been leaving him secret messages. She could not find any of them. She asked that I speak to him. After I confirmed his delusions and the fact that his temper was somewhat dangerous, I began a regime of treatment. I have, along with my staff, cared for him for several years."

"So, his delusions have changed over the years?" Adrian asked him.

"Yes, and the specificity of these is most striking. I know he on occasion receives visitors, and after those visits, he is very animated. That is fairly normal for patients though."

"And these delusions are very particular?"

"Yes, but my belief is the information was being sent to him. I cannot forbid a visitor unless the patient exhibits violent behavior. And in this case, there was no violent behavior. Had I known that the visits were encouraging these delusions, I would not have tolerated them."

"So once more, to be very clear, Mr. Edwards is

delusional, and he is not related to Her Grace, the Dowager Duchess of Bridgewater?"

"Mr. Edwards is the child of Mrs. Edwards, not Her Grace. He has delusions and believes he is a person he is not. Depending on what he has recently seen, that identity can shift. It is my belief that something made him choose this identity."

"And recently a woman came to remove him from the asylum, correct?" Adrian asked. He was staring at the gallery instead of Dr. Dolan.

"I refunded Mrs. Edwards' payments, and a woman came to check him out. I do not see that woman here today."

"Thank you, Dr. Dolan. Those were my questions." Adrian started to whisper to Lily and made her blush. This caused a little jealousy, so Ralph squeezed her hand tighter.

"Dr. Dolan, are you a genealogist?" Sedgwick started. He stood up to do this questioning.

"No, I am not."

"Have you examined the family records of the Dowager Duchess of Bridgewater and Mrs. Edwards?" Sedgwick was clearly scheming, but Lily was more important. Ralph drew closer to her.

"No, I have not."

"And so," Sedgwick said, sitting back down, "you have no familiarity with whether or not Mrs. Edwards or the Dowager Duchess of Bridgewater ever had children."

"Is that a question? No, and it is not customary practice to conduct a survey of a family before—"

"Please just answer yes or no. So, you do not know for a fact that Mrs. Edwards gave birth to Mr. Edwards or the truth of whether Her Grace ever had children?" Sedgwick's condescension was so potent it seeped into the air and hung.

"No, I do not."

"And is your ignorance of such facts equal?"

A sharp inhale swept across the room right after the insult. Apparently, there were still certain things one does not do to doctors.

"I do not know either."

"You stated that Mr. Edwards received visitors. Are these documents an accurate accounting of those visits?" Mr. Sedgwick brandished the visitor's book at Dr. Dolan.

"That is our visitor's log. If there is a false entry, that is the fault of the person putting a name in there falsely."

"So, unless it is a lie, then we can rely on the logs?"

"As I stated, they are only as reliable as the people who write their names in the book."

"So, in summary you do not know Mr. Edwards' parents, the contents of your own visitor's log, or any relevant information regarding Her Grace?"

"I do know that the man you represent is mad, that someone has directed that madness, that his mother brought him to me for help, and that if I were the sort of person to convince a madman they were a secret noble, I wouldn't give my real name in the visitor's log."

Lord Cornwall chimed in. "I think that is sufficient from Dr. Dolan. Thank you, Dr. Dolan. You may leave."

As Dolan exited, Adrian caught him by the arm and whispered something to him that resulted in a frown. There was an uneasy whirling in Ralph's head after the questioning. However, Lord Cornwall seemed content in his judgment that the doctor was credible. He needed to be close to Lily. He put his hand under Lily's back and stroked her side. She leaned into him.

"What is wrong, my dear? You seem upset?"

Lily half pouted in the way that was very childish but endearing.

"What did Mr. Rose say to make you blush?"

"Oh, that he thinks that Mr. Cartwright may have, to be kind, had a secret desire for Mrs. Bertram based on how defensive he became."

"Oh, that is all?"

"Yes, what did you think it was? I doubt Mr. Rose has the capacity for salaciousness. His sister took the wit and humor out of that family."

"People say that about Vincent too. But I will learn to make you laugh, if you want."

"Oh no, Ralph. You do many things I like a great deal more." Lily pursed her lips in a flirtatious pout. Ralph was so overcome with those lips that he failed to notice Mrs. Edwards enter.

Chapter Thirty-Four

Love is not the same as glory. It will require devotion and endurance, and even when requited, it can contain long bouts of pain with no promise of elation. Love must be a labor, elsewise it is merely pleasure playing a trick on the mind.
~Aunt Penny's Advice on Living, July 1885

Lily was as lethargic as a panting cat. Her deflated posture sank with boredom and fatigue, but she needed to remain awake. Last night had turned out to be unexpectedly passionate, with numerous risings and quakes. As usual, after she and Ralph coalesced into a nest of satisfied serpents, entangled in blankets, limbs, and sweat, she had stayed awake for long while. So, of course this procession of highborn and lowborn people being questioned in front of a crowd was boring by comparison. She had twice caught her hands adjusting her corset and all-in-one from the horrible heat.

Ralph's little jealousy created a storm of upset and amusement. She loved him and did not want any sense of disloyalty to come from her actions. On the other hand, laughing at a stray remark was not a big transgression. She laughed at Vincent quite often. But to be fair, people thought she was marrying Vincent. It was hard to escape, considering he made her laugh and she tolerated his ribald humor.

"Mrs. Edwards, is Mr. Edwards your son?" Lord Cornwall cut straight to the quick. Lily strived hard to smother a smile. This old curmudgeon was probably a bit afflicted by the heat as well. His wig probably smelled of death.

"Yes. Of course. My tiny Bartholomew. My Batty. He is my son. And to the Mandevilles, I am so sorry for this accusation." Her guilt and pain were so palpable. Lily's eyes swelled with mournful dewdrops. This woman's first instinct in the butcher shop when she had met her was to express fear and shame. Her face was a mixture of humiliation and guilt. She was staring across the room and naming her son a madman. He was disclaiming her parentage and claiming to be a noble. The pain shone dark on her face. What impossible demands were made of mothers.

"So, why was he in the York Asylum? Why did you commit your own child to the asylum?" Lord Cornwall appeared genuinely interested.

"He believed he was the son of the king. He had told a number of our neighbors and friends. I thought…" She took a second to breathe and blink. "I thought he would grow out of this, get older, and be decent. But he didn't. He would read about the queen and king, and then he would say that he had been party to their privacy and that the stories were wrong. When people were nasty about the queen, he would become angry. And if I tried to tell him, 'you are my son,' he would tell me I was lying." She began to actively tear up as she looked across the room. Mr. Edwards looked defiantly toward her, with eyes like tiny beady daggers. Lily's sympathy for his madness ignited into anger.

"Do you wish to address your son?" Lord Cornwall

asked.

"What did they tell you, Batty? Who did this to you? Please come back. The doctor promised he will keep trying to help you. I am begging you, little boy, come back."

"Lord High Steward, I beg your pardon. I ask that such questions be disregarded as they are from one witness to another. May I ask Mrs. Edwards a question?" Sedgwick was tight, controlled, and speaking through his teeth.

"Only for a moment, Mr. Sedgwick," Lord Cornwall added, red faced and full of heavy breaths.

"Mrs. Edwards, did you bring the register of your county or church with you?" Sedgwick asked. His voice strained to perform after a day of harsh questioning.

"What's that? Register? I do not know what you're talking about." Of course Mrs. Edwards would be confused. Rural bureaucracy was not her forte.

"A registry of births is a book that all births in a county should be recorded in. Sometimes a church makes a record of the birth instead. Did you bring those records?" Sedgwick cocked his head at the gallery and looked pleased with himself. How detestable! To beam like a proud puppy at your own cruelty!

"No, why would I? You expect me to steal that? What sort of idiot are you?" Mrs. Edwards was not a mother to be reckoned with.

"Mrs. Edwards, I have stated it already, but decorum cannot be breached. Please refrain from such names, or I will have you escorted out." Lord Cornwall had turned a paler, more patrician color. Probably because of the occasional blast of chilly air from the cracking windows and walls.

"I apologize, my lord."

"Anything further?"

"So just to be clear, we do not have anything but your word on the heritage of Mr. Edwards?" Sedgwick asked, louder than before.

"No, only my words and tears."

"And who paid for your passage here? Who paid for your lodgings? Was it the Mandevilles?" Sedgwick feigned a serious tone and narrowed his eyes on Mrs. Edwards.

"I paid for it myself, on account that this is my responsibility," Mrs. Edwards answered, trembling and clearly unhappy with the question. Sedgwick's mouth drew tight, as this was obviously not the answer he thought he would hear.

Adrian rose and looked at Lord Cornwall. "Lord High Steward, is it possible that I ask two questions?"

"Two is two more than I am inclined toward, but I ask that you make them fast."

"Mrs. Edwards, did you pay the asylum for many of Mr. Edwards's necessities even after he had refused to acknowledge your parentage?" Adrian sat up as straight as possible. Lily reflexively adjusted her own posture and remembered her station. But she didn't like it.

"Yes, I did. As a matter of fact, they sent me my money back after he left."

"And do you still love your son, in spite of this great hardship?"

"He is my son." Mrs. Edwards fought her weeping, although her homespun collar and dress were tense with tears and sweat.

Lord Cornwall cleared his throat, probably more

for effect than for coping with heat. "Mrs. Edwards, you are dismissed with the thanks of Parliament." The clerks listened closely to Lord Cornwall, and then began to unlock the back doors to the room. "Witnesses are dismissed. Messrs. Rose and Sedgwick, you may both make a brief closing statement."

Sedgwick rose like an eager weasel and proclaimed, "I will go first and…" He paused. "I will also be brief."

Lord Cornwall stared, and for a second his eyes shut and he looked like he would faint. But he did not. How unfortunate.

"This is going to be so ridiculous I will need to stifle Vincent's laughing. May I borrow a fan or your bag?" Ralph asked with a whisper. His smile was a little too wide and a little too toothy, either giddy with fear or supreme confidence.

"I suppose you could shove my handkerchief in his mouth. Make sure his bile does not get on the embroidery." She mirrored Ralph's nervous smile.

"I think Vincent's bile could get on it even if it were still in your bag."

"I love you. This is going to be fine."

Chapter Thirty-Five

Uncertainty is a plague. To labor in the name of something great or harsh with certitude but not certainty is the nature of life. But to demand that others spend their short lives in the twilight of your indecision is pure sadism. My advice is to both decide quickly and apologize even more quickly when one is wrong.
~Aunt Penny's Guide to Living, July 1885

"This hearing was conducted to ascertain whether there is a basis for convening the House of Commons on the subject of the Duke of Bridgewater's impeachment. The question is whether there is reason to believe the word of a man who some have labelled mad out of spite. Whether to believe his documents and his convictions. Or whether we should believe the chasm of nothing that has been brought out to contradict it." Sedgwick stood with both hands on the desk, like he was shoving down his expanding ego. "Mr. Edwards has stated his professed heritage, provided proof he was in contact with members of Her Grace's household, and illustrated that there is no credibility to the story of Dr. Dolan or the people arrayed against him. But take a step back. This is an ancillary proceeding. This is not designed to prove to a certainty his identity. It is to decide whether there is enough proof to allow the House of Commons to consider this case. And so, the question we must ask is whether the allegations have been so thoroughly refuted that it is the Lord High Steward's opinion that they do not merit deliberation in the specific body designed to accomplish such a task."

A tremor of fear ran through Lily. Her stomach tightened and clenched under her dress, and her shoulders tensed. This was hardly a surprising argument. "Doesn't that favor his side quite a bit?"

"That is probably why he is addressing that instead of his own case," Ralph replied quietly.

"First, Mr. Edwards truthfully stated his whereabouts, his history, and his basis for his allegations. He never hid anything. He then provided evidence that a Mrs. B had been writing him while in the asylum. We know from Mrs. Bertram's testimony that she signs her letters Mrs. B. He has provided evidence of visits to deliver such letters. Unless it is the allegation of the Duke of Bridgewater that there is a conspiracy to dupe Mr. Edwards into this belief, then it is sincere. It is motivated by the facts.

"Second, there is not any credible evidence against this claim. Ms. Bertram and Mr. Cartwright are servants. Both of them demonstrated ignorance of elementary facts about Her Grace. They might believe a claim against Her Grace's estate would put them out of work. Dr. Dolan performed no investigation of the parentage of Mr. Edwards, and yet he somehow expects to be an authority on the matter of his lineage. And Mrs. Edwards could not muster a single witness in support of her claim that she was indeed his mother. The duke has every opportunity to procure witnesses to my client's adolescence and Mrs. Edwards' claims.

They could have prepared a genealogical record. They have not done so. I do not believe it is because Mr. Rose is a bad barrister..." He paused in thought and turned to face Adrian.

Adrian was biting his cheek.

"Instead I think it is because they cannot do so. Because Mr. Edwards is telling the truth. And this leads me to my final assertion. The duke made this a political matter. Rather than let the trial proceed as a civil matter, he claimed the privilege of his peerage and made it a question for Parliament. They chose that path. And if they want this matter to go Parliament, why shouldn't it? If the House of Commons is the appropriate place for these allegations to be heard, then why are they fighting so vigorously against that happening?

"In summary, the question is still in dispute, and the facts are still being uncovered. Since the House of Commons is the appropriate body for finding those facts—which position Mr. Rose agrees with—I ask this simple thing. Let them decide whether the impeachment is warranted on its own terms. Thank you for your service, Lord Cornwall."

Sedgwick sat down next to Mr. Edwards. Adrian stood next to the Mandevilles and then paced toward Lord Cornwall. The air was perfectly still, like an early morning. After that, Adrian started to pour his words into the complete silence.

"Dignity is costly. And this matter concerns nothing more than dignity. The dignity of the Duke of Bridgewater in facing this accusation. The dignity of Mr. Edwards in alleging such a great conspiracy. The dignity of the House of Commons in hearing such a case. And then there is the dignity that has been lost. Mrs. Edwards confessed her son's illness. The Duchess of Bridgewater faced rumors and accusations. The Mandevilles have stood up to a mountain of accusations. Dignity is costly.

"The price of levelling these allegations is next to nothing. To state that you are a wronged noble costs only the air in your lungs. That is the case no matter how false the claim. And once it is stated, it becomes rumor, intrigue, and gossip. And that is halfway to making it true in the eyes of many. But Parliament is more than gossip and intrigue. Truth is more than gossip and intrigue. Mr. Sedgwick and Mr. Edwards have stated that to stop these allegations, that we must provide evidence of every minute of Mr. Edwards' life. They have reversed the burden in our system.

"But an accuser must prove his accusation." Adrian pointed his stony face at Lord Cornwall and persisted. "And even after his doctor travels here to call him mad, and his mother pleads with him to come home, they cry they need more proof. Even after the Dowager Duchess of Bridgewater's own servants state she was never with child, they cry out that they need more proof. Even when they, by their own admission, offer none.

"And so, I ask you to reflect on what Mr. Edwards said yesterday. He said you should believe Dr. Dolan. That Dr. Dolan was credible. And Dr. Dolan stated that Mr. Edwards is deluded. Dolan said Mr. Edwards is insane. Unless there is ample evidence to contradict him, this is a simple matter to resolve. Mr. Edwards is not the Duke of Bridgewater. Her Grace the Dowager Duchess had no children. And if she had, she could easily prove it herself. Or Mr. Edwards could have provided evidence of it from a county or church registry." Lily couldn't help as a warm grin spread across her face. This remark seemed specifically designed to irritate Sedgwick for his ridiculous claims about Mrs. Edwards not having those same types of documents.

"Reflect for a moment on the outcome of this case if we allow it to go to the House of Commons. Imagine the great asylums emptying. Imagine the great march of princes and queens in waiting that shall come to Parliament. Each will claim that they are like Mr. Edwards. Every one of them will say they had a secret visitor who whispered to them of their hidden greatness. And then, armed with nothing but a stack of assumptions, they will each command an audience. They will cause a scandal and call into doubt the very basis of our government. To let this matter go forward with no proof would be to render the whole of our country susceptible to the claims of the mad. It would replace prudence with chaos and truth with gossip.

"And so, I ask you to dismiss this matter. Not only for the good of the Mandevilles and Mr. Edwards and Parliament. But for the good of the multitude who are seeking to profit from publicizing this unfortunate event." In a breach of decorum, Adrian spun to face the people seated behind him, the reporters from London's most highly circulated papers. He stared at the absorbed faces of the people writing down his words. Great anger was written on his brow in premature wrinkles.

"To get to this point, there had to be money. Mr. Sedgwick does not work for nothing. There had to be an accuser, propped up with letters designed to manipulate the delusions of a madman. There had to be someone to send rumors and innuendo to these people who have defamed the Mandevilles. If the impeachment is voted on, then it will go to the House of Lords for a trial—the House of Lords where the Duke of Bridgewater is very well liked—and the matter would be resolved by a majority vote.

"Only then, it will not be gossip. It will be a legal fact that the accusation is false. Which means that actively propagating it will be defamation. And that every person and institution that profited from reporting or publishing these matters will be liable to the Mandevilles for any damage to their reputation. And that if, Heaven forbid, someone orchestrated this matter to damage that family or commit a fraud, then under the laws of conspiracy every person to publish these allegations in furtherance of that goal would be an accomplice. They would lose their wealth and go to jail. And from what I hear, the Mandevilles have a very eager attorney."

The assembled press gathered their things and clutched them as tight as possible. Adrian held his gaze toward them until he individually glared at every reporter he could. Lily felt guilt sting for a second; it was hard not to enjoy their vulnerability, since the people who had profited from her private pain were probably up in that gallery.

"I will adjourn until I have decided the matter. You may remain in the room, or you may leave. But if you depart, it is not my duty to remind you that this tribunal will convene to deliver a decision." Lord Cornwall appeared halfway out of the room before Mr. Sedgwick interjected.

"But, Lord Cornwall, do you know when you will

finish your—" he stammered. He appearing to vainly grasp for some idea of how long he could escape the sauna and icebox of the people and the case.

"I do not, and I would encourage the parties to remain."

"I understand."

Lily lifted herself up, and Ralph embraced her with abandon. They walked arm in arm out the cracked doors. She used to be conscious of such public affections. But given the pedigree and intensity of the scandals they were leaving behind in the room, this light thing was of small importance. And it was impossible to care what villains thought anymore.

"How do you believe he will decide, Ralph? I have my own ideas on the matter." Ralph would keep his opinion sequestered unless she pressed him.

"What are your ideas, Lily?" Ralph looked forward and cocked his head quickly toward her, as if he only remembered after the fact that she was there at all. How troubling.

"I think that Mr. Edwards did not do his case any favors. I believe that Adrian was correct about the burden of proof, and he was right that the burden was not carried. Also, Mrs. Edwards was very convincing. As was Dr. Dolan."

"I hope you are right. I think that their intention is that the matter goes to Parliament. In which case we still win. But it is very public, and we must rely on the kindness of the peerage." His voice was quick and soft. Obviously, he did not enjoy what he was saying.

"But then we win. If we agree that it is likely we prevail, then why all the melancholy?"

"Because it is not, in my mind, a case that should

have been a close call. Her Grace the Dowager not appearing, the letters, and the arguments about other things we should have done—they all point to an ulterior motive." Ralph's arm held fast to her, and they stopped about a block away. Any of the press that had been nearby had been lost in their journey. They were just two lovely people again. She could breathe again. The cooler air tasted like crisp apples compared to the courtroom's alternating heat and chill. It was still warm from the July heat, but it was not nearly as hot as that dreadful, inconstant room. Hopefully, she could forget it soon.

"You know, I am glad we are to be married. A single person's optimism is like a ray of light. It can be bright or dim, but it is solitary. But love is like a mirror to that light. It multiplies it. So everything can be bright when we are together." Ralph smiled at her, so overfull of kindness and love. It was hard not to demand they return to their comfortable, lusty bed.

"How poetic. You must have been thinking of that for some time." Lily smiled deviously, trying so hard to make her thoughts known without saying them.

"I was inspired. I could not help it. You do that to me, *miliy*."

"Oh, Ralph, I do hope this is your real opinion. If it is not, and we are facing harder times, and your family needs more of you, please tell me that. I couldn't tolerate the notion that you would resent me later for not persisting with your family in a cruel and difficult situation." He needed to be as close as possible when she said this to him. She knew him. If he were lying, then his breath would catch, and his heart might speed up.

"I do not think this is the end. I think that the machinery of Parliament is designed to stop this sort of accusation. I also think that Adrian would have instructed us differently if that appeared likely." His breath was still even, but his heart racing. His hands were on her back, and she saw his face descending passionately toward hers.

"The steward is back. Let us reconvene." Of all the times for Vincent to drolly interject! His pale face and heavy breath indicated he had jogged to find them. The idea of Vincent being made to run, in the heat, in a suit, only to find them embracing, was humorous enough to dull her irritation.

The three journeyed back to the room with barely a word between them.

Chapter Thirty-Six

*Hold tight to your reputation, as without a good
name the world can be cold and cruel.*
                    ~Aunt Penny's Advice on Living, July 1885

"You have asked me to destroy a great family and
flood our system with so many disputes that I would go
to my grave before they were adjudicated. I have never
seen such a crass display of unfounded accusation and
impertinence in my life. In making a ruling on a case
such as this, it is important not to substitute my
judgments for those of my peers. The system of peerage
and our Parliament make the proper route for such a
dispute a formal vote in the House of Commons and a
trial in the House of Lords. And that is the normal
course for a reason. It is a political matter, and
resolution by the political branch of our government
makes sense."

She leaned into Ralph and smiled. This long hard
road had led to a more peaceful place.

Lord Cornwall had paused to collect his thoughts,
and then he expounded again. "And although there are
questions that have not been answered, it is my belief
that the House of Commons would not vote for
impeachment. The House of Lords, where, as Mr. Rose
has pointed out, the Duke of Bridgewater is extremely
well liked, would not vote to impeach him no matter

what. And that is perhaps the great folly of this charade. We may never know the truth of the allegations. But even if I allowed these allegations to be voted on, we would not know the truth. What you see here may be a grave injustice. It may be justice personified. That is the nature of power. Those that see it and wield it are not neutral, and any matter involving a peer is one of power. What is more—" Lord Cornwall stopped to catch his breath, staring directly at Mr. Edwards and his attorney. "If I let this matter go forward, I would live every day in the company of those peers whose slander I facilitated. I would see the lives I placed in jeopardy by making it an easy thing to impeach them. Our system is not built for the remedy of social ills and injustices or for revolutions. These allegations ask too much of Parliament and too much of me with too little evidence to back them."

Adrian grabbed Sebastian by the arm, and both men obviously pleased to the point of giddiness. Their smiles shone, bright and clean, like new Easter bonnets.

Lord Cornwall appeared to be nearing the end of his ruling. His tone became darker, and his delivery was hurried and stumbling. "The allegations have little chance of success in either House, and the impeachment of a lord on such evidence would be an imprudent use of our limited resources. I rule that the allegations are unproven, and that the matter should be disposed of without further deliberations by either House. Although the House of Commons could, independent of this ruling, vote on the matter, I ask you to remain aware this ruling is to be written and circulated to them. If it is raised, they will know that the House of Lords shall likely reject it." Lord Cornwall rose again, and his clerks flanked him. "We stand adjourned."

The courtroom simmered like a fuse, sputtering with suppressed words and the occasional scowl. But after the clerks and Lord Cornwall left, the room boomed. Sebastian, Adrian, and Vincent walked slowly toward the door. They brushed away any questions from the press. Sebastian wore a wavering scowl. Clearly, he had to exercise restraint in front of them. Lord, he walked like a politician already. God save him. Ralph closed the gap, rushing impolitely, then grabbed Lily by her arm and whisked her from the aisle to the door. He looked in her eyes, and his smile was wider and lighter than ever. There was a vigor in him that had been absent for days, and she stirred in response.

"I want us to go. I want this moment frozen, so we never lose it. But we also never have to come back to it. Will you help me hurry?"

She beamed back and laughed. She wanted to leave more than anything she had ever wanted in her life. "I have rarely run in slippers, but I will try."

Chapter Thirty-Seven

When choosing a gift for your husband or father, a good bottle of Scotch whisky is truly the best gift. Of course, most ladies are not privy to enough knowledge about whisky to make an informed decision. But Aunt Penny is here to help you. First and foremost, make sure you have proper Scottish whisky. I am certain Wales and England make a fine whiskey, but the Scots have perfected the technique. Second, most refined gentleman will prefer a lowland whisky. And finally, one must observe the whisky in the bottle. It should be liquid amber, free from any debris or cloudiness.
~Aunt Penny's Advice on Living, August 1885

Ralph's townhouse felt uncomfortable on the eve of his wedding to Lily. His brothers and friends had gathered to celebrate, but the night was sedate. Amesbury, Barton, Southampton, and Adrian were invited for whiskey, cards, and discussion. It was amusing to think that masculinity could be distilled into flimsy things like paper cards and glass bottles. Due to Barton and Southampton's presence, they could not discuss the Shadow Society or the Black Swan. But a banal evening with polite conversation was quite a relief after the exhausting summer.

Earlier, Ralph had picked up the jewelry he commissioned for Lily. He had ordered it before the lawsuit was a looming threat, but he held off giving it to her. Now, he could give it to her and have no attachment of memory to the trial. They would only have happy memories of their wedding and marriage. Hopefully, this nightmare was finally over, and they could live in peace. If not peace, simply happiness. Although, maybe he should pretend he had an illness, so he could have a month in his bed with Lily.

"This is excellent scotch. Where is it from?" Sebastian asked.

"The Marquess of Annadale has a distillery on his estate. I believe Annadale also has an abundance of heather that perfumes the air and adds a depth of flavor to the whiskey," Amesbury answered elegantly.

"I taste a smooth honey in it. It is truly delicious. Congratulations on your wedding, Mandeville," Southampton said while raising his glass at Ralph.

"Thank you. I am the happiest man in all of history." Ralph knew he sounded like a simpleton, but he was the most eager groom the world had ever known. Eager and less sober than ever, where the haziness pleasantness started to make him giggle.

"Is it true that Lily is refusing to see the queen?" Barton asked.

Ralph flinched. "Lily has not informed me that she refuses, but I have not asked. I believe Lily has already met with the queen and that should suffice." What an unfortunate topic.

"I don't understand. Why would Lily not wish to meet with the queen? If she enjoys Lily, then you both will be invited to events hosted by her." Southampton shook his head.

"Because Lily will always stand by her friends.

The queen has decided to ostracize Lady Olivia, and therefore Lily has decided to snub the queen right back. And she is absolutely correct," Vincent blathered.

"I had not heard Lady Olivia was ostracized. It is unfortunate for her but excellent for me," Southampton quipped.

"How does it benefit you?" Barton asked.

"Lady Olivia is so beautiful and very desired. The ambitious men will no longer court her." Southampton gestured to Rose. "Am I correct?"

"Unfortunately, yes. Although I do not believe she would have settled for a mere gentleman," Rose answered.

"And so, as a duke I will be a wonderful match for her. She can have all my resources for her agenda. It's not likely that anyone will try to strip my title or lands because my wife is a suffragette," Southampton concluded.

"Do you not have ambitions?" Sebastian asked.

"What could I possibly want that the queen could bestow? I am a duke. I own five estates, one of which is a castle. My life is a storybook, except I am missing the thin blonde bluestocking I desire. The queen is never going to be able to give me more than what I have. I could want to be prime minister, but I truly believe that it is better to be friends with the prime minister than to be the man himself," Southampton lectured.

The duke's words were powerful and hung in the air. While the queen could discourage people from trusting him with their money, she did not have much power over him. If the cost was sufficiently high, the queen might quietly let this debacle go and allow Olivia to be invited to events. Especially if Olivia married a duke.

"Well, regardless of the queen and her anger, I will be vowing to honor Lily. Therefore, I will abide by her wishes. Olivia was fiercely loyal to our family during our time of need, and only a coward would refuse to stand by her now." His bride deserved his loyalty above all others.

"Oh dear, Ralph called Mother a coward," Vincent teased.

"Mother does not want to stand by Olivia? But Olivia warned us of the suit and braved an asylum for us! How could she do that?" Ralph asked.

"Mother desires a prime minister for a son," Vincent answered and gestured toward Sebastian. "And oddly enough, Ralph, he happens to look like our eldest brother."

"Somehow it always comes back to me. I wish she would trust me to manage my own life," Sebastian murmured into his glass.

"Cut the leading strings. Now that the season is over, Ralph and Lily will be in Norfolk. Move in here," Vincent offered.

Ralph took a step back. Was this real or was the whiskey that strong? He may never recover from the shock of Vincent's words. How strange; a glimmer of hope that his brothers would be friendly. But for Vincent to invite Sebastian to live with him was amazing. This hope needed fostering. "Absolutely! It is a great house for a bachelor."

Sebastian considered the offer. "Very well."

"Wonderful. And now I have a gift for Ralph." Vincent presented Ralph with a small box.

Inside laid a pair of gleaming cufflinks, adorned

with enameled lilies. "Thank you, Vincent."

"Well, that is not the gift. I spoke to Barrowman, and we decided he will be your valet. But he will assist in finding a replacement valet. So, I have given you the most important woman and most important man in your life. Kiss them both for me. With similar passion," Vincent said with a grin.

"Thank you!" Ralph hugged his brother sincerely. He knew the sacrifice Vincent had made for him.

"I have no idea who Barrowman is, or what is going on, but I would love more whiskey." Southampton shook his glass. Of course, the duke was quite accustomed to having things appear for him through mere invocation.

"It can be difficult to be friends with brothers. I believe Adrian and I are the only two here without a brother," Barton said as Amesbury poured more whiskey.

"Yes. As a man who has lived with three women all my life, I have some advice for you, Ralph. Choose your battles wisely. There will come a time where Lily feels very strongly about something. And trust me, just give it to her. Also, never use the words 'reason' or 'logic.' From what I have heard, that is how men silence women and control them. Unless she is truly behaving like a madwoman, simply listen to her arguments and if her intended actions will not harm anything, agree," Adrian pontificated.

"That was a verbose way to say the old axiom 'Happy wife, happy life,' " Southampton said, grinning as he tried to mimic common wisdom. "But Rose is correct. Even my lovely sister Aurelia can be passionate about things I have no interest in, and it is better to simply give her what she thinks is best. Women typically have formulated arguments in advance of a discussion and will rapid fire at you."

"How is Aurelia?" Sebastian asked.

Southampton shook his head and ran his hand through his hair, clearly distressed. "I believe you were all at the garden party I hosted earlier this summer?"

The men all nodded. Ralph bit deeply into his lip. What a fond memory. It was the afternoon Lily tried to seduce him. And it had inspired the purchase of their townhouse.

"I had the unfortunate experience of overhearing a couple of so-called gentlemen discussing my dear sweet sister, who is only seventeen. I have been present for a distastefully long conversation about the size and taste of her bosom. I have found it harder to tolerate my own gender with every passing comment. She was such an adorable and sweet child," Southampton lamented.

"You should spend time with Berkeley. We were at a ball, and we had to listen to three men discuss Berkeley's sister at length and in terms that no man should have to hear about his sister. Of course, I have had to listen to Vincent's remarks about Stella. That was unpleasant," Amesbury added.

"Perhaps we should arrange for our sisters to have tea one of these days. Aurora is coming out next season and could use friends. If we are lucky, they could have something similar to Honoria's friendship with Lily, Olivia, and Bella," Rose suggested.

"For Christ's sake! We are men, together on the eve of Ralph's wedding, and you lot have been discussing women without mentioning which one you would like to tup and in which way. We could even discuss politics or sport, but I refuse to arrange teas for the debutantes," Vincent railed. Clearly the trappings of adulthood were shackles to him.

"I will host this tea, if you gentlemen would like to choose a day," Southampton said while grinning at Vincent.

"Thursday would suit well for Aurora." Adrian further annoyed Vincent.

"That's it. I vow to ruin one of the women mentioned tonight. It might be someone's sister, or Lady Olivia, or Miss Beauchamp, but I will seduce one of the women," Vincent swore.

"Stella is far too savvy for the likes of you. She will help Miss Aurora Rose and Lady Aurelia. I wish you luck on your seduction," Amesbury quipped.

Ralph sat back in his chair and smiled. This was everything he had wanted for so long. His brothers were friends for the first time, Lily was soon to be his wife, and he had new friends. Yes, the trial had been difficult, and the press had run amuck. But his virtue was rewarded. Nothing worse could strike him now, and he was finally at peace.

Tomorrow they would be in Surrey, and it would be his wedding day. This day and the next would be a bright watercolor, full of promise and feeling.

Chapter Thirty-Eight

Good stories end with a wedding or a funeral. Weddings for comedies and funerals for tragedies. This disturbs me, as I believe the human spirit can endure a tragedy and conquer all. I am also bothered by a wedding being the apex of anyone's life. Of course, this is only for literature. We all know life continues for the subjects of these tales.
~Aunt Penny's Advice for Living, August 1885

Lily's eagerness to debut her wedding dress matched her enthusiasm for marriage. The dress was worthy of display. It wrapped tightly around her in a shade of white nearing silver, with a basque waist and pearls sewn into the neck and waistline. The lace overlay was woven in an orange blossom pattern, and it settled delicately over the satin gown as a quiet mother hovers over a sleeping child. To hold in place the pleated sashes of lace, Lily had silver and diamond ivy leaves serving as pins. The train of her dress was her favorite part. It was twelve feet long with pearl embellishments, three of which were buttons so that the train could be bustled into the rest of her skirts. It was a trail of bright pillowy clouds, speckled with daytime stars. Her heart and pride swelled for this dress. Maybe she could give it to her daughter one day.

Bella helped Lily don her veil, floor length and

made of lace. She carefully and quickly added the wreath of orange blossoms and dug the pins into Lily's hair. "You look beautiful, Lily."

"Thank you." Lily beamed. She was finally beautiful, loved, and happy. She would always remember this morning.

"Lily, we have been discussing it and have decided that we will have to change Cards and Scandal," Honoria said as she walked to Lily.

"Must we?" she whined. She faintly remembered that years ago, they had agreed married women would not be invited to Cards and Scandal.

"Oh, don't look so maudlin. We are simply doing away with the single-ladies-only rule. We don't want to have the games or house parties without you," Olivia explained. "And now, for your adornments."

"I have something old," Bella said as she fastened earbobs to Lily's ears. They were a bit tight, but they would stand firm throughout the ceremony. "I found these at auction. According to the auction house, they are from the Elizabethan era."

"I have something new." Even when she was clear, Honoria's words carried a little mystery. Honoria fastened a necklace with a cameo attached to it. The face was handsome and unyielding, set in buttery-looking stone.

But whose pretty face was in the cameo? "Is that...?"

"Ralph. I spent two weeks carving it. I hope you like it," Honoria offered.

"I love it!" Lily hugged Honoria close, which must have looked like a warm cloud hugging a bright red sunset. She closed her eyes and tried to remember this moment forever. Life could never be sweeter than it was today.

"Ahem. I have something borrowed and blue. My mother expects this to be returned," Olivia interrupted before clasping a sapphire and diamond bracelet on Lily's wrist. The bracelet sparkled and reflected light onto Lily's hand that spun like falling snowflakes. "Don't forget the sixpence for your shoe." How exquisite!

"Are you nervous for the wedding night?" Bella asked.

Olivia laughed. "Oh, no. From what I could hear, Ralph is skilled in producing this sound all night long— 'Ooooooh, yes!' "

Lily's face was hot. She must have turned a color of red only found in ladybugs.

Bella scowled at Olivia. "Olivia, help me set up for the photographs."

Once Olivia and Bella left the room, Honoria fixed Lily's veil. "Did he use his mouth before entering you?"

Lily's mouth opened in shock. "Yes! How did you know?"

"It makes the act much more pleasurable, but it usually feels nice even without that." Honoria handed Lily her bouquet. "Let's go take portraits."

"Honoria, how do you know all of this? Have you and Berkeley...?" Lily started to ask. She couldn't just allude to scandalous lovemaking and not pique her interest. Especially not today.

"No! Frederick has been a perfect gentleman. I told you I had fallen in love before," Honoria answered.

"Will you tell me what happened? As a wedding

present?" she pressed. It was maddening to know Honoria had been in love and made love and yet was alone.

"The lovingly handcrafted cameo of your husband is not enough?" Honoria teased, but waved her hand when she saw the guilt flood Lily's face. "I was young and fell in love with him. I cannot recall when it happened. It was around when I understood love as a concept. His family did not approve of my family, and he fled the country rather than stand up to them."

Honoria's story broke Lily's heart. "Do you still love him?"

A sad smile graced Honoria. "So much that I hate him." How could sadness and love be such close friends in her heart?

They slowly left the room together and joined Bella and Olivia outside to take wedding portraits. An elaborate set had been constructed, complete with a chaise longue and a bamboo tree in a planter. There were traditional poses of the bride on her own and with her maids. Then, because Honoria was the photographer, they took a picture that made it look as though they were trying to kill each other. Lily throttled Olivia, Bella had her shoe in a threatening position above Lily's head, and Olivia held Honoria at bay. Of course, the camera required them to hold these positions while being perfectly still for far too long, but Lily would keep the picture in a silver frame on her vanity until the day she died. The joy-filled women were still as mannequins, although not one could keep from laughing.

After their pictures were taken, she handed each lady a small gift. Their faces were confused when they pulled out small measuring tapes. "My gift to you is to design and have made three dresses for next season for each of you," Lily announced.

"This is too generous!" Bella exclaimed.

Lily shook her head. "Once I have given Ralph two children, I may wish to begin a fashion house. You will be my walking fashion plates, so it is an investment."

"Oh, that is wonderful!" Olivia clapped.

"I will be a loyal customer," Bella vowed. Her smile was delicate and sweet.

"As will I," Honoria agreed.

"There is something I want to tell you ladies. I hope I don't cry," Lily said. She blinked back the fat tears welling in her eyes. Why did one cry when they were happy? "I have loved every moment of our friendship, and you three have meant more to me than anything in the world. I know they say that blood is thicker than water, but in my life this friendship has strengthened me and shown me how truly great the world can be." The tears were rolling now, and her nose was running. She fetched her handkerchief hidden under the dress and tried to stop her voice from growing oddly high-pitched. "To me, you are my sisters, and I love you more than you will ever know."

Lily was crying now and dabbing her eyes while sniffing her nose. As was Bella. As was Honoria. As was Olivia. They stood awkwardly and tried to stop crying with no effect. That is, until Olivia blew her nose with a goose-like honk. Honoria began to laugh, as did Lily and Bella. This contagious silliness flowed through the group until they were all laughing and honking, which must have looked ridiculous. The seriousness was commuted into love, and the women prepared for

Lily's wedding.

After the tears were dry, Papa collected her to give her away. The ceremony was lovely, and she recited her vows with vigor. She fully felt her words, and they sang from her beating heart and ran through every vein and capillary, as if the moment were pure music. She was telling the entire world that she would stand by Ralph whether he was poor, sick, or just somehow worse. Her heart and body were overflowing with love and happiness. The morning sun of her love had banished every piece of darkness from her. Every part of her was caressed by warm winds of a new birth into the world she had always wanted. This was the man she bound her soul to, and not even death could tear them apart. She would follow Ralph to the gates of Heaven or Hell and berate whatever fool creature kept her from him. After their first kiss as man and wife, they left the small chapel on her father's estate to be pelted by rice.

The lawn of her father's estate glittered in a brilliant arrangement for the wedding breakfast. The soda fountain was prepared with syrups with flavors she had stolen from her travels, such as blackberry mint and strawberry basil. Honoria had envisioned floral sculptures of monogamous animals (though they decided on swans and butterflies) and had decorated the garden with more color than any wedding Lily had seen. It was outrageous enough to be fashionable but serene enough to be accepted. It was emblematic of Lily and Ralph's union. Just them. It was more than a perfect picture. It was a Heaven designed just for her.

She hadn't realized how hungry she was until she tested the wedding breakfast. It was all too tempting. The ferocious growl of her anxious stomach made her shake. Yet Lily resisted eating everything before her and only took small ladylike bites. But secretly she knew that she had to have room for the ice cream service. Again, she had chosen bold and exotic flavors: vanilla, raspberry, and chocolate. In the time of penny licks, she alone would serve her guests three flavors of pure luxury.

She had rhapsodized too intensely about ice cream, and she had not noticed Vincent standing up, glass in hand. "Attention please, ladies and gentlemen. Paying too much attention to the bride and groom is déclassé. It prevents them from kissing. I would like to propose a toast to my two favorite people in the world, Ralph and Lily. Weddings and great loves are beautiful because they are the only things that contain their own contradictions. A wedding is both born of great tradition and an insurrection of two against fate and circumstances. Great love is both fragile and invincible. If one were to ask most guests here, they would tell you Ralph and Lily's romance began at a ball, as many marriages do. After all, that is why mothers host them. But that was not the beginning of their romance. If you were to ask Ralph and Lily where their love began, they might tell you it was the fateful day they sat next to one another at a wedding. But they would be wrong too. Believe me, as the only person who knows them better than they know themselves, I say with confidence they are wrong." Vincent paused to ensure the attention of the audience, then continued with a grin born of showmanship.

"No. Instead, it began when four-year-old Lily met nine-year-old Ralph at the train station coming from Eton. When I saw them playing together, I felt a quaking in my bones. The way you know you are witnessing great love. That quaking, that tense feeling, is what happens when love, so great and humble, reaches past the flaws of the present to find its place in something bigger. Over the years, I befriended Lily. I knew she would be my sister. I have come to know her as pure good, almost as good as Ralph, who I think of as a saint. I could not be happier than I am today, to finally see true love united. And so I say, Ralph and Lily, in a world of darkness, you are a light. The entire world is better for the both of you, and I know your love, so strong and delicate, shall preserve itself forever and renew our faith in all good things both old and new."

Lily would not be able to hold back her tears, yet again. To feel so accepted and cared for was too warm, and her eyes simmered with tears like a teapot left far too long over heat. Did all brides cry with so much joy on their wedding day? She dabbed her eyes and leaned across Ralph to playfully hit Vincent's arm. "Thank you for the speech, but try not to make ladies cry on their wedding day."

"Yes, bad form, old man," Ralph said, blinking his own tears away. At Lily's questioning glance, he shrugged. "I'm not crying. I'm simply allergic to Vincent."

Vincent began to laugh. It was good to cut the sincerity with levity. "Ha! You think I would not make you cry today? Of course, I had to make you cry today. Just wait, I will make you weep at every special occasion for the rest of your lives. Welcome to the family, Lily."

She beamed and slipped her gloved hand into

Ralph's gloved hand. She finally had a family. She would spend the rest of her life with the man she loved and wake up every morning next to someone who labored entirely for her. Never again would she be alone. Everything she had endured—her mother, Christopher, the stories in the papers, the trial—was all worth the fight so that she could sit with the man she loved as her husband. The banal spirit of her past departed her side, and her new companion slid into place. She had spent her life preparing for this without even the faintest hope of it ever happening. Her life was beginning again with all of her wishes granted.

"I love you, Ralph," Lily declared, smiling at him.

"I love you too, *miliy*," Ralph answered. "Are you sad that our adventure is over?"

"My darling, we are young and in love. Our adventure has only begun," Lily declared, and her words faded into a kiss.

Chapter Thirty-Nine

I never consider a tale ended unless the villain hangs. I persist in imagining the characters long after and dream of their adventures.
~Aunt Penny's Advice for Living, August 1885

Vincent led Marlene away from the hot, teary crowd of the wedding. It was bad form to propose marriage at someone else's wedding, but he wanted to secure Marlene's hand. August meant the end of the season, and with Marlene's precarious situation, he wanted her to know she was going to be taken care of. Depending on Marlene's feelings, he hoped for a short engagement with a small wedding. Quick, quiet, and married was ideal. Quick and quiet things left less room for meddling or doubt. As an experienced meddler and skeptic, he knew this was true.

Vincent walked under a flowering tree, and the branches tousled his hair. That was unusual for August, but it was riddled with white flowers. "Marlene, I have wanted to speak with you about something that has been much on my mind for the past month."

Marlene leaned against the tree and gave a coy smile up at him. "I am most eager to discuss something with you as well." She purred a bit when she talked, as if she savored her words.

He smirked. She was likely anxious about his lack

331

of proposal. Very well, he would let her speak her mind before he eased it. "By all means, please begin."

"While you were off in the countryside, your mother was kind enough to invite me to tea. Sebastian was present," Marlene began.

Vincent began to feel a heaviness in the pit of his stomach. She had sneered at his trip to Lancaster, but he explained that it was necessary for his family. And why would she call Sebastian by his Christian name? How unnerving. It was hard to be calm. Surely, she knew about his ever-present jealousy of Sebastian. But Lily also called Sebastian and himself by their Christian names. Maybe this was an ant hill and not a mountain.

"Sebastian treated me so kindly. He escorted me home, and we began to meet at events. Neither one of us planned it, but we fell in love," Marlene continued. She held the grave words in the air, admiring her handiwork. They fell like a tombstone on him. The empty air in his mouth felt like dry lightning. How could words fail him now?

"I beg your pardon?" This could not be true. She was teasing him. Having a laugh at his rivalry. Something. Anything but what she was claiming. She had found his hidden heart and was trying to stab it.

"I know you have an attachment for me, but we did not have an understanding. I hope you can be happy for Sebastian and me. I expect a proposal soon." Marlene smiled wistfully at the notion. Her feline features and cow eyes were more repulsive than anything he had seen before.

He had never hit anyone. He had boxed, but never truly lashed out in anger. After all, words were better weapons than fists. But in this moment, he struggled not to strike her. This harlot had led him on and asked him to be happy while she fucked his brother. His goddamned brother. It would be insulting enough if she had tossed him over for a stranger, but to leave him for Sebastian was devastating. No, this had all the earmarks of intentional harm.

"Do you truly think you will be countess? You, with no dowry or connections, actually think he will marry you?" Vincent sneered.

"I believe he truly loves me and wants me no matter what I have, but for who I am," Marlene countered while jerking her head up.

He had injured her pride. Good. "Oh, I see. Well then, what kind of speech should I give at your wedding? I am certain I can create a limerick, although it may not be flattering. I could describe how eagerly you let me touch your breast. Or perhaps I could recite a poem I shall write about the noises you make when you come, that high-pitched mewling. You are trying to make it seem as though I formed this attachment alone. You encouraged and nurtured it," he seethed. He wanted to spit fire on her until she burned from the inside.

"No one would believe you. Everyone knows how spiteful you are and how much you hate Sebastian." Marlene smiled at him.

"I could ruin you right now," he spat. She wasn't even apologetic. She kept smiling at him as though he were a child.

"But you won't. This is your beloved lion tamer's wedding to your favorite brother. You will not say or do anything. You are powerless, impotent. You will simply go home and accept the reality of the situation. I will marry Sebastian, and you will no longer be welcome in our home," Marlene sang. She glowed with heavy spite. All traces of beauty left her. Her skin was pale, her hair stringy, her eyes dour and mechanical. How had he been so fucking stupid?

He needed to leave. His legs tensed, eager to run. She was right, and he would lose his entire family. His parents, especially his mother, would find a million reasons why this was his fault and to excuse Sebastian's actions. She correctly assumed that the one place he would behave was at Lily and Ralph's wedding. The anger and fear of a million unspoken insecurities, nourished by his stature as a second born, roared in his brain. He was trapped like a wild animal, and he needed to get out. If he couldn't get free, he would do something he would always regret. In this panic, his thoughts raced; he should kill her, kill Sebastian, kill himself.

But he said nothing and stormed away. How sad and dutiful. If she said one more word, he really would snap her neck. As he walked through the wedding party, but somehow nothing had changed. His head was exploding with rage while they ate ice cream. Sebastian was talking to Ralph, both smiling. Sebastian, that son of a bitch, had stood in Vincent's house and agreed to live with him, and he was wooing Marlene behind his back. He had never hated Sebastian before, through years of bitterness and hard feelings, but after today he would always hate him.

"Vincent? Are you ill?" Lily asked as she jogged inelegantly to him.

"No. Yes. I must leave," Vincent growled, though Lily did nothing to deserve his terse tone.

"Very well. Will you be in Norfolk soon? We would love to have you be our guest often," Lily asked as she cocked her head at him. Lily had always known when something was amiss with him. She could always see his true self. But she didn't deserve this unwanted revelation.

Norfolk wasn't far enough away. Anywhere in England wasn't far enough away to keep his mother from guilting him to coming to Sebastian's engagement dinner. But nowhere in Europe was far enough away. What about another world, perhaps China or Africa? Of course, he had a world traveler right in front of him.

"Lily, do you trust me?" he asked.

"Of course. You may doubt whether the sun will rise, but never doubt my trust in you," Lily said as she reached for his arm, giving a little squeeze.

"I need to go far away. For a couple of months. I promise to write and explain myself. But for today, I need you to trust me. Where should I go?" He was babbling, and he knew it. But who cared at this point?

Lily's face stormed with concern and unasked questions. "America? Berkeley, Melgum, and Lady Serena are touring Canada and America. They speak English there—well, a sort of English—so it might be easier to live there for a couple of months."

"Yes! Oh Lily, you are a genius! Where do you suppose Berkeley is in America?" Vincent had forgotten about Berkeley's voyage to find a wife.

"I am unsure. I know they went to Dublin and Spain first, as well as possibly Paris for Serena to freshen her wardrobe. They planned on a brief visit to Canada. Montreal and Toronto to be specific. You may wish to begin with Boston? From what Papa says, it's a magical city," Lily answered. Her face was still glowing, even in this tense and difficult conversation.

"Yes. I'll leave tonight for Dublin. Please wait to tell Ralph I am leaving for a few days. I will write you from Dublin explaining everything. I promise," he swore.

"Are you in trouble, Vincent?" Lily asked.

Yes. If only she knew. He would be hanged for beating Sebastian until he was bruised and bloody. "No. I will explain, but I cannot now."

"You will come back, won't you? I am tired of family abandoning me." Lily frowned. Of course Lily deserved his friendship, but could he restrain himself?

He sighed and shook his head because, well, she deserved his honesty even in his foul mood. "Of course I will, lion tamer. Marlene rejected me, and I cannot hold my venom."

"Oh, thank God!" Lily cried loudly, attracting some glares. Who glared at a bride during her own wedding, except maybe the mistress? At his clear shock, she whispered like a savvy lady in waiting, "She annoyed me to no end. I could never place why, but Ralph and I decided to play nice because you were intent on wedding her."

"Why did you never say anything?" Both his closest friend and brother hated Marlene, but they never said so? Should he feel supported by their silence or betrayed by it?

"Darling, we want you to be happy. And you never asked," Lily explained.

"I must go now. Congratulations on your wedding. I hope this doesn't cloud any of your happiness," he whispered before he dashed away as fast as the gathered patrician eyes would allow.

Tomorrow, he would write Lily to tell her Marlene had jilted him for Sebastian. Tonight, he would go to Dublin and drink the city dry. After a lifetime of competition and rivalry, Sebastian had finally won. Vincent was without a family and without a home. He was tired of the pretty lies. In truth, there was no justice, and happy endings never came for men who made their names by being cynics. It was time to stop pretending he was wanted or loved. He should embrace the life of a churl. For the rest of his life, he would be a dark cloud blown by harsh winds.

Epilogue

The Cat sauntered down Tothill Street while delicately weaving between the pedestrians. She ducked down an alley that smelled like dank laundry and entered through the back entrance to a restaurant famous for shady negotiations between members of Parliament. She slipped past the wait staff and into the red and white dining room. Her instructions were to meet the Spider at the fourth booth, so when she found it, she peeled back the curtain and disappeared behind it. The rich fabric and awkwardly intimate smallness of the booth felt like a brothel, but she took rest on the padded bench. She had become accustomed to dirty work.

The Spider sat across the small table from her, and he was clearly annoyed at her tardiness. In truth, the Cat adored the Spider. He was terribly handsome with pine-colored eyes, a strong jaw, and a muscular body. However, the Spider had never looked twice at her and showed no interest. It was a disappointment, but she was learning she could play with her prey and didn't need to dwell on any one man in particular. After all, that was the point of being a cat.

"Where is Vincent now?" the Spider asked.

"On his way to America. He will not interfere with our plans," she answered with a smile. Hopefully, this bravado wouldn't seem false. "Our next attempt to destroy the Mandevilles will be successful."

"The trial was foolish. If the Dragon had called in his favors, there would be no Duke of Bridgewater," the Spider sneered. The Spider was always so convinced of his own intelligence.

"The point was never to strip the duke of his title. It was to humiliate the family. That is why you dropped the stories to the press. They think they are strong, but they are at their weakest. Ralph is off, newly wed and completely distracted. Vincent has fled the continent and won't be coming back any time soon. And due to your brilliant mind, Sebastian will not be pursuing Olivia."

"Do you really think he will believe she is ostracized without verifying it? Why would he not ask someone?" The Spider frowned at this idea, as he did at any loose ends. His plans always included contingencies, but he did not like relying on an easily disproven deception. "The point of any good strategy is to give your opponents only bad choices. If you promise to shoot a group of men, you will hurt some, and then they will hurt you. But if you simply inform them that you plan on shooting one of them and make them decide, then they will hurt each other to avoid the pain."

"When a man is ambitious as Sebastian is, he is blinded by the prejudices of power. He needs approval from the queen and will not risk alerting her to his affection for Olivia by inquiring. In this world, a whisper is deadlier than a loaded gun. Sebastian will feel alone. He will be ripe for seduction by someone who is scandal free," she answered.

"I cannot imagine giving up love for anything," the

Spider mumbled.

Huh? She couldn't believe her ears. This was the Shadow Society. They didn't join for love. They joined to destroy those that had injured them. They joined for vengeance. "Be that as it may. We are poised perfectly to control the Mandevilles, and we will be done with them soon."

"Excellent, but I am not satisfied that your methods are without unnecessary risk. We need to place an operative with Sebastian. I have also recruited someone who will revolutionize our organization," the Spider bragged. His eyes were bright with hubris.

"Oooh. Anyone I know?" the Cat asked.

"No, but I will try to make arrangements for an introduction soon. Try to encourage Sebastian to hire a new valet. I will find someone who can spy on him for us," the Spider said as he threw his money close onto the table. He was clearly ready to leave, although he never announced it. His face never changed, but his words sneered and roiled like angry smoke. So much ceremony for a spy. "I will be in touch."

The Cat had to wait a few minutes before she could leave. The bright day blinded her temporarily, so she bumped into a passerby. How unfortunate and compromising.

"I beg your pardon. Oh! Miss Haverford, how do you do today?"

Marlene could not recall the paunchy man and his common, round face at first. Her thoughts raced for a reasonable explanation. "I am a bit lost, sir. Could you advise me on how to return to Mayfair?"

"My dear, you are quite far from home. Allow me to escort you back," the old man blustered.

"Thank you, sir," Marlene purred. It was not every day a merchant's daughter could lay a highborn family low.

A word about the author...

Christine lives in Austin, Texas, with her husband, daughter, and three black cats. She studied Western Civilization in California and traveled in Europe before moving to Texas. She is passionate about writing, cooking, art, and her family.

Thank you for purchasing
this publication of The Wild Rose Press, Inc.

For questions or more information
contact us at
info@thewildrosepress.com.

The Wild Rose Press, Inc.
www.thewildrosepress.com
https://www.facebook.com/TheWildRosePress/